PENGUIN

THE DESTINY OF CANADA

CHRISTOPHER PENNINGTON holds a doctorate in history from the University of Toronto. He specializes in the history of Canadian politics and foreign relations, has taught at U of T, Ryerson University, and Trent University, and currently works as a manuscript editor for the *Dictionary of Canadian Biography*. He lives in Pickering, Ontario, with his family.

ALSO IN THE
History *of* Canada Series

Death or Victory: The Battle of Quebec and the Birth of an Empire by Dan Snow

The Last Act: Pierre Trudeau, the Gang of Eight, and the Fight for Canada by Ron Graham

War in the St. Lawrence: The Forgotten U-Boat Battles on Canada's Shores by Roger Sarty

Ridgeway: The American Fenian Invasion and the 1866 Battle That Made Canada by Peter Vronsky

The Best Place to Be: Expo 67 and Its Time by John Lownsbrough

Two Weeks in Quebec City: The Meeting That Made Canada by Christopher Moore

Ice and Water: The Future of the Arctic by John English

Trouble on Main Street: The 1907 Vancouver Race Riots by Julie Gilmour

Death on Two Fronts: Newfoundland by Sean Cadigan

THE DESTINY OF CANADA

Macdonald, Laurier, and the Election of 1891

CHRISTOPHER PENNINGTON

General Editors:
MARGARET MACMILLAN
and ROBERT BOTHWELL

PENGUIN
an imprint of Penguin Canada

Published by the Penguin Group
Penguin Group (Canada), 90 Eglinton Avenue East, Suite 700, Toronto, Ontario, Canada M4P 2Y3
(a division of Pearson Canada Inc.)

Penguin Group (USA) Inc., 375 Hudson Street, New York, New York 10014, U.S.A.
Penguin Books Ltd, 80 Strand, London WC2R 0RL, England
Penguin Ireland, 25 St Stephen's Green, Dublin 2, Ireland (a division of Penguin Books Ltd)
Penguin Group (Australia), 250 Camberwell Road, Camberwell, Victoria 3124, Australia
(a division of Pearson Australia Group Pty Ltd)
Penguin Books India Pvt Ltd, 11 Community Centre, Panchsheel Park, New Delhi – 110 017, India
Penguin Group (NZ), 67 Apollo Drive, Rosedale, Auckland 0632, New Zealand
(a division of Pearson New Zealand Ltd)
Penguin Books (South Africa) (Pty) Ltd, 24 Sturdee Avenue, Rosebank, Johannesburg 2196, South Africa

Penguin Books Ltd, Registered Offices: 80 Strand, London WC2R 0RL, England

First published in Allen Lane hardcover by Penguin Canada, a division of Pearson Canada Inc., 2011
Published in this edition, 2012

1 2 3 4 5 6 7 8 9 10 (WEB)

Manufactured in Canada.

LIBRARY AND ARCHIVES CANADA CATALOGUING IN PUBLICATION

Pennington, Christopher John, 1977–
The destiny of Canada : Macdonald, Laurier, and the election of 1891 / Christopher Pennington.

(The history of Canada)
Originally published: Toronto : Allen Lane Canada, 2011.
Includes bibliographical references and index.
ISBN 978-0-14-305282-1

1. Macdonald, John A. (John Alexander), 1815–1891. 2. Laurier, Wilfrid, Sir, 1841–1919. 3. Canada—History—1867–1914. 4. Canada—Politics and government—1878–1896. I. Title. II. Series: History of Canada (Toronto, Ont.)

FC520.P46 2012 971.05'4 C2012-900516-9

Dedicated to
Chris,
Ian, Emmett, and Winston

CONTENTS

INTRODUCTION TO THE HISTORY OF CANADA SERIES

Canada, the world agrees, is a success story. We should never make the mistake, though, of thinking that it was easy or foreordained. At crucial moments during Canada's history, challenges had to be faced and choices made. Certain roads were taken and others were not. Imagine a Canada, indeed imagine a North America, where the French and not the British had won the Battle of the Plains of Abraham. Or imagine a world in which Canadians had decided to throw in their lot with the revolutionaries in the thirteen colonies.

This series looks at the making of Canada as an independent, self-governing nation. It includes works on key stages in the laying of the foundations as well as the crucial turning points between 1867 and the present that made the Canada we know today. It is about those defining moments when the course of Canadian history and the nature of Canada itself were oscillating. And it is about the human beings—heroic, flawed, wise, foolish, complex—who had to make decisions without knowing what the consequences might be.

We begin the series with the European presence in the eighteenth century—a presence that continues to shape our society today—and conclude it with an exploration of the strategic importance of the Canadian Arctic. We look at how the mass movements of peoples, whether Loyalists in the eighteenth century or Asians at the start of the twentieth, have profoundly influenced the nature of Canada. We also look at battles and their aftermaths: the Plains of Abraham, the 1866 Fenian raids, the German submarines in the St. Lawrence River during World War II. Political crises—the 1891 election that saw Sir John A. Macdonald battling Wilfrid Laurier; Pierre Trudeau's triumphant patriation of the Canadian Constitution—provide rich moments of storytelling. So, too, do the Expo 67 celebrations, which marked a time of soaring optimism and gave Canadians new confidence in themselves.

We have chosen these critical turning points partly because they are good stories in themselves but also because they show what Canada was like at particularly important junctures in its history. And to tell them we have chosen Canada's best historians. Our authors are great storytellers who shine a spotlight on a different Canada, a Canada of the past, and illustrate links from then to now. We need to remember the roads that were taken—and the ones that were not. Our goal is to help our readers understand how we got from that past to this present.

Margaret MacMillan
Warden at St. Antony's College, Oxford

Robert Bothwell
May Gluskin Chair of Canadian History
University of Toronto

PREFACE

Why write a book about the election of 1891? Is it a story that needs to be told? No one seems to have thought so, admittedly, in the one hundred and twenty years since it took place. Historians have penned a few articles about particular aspects of the subject, and it has made notable cameo appearances in several books situated in the late nineteenth century.[1] But it has never been regarded in its own right as a turning point in Canadian history. Perhaps the most representative example of the traditional lack of appreciation for this election is *Fights of Our Lives*, a 2002 book by John Duffy, a Liberal strategist. Duffy focuses on what he considers to be the most significant federal campaigns since Confederation, and in his view the election of 1891 utterly fails to make the grade. It is hardly mentioned at all, in fact, being dismissed in one paragraph as "a run-of-the-mill post-Confederation election with a great issue in it, but no more."[2]

That's wrong. There was nothing "run-of-the-mill" about the election of 1891. The "great issue" at stake was nothing less than the future of the relationship between Canada and the United States, and by extension, the future of Canada itself. The most immediate matter was the proper trade policy to pursue with the Americans. Was it best to keep up the National Policy of Sir John A. Macdonald and his Conservative government? Its high tariffs against British and American imports protected Canadian manufacturers from foreign competition, but also tended to stifle trade with the United States. Canada was then in a very bad way economically, particularly in relation to the United States, and by 1891—twelve years after the National Policy had taken effect—many Canadians had lost faith in the wisdom of fighting a never-ending tariff war with their vastly larger and more prosperous southern neighbour.

In the election of 1891, for the first time in Canadian history, the electorate was presented with a clear and radical alternative to the National Policy. Wilfrid Laurier and the Liberals, throwing caution to the wind, ran on a platform of unrestricted reciprocity. At first glance it was a simple and appealing proposal: absolute free trade with the United States and, as a consequence, free access to the sixty million potential customers in the American domestic market. Its achievement would be a dream come true for Canadian exporters, especially the farmers who still made up three-quarters of the population. It was widely hoped in Canada that this heroic remedy would rescue the country from the economic doldrums, bring an end to a long era of gloomy pessimism, and reinforce the trembling foundations of Confederation itself.

That was at first glance. Upon closer inspection, there were reasons to suspect that unrestricted reciprocity was a reckless, unpredictable, and perhaps even dangerous policy. There was no guarantee that the United States would agree to it in the first place, or that it would play by the rules and honour the deal once it had taken effect. Even if the Americans did play fairly, there were legitimate concerns about the threat to Canadian manufacturers represented by the torrent of cheap and desirable U.S. imports that would flood the Canadian domestic market. There were also worries about whether American customers would actually want to buy what Canadian exporters were selling. Most of all, though, the issue of free trade with the United States proved impossible to separate from the even more momentous question of the "destiny of Canada," which was the cause of chronic anxiety at the time. Was Canada to remain a self-governing colony of the British Empire? Or would it inevitably be drawn, either through mutual agreement or forcible annexation, into political union with the United States? To speak in favour of such a thing was seen as taboo, if not outright treasonous, in the eyes of the vast majority of Canadians. If unrestricted reciprocity was merely the first step toward the American conquest of Canada, then Canadian voters were sure to reject it.

Sir John A. Macdonald was keenly aware of this sentiment, and used it to shrewd advantage in the election of 1891. He framed the campaign as a contest not between two different trade platforms, but as a life-or-death battle between heroic Canada-loving Conservative nationalists and sinister Yankee-loving Liberal annexationists. It is because of that strategy that the campaign has been remembered by historians, echoing the words of the Old Man himself, as the "Loyalty Election." Its most enduring images have related to Macdonald's brand of British-Canadian nationalism, such as the Old Man wrapped in the British flag and the Liberals conspiring in secret with greedy American leaders. The decision of the prime minister to turn the election into a flag-waving contest raised the stakes, created bitterness on both sides, and cemented a perceived link between free trade and the disloyal policy of annexation. He thus ensured that the effects of the election of 1891 would continue to be felt throughout the next century.

The infuriating thing about all of this is that the "Loyalty Election" should not be remembered as a contest between patriotism and disloyalty, no matter how effectively Macdonald distorted the trade question to create that impression. There were genuine schemers in this election who supported the annexation of Canada to the United States, but these were a minuscule few, and their importance was enormously exaggerated by Macdonald and the Conservatives. The truth is that both the Conservatives and the Liberals acted patriotically during the campaign. They simply had contrasting ideas for the future of the country, ideas rooted in different but equally legitimate conceptions of the meaning of Canadian nationalism. The clash of these ideas was the real "great issue" of the election of 1891.

This is one reason why the story of this election deserves to be told, but it is not the only one. The campaign also helped to establish certain political traditions and patterns of thinking that continue, even today, to influence how Canada is governed and how Canadians think about themselves. Trade was only the first of the two great issues in Canadian politics at that time. The second, which in many respects was more dreaded and dangerous, was the race-and-religion question. These were intolerant times. Leading politicians, Macdonald foremost amongst them, were aware of how volatile controversies over race, language, or religion could be in a country that was militantly divided along English-French and Protestant-Catholic lines. There was good reason to believe, given the simmering tensions that prevailed in the Dominion in the late 1880s, that the next campaign would not revolve around trade at all, but would deteriorate into a disastrous, possibly even violent conflict between English and French Canadians.

That racial showdown never took place during the election of 1891, despite the energetic efforts of certain bigoted political and religious leaders to incite it. This was all the more surprising given that one of the two parties was, for the first time in Canadian history, led by a French Canadian Roman Catholic. The opportunity was certainly there for Conservative candidates in English Canada to play the "French domination" card, and the reverse was true in Quebec, where the Liberals could have played a winning hand by presenting Wilfrid Laurier strictly as a champion of the French language and the Catholic faith. In some constituencies across the country, undeniably, appeals were made to racial or religious sentiment.

Yet the most remarkable feature of the election—more remarkable than the debate over the trade question—was that all of the leading politicians, Conservative and Liberal alike, refused to give in to these temptations. On the contrary, they worked together in the years leading up to the election, and through their independent actions in the campaign itself, to prevent the race-and-religion question from becoming the "great issue" of the election. Historians have given them little credit for this, but it was an important achievement, one attained even as Liberals and Conservatives were bitterly assailing each other over their respective positions on the trade question.[3]

This intriguing tale of how Canadian politicians came together to prevent racial and religious conflict from poisoning the election of 1891 is told, for the most part, in the first half of this book. It doesn't figure prominently in the second half precisely because they succeeded so well at steering the debate toward the trade question instead. Only the most cynical Canadian today, it seems fair to say, would deny that this was an admirable joint effort in the cause of national unity. But many Canadians today might be surprised that politicians were capable of doing anything admirable in the late nineteenth century, an era that has become synonymous with patronage, corruption, and Macdonald, a prime minister who is most commonly remembered for being an alcoholic.

There is no point in glossing over the failings of the Canadian political system in these years. The satirist Stephen Leacock was perceptive when he wrote that Canadian politicians too often resembled "little turkey-cocks ... fighting all the while as they feather their mean nests of sticks and mud, high on their river bluff."[4] Patronage and corruption existed on a scale that was criticized then and that would be shockingly unacceptable today. Notwithstanding rare political truces, a malodorous and extreme partisanship permeated all aspects of politics and society, including the press, which did little more than cheerlead for one party or the other. The democratic system itself, though better than it had been in the bad old days of open voting, was fundamentally unfair: more than half the adult population was excluded from voting or running for office on grounds that were illegitimate by any reasonable standard. And yes, the prime minister liked to take a drink now and then.

This is all true, and yet it is not the whole truth. The late nineteenth century was indeed an era of corruption, squalid tactics, and limited democracy by modern standards. But it was also, paradoxically, an era resplendent with larger-than-life political figures, passionate and often eloquent national debates, and above all, a Canadian electorate that cared deeply about democracy. The public followed political affairs closely in their daily newspapers, which, partisan though they were, provided remarkably good coverage, including careful scrutiny of party policies and verbatim reports of speeches made by leading politicians. Constituents packed political meetings by the hundreds even between elections, and by the thousands when national leaders came to visit. Party organizers staged elaborate parades and produced delightful public spectacles. Voter turnout was always impressive, in spite of the difficulties voters faced getting time off from work and travelling to polling stations. And both the people and the politicians had respect for Parliament. The House of Commons was the acknowledged forum for important national debates, and a place where reasoned argument and skilful oratory were not only admired but also capable now and then of actually changing the votes of some honourable members.

This, the environment in which the election of 1891 took place, is the final reason why this story is one worth telling. This book is not intended as a critique of modern Canadian democracy, but after being immersed in the raw and colourful nineteenth-century political world, it is difficult not to feel a touch of regret that so little of the enthusiasm that Canadians once invested in their election campaigns exists in the twenty-first century. At a time when voter turnout is at an all-time low and Parliament is treated with diminished respect even by politicians, and when it is almost impossible to imagine a campaign rally attracting thousands of people, it is worth recalling what once motivated Canadians to take such an active part in political life. Here, then, is the story of the election of 1891.

PART 1
The Dominion

ONE

The March of the Boodle Brigade

It was half past nine on the evening of February 22, 1887—general-election day in the Dominion of Canada—and the results were trickling in over the telegraph wires. The windows shone brightly in newspaper offices across the country as journalists posted the latest numbers on broadsheets for the benefit of anxious crowds that were gathering in the frozen streets. The early returns suggested that a long night lay ahead before a winner could be declared. And in the downstairs library of Earnscliffe, his stately Ottawa home, the prime minister of Canada rose from his chair, took his candle, and addressed a small circle of advisors and friends. "Good night, gentlemen," he said calmly. And with that, Sir John Alexander Macdonald retired upstairs to bed.[1]

The Old Man could be forgiven for turning in early, even if it meant not knowing whether he would still be leading the country in the morning. It had been an exhausting campaign, a five-week whirlwind of winter travel, late-night rallies, and fitful sleeps in unfamiliar beds.

He had borne it all with his usual vigour and good cheer; after all, the Liberal-Conservative Party depended heavily on his leadership. Still, it was a lot to ask of a politician who had celebrated his seventy-second birthday on the campaign trail. Sir John was worn down and looked it. The Old Man's famous features—wry mouth, bulbous nose, craggy pockmarked cheeks, curly grey hair—seemed more haggard than they had been only months before. He still stood quite erect, about six feet in height, and there was a spring in his step when he mounted a platform to address his supporters. But Sir John was so slight-shouldered and frail that it sometimes looked as though a strong wind might blow him away.[2]

His condition was hardly a surprise. Macdonald had always taken on too much. To ready the party for this campaign, in fact, he had already been stumping for the better part of a year. In the summer of 1886 he had made his first-ever trip out West, aboard the recently finished Canadian Pacific Railway, on a three-month sightseeing adventure. It was supposed to have been a vacation with his wife, Agnes, but politics had intruded, as it always did, and much of his time had been spent shoring up Western support. In the autumn he had toured the Maritimes, getting his followers there in election-fighting trim. After that he had found time for a rabble-rousing swing through his native Ontario, displaying a zest that astonished his younger colleagues. And then, beginning in early January, there had been the gruelling five-week campaign. The prime minister had barnstormed the Dominion throughout, sometimes addressing two or three meetings a day and regularly entertaining the leather-lunged crowds that came to see him until the early hours of the morning. It had been a remarkable effort, one that would have been taxing even for a man half his age.[3]

Macdonald feared that it had not been enough. He had the unsettling feeling that Canadians had grown weary of his government, and the outcome of the election was, in fact, uncertain in practically every region of the country. Only western Canada, which he had personally lured into Confederation and endowed with a transcontinental railway, seemed to be completely safe. British Columbia would almost certainly re-elect Liberal-Conservative candidates in each of its six seats. The North-West Territories, still under strict federal control and voting for the first time, would probably follow suit in its four constituencies. Manitoba, which occasionally elected a few Liberals, also seemed on course to elect a strong Tory contingent. All this was happy news for Macdonald, except for the fact that western Canada, with by far the sparsest population in the country, possessed only 15 of the 215 seats in the House of Commons.[4]

There was trouble brewing for the Conservatives in Ontario, where ninety-two seats were at stake, far more than anywhere else. The Tories normally did well to the east of the provincial capital of Toronto, especially in the old Loyalist towns such as Cornwall and Kingston, and with the substantial French-speaking population in the Ottawa region. The province was also, however, the heartland of the Liberal Party, especially in the rural constituencies west of Toronto. Since Confederation the government of Ontario had been continuously in Liberal hands. For the last fifteen years it had been led by Premier Oliver Mowat, a tubby, clever, invincible politician—and one-time Macdonald protégé—whose support of the federal Liberals had given them a welcome organizational boost during the campaign. The federal leader, Edward Blake, was also an Ontario man, a renowned Toronto lawyer whose reputation for standing on principle was much respected in the province. With all of these factors favouring the Liberals, the results in Ontario, where the Tories had won fifty-five of ninety-two seats in 1882, seemed to be a toss-up.

The situation was also uncertain in Quebec, and that was especially alarming for Macdonald because the *belle province* had been the stronghold of his Conservatives since Confederation. The powerful Roman Catholic Church in Quebec traditionally supported them—parish priests were known to warn their flocks that Tory *bleu* was the colour of heaven and Liberal *rouge* the colour of hell—and the Conservatives normally carried the vast majority of the province's sixty-five seats. These Quebec members had always been a vital component of the Macdonald government, occupying important cabinet positions and demonstrating that French Canadians were fully represented in the halls of power in Ottawa. Macdonald's skilful accommodation of French Canadian interests was one of the leading reasons for his success in easing French-English tensions over the course of his long career.

Now the situation seemed to have soured. In the last two years there had been increasing discontent with the party in Quebec at both the federal and provincial levels. A charismatic opposition politician, Honoré Mercier, had recently become premier by campaigning not as a party follower, but as an unabashed Quebec nationalist. His adherence to a vision of a French and Roman Catholic Quebec, and his apparent lack of interest in relations with the English-speaking provinces, did not exactly make him an advocate of "separation" from Canada. But there was no question that his loyalty lay with his province, not with the Dominion, and that was a marked change from the moderate Quebec leaders who had typically allied with the Conservatives and helped govern the country since Confederation. That a man like Mercier could become premier was an ominous sign.

The outlook was just as troubling in the Maritimes, where Tory fortunes had gone into a steep decline along with the region's depressed economy. The results in recent provincial elections spoke volumes. Not long ago the Tories had been dominant, but now only tiny Prince Edward Island still had a Conservative government. In April 1886 the Tories in New Brunswick had taken an electoral kicking, winning just eight of forty-one seats in the provincial legislature. Two months later the Nova Scotia Conservatives had been crushed by an incumbent Liberal government that wanted *to secede from Canada*. Were things so bad that Nova Scotians preferred a party that was hoping to break up the country? Yes, apparently. Macdonald threw his Nova Scotia cabinet ministers into the fray, hoping to knock sense into the electorate, but the Liberals triumphed anyway. To make matters worse, W.S. Fielding, the popular Liberal premier, had involved himself in the federal campaign. He was privately predicting that the federal Liberals would make enormous gains in the province.

If Fielding was right about Nova Scotia, and if this apparent trend in favour of the Liberals proved to be consistent across the country, there was little chance that the Tories could win the election. If they did lose, it would be a shock. The Conservatives were the natural governing party of the Dominion. Under the leadership of Macdonald they had been in office for fifteen of the twenty years since Confederation. They had won four of five federal elections, and the last two, in 1878 and 1882, had been blowouts. The Tories called themselves the nation-building party, and they had a good claim to the title. Three new provinces—Manitoba, British Columbia, and Prince Edward Island—and the vast North-West Territories had entered Confederation on their watch. They had overseen most of the construction of the Intercolonial Railway, a 680-mile line connecting Quebec with the Maritimes. Most important, they had championed the Canadian Pacific Railway, the 2500-mile "backbone of steel," completed in 1885, that ran between Montreal and Vancouver. A testament to their determination and vision, the C.P.R. was the Tories' greatest, most improbable political achievement.

Would it all be enough? There were two main reasons why Canadians were disaffected in 1887. There was a bit of voter fatigue, of course—Macdonald and his Tories seemed to have been governing forever, and many grievances had accumulated over the years—but voter fatigue was a minor element of the election campaign. In late nineteenth-century Canadian politics there were really only two subjects of life-or-death importance: the trade question, and the race-and-religion question. In its most recent term of office from 1882 to 1887, the Macdonald government had struggled to find the answers to each of these questions. And that, in a nutshell, accounted for its perilous position in the election campaign that had just concluded.

The Trade Question

Trade policy was a deadly serious and highly emotional issue in nineteenth-century Canada. Foreign trade was necessary to create and maintain jobs in what was then an immense, industrializing, and lightly populated colonial nation, and the world was a bleak and frightening place for those who found themselves out of work. People were expected to pull their own weight in Canada; there were no social assistance programs to shield the unemployed from poverty. Families risked literally freezing in their homes when the money ran out to pay for fuel in winter. Others lost their homes entirely and were reduced to begging in the streets and alleys of the larger cities. There was a little aid to be had from churches and private charities, but it was shameful and humiliating to ask for it. Many would have rather died, and during the 1880s some did. These were times when it was still possible for Canadians to starve to death if they could not find work.

For this reason alone it was no wonder that trade policy was a concern of the first rank in Canadian politics. But it was not the only reason. The trade question also aroused deep feelings because it was entwined with the broad question of national identity. This was a constant source of worry and speculation. Would Canada remain part of the British Empire, attached firmly to the Motherland by a strong transatlantic trading relationship? Or was Canada destined to be pulled into the orbit of the United States? Canadians then, as they do now, had mixed feelings about their southern neighbour. On the one hand the U.S. domestic market was huge and inviting, and most Canadians—particularly farmers—wanted to get unrestricted access to those millions of customers. On the other hand they worried that free trade would expose them to ruinous competition, and that the lopsided economic relationship might, worst of all, lead to the eventual absorption of Canada by the territory-hungry United States. Canadians could not agree on many things, but they were almost universally agreed that they did not want to become Americans.

Macdonald's solution to this predicament was the National Policy, his party's trade policy and long-term economic strategy. Devised in the mid-1870s in the midst of a depression, the N.P. imposed high tariffs, usually around 30 percent, against British and American imported goods. The idea was that the American government, which was already applying high tariffs to Canadian imports, would be induced by this retaliation to negotiate free trade with the Dominion in natural products that U.S. businesses needed and that Canadians excelled at producing. (Macdonald had always made clear that free trade in manufactured goods, where U.S. corporations were thought to have a major competitive edge, would not be put on the table.) Meanwhile, the high tariff wall would make American imports too expensive for most Canadians to buy, providing Canada's "infant industries" with guaranteed customers in their home market and encouraging the growth of an independent industrial economy.

All Canadians could cheer the National Policy's defiant tone, and most approved of its not-too-subtle anti-American thrust.[5] Best of all, Macdonald had christened it with a brilliant name. The National Policy not only sounded visionary and patriotic; it also implied that any other trade policy was the opposite. This had confounded the Liberals. What were they supposed to put up against it? The Anti-National Policy? It was no wonder, given the emotional resonance of the N.P.—along with the generous campaign contributions flowing to the Conservatives from grateful Canadian manufacturers—that the Liberals had been soundly defeated in the elections of 1878 and 1882.

Now, in 1887, the National Policy might well have become a liability. Farmers, the largest voting constituency in Canada, were frustrated that its high tariffs had failed to produce the slightest American interest in freer trade. Meanwhile, it was forcing them to pay steeper prices for Canadian goods than they might otherwise have paid for cheaper American imports. These farmers longed for the blissful days of the Reciprocity Treaty of 1854, when natural products had crossed the border freely and farmers had, as one reminisced, "sent their produce to the United States and brought back gold."[6] Now they were struggling badly. In 1878, when he introduced the N.P., Macdonald had promised to get farmers a trade deal that would win them access to the U.S. market within two years. He had been renewing that promise every two years, more or less, ever since, but still there was no deal.

That broken promise might have been forgiven if the country had been enjoying prosperous times. It wasn't. The economy had been mired in a slump for most of the last decade. Canadians looked enviously to the south, where Americans enjoyed a robust economy and a higher standard of living. A million Canadians—at a time when the population of the Dominion was only four and a half million—had emigrated to the United States over the last twenty-five years, mostly to find work in the big cities of the industrial northeast. That was an appalling statistic, and the Liberals, of course, dwelled on it constantly. The Conservatives had a long-standing habit of denying that hard times even existed, instead hailing the long-promised (but not yet achieved) settlement of the West as the stimulus that would bring back prosperity. That argument had worked in the past, but in this campaign Macdonald had sensed increasing frustration and pessimism among the electorate. Even the perennially optimistic Toronto Board of Trade conceded in its latest annual report that "only a few of the conditions which have started the United States into a new period of activity and prosperity of the most pronounced kind, exist in our midst."[7] That, coming from an organization that existed solely to cheerlead for Canadian business, was a discouraging assessment. Nor was the depressed economy the worst of the bad news for Macdonald. The trouble on the trade front was, in all probability, less dangerous than the other great and terrible question in Canadian politics.

Race and Religion

Macdonald knew better than anyone that the Dominion of Canada was built on shaky foundations. It was only twenty years old in 1887, and the "new nationality" that its founders had expected to emerge was still an abstract concept. Canadians were a tribal people, dividing themselves along sharply drawn lines of race, region, religion, and language. They were moved by clannish loyalties and senseless prejudices, and the oldest and deepest fault line was the one that separated the English Protestant majority from the French Catholic minority. For 130 years, since the British conquest of New France, this had been the insurmountable issue, the constant fact of life, the great unresolved question in Canadian politics. So much history and so much bad feeling stood between the nation's two founding groups that there had been no easy way for the politicians to make them coexist happily, let alone work toward common nationality.

There were several explanations for the persistence of this distrust and hostility. First, there was the language barrier, which was almost impossible to underestimate as an impediment to good relations. The Dominion was not bilingual in any practical sense. English Canadians spoke English, and French Canadians spoke French. Only a small number spoke both languages, and most of those were francophones who had adjusted to the reality that English was the de facto language of business and politics. The British North America Act of 1867 specified that either language could be used in Parliament and the courts. But that was not much consolation to the unilingual francophones. Even those sitting in Parliament were ignored by the English-speaking majority and they had to sit, helplessly, as most parliamentary proceedings were conducted in English. This had spurred many francophone politicians to become bilingual, but few anglophones, not even Macdonald himself, had bothered to do the same.

Second, there was geography. Most English Canadians lived in the six provinces of English Canada, and most French Canadians lived in Quebec. There was little mixing. Quebec had a substantial English-speaking minority of about 20 percent, but it was concentrated primarily in Montreal, Quebec City, and the Eastern Townships.

In these areas the anglophones tended to live separate lives from the francophones. In Montreal especially, despite the two groups living close together, it was often possible for well-to-do anglophones to live their entire lives without speaking a word of French. It was different for the isolated French-speaking populations in English Canada, who were under constant pressure to learn English, and whose right to send their children to French-language schools was also under threat. In these strained circumstances there was little hope of tolerance developing, let alone genuine friendship.

Third, there was history. The French Canadians were a conquered people. Their ancestors had fought for New France, the colony that had fallen permanently into British hands in 1763, and generations of French Canadians had since lived and died under the rule of either the British government or, since Confederation, the English Canadians who dominated Canadian politics. The British considered themselves to be moderate rulers—benevolent even—but whether or not they were hardly mattered. It mattered only that they were rulers, the first-class citizens of Canadian society. Among French Canadians the Conquest had left a scar that would probably never heal. How could any politician overcome a wound as deep as this? How could French and English Canadians look past all this history and view one another with anything but suspicion and distrust? One ill-judged statement or action and a new crisis was likely to erupt.

Fourth, there was the tragic saga of Louis Riel.

The Hanging of Riel

Riel never should have become a martyr. He had once been the Father of Manitoba, a popular and respected Métis leader who had led the resistance in 1869–70 after the government tried to take possession of the North-West without bothering to consult the Métis and aboriginal populations that held the balance of power in the region.[8] Riel had acted coolly then. His disciplined forces had taken control of Red River, the one important Western settlement, then dispatched a list of demands to Ottawa. Macdonald, lacking either the troops to combat the resistance or the means to get them out West, had relented. The result was the creation of Manitoba.

It might have ended there had Riel not seen fit to make an example of a prisoner, Thomas Scott, who refused to respect the authority of the provisional government and attempted to escape custody on several occasions. Riel ordered Scott executed on the charge of insubordination. "We must make Canada respect us," he said at the time.[9] It was one of the most tragic decisions in Canadian history. The execution of Scott, a member of an ultra-Protestant fraternal association known as the Orange Order, enraged English-speaking Protestants across the country and turned Riel, a French-speaking Roman Catholic, into a national villain. The Macdonald government sent a hastily assembled military force to the North-West to apprehend him, and the Father of Manitoba was forced into humiliating exile in the United States.

While he was gone, the living conditions of the Métis and aboriginals deteriorated across western Canada. The immense herds of buffalo, relentlessly hunted for decades, disappeared. The settlement of the region by white Ontario Protestants displaced many Métis and aboriginals, who kept moving west in a vain search for the buffalo and food to sustain their starving peoples. Macdonald largely ignored their legitimate land claims, their pleas for assistance to make the transition to farming, and their desperate need for government rations to relieve their suffering. In 1884 the most disaffected Métis and a few aboriginals called on Riel to return to lead them. An armed rebellion broke out in March 1885. This time, thanks to the Canadian Pacific Railway, the government was able to send thousands of troops to the region in a matter of days. The rebellion was crushed, and Riel soon surrendered. He was tried for treason, convicted by an English Canadian jury, and sentenced to death.

The severity of the sentence divided the country. In English Canada, particularly Ontario, Riel was seen as a traitor who deserved to die.

But in Quebec he won sympathy for being a fellow French-speaking Roman Catholic who had protected his people from English-speaking Protestant interlopers. His troubled mental state reinforced the case for clemency. Riel was delusional—he believed himself to be a prophet and had gone about renaming the days of the week—and it was assumed in Quebec that this pathetic figure would have his sentence commuted to life imprisonment. Macdonald showed no mercy. He pushed to have Riel declared legally sane, then moved ahead with the execution, stating defiantly that "Riel shall hang though every dog in Quebec bark in his favour."[10] Politics had played a part in his decision: hanging Riel would lose the Tories votes in Quebec, but sparing him would lose them even more in Ontario. Riel was hanged on November 16, 1885. French-speaking Quebecers were outraged, and the fortunes of the Liberal-Conservative Party in the province were now in jeopardy as the votes were being counted in the election of 1887.

Macdonald had mishandled the Riel affair from the beginning. His long-standing neglect of the region had helped to spark the rebellion in the first place, and his decision to execute Riel was the most callous of his political career. Nor had his handling of the trade question been unassailable. The National Policy had a perfect name but a decidedly imperfect record of success, and not even the most stringent denials by the prime minister could blind Canadians to the fact that the country was mired in depression. Now Sir John was facing an unhappy electorate and there was a good chance that his government was about to be defeated.

Here a question begs to be asked. How could Sir John A. Macdonald, a prime minister who seemed to have mishandled the most vital political questions of his time, have stayed in office for fifteen of the twenty years since Confederation? How had he, furthermore, become the most legendary politician in the history of the Dominion? There is no simple answer to that question, except to say that his personality and political style were a great deal more complicated, and in many ways more remarkable, than his superficial historical image would suggest.

The Master of Men

The enduring popular memory of Sir John A. Macdonald is that of a drunk. Generations of Canadian historians have painted him that way, and that's understandable. Drinking stories are entertaining. It is hard to resist recalling the time he showed up so inebriated for a campaign debate that he threw up on the platform, then grinned and said, "Every time I hear this Liberal speak, it turns my stomach!"[11] There is also a fair bit of truth to the caricature. Macdonald had sporadic bouts of heavy drinking, and sometimes they affected his career. In 1862, for example, he disappeared for several days in the middle of a key legislative debate. His government had been turned out of office by the time he sobered up. In 1867, when he was in London shepherding Confederation through the British Parliament, he fell asleep after failing to snuff the bedside candle. His sheets and then the room caught fire and he narrowly escaped with a few painful burns. That near miss, politely explained as a freak accident, was probably the result of his passing out after heavy drinking. There were occasions when his private secretary found him in bed, inebriated, with empty bottles of sherry strewn about. Worse still, there were inglorious instances when he had been pulled, staggering and hollering, from the floor of the House of Commons itself.

Why wasn't it more scandalous, in an era defined by notions of respectability, that the prime minister was at times too drunk to conduct the nation's business? Most likely it was because Macdonald was totally open about his drinking. He never tried to hide it and never pretended to be more respectable than he really was. There was, it seems, something endearing about that. Macdonald's weakness for the bottle became a long-running national joke, complete with punchlines supplied by the prime minister himself. He once confronted D'Arcy McGee, a popular cabinet minister and an even more notorious drinker, about his troubles with alcohol. "We cannot have two drunkards in the cabinet," the prime minister said cheerfully. "You must stop." Asked the secret of his success against George Brown, his morally upstanding but humourless Liberal archrival in the pre-Confederation era, Macdonald wryly observed that "the people prefer Sir John A. drunk to George Brown sober."[12]

Perhaps it was also a cultural thing. Macdonald grew up at a time when alcohol was everywhere and it was not unusual to consume it generously, even to the point of getting staggeringly drunk. He enjoyed being at the bar with his friends and colleagues, but he did not really drink socially, in the modern sense that people go out and have one or two to get a buzz going. Macdonald was a binge drinker. He could stay sober for long stretches, then suddenly he would fall off the wagon and get so drunk and sick that for days he would be incapacitated. Why did he lurch back and forth like this? Why such extremes in such a normally level-headed man?

Macdonald drank when he was under pressure, and that was most of the time. His finances were a disaster (at the time members of Parliament received a small stipend, not nearly enough to sustain their families without outside income) and his personal life had been marred by tragedy. When he was five years old he watched helplessly while his brother was beaten to death by a drunken family servant. His father died when he was fifteen, leaving him as the family breadwinner. His first wife, Isabella, suffered from a mysterious, devastating illness that kept her bedridden for most of their marriage. Their first child, John Alexander, was found dead in his crib when he was a year old. A second son survived, but he would never have a close relationship with his father; Isabella died in 1857, and with Macdonald attending to his legal and political career, Hugh John was raised by family friends. Macdonald found happiness with his second wife, Agnes, whom he married in 1867. But their only child, Mary, was born with hydrocephalus, or, as it was then called, "water on the brain." It crippled her mental and physical development, and her incurable disability was an ever-replenishing well of sadness and frustration for her parents.

These tragedies did not absolve Macdonald of all responsibility for his destructive drinking habits. They did not then—his career and reputation suffered undeniably during his worst periods, when he was a younger man—nor should they now. Neither is it fair to suggest that his drinking contributed much to his success as a politician. It's true that he liked to have a drink with colleagues, and there was political value in that. No doubt some voters could sympathize with his weakness for the bottle. But the Canadian people did not love Macdonald because he was a drunk. They loved him—those who supported him, and especially those who knew him—because he was a talented political leader and a likeable human being.

The most striking thing about Sir John was that he seemed to enjoy life so much. Canadian society in the late nineteenth century was deeply imbued with Victorian values. People were supposed to be hard working and God fearing, with little time or concern for simply having fun, and politicians frequently reflected those sober ideals. The House of Commons was a forbidding chamber filled with righteous, religious men (on the Liberal side especially) who took themselves very seriously. Certainly the issues that the young Dominion faced were grave, and the source of much stress and anxiety. But Macdonald had a natural and irrepressible good cheer. He enjoyed what he did for a living. He relished the challenge of governing. He found people fascinating. He had a wicked sense of humour that often revealed itself when he was in the House, and he found the world around him perpetually amusing. He had a deserved reputation as a storyteller, and if he had a habit of retelling the same old stories, his friends and colleagues were always happy to hear them again.

Macdonald always kept up friendly personal relations with his fellow party members. He hosted frequent banquets at Earnscliffe for Conservative members of Parliament—often along with some "loose fish," independent members who might yet be cajoled to join the ranks—where the booze flowed freely and everyone shared war stories from the campaign trail.[13] In the House of Commons he allowed his colleagues to take the lead, rarely giving prepared speeches and preferring instead to interject with his signature sardonic wit when the occasion called for it. He would listen attentively to speeches in the House, even dreadful ones, when others were at the saloon or sleeping at their desks. No member of Parliament was ever taken for granted. He would make a point of putting an arm around a backbencher who had just made a dismal speech, letting everyone in the House know that he was proud of the fellow's effort. When he made a speech himself, Macdonald liked to turn his back on the Opposition and speak directly to his supporters, as if letting them in on a delicious inside joke.

He had pleasant relations with practically everybody, including his most bitter rivals. As a rule Sir John did not hold grudges—"a public man can have no resentments," he said—and he was often as considerate to opposition politicians as he was to fellow Tories.[14] A Liberal backbencher who had returned to the House after a prolonged absence told a story that illustrated the point. When he walked into Parliament he was met by his own chief, Edward Blake, with a curt nod and cold silence. Another leading Liberal, Sir Richard Cartwright, ignored him entirely. But Macdonald rushed up to grasp his hand and slap him heartily on the shoulder. "Davy, old man," the prime minister exclaimed, "I'm glad to see you back. I hope you'll soon be yourself again and live many a day to vote against me—as you have always done!" This devout Liberal never did vote for him, but confessed how difficult it was, as he put it, "to follow the men who haven't a word of greeting for me, and oppose a man with a heart like Sir John's."[15]

This personal kindness was a Macdonald trademark. There is an old saying that a knight is not a hero to his squire, but those who worked for the prime minister tended to adore him most. His extremely efficient private secretary, Joseph Pope, loved him as a son would a father and travelled with him everywhere to ensure his safety and comfort.[16] Many others were just as loyal and affectionate. Sir John won people over with his bear-trap memory for names and faces. He could go around a room, meet twenty or thirty new people, and then recall them all by name when saying goodbye at the end of the evening. He regularly astonished people whom he had met only once, sometimes decades earlier, by recalling not only their names but also the circumstances of their first encounter. He attended personally to all of his correspondence—an extraordinary task, accomplished with the aid of the tireless Pope—and took care that the name of even the most humble recipient was spelled correctly. Even the Liberals grudgingly admitted that the Old Man was a "master in the management of men."[17]

Macdonald was one of the most engaging public speakers of his times. That was important, because political gatherings in nineteenth-century Canada were completely different from the sterile, scripted, sparsely attended photo-ops that pass for "rallies" in the twenty-first century. In Macdonald's day Canadian politics was a raw and raucous business, and rallies were delightful spectacles for ordinary people who had few chances to enjoy free public entertainment. Hundreds attended these meetings even in rural areas, where the local church or town hall or school would be crammed with sweating, jostling supporters from both parties. In the cities it was not unusual to have thousands come out for a campaign rally, and those city events could be truly spectacular. Politicians would be carried in torchlight parades on their way to the venue, usually the largest theatre or the local militia drill shed. Party workers cheered and sang lusty campaign songs as they marched. At least one brass band would lend a hearty oom-pah-pah to the proceedings. Finally, when the procession reached its destination, the evening would really get going.

Macdonald was never particularly good at giving prepared speeches, and tended to have a somewhat stuttered delivery when addressing the House of Commons. But in front of a boisterous crowd at a late-night rally, his easy confidence and quick wit delighted his supporters. He was always ready with smart replies to hecklers who tried to trip him up. He had a self-deprecating style, referring frequently to his homely looks or advancing age to draw a laugh from the crowd. And a remarkable number of Canadians knew him personally, or at least felt that they did. They had become familiar with his voice and appearance. They knew his curious little mannerisms, such as the way he liked to cock his head slightly in a quizzical fashion and wag it back and forth when he walked. There was hardly a Canadian alive who had not grown up thinking of him as a fixture in the politics of the country, and in all those years the Old Man's irrepressible personality had grown on them. Still, the prime minister was not just a charming rogue. He was also a brilliant politician.

The Master Strategist

For all the stories about his drinking and easygoing ways, Macdonald was in reality a dedicated and hard-working politician. He frequently worked six days a week, twelve to fourteen hours a day, and many of those eye-straining, unglamorous hours were spent alone at his desk. In addition to being prime minister he normally served as the minister of a major government department, and a steady flow of administrative work went along with that. He was also, of course, the leader of the Liberal-Conservative Party. That job required him to constantly keep in touch with scores of party organizers and to utilize his talents for massaging egos, smoothing over internal conflicts, and keeping everyone united under his leadership.

Of great importance was his talent for managing the federal cabinet. Macdonald, who once listed his profession as "cabinet-maker," chose his ministers carefully, making sure to include representatives from all provinces and every important voting bloc in the country.[18] Sometimes it was painfully obvious that someone was in the cabinet simply to represent a certain region, race, or religion. For example, Mackenzie Bowell, a newspaper publisher from Ontario, was a man of unspectacular talent or intellect. But he was a former Grand Master of the Orange Order, an association representing hundreds of thousands of Protestant votes, and thus Macdonald entrusted Bowell with the Customs Department. Frank Smith, an Irish Catholic Ontario businessman, was even less distinguished than Bowell. He had not been elected (Sir John had to appoint him as a senator to make him eligible for inclusion in the cabinet) and he was merely a minister of state, a euphemism for what might as well have been called the portfolio of "minister for Irish Catholics from Ontario." Political usefulness usually trumped personal ability when it came to fixing the cabinet. But that was all right. "A good carpenter," Sir John insisted, "can work with indifferent tools."[19]

Fortunately, it was sometimes possible to find party members who fit the needed political criteria but were also competent. John Thompson, a portly and good-natured man who had been a brilliant lawyer, judge, and premier of Nova Scotia before Sir John made him minister of justice in 1885, was a lucky find. The important Quebec ministers—Hector Langevin, Joseph-Adolphe Chapleau, and Joseph-Adolphe Caron—were all highly capable, even if they had a distracting tendency to wage political turf wars with each other. Then there was Sir Charles Tupper of Nova Scotia, who was probably the Canadian politician with the greatest stature next to Macdonald himself. Tupper was an arrogant, bullying, self-aggrandizing person whom Sir John had struggled to get along with in the past. But the "War Horse of Cumberland" had tremendous ability, and his thundering presence on the campaign trail was vital to Conservative prospects. For this reason, Sir Charles had been recalled from a diplomatic post in England—"you must take hold of Nova Scotia," Macdonald had insisted—and installed as minister of finance only days before the election of 1887 had begun.[20]

Tupper preferred his post in England, and it says much about his loyalty to the prime minister that he returned. Even with his exceptional personal skills, however, Sir John could not have kept such a disparate cabinet functioning without a philosophy that suited both his party and the times. Here, again, he has often been misunderstood. His opponents claimed that he had no principles at all. According to this theory, Macdonald was a political jellyfish, a spineless creature buffeted aimlessly by the prevailing currents of public opinion. Staying in power was the only thing that mattered to him, the story went, and this accounted for the seemingly endless compromises and policy reversals that had marked his career.

This view of Macdonald is wrong. He was neither stubborn and doctrinaire nor spineless. He had certain unshakable principles, and fortunately, they coincided with the principles held by most Canadians in the latter nineteenth century. He was, first of all, deeply British. Macdonald loved Britain's Empire, its parliamentary system, its tradition of common law, and even its style of spelling (it was Sir John who passed a minute of council to ensure that Canadians would forever retain the "u" in "colour"[21]). At the same time, he had a healthy distrust of the United States, and this too was a common prejudice among Canadians. Beyond that he pursued broad, simple goals: to encourage economic progress and to prevent racial or religious conflict; and by doing those things, keep the country together. For fifteen of the last twenty years Macdonald had managed to do exactly that.

To achieve these goals was, of course, a complicated business. Nineteenth-century Canada was, we have seen, a factionalized place. People identified themselves by their religion, language, or region more readily than with any "Canadian identity." English Canadians suspected French Canadians, and those suspicions tended to be mutual. People from central Canada had little in common with those from the Maritimes. British Columbia, thousands of miles away, was like a separate universe. Then there were more precise divisions: Ontario society was vastly different from that of Quebec, and each Maritime province cherished its distinct history and culture. Western Canada was rarely visited by anyone who was not settling there, and the plights of aboriginal and Métis populations were ignored by everybody. There were other differences, and they were all divisive. Catholic versus Protestant. Rural versus urban. Rich versus poor. It went on and on.[22]

Macdonald had almost always found a way to smooth over these differences. His great assets, aside from his core political values, were his tolerance, patience, and pragmatism. It is difficult to single out one trait from the others, but his tolerance was probably of paramount importance. Sir John was an English Canadian through and through. Yet, from the early days of his political career, he understood the essential truth of Canadian politics: that French and English politicians must build a coalition within a single party in order to wield power in federal politics. He had not pioneered the concept—the Liberals had actually formed the first "bi-racial" ministry in the old Province of Canada between 1848 and 1851—but Macdonald's superior ability to form strong bonds with his French Canadian counterparts had made his party dominant since that time.

He believed in the "two nations" concept of Canada, which basically maintained that English Canada was the home of English-speaking Canadians and that Quebec must be acknowledged as the home of French-speaking Canadians. Macdonald believed that, given their own sphere of influence and treated with respect by the rest of the population, most French Canadians would take their place in the federal government and feel part of the Dominion of Canada. "Treat them as a nation," Sir John said, "and they will act as a free people generally do—generously. Treat them as a faction, and they will become factious."[23] He followed his own advice. His governments relied on strong contingents from Quebec, and he always had a trusted Quebec lieutenant to manage political affairs in the province.

In matters of policy, Macdonald was an original progressive conservative. It was in his nature to lean toward tradition and to keep things as they were. He saw no point, however, in clinging to views that had become outdated. Sir John was too pragmatic to lose elections simply by failing to acknowledge changes in public opinion. "You must yield to the times," he once said.[24] He had made an art of it during his career, patiently waiting until the moment was right, then suddenly embracing a policy that he had until that moment opposed. It seemed outrageous, but it worked. There were almost too many instances to list. He had opposed responsible government in the 1840s, for example, until the tide in its favour became irresistible. He had opposed representation by population, or "rep by pop," only to support it when it became a part of Confederation. He had even opposed Confederation itself until, after yielding to the times, he had thrown himself merrily into the business of nation building.

There was always a risk that this behaviour would be interpreted as opportunism rather than pragmatism, and the charge of inconsistency dogged Macdonald throughout his career. Fortunately for him, Canadian politics did not revolve solely around matters of public policy. There were other ways to win elections, and no one knew the tricks of the trade better than Macdonald.

The Ruthless Bully

The least glorious factors contributing to Macdonald's success were his distribution of government patronage and his penchant for cheating in elections.

Sir John had not invented the practice of giving favours to political supporters, of course. It was the oldest practice in politics. Everyone had done it before him, Liberals and Conservatives alike, although the Liberals liked to preach principle over patronage (easy to do, by the way, when sitting on the Opposition benches). The general concern was how blatantly Sir John employed patronage as a means of staying in power, without even a casual regard for the traditional conception of fair play.

The distribution of patronage served a number of purposes. First, it was a way to reward loyal Tories for their years of service to the party. The procedure was informal but well known.[25] Applicants for government jobs—everything from postal clerks to judges to federal senators—applied not to the department where the position had been posted, but to the executive committee of the local Conservative constituency association. This committee (along with the local member of Parliament in many cases) would write a letter of recommendation to the prime minister. If the applicant had sweated blood for the Conservatives and had never once strayed to the Liberals, Macdonald would probably approve the application. His endorsement would be forwarded to the relevant cabinet minister, and another faithful Conservative would be confirmed in his allegiance for the rest of his working days. The same rule held for other forms of patronage: contracts for the construction of public works, for example, and government advertising that was sold only to Tory newspapers.

This system did more than reward supporters for good behaviour. It made it clear that anybody who wanted a government job—and these were prized as generally steady, well-paid, long-term positions—had better start knocking on doors for the Conservative Party. This was not an incidental side effect of the system; it was a deliberate strategy to discourage people from supporting Liberal Party candidates. Macdonald even withheld patronage from constituencies that failed to elect Conservatives, sending a message to party workers and voters alike. When Toronto Tories once complained that patronage had not been flowing into their Liberal-held constituencies, Macdonald replied matter-of-factly, "When Toronto elects Conservative members, Toronto will get Conservative appointments. But not before."[26]

Even the way that elections were run was affected. Macdonald had extended his ruthlessly partisan style of allocating patronage to the selection of returning officers, who oversaw voters lists and polling stations. In 1885, after an enormous struggle in Parliament, the Conservatives had passed the Franchise Act. This legislation took control of the federal franchise away from provincial governments (too many of which were Liberal for Macdonald's taste) and placed it in the hands of his own federal government. The rules regarding voter eligibility were a nightmarish labyrinth, and great discretion was assigned to returning officers who would now, presumably, interpret their lists in a manner that favoured the Conservatives. The Franchise Act, the Liberals howled, had been designed to tilt the playing field hopelessly against them. They were right. In a political career that spanned more than forty years, Macdonald confided to a close friend, he considered the passage of the Franchise Act his "greatest triumph."[27]

This heavy-handed use of patronage distorted Canadian politics in several ways. First, because the actual merit of applicants was irrelevant in comparison to their political allegiance, the federal civil service had acquired a shabby reputation. Second, the confidence of many Canadians in the basic fairness of their political system had been shaken. Third, the fact that applications for patronage went through the prime minister himself had centralized the Conservative Party to a remarkable degree. It had become a habit for the Tories to run everything past him, to rely upon his judgment, and to defer to his authority on matters large and small. They were no longer the Conservative Party at all, their critics sniped. They were the Macdonald Party.

The Liberals, of course, denounced the whole practice. Always inclined to cast themselves as morally superior, they contended that Tory patronage had led not only to bad appointments but also to the gross misuse of public funds, especially through the awarding of government contracts. There was even a word for this shameful business—*boodle*—which one Liberal newspaper helpfully explained was derived from the Dutch *boedel*, "signifying property or goods obtained in an illegitimate way."[28] The Liberals never tired of finding inventive ways to employ the term. Their opponents were no-good "boodlers," practising the odious politics of "boodleism." Macdonald himself was the "Boodle King." One widely reprinted campaign cartoon in February 1887 depicted "The March of the Boodle Brigade," a wretched line of Conservative hangers-on and office seekers. All were shuffling with heads down and eyes to the ground, avoiding the light of a rising sun representing "Canada's hopes for honest government."[29]

That was marvellous stuff, but it could not be denied that Macdonald's system had been a tremendous success. For decades he had used its invisible threads to pull the Conservatives together and unite them under his leadership. In every constituency in the Dominion there were Tories who owed their jobs to his government, and he could rely upon their energetic support in the final days of this miserable winter campaign. Nor would they be winning over voters with mere wishes and prayers. The Conservatives had a massive financial advantage over the Liberals, thanks to contributions made by wealthy manufacturers who were grateful for the high tariffs of the National Policy. Macdonald had assembled them, as he had done in previous elections, in the Red Parlour of the Queen's Hotel in Toronto. In that infamous smoke-filled room he had made his regular plea for support, and the manufacturers had responded with undisclosed sums of money. In an era when votes could be bought for a few dollars apiece, whatever the issues of the campaign might be, having that kind of money to throw around was sure to breathe life into the Conservative Party.

The March of the Boodle Brigade

In the end it was just as well that the prime minister had gone to bed before all the votes had been tallied in the 1887 election. The Old Man needed his sleep, and nothing was settled on election night anyway. It was not until the third or fourth day afterward that Liberal newspapers began to come to grips with the results. They could not change the meaning of the columns of polling numbers that crowded their front pages. They were loath to admit it, but Sir John A. Macdonald and the Conservative Party had triumphed. Canadians who desired an explanation for this outcome were obliged by journalists who painstakingly crunched the numbers region by region, province by province, riding by riding, and poll by poll.[30]

First, all eyes looked to Quebec. The Tories had won massively there in the last two elections—fifty-one of sixty-five seats in 1882—and if the Liberals had managed merely to break even they could celebrate a dramatic reversal of their fortunes. They had not quite done it.

Twenty-nine seats had been won by the Liberals and another three had been won by the National Conservatives, a cadre of politicians who called for the defence of Quebec against the Riel-hanging Macdonald government. They had not been opposed in their own ridings by the Liberals, who could probably count on their support in the House of Commons.

That added up to thirty-two seats, but Macdonald and the Liberal-Conservatives had done them one better—literally. They claimed thirty-three seats and a very narrow advantage in the popular vote, thus preserving their hold—a tenuous one indeed—on the province. There were several explanations for their success. Party affiliation ran deep in Quebec and was not easily altered even by events as traumatic as the hanging of Riel. The Catholic Church, though indignant at the hanging, had largely remained loyal to the government. So had Macdonald's French Canadian lieutenants: Chapleau, Caron, and Langevin. They had faced withering criticism on the campaign trail, particularly the nefarious charge of *vendu* (sell-out), but they had defended the government's actions and probably salvaged precious seats by doing so. It also helped that the Riel affair had occurred more than a year earlier, allowing emotions to subside. Finally, a narrow majority of the people of Quebec apparently still trusted the Old Man to look after their interests, as he always had. Even so, the results in Quebec were exciting for the Liberals.

However, the outcome in their own stronghold, Ontario, was a deep disappointment. The Tories had beaten them there in the last two elections and, despite the economic depression, had beaten them again. Their margin of victory, fifty-five seats to thirty-seven, was exactly the same as it had been in the election of 1882. The Liberals had lost a number of close races—in Haldimand riding their sitting member of Parliament, Charles Coulter, lost by a single vote—and they had not managed to beat any important Tories in their own ridings.[31] The prime minister himself had come within seventeen votes of failing to reclaim his seat in Kingston.

The West, as expected, voted overwhelmingly for the Tories. British Columbia gave all six of its seats to the government, and it was the same story in the four newly created ridings of the North-West Territories. Only in the Marquette riding of Manitoba did the Liberals win a seat, one that they already held. Across the region the count was a fourteen-to-one landslide for the government. Still, if only because they had expected to lose in the West, this was not the worst of the news for the Liberals.

Their greatest disappointment came in the Maritimes. There they actually won the popular vote in the region by a razor-thin margin—about 500 votes out of 175,000 cast—but somehow that slight majority was not translated into substantial gains. They picked up two seats in Prince Edward Island, giving them all of its six seats, and they gained one in New Brunswick, nudging their tally there to six of sixteen seats. But that was it. Nova Scotia, where Liberal hopes had run high, had returned Conservative M.P.s in fourteen of twenty-one constituencies, the same outcome as in the previous election. For Macdonald, who had feared a disastrous defeat in the province, just holding steady was a triumph. The Tory newspapers crowed that Sir Charles Tupper's speaking tour had single-handedly turned the Nova Scotian elections around. The Liberal newspapers grumbled that the traditional Conservative tools of booze, boodle, and bribery had again defeated the true will of the Nova Scotia electorate. They could grumble all they wanted. The outcome in the Maritime provinces, even after a bitter round of petitions launched by both parties, was solidly Tory.

In the final tally, Sir John A. Macdonald and the Liberal-Conservatives were comfortably re-elected with 126 of 215 seats in the House of Commons. It was a drop of thirteen seats from the election of 1882, but that hardly mattered. The party still had a serviceable majority. None of the factors that had worked against the party during the campaign—its lengthy tenure in office, its struggle to end the depression, its mishandling of the Riel affair—proved to be enough to oust the government. Sir

John A. Macdonald, at seventy-two years of age, had once again proved himself the most resilient politician in the young country's history. He again pulled out all the stops, and the voters rewarded him with another majority—another four, perhaps five, years in which to govern the Dominion of Canada.

The Liberals cried foul. The Boodle Brigade marched on.

TWO

The Fearful Blunder

The election had taken a heavy toll on Edward Blake. Tired and frustrated, the Liberal leader searched vainly for answers in the study of Humewood, his Toronto home. How could Macdonald have won again? The National Policy was a failure. The West had been neglected. Riel had been hanged. And there had been, as always, the boodling. How had so many sins gone unpunished? Blake's bitterness was plain in a post-mortem letter to Wilfrid Laurier, his close confidant and Quebec lieutenant. "The case against the government was so overwhelming," he reflected, "it ought to have so absolutely enlisted the more intelligent and independent and moral parts of the community." Blake found it almost impossible to bear the country's failure to rise to the occasion. "The moral tone is so low, the game of grab is so openly played," he continued, "that I think it more likely that we shall see a cynical expansion of the iniquitous system of the past than a revulsion against it."[1]

This was something more than the usual post-election sour grapes. Blake wasn't just discouraged by another Liberal defeat. He was disappointed with the whole electoral system, and with Canadians themselves.

He was tired of seeing them rally to Sir John A. in spite of his flaws. He was tired of the stresses of the Liberal leadership, of the long hours and the pressure and the little indignities of public life. He wanted out. The call of duty tore at his conscience and kept him agonizing for a couple of days, but in the end the "game of grab" was too much for him. On March 3 he sent a letter to his fellow Liberal members of Parliament, announcing his intention to resign the leadership before the opening of the next session.

This was appalling news, and all hell promptly broke loose in the Liberal Party. Blake had led the party for seven years, and in all that time there had been hardly a whisper about replacing him. There was a remarkable consensus within the ranks that he was the best man for the job and that his departure would be a disaster for the party. As the news of his intentions filtered out, dozens of letters flew back and forth between frantic Liberals who debated how they could best persuade their leader to stay at his post. More poured into Blake's study from all over the country. Every one of them pleaded with him to reconsider.

A leading Liberal in Prince Edward Island, Louis Davies, assured Blake that his constituency supporters had told him "they were voting for *Blake* and so it was throughout the Island and doubtless through the other provinces." Charles Weldon, a senior M.P. from New Brunswick, noted that throughout the Maritimes Blake enjoyed not only the "esteem and respect of the Liberal Party but their entire confidence." From Manitoba, James Fisher, a party worker, claimed that "in no part of the Dominion have you firmer friends than here." From Quebec came a concerned message from Laurier, who was Blake's parliamentary deskmate and probably his closest confidant. "I am quite sure, my dear Blake, that you do not realize the real position which you occupy in the party," Laurier wrote, "nor the respect, admiration and affection which every one of your followers entertains for your talents and character." And from Ontario, the traditional fortress of the federal Liberals, came the most desperate pleas of all. J.D. Edgar, a key organizer in the province, best summarized the feelings of panic and denial that had gripped his Ontario colleagues. "I do not think the caucus will choose any other leader," Edgar wrote flatly, "and you can't make them do it."[2]

The Hamlet of Canada

It was no wonder that the Liberals were anxious to keep him at the helm. Edward Blake was first-rate material, a politician whose intelligence, integrity, and eloquence were admitted even by the Conservatives. He came from a famous Toronto family—his father, William Hume Blake, had been one of Upper Canada's great legal minds—and Edward had followed in his footsteps, earning a reputation as an outstanding lawyer in his own right. He was a founding partner of one of Canada's most prestigious firms, and widely acclaimed for successfully representing Ontario in several landmark constitutional cases against the Macdonald government.[3] Blake was a master of logic and argumentation, capable of making relentless, devastating speeches in the House of Commons. His knowledge of political issues was unsurpassed by anyone but the prime minister himself. At fifty-three he was in the prime of life. In many ways—even in his tall, broad, imposing presence—Edward Blake could be judged the equal or better of Sir John A. Macdonald.

Yet, he had never become prime minister. Blake's twenty-year career in politics had been, after a fine beginning, an exercise in frustration and disappointment. He had entered public life in 1867 largely out of a sense of obligation to lend his services to the country. (He also had a famous family name to uphold and, no doubt, at least some attraction to power.) In the elections of that year he won a seat in both the House of Commons and the Ontario legislature. He focused mainly on provincial politics and rose quickly through the ranks; he was soon a cabinet minister and, by 1871, he was premier of Ontario. After only a year in that office, however, he decided to abandon provincial politics in favour of the national stage.

Though he was touted as a natural leader of the federal Liberal Party, Blake was at first reluctant to take the job, citing his delicate health. The leadership went instead to Alexander Mackenzie, under whom Blake served an awkward apprenticeship from 1873 to 1880. Mackenzie was a common man, in the very best and worst senses of that term. A former stonemason, he was remarkably honest and diligent. He was neither power-hungry nor pretentious (both Mackenzie and Blake refused British knighthoods on the grounds that they were no better than their fellow Canadians), and his sincerity and work ethic were great assets to the party. The trouble was that Mackenzie entirely lacked charisma and imagination. He was a shy, humourless man who drew little joy out of life. (He disliked sports, for example, because he couldn't see the point of getting tired for no constructive purpose.) As a leader he was uninspiring, and his political skills were certainly no match for those of Macdonald.

Mackenzie became an "accidental" prime minister in 1873, after a particularly egregious case of boodling, the Pacific Scandal, forced the Conservatives from power. It was bad luck that his five years in office were marred by a severe economic depression. Blake was unhappy serving under Mackenzie, and drifted in and out of the cabinet as his conscience and unsteady health dictated. This did not help the government, which was star-crossed anyway and did not need a man of Blake's stature undermining Mackenzie. When the Liberals were beaten badly in the election of 1878, the knives came out. The old stonemason was angry to be forced out, but grudgingly accepted the will of the party. Blake again claimed that he did not want the job, but this time, perhaps, he did not need quite so much coaxing. In April 1880, Edward Blake assumed the leadership of the Liberal Party of Canada.

There would come a time when becoming Liberal leader practically guaranteed becoming prime minister. This was not the case in the 1880s. As a cohesive political organization, the Liberal Party of Canada hardly existed at all. It was really a loosely stitched coalition of the former colonial parties—Reform or Liberal or *rouge*—that had developed separately in the early 1800s. Unlike the Conservatives, these Liberal factions had never quite coalesced into a national party after Confederation. At the local level members were often more loyal to the provincial party than to its national counterpart. Support for the federal party was pathetic in British Columbia and the North-West, modest in Manitoba, up and down in the Maritimes, historically weak but improving in Quebec, and reliably strong only in Ontario. In the six federal elections since 1867, the Liberals had won only once, in 1874, and that victory was due more to the temporary unpopularity of the Conservatives than to any outpouring of excitement about the Liberals.

How could this lack of success be explained? The most obvious explanation was the great strength of the Tories. Macdonald's personal appeal, his skilful distribution of patronage, and his government's manipulation of the electoral system combined to make the Conservatives nearly unbeatable. No one said it better than one of the Ontario party organizers, W.T.R. Preston, who had a simple explanation for the inability of his leader to beat Macdonald. "It was not that public opinion had failed to support him," Preston later lamented of Blake, "but that public opinion was not free to express itself."[4]

Policies mattered, too. The Conservatives had taken the lion's share of the credit for Confederation itself, and they had since established themselves as Canada's forward-looking, "nation-building" party. They had implemented the National Policy, added three provinces and the vast North-West to the country, and built the Canadian Pacific Railway. The Liberals, being in opposition, had been the ones to criticize the Conservatives at every step. "Little Canadians," Sir John A. liked to call them, and there was some truth in the name. The Liberals, with their lack of interest in the settlement of the North-West, their disparagement of the railway, and their attachment to "provincial rights," seemed to possess less of a national vision—less *courage*, above all—than the Conservatives.

For all that, the Liberal Party might have won more elections if only they had been able to challenge the Tories in Quebec. Macdonald and his now-deceased ally, George-Étienne Cartier, had created a French-English coalition in the 1850s that was still the basis of the Conservative Party's electoral success in the 1880s. Macdonald's record of tolerance and respect toward French Canadians, and his long-standing habit of giving important cabinet posts to Quebec politicians, had long ago persuaded the influential Catholic Church of Quebec—inherently suspicious of liberalism in general—to throw its support behind his party. Catholic priests routinely instructed their parishioners to vote Conservative, a flagrant blurring of the supposed line drawn between church and state. That kind of help, coupled with the usual Conservative advantage in campaign funds and patronage, had made for a lot of lean years for Quebec Liberal politicians.

Nor had the traditional attitude of Ontario Liberals toward Quebec helped matters. Once, there had been a successful French-English Liberal partnership. From 1848 to 1851, the Province of Canada had been governed by a "Great Ministry," the first to operate as a truly responsible government, under co-premiers Robert Baldwin and Louis-Hippolyte Lafontaine. Since the early 1850s, however, Liberals in Ontario had tended to espouse an angry and loud-mouthed liberalism that was often hostile to the French language and the Catholic faith.[5] George Brown, bombastic founder of the Toronto *Globe* and the leading Liberal in the province from the mid-1850s to early 1870s, had often rallied supporters by invoking fears of "French domination." That strategy had won him votes in Ontario, but had devastated the federal party in Quebec. Mackenzie had been better than Brown in this respect—he had never pandered to anti-French sentiment—but he was never quite a genuinely national leader either.

Edward Blake was a broad-minded politician, and sometimes a practical one too. It was obvious to him that the Liberals could not win a majority government with appeals to anti-French or anti-Catholic prejudice in Ontario and the Maritimes. The country was both English and French, and so the Liberal Party must be as well. During his years as Liberal leader, Blake had championed a moderate and inclusive liberalism that was designed to make French Canadian Catholics feel welcome within the party. His close friendship and political alliance with Wilfrid Laurier was a testament to his sincerity. At the same time, Blake had tried hard to expunge lingering anti-Quebec sentiment in the party, especially in its Ontario wing. Most important, he had refused to condone the execution of Louis Riel. It would have been popular in Ontario to cheer it; indeed, several Ontario Liberals refused to support Blake's position. But his stand against the execution was appreciated in Quebec, and the Liberals won nearly half the seats in the province in the election of 1887.

On the race-and-religion question, then, Blake was a major improvement over Liberal leaders past. On the other vital question of the day, trade with the United States, he was less decisive. Free trade was one of the party's fundamental principles. Blake accepted the principle, but worried that American influence over Canada would be too great if complete free trade prevailed. He also doubted that the federal budget could stand the loss of revenues that would result from abolishing the tariff on American imports. He said as much during the 1887 campaign in a speech delivered at Malvern, Ontario. The Malvern speech was a candid admission that in the present circumstances free trade was impossible and that the National Policy would not be much altered by a Liberal government. That was honest, but discouraging. Canadians craved bolder solutions to their economic misery, and instead, Blake had basically conceded the all-important trade issue to the Conservatives. That strategic error was a leading reason for their recent defeat.

There was another, perhaps more fundamental reason for the consistent failure of Edward Blake to defeat Sir John A. Macdonald. Canadians had famously preferred Sir John drunk to George Brown sober; now they seemed to feel the same way about Blake. Macdonald privately admitted that he enjoyed running against Blake because he was the weakest opponent that the Liberals could possibly put up against him. That was harsh, but perceptive. The truth was that Edward Blake had personal failings that prevented him being an effective leader.

The most obvious problem was that he hated politics. Blake would have been happier if he had never left the courtroom. In that rational setting, meticulous research and precise reasoning were rewarded. Canadian politics was not like that at all. The issues were never black and white; they were shrouded in maddening clouds of grey, and the need to find common ground between so many groups of people made it exceedingly difficult to adopt a principled position. Blake hated grubbing for votes. He was never comfortable mingling with the masses in the endless succession of small-town meetings that he encountered on the campaign trail. Crowd-winning raunchy jokes and simplistic slogans were beneath him. He refused to pander. Blake could not in good conscience tell the people what they wanted to hear. That was principled, perhaps even admirable, but it didn't win elections.

Blake commanded respect from his followers because of his intellect and ability, but he was not a people person. He was notoriously snobbish and self-absorbed, and completely uninterested in the friendly camaraderie—the boozing and backslapping—at which Macdonald so excelled. He frequently slept at his desk while his followers were making speeches in the House. He hardly seemed to notice them when they passed him in the hallways. This was not entirely his fault, actually: Blake had poor eyesight and often failed to recognize familiar faces. He privately lamented this shortcoming, but it was hardly the one that mattered most.

The fundamental problem was that, deep down, Edward Blake was an anxious and unhappy man who constantly wrestled with a menagerie of personal demons.[6] He had grown up in an extremely driven family, and the pressure to succeed had been a heavy burden. His mother, Catherine, had raised him to be a devout Anglican, but in adulthood he had doubted his faith, causing him to be racked with guilt. Blake was obsessively preoccupied with telling the truth and remaining morally incorruptible: he felt that it was better to be right than victorious. And so he was often right and never victorious. For him to pass up political opportunities rather than offend his conscience, particularly when competing against Macdonald, was like playing the game of politics with one hand—perhaps both hands—tied behind his back.

Blake's health, both mental and physical, was another issue. He was afflicted by chronic "neurasthenia," a mysterious nineteenth-century illness associated with anxiety, headaches, and an inability to function under stress. This condition—exasperating both to himself and his followers—had worsened. The demands of leadership were great, and he was all too often felled by the strain. There was no remedy but rest. For this reason Blake was fond of taking long recuperative vacations at the family cottage in Murray Bay, Quebec. Off he would go whenever his affliction hit, no matter how desperately the Liberals might need him at that particular moment. When the going got tough, as the saying goes, Edward Blake got going—to Murray Bay, where he could find peace and a refuge from politics.

This behaviour, even if dictated by his medical condition, gave the impression that Blake was concerned first with himself and only second with the fortunes of the Liberal Party. The impression was reinforced by other aspects of his conduct. He had never been a good party man, never the type who could submerge his own feelings and opinions for the party's benefit. He was guided by his principles, not the exigencies of party politics, and it showed, for example, in his titanic speeches (which of course he expected his followers to listen to without sleeping). Blake was very fond of—to use a charming nineteenth-century term—speechifying. He would address the House for five, six, even seven hours at a stretch. These speeches were monuments of preparation and detail, but they were boring, draining, and demoralizing to those who had to speak after him. "Blake exhausted every subject he touched," one Liberal M.P. complained. "Nothing was left for his followers to say."[7]

Blake's most infuriating trait was his total lack of enthusiasm for the job. He was always dwelling on the difficulty of leading the party, always complaining that he wasn't suited to public life. He had a habit of threatening to resign, and every time he did so the Liberals dutifully assured him that they could not carry on without him. That had always been enough to convince Blake that he should stay, but this behaviour was deeply distressing to the party. Recently his desire to leave politics had become even more pronounced. Just before the election of 1887, Blake tried to persuade Oliver Mowat, the long-serving premier of Ontario, to take over the federal party. When that effort failed, Blake was obliged to carry on, "obliged" being the key word. He waged a sulking and half-hearted campaign, refusing requests to speak across the country and appearing only in friendly rural Ontario constituencies. He hadn't even made a speech in Toronto, where he actually lived.

Clearly, Blake was a flawed leader. Nevertheless, the Liberals couldn't imagine moving forward without him, and again they urged him to stay, and again he was moved by the argument that he could not abandon the party. As J.D. Edgar put it, "It would humiliate every reformer in Canada to think that the tories had driven you from your position."[8] Blake was tormented by the jibes and taunts of the Conservative press when rumours of his threatened resignation leaked out. When he returned from South Carolina at the end of March (he had gone there after announcing his intention to resign, on another restorative vacation), Blake sat down and reviewed his options.

On March 28, after much agonizing, he drafted a letter to his colleagues pleading for their understanding. He was mentally exhausted and physically very ill. His legal practice and family life had suffered because of his devotion to public duty. He simply could not do the job anymore, he confessed, because of "impaired health, diminished means, vanished business and neglected home affairs." Plus, he admitted frankly, "the ambition to rule a free country is a high and honourable ambition ... but it unfortunately happens that I am by temperament averse to rule."[9] Had they read this anguished letter, it would have been difficult for the Liberals not to feel some sympathy for their leader. It was a shame they never saw it.

Blake decided that this letter was too personal, and crafted a second that actually went out to the party. It was flat and unemotional, stating only that he had his reasons for leaving. It did, however, offer hope to those who urged him to stay. Acknowledging that some had suggested that he share the burden of the leadership instead of quitting entirely, Blake reluctantly expressed a willingness to retain the "nominal lead" of a committee that might be created to direct the party in the current parliamentary session. "I believe this plan will be unsatisfactory as a makeshift," he warned, "while as a permanency it would be intolerable."[10] But the party was thrilled. On April 14, the day after the opening of Parliament, the Liberals held a full caucus and Blake was unanimously re-elected. The committee that would shoulder the workload consisted of eight leading Liberals (two each from Ontario and Quebec, and one from each Maritime province and Manitoba). And so the Liberals began the parliamentary session in April 1887 guided by committee.

It didn't last. Despite the high hopes, the new arrangement began to fall apart in a matter of weeks. It was too hard to make decisions with so many individuals involved, and uncertainty gripped the backbenchers. Sir Richard Cartwright, a member of the committee, complained of "half our men seeking by any and every miserable way to shirk a vote on the very simplest and plainest questions."[11] Nor did the committee bring much relief to Blake. By mid-May word had gotten around that he was thinking of resigning entirely. His health seemed to be getting worse. He looked awful in the House of Commons on May 26, and was sufficiently stricken by illness to spend the next week in bed. It was becoming painfully clear that he was not going to be able to stay on, even in a reduced role.

The Pretenders

Doctors hurried to and from Humewood all that week as the Liberals waited anxiously to see Blake. The challenge of choosing a successor had settled gloomily upon them. There was no obvious successor. Blake himself had tried to woo Oliver Mowat, but the Ontario premier had declined to leave Queen's Park, where he occupied a dominant position, to take over a federal party that lacked access to power or patronage. Now, since the most recent Liberal defeat, there was even less reason for him to take the job.

Perhaps someone could be found from within the federal ranks. Party newspapers wondered if David Mills, M.P. for Bothwell, Ontario, might be suitable for the job. Mills was a "Blake man" with a long record of service to the party. He had held his rural riding since Confederation and had served as minister of the interior in Mackenzie's cabinet. A lawyer and professor, Mills was a fine constitutional theorist and expert on Canadian federalism. Leadership material, however, he was not. He cared little for French Canada and was denounced in the Quebec press as "a man of narrow and extremely partisan views."[12] His personality was uninspiring and so were his windy, pretentious, know-it-all parliamentary speeches. Someone—probably Macdonald—had once called him "the Philosopher from Bothwell." That this mocking nickname had stuck was strong evidence that Mills was not a serious candidate for the leadership.

Also publicly mentioned as a possible successor was J.D. Edgar. Though he was M.P. for Ontario West, east of Toronto, it was not his presence in the House of Commons that made Edgar important. For years he had been the indispensable organizer of the federal party in Ontario, ensuring that local constituencies fielded strong candidates and remained in a state of campaign readiness. He had also been their bagman, the person with the unhappy task, especially in a party out of power, of squeezing supporters for financial contributions. Over the course of the 1880s Edgar had made some headway here, creating a strategy for soliciting funds. He was also the parliamentary whip, enforcing party discipline on important votes in the House of Commons. Resourceful, dedicated, and trusted, Edgar was an important figure within the party and one of its most capable members.

Like Mills, however, Edgar lacked the charisma that was (if one can disregard the example of Blake himself) thought to be important for party leadership. He was a broad-minded politician for his day, sensitive to the concerns of French Canada, but this quality had not increased his popular appeal in Ontario. Better at wire-pulling behind the scenes than getting elected himself, Edgar had been defeated *nine times* in provincial and federal campaigns before the Liberals had finally, in 1884, secured him a safe seat. That was not an auspicious track record for a potential leader. Given that his talent was for organization rather than campaigning, it was hardly surprising that Edgar was not being widely considered for the top job.

By far the most obvious candidate to succeed Blake was the number-two man in the federal Liberal party, Sir Richard Cartwright. A picture of grim dignity, adorned with sprouting sidewhiskers that made him instantly recognizable (and to later generations of Canadians, faintly ridiculous), Cartwright definitely looked like a statesman. He had the experience needed to lead, having earned a British knighthood for his service as minister of finance in the Mackenzie government. He was respected for standing on principle—originally a Tory, Cartwright had grown so disenchanted with Macdonald's methods that he had crossed the floor just after Confederation—and for selfless honesty. He favoured free trade with the United States, a policy that a long-repressed faction of the Liberal Party would eagerly support. Most of all, Sir Richard was a heavyweight who seemed to have the *gravitas* to go toe-to-toe with Macdonald. Though his own efforts to persuade Blake to stay had likely been sincere, he was also, almost certainly, ambitious enough to accept the leadership if it was offered it to him.

Alas, as with the others, he had shortcomings. Cartwright was well respected in his native Ontario, but he had voted with the Conservatives over the Riel hanging and probably would lose the Liberals whatever ground Blake had gained for them in Quebec. His performance as minister of finance had been controversial; his austere policies had failed to remedy the depressed economy. Most of all, perhaps even more than the other leadership candidates, Cartwright did not inspire Canadians. He could inform them, in excruciating detail, of what was wrong with the Tories and the National Policy. But his speeches were like funeral orations. Macdonald endlessly mocked him as the "Blue Ruin Knight," a man who had no faith in the future of his own country. Even J.W. Bengough, the splendid cartoonist who usually sympathized with the Liberals, delighted in lampooning him. One of his best cartoons in the popular magazine *Grip* depicted Cartwright as a painter, standing proudly beside a freshly finished work, "The Future of Canada." The canvas was smothered in black paint. Another had a portrait artist attempting in vain to paint him, begging him to "try to look pleasant." "Impossible," his subject replied. "I am Sir Richard Cartwright."[13]

Still, the Blue Ruin Knight was the best of the Liberal lot, and widely considered the front-runner to succeed Blake. How that decision would be made was, unfortunately, another problem. The Liberal Party had no established process for replacing its leader. There had never been a popular vote by the rank and file to fill the position, nor had there been a party convention. Blake himself had taken the job from Alexander Mackenzie in an awkward fashion. At any rate, this situation now was different: Blake, unlike Mackenzie, clearly wanted to go. The closest thing to a custom in Canadian politics, one established by past practice, was that the outgoing leader would have the final word on the choice of his successor.

Whom would Blake choose? On June 1 he was well enough to receive a two-man Liberal deputation. David Mills and Charles Burpee, a recently defeated M.P. from New Brunswick, were given the task of visiting him at Humewood. Upon entering the house they found Blake lying on a sofa, tended to by his wife, Margaret. He looked terribly weary. Regarding the issue of the moment, however, Blake was able to muster surprising energy. In a dramatic and emphatic fashion he informed his colleagues of what would turn out be the most important decision of his political career. The man he named was neither Edgar, nor Mills, nor Cartwright. "There is only one possible choice," Blake announced firmly to the astonished delegation. "Laurier."[14]

The Elegant Dilettante

Mills and Burpee could hardly believe their ears. They left the room incredulous, and the reaction was basically the same throughout the Liberal Party as the news quickly spread. Laurier? Was Blake serious? For three months the party had agonized over his possible successor and no one, not even in private correspondence, had seriously put Wilfrid Laurier's name forward. It just didn't make sense. Laurier had political experience, of course. He had grown up in an intensely active Liberal family; he had been in the federal Parliament since 1874, most of that time representing Quebec East; and he had briefly served as minister of inland revenue in the Mackenzie government. He was thought by many to be the most eloquent speaker in Parliament in both English and French. And everybody liked him. Laurier was a good fellow. He was kind and well-mannered, handsome and charming. For a multitude of reasons, however, Wilfrid Laurier was not considered suitable material for the Liberal leadership.

The first problem was, of course, that he was a French Canadian Roman Catholic. There had not been either a French Canadian or a Roman Catholic leader of a federal party since Confederation, for the simple reason that such a leader would not be acceptable to a clear majority of Canadians. Outside of Quebec the country was dominated by English-speaking Protestants, and many were full-fledged Orangemen, solemnly pledged to resist the supposed encroachment of Catholicism in Canadian society. Surely there would be a mass defection of support from the Liberal Party in Ontario, and perhaps the Maritimes as well, if Laurier were made leader. It might be worth it, if Laurier inspired significant Liberal gains in Quebec. But the province had been a Tory bastion since Confederation, and the Liberals there were still vigorously opposed by the Catholic Church. It hardly seemed worth throwing away hard-earned votes in English Canada without a guarantee that the ground lost could definitely be made up in Quebec.

Laurier was potentially a liability in other respects. He was known throughout the Dominion as a stirring speaker who had weighed in on the issues of his times, and over the years he had said many things that had stung the ears of English Canadians. In the 1860s, editing a small *rouge* paper, *Le Défricheur*, a youthful Laurier had denounced Confederation as "the tomb of the French race."[15] If few Canadians remembered that slight, almost all remembered what Laurier had said after Louis Riel's execution. The week after the hanging, in front of forty thousand cheering French Canadians at the Champs de Mars in Montreal, he had declared, "Had I been born on the banks of the Saskatchewan, I too would have shouldered a musket!" His words came back to haunt him a year later when, addressing an unruly crowd in Toronto, he had struggled to make himself heard. "Where's your musket?" hecklers had jeered. "Where's your musket?"[16]

Even if one could accept the notion of a French Canadian Roman Catholic leader, Laurier in particular seemed a dubious choice. He liked his life in Arthabaskaville, where he and Zoe, his wife of twenty years, happily resided.[17] He had never shown any desire to lead the party or, for that matter, to become a prominent figure on the national stage. His eloquence was unforgettable, but he lacked the work ethic to do intensive research and produce the titanic parliamentary speeches of a man like Edward Blake. In the House of Commons, Laurier had for years served as a kind of personal assistant to Blake, keeping his papers properly shuffled and his glass of water full, while speaking himself only on rare occasions. Nor did he seem to have much liking for the smoke-filled rooms where Liberal Party organization and strategy were hammered out.

There were two other significant concerns. First, Laurier lacked the financial security that would allow him to give his full attention to the demands of the leadership. He made about two thousand dollars a year from his legal practice—good money for the times—but already he was spending only half his time tending to the practice, while the rest was consumed by politics. "I am not a wealthy man," he confessed in a letter to a friend, "and my health is poor."[18] His questionable health was the second concern. His family had been stalked by tuberculosis—his mother and sister had died from it—and an ominous dry cough was his near-constant companion. Laurier always looked pale, sometimes alarmingly so, and at times he could be witnessed coughing blood into his handkerchief. His doctor assured him that this was chronic bronchitis, but Laurier was prone to fear the worst, and his Liberal friends also worried for him. François Langelier, a friend and fellow Quebecer, was one of the few Liberals who had thought of Laurier as a possible successor. But for Langelier the problem of Laurier's health was paramount. In March he had told Blake, "Laurier would scarcely do on account of his want of physical strength."[19]

Finally, there was the question of his character. Laurier was elegant and a fine public speaker, but these qualities only counted for so much in the cut-and-thrust world of Canadian politics. Campaigns were conducted with no holds barred. Constituencies were won through scrapping and scuffling for votes that were often collected with the help of booze, bribes, and whatever else might be necessary. There was little evidence to suggest that Laurier had the stomach for the brawling reality of a nationwide campaign. He had never been called upon to make the really hard decisions that determined a party's fortunes. Some months later an Ontario Liberal, a veteran of many political battles, would remark to a journalist, "Laurier will never make a leader; he has not enough of the devil in him."[20]

Laurier himself tended to agree. On June 7 the Liberals held a caucus at which they accepted Blake's resignation and nominated Laurier for the leadership. He declined to accept, in spite of the dutiful protests of leading members of the party. To his friend Ernest Pacaud, a prominent journalist, he insisted, "I do not want to be leader. That is not my aspiration ... my friends are imposing too heavy a burden on me."[21] To Blake, Laurier insisted that everyone, Blake included, had gotten it wrong and that he was not fitted for the job. Eventually, though, he came around. On June 18 Laurier again wrote Blake to announce that he had changed his mind. Five days later, at the end of the parliamentary session, Laurier made public his decision to accept the party leadership. The news was duly transmitted to Canadians through the press.

That he accepted the leadership at all was an indication that there was something more to Wilfrid Laurier than his Liberal colleagues suspected. There was more ambition and self-confidence within him than he had let on, and perhaps he was tougher than his delicate health and suave demeanour suggested. Laurier came from the *rouge* tradition of Quebec politics, and in nineteenth-century Canada you did not survive as a *rouge* unless you were willing to do battle with the Roman Catholic Church. The merciless attacks by the bishops were cruel treatment for *rouges* such as Laurier, who were almost always faithful Catholics, and thus needed thick skins. On one occasion, when Quebec Catholic leaders warned parishioners that a *bleu* defeat would result in their wading "knee-deep in the blood of priests," one old *rouge* is said to have sighed, "Oh well. We'll put on high boots."[22]

Laurier had long possessed this kind of mettle. He had championed liberal views from a young age, and had suffered as a result. In 1867 he lost his job at *Le Défricheur* because the Church launched a vicious campaign against him; in his columns Laurier had defiantly replied, "You want war; you shall have it!"[23] He had lost that war but won many others since, and his constant preoccupation had always been the ever-controversial "race, language, and religion" issue. He believed that

Canada could be a great nation, indeed an example to the rest of the world, but only if its citizens were willing to live together on terms of genuine tolerance and respect. To achieve this, he contended, the liberal values of freedom of speech, freedom of the individual, and equal justice for all Canadians were of paramount importance. Laurier had fought for these things all his life. Now he would fight for them as leader of the Liberal Party.

Still, his acceptance of the leadership was not without regret or worry. He was not at all sure that English Canada was ready for a French Canadian party leader, or that it would ever be. He had seen what the leadership had done to Edward Blake, the toll it had taken on his health and family life. Laurier was happily married to Zoe—their only source of sadness was that they were childless—and their lives would now be intruded upon even further by politics. He also had doubts about how well he would handle the role. In his letter to Blake of June 18, the one in which he accepted the leadership, he revealed his feelings: "I know that I have not the aptitude for it, and I have a sad apprehension that it must end in disaster."[24]

Many Liberals agreed. Most English Canadian Liberals preferred Sir Richard Cartwright and had acquiesced to the selection of Laurier only because they believed it was temporary; surely Blake would return to the leadership once his health improved. In Ontario, Cartwright received a letter from a discouraged supporter who warned, "Do not be disappointed if you hear that I have turned Tory over the appointment ... the party is playing too much into the hands of the Catholic party ... a large amount of the best support of the Liberal party in Ontario will be alienated by the selection."[25] That was just what the Liberals were afraid of. J.D. Edgar, who as the chief party organizer in the province was finely attuned to such sentiments, confessed his dismay in a letter to his wife. "It is," he wrote simply, "a fearful blunder."[26]

THREE

The Business Proposition

Wilfrid Laurier had been Liberal leader for all of three weeks when he received a breathless letter from Sir Richard Cartwright. "Matters have been moving fast in Ontario within the last two weeks," the letter began. Then, somewhat ominously, "it is doubtful whether any public meeting can be held in a rural district without expressing a pretty decided opinion as to Commercial Union and I am beginning to think we may as well face the music ... Turn the matter over and write me."[1]

Turn it over, indeed. This was an entirely unexpected development. Commercial union, an idea that had been kicked around since the 1850s, was a radical proposal for free trade between Canada and the United States. It was more than radical, actually. It was revolutionary. C.U., as it had come to be called, would abolish the customs houses along the Canada-U.S. border, create a common external tariff against other countries (even Great Britain), and share the revenues raised by that tariff. For all practical purposes it would fuse the Canadian and

American economies, and to function properly it would require a vast and unprecedented degree of cooperation between the two governments. If it worked, the theory went, there would be a tremendous expansion of trade between the two countries. Resource producers and manufacturers alike would be free to sell their products in this enormous open market—no more tariffs to be paid, no more government favours to be curried—and on this theoretically level playing field, the most competitive players would lead the way toward greater wealth and prosperity for both countries.

That sounded good to many Canadians, but it alarmed many others. Sir John A. Macdonald and the Conservatives had always distrusted the idea. They suspected that commercial union would be disloyal to Great Britain and ruinous to Canada's perennially developing "infant industries." Resource producers—farmers, fishers, foresters, miners—would thrive, but like many Canadians, Macdonald feared that American manufacturers were too large and well established for Canadian manufacturers to compete against them without tariff protection. As the prime minister had put it in a private letter to Sir Charles Tupper back in 1884, "Our manufacturers are too young and weak yet ... they would be crushed out just now."[2] Worse, commercial union might also be politically entangling, a devious thin edge of the wedge toward the unthinkable: the annexation of Canada to the United States. It was no wonder that Macdonald was content to stay loyal to his Yankee-bashing, patriotic-sounding, election-winning National Policy. He knew better than to mess with a good thing.

Commercial union was a more complicated subject for the Liberals. Their natural inclination, as nineteenth-century classical liberals, was to sympathize with the principle of free trade between men and nations. An important wing of the party, led by Sir Richard Cartwright, favoured intimate trading relations with the United States. Yet a larger wing, led by Edward Blake, had always been doubtful. Commercial union would not be easy to implement. The day-to-day conditions of free trade would have to be enforced. The common tariff would have to be set and periodically revised. A reasonable formula for sharing customs revenues would have to be invented. And all these details would have to be worked out with the U.S. Congress, a legislative body that was fond of protectionist tariffs, suspicious of foreign entanglements, and inclined to regard Canada as a sleepy colonial backwater rather than a sovereign nation.[3] It seemed unlikely to doubters such as Blake that Ottawa could avoid being bullied by Washington. For all these reasons, the Liberal Party had always kept a safe distance from commercial union.

Neither party, then, had made the slightest effort to promote C.U. in the spring of 1887. And yet, as Cartwright informed Laurier, the subject was rapidly emerging from the grassroots as the hottest topic in the country's most populous province. Starting with a central convention in Toronto at the end of April, Ontario farmers had begun organizing "Farmers' Institutes" at the county level and holding public meetings to discuss the trade question. These meetings, in places like Owen Sound, Stratford, and Ameliasburgh, had been drawing crowds of between a few dozen and a few hundred. Party affiliation did not apply (Liberals and Tories had been mingling happily, which was uncommon indeed), and unanimous resolutions had been passed, frequently to rousing applause, in favour of commercial union or a similarly bold free-trade proposal.

By the middle of June it seemed that one of these meetings was being held almost every day in Ontario. The newspapers could not help but take notice, and some of them—including major Liberal organs like the Toronto *Globe*, Manitoba *Free Press*, and Halifax *Chronicle*—jumped on the bandwagon without getting permission from the federal party leaders. Even in some American newspapers, whose apathy toward the Dominion was legendary, there were some stirrings of interest and even support. The New York *Times* was most impressed, declaring grandly near the end of May that "commercial union has become the question of the hour in Canada."[4] It was an accurate assessment. And it had all happened, somehow, without the encouragement of the two Canadian political parties.

If neither the Conservatives nor the Liberals wanted commercial union to become a live issue, how was it making such headway? The obvious explanation lay in the times themselves. Farmers, still the largest voting constituency in Canada, were suffering in the late 1880s, trapped in a prolonged economic depression. For them the effects of the National Policy had been devastating. The towering tariffs at the Canada-U.S. border had been gouging the farmers coming and going. American-made manufactured goods had a fine reputation in Canada; quite often they were better made and cheaper than their Canadian-made equivalent. These imports were too expensive for Canadian farmers to buy under the National Policy because U.S. companies simply passed the cost of the tariff (usually about 30 percent on top of their usual price) on to their customers north of the border. Having paid extra for U.S. goods, Canadian farmers then had to pay punishing tariffs on their own crops before exporting them into the U.S. market. This extra expense made it almost impossible for them to compete with American farmers, who could of course sell their crops freely in their own market. Rural families had consequently been struggling to keep their farms afloat, cursed by inflated prices on things they wanted to buy and profit-sapping tariffs on things they needed to sell.

Under the circumstances, it was only natural that many rural Canadians would be interested in heroic remedies. But movements need leaders, too, and just at this moment an interesting collection of businessmen and journalists emerged to promote the policy in Canada and the United States. Their efforts were more or less independent of political parties in both countries, despite trying to interest politicians in their cause. Their campaign was a great success, though it was loosely coordinated and—this would only be revealed later—some of its leaders had scandalous ulterior motives. In a few short months, beginning in

February 1887, this eclectic band of promoters took advantage of the prevailing popular discontent and turned commercial union into a live issue in Canadian politics.

The Ringleaders

Two of the leading commercial unionists were, surprisingly, Americans. In fact the first noteworthy public expression of support for C.U. in 1887 was voiced in, of all places, the U.S. Congress. On February 14 Benjamin Butterworth, Republican from Ohio, introduced a resolution in the House of Representatives seeking "to extend the trade and commerce of the United States and to provide for full reciprocity between the United States and the Dominion of Canada." The resolution never used the term "commercial union," but it did propose to abolish customs houses along the Canadian-American border plus—most dramatically—establish a common tariff against the rest of the world. This was commercial union in fact, if not quite in name.[5]

It was a little odd that this resolution was the work of a Republican, because the Republicans were the party of protective tariffs. It was odder still that Ben Butterworth, a self-proclaimed "Republican of the straightest sect, and a protectionist on principle," was its author.[6] Butterworth stood out among politicians because of his uncommon honesty and good humour (not to mention that he was six foot six and weighed more than three hundred pounds). He was popular on Capitol Hill, a funny after-dinner speaker, and a kind of friendly giant of Congress. But the inspiration behind his commercial union bill had actually come from one of his constituents, Samuel J. Ritchie, a prominent Ohio businessman. Sam Ritchie was a born schemer who lived a chaotic life that consisted of pushing risky development projects, scrounging government subsidies, and dodging a small army of frustrated creditors. He had mining and railway interests in Canada that would benefit from commercial union, and political friends in Ottawa and Washington whom he hoped would assist his cause. They were an odd couple, these two, with Butterworth as the front man and Ritchie lobbying behind the scenes to drum up support for their scheme.

They did not expect the Butterworth bill to pass. The congressional session was nearly over, and no serious effort was made to ensure that a vote would be taken in the House. The point of bringing it forward was to attract press attention, and on that score they enjoyed some success. Such major U.S. newspapers as the Washington *Post*, Boston *Globe*, and New York *Times* reported on it with interest, and more important, the story appeared—along with a ringing editorial endorsement—in the greatest independent newspaper in Canada, the Toronto *Mail*. Once the official mouthpiece of the Tories, the *Mail* had abandoned the party in the mid-1880s under the direction of Edward Farrer, another of the ringleaders of the commercial union movement. A stocky man with a bushy black beard and owlish looks, "Ned" Farrer was the most acclaimed journalist in Canada. His notorious boozing sprees had gotten him tossed from editorial staffs, and his mercenary habit of taking political positions based solely on who would pay him the most unsettled other journalists. His capacity for mischief was legendary. He regularly amused himself by penning editorials for both the *Mail* and rival news-papers, effectively having a debate with himself, and during the election of 1882 Farrer was even rumoured to have written the platforms of both parties. He was frequently suspected of being up to no good, and in *Grip* magazine he was frequently portrayed as a cartoonish, troublemaking leprechaun.[7]

Farrer was the key figure behind the *Mail*'s sudden embrace of commercial union. It was a shrewd decision. In February 1887 the time was right to be pushing free trade, and the popularity of C.U. soon showed in the swelling circulation numbers of the *Mail*. That caused a chain reaction among Ontario newspapers. The Toronto *Globe*, which was already hemorrhaging readers and sensed the public mood, soon began leaning toward C.U. even though its political masters, the Liberals, had not yet approved of it.[8] By April the transition was complete, and that paper too had come out strongly in favour of commercial union. As the *Globe* went, so went many smaller Liberal organs in Ontario, and in this way the editorial shift of the *Mail* was amplified across the province. With paper after paper taking up the cause, the impression was created that commercial union was gaining dramatically in popularity, which helped to further encourage the movement.

Farrer wasn't the only prominent writer booming the policy. Also lending his pen to the cause was Goldwin Smith, a world-famous British history professor who had lived in Toronto since 1871. Smith was a thin and snobbish man with a talent for brilliant and infuriating social commentary. He wrote prolifically, usually against the majority viewpoint, and styled himself (with some justification) as Canada's resident intellectual. From the study of the Grange, his English-style mansion set in the heart of Toronto, the professor dispensed his views. He couldn't have cared less that most Canadians regularly disagreed with his positions. Indeed, he seemed to enjoy railing against what passed in Canada for conventional wisdom.

What Smith wanted most was, as he wistfully called it, a "re-union of the English-speaking peoples of North America."[9] He saw the American Revolution as a tragedy that had separated two English-speaking populations with essentially the same culture, history, and interests. Canada, he argued, was an artificial construct, a "crazy quilt" of competing regions, languages, and identities that could never become a real nation. Its inevitable future was political union with the United States—he never used the term "annexation," which implied coercion—and he supported commercial union for the simple reason that he assumed it would be a step in that direction. The fact that Goldwin Smith longed for political union, of course, made him a dubious commercial unionist. Most Canadians found the notion of merging with the United States disgusting, if not treasonous, and they were inclined to regard Smith's motives with the deepest suspicion.

Smith's personality also made him a doubtful champion for the cause. He was a sour old man whose mind was poisoned by irrational prejudices against women, French Canadians, and Jews. His English snobbishness was off-putting to ordinary Canadians, and he completely lacked the warmth and good cheer required of a man who aspired to lead a popular movement. No one has ever offered a more devastating assessment of Goldwin Smith than his youthful protégé, W.D. Gregory, who in 1887 was a Liberal journalist. Gregory, who admired the professor enough to name his first-born son after him, wrote that "Goldwin Smith, I think, had no deep affection for anyone."[10]

They had their talents, but none of these four men—Butterworth, Ritchie, Farrer, or Smith—could lead the campaign for commercial union in Canada. The first two were Americans. The third was a behind-the-scenes type. And the fourth wanted to surrender Canada to the United States. Each was playing his part, but someone else was needed to serve as the public face of the movement, someone who was engaging and inspiring, capable of giving rabble-rousing speeches and then climbing down from the platform, chatting up the people one by one, and convincing them that this was a risk worth taking. To have any chance of success, commercial union had to have this kind of champion.

In the spring of 1887, it had Erastus Wiman.

The Renegade Canadian

Today he is completely forgotten, but in his day Erastus Wiman was a household name. He was a businessman, born in 1834 into a humble family in rural Ontario, whose life was a classic rags-to-riches story.[11] He earned his first cent as a nine-year-old Toronto newsboy (the first in Canada, he was fond of boasting). At sixteen he was apprenticed to the *North American*, the newspaper owned by his cousin William McDougall, a Reform politician, and at twenty-one he was named the Toronto *Globe*'s commercial editor. Never content with just one job, Wiman also founded his own publishing company, edited a humorous newspaper called the *Grumbler*, and served briefly as a city councillor.

In 1860 a U.S. credit rating agency, R.G. Dun & Company, recruited him to manage its Toronto office. Two years later he was relocated to Montreal to oversee the firm's Canadian operations. In 1866 Wiman was made a partner in the company and again relocated—for good this time—to New York City.

As general manager of the R.G. Dun & Co. Mercantile Agency (known as Dun & Wiman in Canada), Wiman occupied a lucrative and influential position in the world of North American business. But his talent for promotion, and improbable achievements in the transportation and entertainment industries, were what had made him one of the best-known Canadians on the continent. He was determined to transform sleepy Staten Island into a bustling metropolis. He acquired the famous ferry service, built a port (rather immodestly named Erastina) and a railway, and entered into an arrangement with the mighty Baltimore & Ohio Railway to ensure a large flow of traffic to the island. After founding the Staten Island Amusement Company, Wiman lured record numbers of visitors to the island with colourful attractions such as Buffalo Bill's Wild West Show and the New York Mets baseball club (which he bought and moved to Staten Island over the bitter objections of the league commissioners). He also had business interests in his homeland, most notably the Great North Western Telegraph Company, which controlled all the telegraph lines in Canada.

Wiman was a striking figure. He had a short and stocky build, a fresh rose in his lapel, mutton chop whiskers, and, as one reporter put it, "an intent, earnest, yet good-natured expression on his English-looking features."[12] He usually rose at four o'clock in the morning—a man's most productive time, he was sure—to write a little and reflect on the day ahead. From Staten Island he would commute to Manhattan aboard one of his ferries (his favourite was no doubt the *Erastus Wiman*) and arrive early at his Broadway office. Throughout the day he was a whirlwind, striding up and down a hectic main floor filled with the clatter of typewriters. Several secretaries struggled to keep up while he dictated his correspondence, a job that was never done given that Wiman was in regular contact with, by his estimation, more than two thousand leading businessmen across North America. At six o'clock he took the ferry home, played the family man to his wife, Eleanor, and their six children, and entertained prominent guests at Tantallon, their Scottish-themed mansion. For good measure the couple owned sprawling acreage on the island and a farmhouse by the water called the Woods of Arden. It was here that Wiman liked to putter about, tend to his stable of prize horses, and play the role of gentleman farmer.

In 1887 Wiman's career was at its peak and his personal worth was estimated at two or three million dollars, a tremendous fortune at the time. He was the quintessential self-made man, his success the product of an extraordinary work ethic and a fondness for taking chances. He was filled with "Yankee boldness," as some Canadian newspapers disapprovingly called it, and quipped that he was never really happy unless engaged in some lawsuit. He was, above all else, a shameless self-promoter. Erastus Wiman yearned to be not only rich but also famous. He wanted it so badly, in fact, that it was almost embarrassing. It was rumoured that he had cut corners to get where he was. His enemies complained that he slipped exaggerated stories about his accomplishments into the newspapers (this was true) and wired them reports of speeches that he had never delivered. A cloud hung over his business dealings, particularly those relating to his monopoly over the telegraph system in Canada. In later years he would be convicted of defrauding his own company and would spend time in a New York prison before being exonerated.

None of these shortcomings—vanity, self-absorption, sketchy business ethics—create the impression that there was anything especially admirable about Erastus Wiman. Certainly he had detractors, notably among the Conservatives in Canada. Typical was the view of the Belleville *Intelligencer*, Mackenzie Bowell's paper, that Wiman was a "greedy renegade" who had turned his back on his homeland.[13] In private, the judgments often were harsher. Many Tories believed that Wiman was secretly trying to bring about the annexation of Canada. Sir John was repeatedly warned that a "Wiman annexation conspiracy" was afoot, that "Czar Wiman" was planning "a crusade against Canadian and British interests," and even that he controlled the minds of Liberal leaders. Even Leonard Tilley, a former minister of finance and normally a fellow of sober views, once wrote to Macdonald that "I cannot help looking upon Wyman [*sic*] as a traitor to his country in the disguise of a friend."[14]

That was unfair. Erastus Wiman was flawed indeed, but he was better than these critiques would suggest. Despite the bluster and self-promotion, there was something endearing about the man. The New York newspapers reported on him with amusement and a certain affection; after all, it was difficult not to like a man who made such good copy. He had a disarming way of admitting his faults. "People say I am a vain man and eager to see my name in the newspapers," a cheerful Wiman once remarked to a reporter. "Probably the first is true, and certainly the second is."[15] His habit of naming everything he owned after himself was a bit much, but that was hardly a unique habit. His schemes were always interesting, and the indomitable enthusiasm with which he lived his life—the Washington *Post* referred to him as "a great good-natured boy"[16]—had made Wiman many friends over the years.

Even his enemies spoke highly of his kindness and humanity. Wiman had a big heart and a broad mind. He supported progressive causes—notably equality for women and generous treatment of religious minorities—which few public figures of his era were willing to take up. He donated his time and money to numerous good works, even to the Staten Island branch of the Society for the Prevention of Cruelty to Children. It was said around New York City that in a roomful of millionaires, Wiman was the only one who would lend an ordinary man a ten-dollar bill. He was most widely respected for having successfully campaigned in the early 1880s to abolish the practice of imprisonment for unpaid debts in New York State. Upon learning that a fellow Canadian had suffered this fate, Wiman promptly paid the man's debts and persuaded the state legislature to repeal the offensive statute. The impact of this reform on the lives of the hundreds of men and women freed from debtors' prison can hardly be overestimated.

Wiman was deeply offended by accusations that he was a sell-out. He was proud of his Canadian roots and had never taken out American citizenship even though it complicated his business dealings in the United States. For daily inspiration he kept a large map of Canada on his desk, and he never tired of informing people about the vast untapped potential of his native land, which he referred to as "the Greater Half of the Continent," even in front of American audiences. He looked out for his compatriots whenever he could, hiring them in R.G. Dun & Co.'s offices to such an extent that one American newspaper dubbed the agency a "Canadian colony." In 1885 Wiman had founded the Canadian Club of New York to give fellow expats a home away from home. He visited Canada regularly on business, made annual hunting trips to Northern Ontario (he claimed once to have shot four marauding wolves in the space of five minutes!), and promoted events such as the Montreal Winter Carnival. In Toronto he earned goodwill by spending thousands to construct the Wiman Baths, a large public swimming facility that he insisted on making equally accessible to the richest and poorest citizens of the city.

While this showy philanthropy failed to impress the Tory papers, the Liberal press could normally be relied upon to defend Wiman's credentials as a patriotic Canadian. Foremost among his cheerleaders were the Toronto *Globe* and Halifax *Chronicle*, the latter going so far as to print some of his favourite sayings as a collection of wise and folksy "Wimanisms."[17] There were other indications that regular folks were proud to see a fellow citizen succeed so spectacularly in the United States. Wiman drew large, friendly audiences on the frequent occasions that he gave speeches in Canada. It was hopefully rumoured in some circles that he might get into politics. His name was even proposed for the leadership of the Liberal Party. (Wiman dismissed these rumours, but not the notion that he was up to the job.) Perhaps the greatest tribute to his Canadian spirit was the fact that a doughnut, that uniquely Canadian pastry, had been devised in his honour. Saturated with rum and smothered in ice cream, the "Erastus Wiman" was decidedly over the top, like its namesake.[18]

The Campaign for Commercial Union

Wiman's greatest ambition was to bring about commercial union between Canada and the United States. He believed that it would be good for both countries but a massive stimulus to the growth and development of Canada in particular. He regarded himself as a kind of unofficial trade ambassador—an "envoy extraordinary"[19]—whose mission was to popularize the issue and get the two governments negotiating. It was all too easy to poke fun at his self-confidence, to suspect that this quest was mere self-aggrandizement, and to dismiss his chances of success. Wiman shrugged off naysayers. "Why should I pretend that I would not like to be considered the great benefactor of my country?" he once asked a British reporter. "The desire of my life is to have my name to go down with posterity with what I know will be the greatest commercial blessing Canada ever received."[20]

Though he had shown interest in commercial union before, it was in the spring of 1887 that Wiman really devoted himself to the cause. A full-out publicity blitz ensued. His talent for manipulating the press stood him in good stead as he published articles, sat for interviews, sent favourable news stories along the wires, and visited newspaper offices in order to converse with editorial staff. One Toronto Tory reported worriedly to Macdonald that Wiman had been skulking about the city's newspaper offices, meeting with the publisher of the *Mail* and allegedly "feeding copy" to the *Globe*. He wondered if it was by pure coincidence that the two newspapers had suddenly become the leading voices in favour of commercial union and warned that "the gang"—meaning Wiman and his allies—"must not get control of our Dominion."[21]

Wiman was not content only to lobby newspaper editors. Using his own funds he published numerous promotional materials, including a *Handbook of Commercial Union*, and saw to it that these were widely circulated in both Canada and the United States. He encouraged the agitation by the Farmers' Institutes of Ontario in an open letter that appeared in the press just before their inaugural convention. He pestered political friends in Washington to make a public statement in favour of the movement. His good friend Ben Butterworth was the most noteworthy convert, but Wiman also coaxed endorsements from Senator John Sherman of Ohio and a couple of other Republicans. He even tried, without success, to entice Sir John A. Macdonald to do the same.[22] Most of all, Wiman did what he had always done best, using his talents as a promoter to boom commercial union in a series of rousing and uncompromising public speeches made in New York, Toronto, and numerous Ontario towns.

Wiman's primary argument was simple. Since the United States was in constant need of raw materials to fuel its great industries, free trade would be a godsend for the Canadian resource producers whose attempts to sell in the American market had so far been stymied by high tariffs. Once this "barbed wire fence" came down (that was one of his favourite lines), the amount of cross-border trade would increase by 500 percent within ten years and the trend of Canadian emigration to the United States would be brought to a halt. The "Greater Half of the Continent" could finally be developed to its fullest potential, and it would be a land of productive farms, forests, fisheries, and mines.

This was the part of the argument that even Wiman's critics agreed with. Canada had plentiful, valuable natural resources, and no doubt the Americans would be eager to get their hands on them. Where they disagreed was about the impact of commercial union on Canadian manufacturers. It was virtually an article of faith among the Conservatives, not to mention the manufacturers themselves, that asking a Canadian to compete with an American manufacturer was like "asking a boy to compete with a man." (That nugget of pessimism came courtesy of the Canadian Manufacturers' Association.)[23] There were good reasons for believing this to be true. American companies tended to be bigger and richer than their Canadian counterparts. They were accustomed to taking advantage of economies of scale, and their brand names were better known in the domestic markets of both countries. Then there was the vaunted American tradition of entrepreneurship, something that Canadians derided as Yankee greed, but secretly feared and admired. Wiman's opponents argued that without the comforting protection offered by the high tariffs of the National Policy, Canadian manufacturers would be helpless.

Wiman had no respect for this kind of self-pitying pessimism. He saw no reason why Canadians could not compete against Americans, because he had been doing it for most of his adult life. In what was probably his boldest speech in the spring of 1887, an address delivered at the Canadian Club of New York, Wiman scorned the notion that American manufacturers would "crowd out the Canadian manufacturer and merchant" if allowed to sell freely in the Canadian market. "Well," he said simply, "all that need be said in reply is: that if the Canadians cannot hold their own when all the conditions are equal, they don't deserve the name of Canadians." That was startling stuff, but there was more. "The talk that any class of Canadians cannot hold their own against any other people on the face of the earth," Wiman soberly informed his audience of Canadian expatriates, "finds no echo in the minds of our fellow-countrymen who have already found a home in the United States. They experience no difficulty in holding their own, side by side, with the Yankees."[24]

This uncompromising confidence, coming from a Canadian businessman who was as familiar with the Americans as anyone, was bound to be heartening to Canadians who read his speech in the newspapers. But more reassurance was needed, on an even more fundamental issue. Many suspected that commercial union was destined to lead to Canada being annexed by the United States. Wiman was never more frustrated or combative than when attempting to put this charge to rest. There was no need for Canadians to fear annexation, he said. The days when a military invasion by the United States was a realistic possibility had long passed. Americans were not the slightest bit interested in Canada's joining their republic unless it was the desire of the Canadian people themselves. As every Canadian knew, this was absolutely not the case. So, then, how would annexation come about? How exactly would Canada's culture and identity be threatened? Wiman scoffed at the idea that Canada's independence would be threatened merely by trading on equal terms with the United States.

On the subject of patriotism, a commodity the Conservatives often seemed to have claimed exclusive ownership of, Wiman was unrepentant. "The discussion of commercial union has been the occasion for a great display of cheap patriotism," he informed the Canadian Club. He went on to provide his own definition of the concept. "Patriotism, as I understand it, consists in the love of one's country for the furtherance of its best and dearest interests. True patriotism should not obstinately stand in the way of the country's best interests." This principle held true even when considering Canada's relations with Great Britain. "Love of British institutions, of British connection," Wiman insisted, building toward a stirring conclusion, "cannot be imperilled by a greater development of Canadian resources. No sentimental consideration should stand in the way of a policy which would benefit Canada."[25]

That was strong stuff, but the central message—that commercial union was a safe and patriotic policy—still needed reinforcing. The Farmers' Institutes became active in Ontario at the end of April, giving the C.U. movement renewed attention and grassroots authenticity that Wiman could not have instilled himself. By early May the Liberal press was coming around. After the *Mail* and *Globe* adopted the policy, other influential regional papers, among them the Manitoba *Free Press* and Halifax *Chronicle*, also climbed on board. They expressed sympathy for C.U. and tried, rather anxiously, to dampen any impression that it was a radical and dangerous idea. Instead these Liberal organs suggested that commercial union was a sensible solution to the economic depression, no more, no less, and no risk at all to Canadian sovereignty. Chiming in from south of the border was Benjamin Butterworth, who gave a major speech on May 19 at a grand banquet of the Canadian Club of New York, an affair arranged by Erastus Wiman and designed to draw the attention of newspapers in both countries. Butterworth was all bonhomie and good cheer that night, praising the similarities of the two peoples and dismissing concerns that the United States might have sinister motives. He had no taste for annexation, he said, and neither did the American people. Commercial union, Butterworth reassured his listeners, was purely a business proposition.

There was no official reaction from the Canadian or American governments, but two days after the Butterworth speech, under conditions of strict secrecy, top men on the two sides met in Washington and discussed the subject of free trade. Here again Erastus Wiman could be seen at work. He and his friend Sam Ritchie had quietly arranged this meeting of Thomas Bayard, the U.S. secretary of state, and Sir Charles Tupper, the Canadian minister of finance. There was little interest in commercial union within the Macdonald government, of course, nor very much, for that matter, on the part of the Cleveland administration. But there were festering issues between the two countries (conflict over the North Atlantic fisheries, for example), and Wiman was hopeful that a sweeping trade agreement would emerge from a face-to-face discussion. It did not happen. Bayard and Tupper were not agreed on many issues, but concerning free trade there was common ground. Neither saw any need to do anything rash, and neither was interested in embracing anything so radical as commercial union.

This should probably have been a death blow to the commercial union movement. There was no chance of a deal being struck, of course, if both governments dismissed the scheme. But Wiman was not the slightest bit discouraged. Things were still going well on the ground, with pro-C.U. meetings being held all over Ontario and more newspapers throwing themselves into the campaign. What was needed now, he concluded, was for himself and Butterworth to take their case directly to the people. Arrangements were made for a monster picnic to be held at Dufferin Lake, a lovely rural venue west of Toronto and close to the town in which Wiman had grown up. It would be held on July 1—Dominion Day—and it was heavily promoted as the greatest Canadian political event of the summer.

Pressing the Case

Dominion Day dawned splendid and sunny. It was still early in the morning when folks began to lay blankets on the gently rolling grounds of Dufferin Lake. Special trains from Toronto let off families eager for a rare day of recreation as much as for the advertised speeches. Those who lived nearby came in carriages, lumber wagons, and dogcarts. They were greeted by fluttering banners with slogans like "BUTTERWORTH, THE BENEFACTOR" and "WELCOME TO WIMAN—HONOR TO WHOM HONOR IS DUE."[26] The *Globe*'s reporter was impressed by the diversity of the crowd. Happy, shouting children roamed the grounds, and ladies in white dresses lent a touch of class to the affair. The picnickers were mostly farmers (the "most intelligent and successful from all parts of the country," the *Globe* assured its readers), but hundreds of businessmen had also come to hear out the man of the hour.[27]

At least two thousand people had gathered near the main platform by the time Erastus Wiman rose to deliver the first speech. He was an emotional man, and he was touched that so many of his old compatriots had come out, as he put it, "to hear what a Peel country boy from abroad had to say."[28] He addressed them for two hours in an ambitious speech that called upon all of his talents as a promoter. Commercial union, he was sure, would be one of the great developments in human history, comparable to the Crusades and the Reformation. It would bring magnificent blossoming prosperity to the Dominion. Instead of young Canadians being forced to seek better opportunities in the United States, commercial union would finally allow them to make their fortunes in their own country.

Wiman was at his most passionate, and he earned his most appreciative applause, when defending supporters of commercial union against the accusation that they lacked patriotism and loyalty to Great Britain. On the contrary, he reasoned, the movement was motivated by "higher patriotism" or what he saw as an enlightened appreciation of the national interest. There could be nothing wrong in pursuing a policy that would benefit the people of Canada, and in fact, by improving relations between Canada and the United States and preventing future conflict, commercial union would benefit the British Empire as well. Wiman saved his best for last. "He is only truly loyal who seeks the enrichment of the vast army of producers that make up the wealth of Canada," he reasoned, "and ... if, under the British flag, with a sturdy love of British traditions, he can accomplish the revolution that opens up the markets of a vast continent, in the name of all that is great and good why should he not be permitted to do so?" It was an impressive speech, and standing there in front of a cheering hometown crowd, Erastus Wiman savoured one of the most triumphant moments of his life.

The real test, however, was the reception that would be given to Ben Butterworth. The *Globe* worried that the American would get a bad reception and reminded readers that Butterworth had "no desire to overthrow or undermine our political institutions or to detach Canada from the Empire," while expressing hope that the congressman would not be intimidated "by the shameful efforts made to shut his mouth."[29] In fact the audience gave Butterworth an even warmer welcome than it had Wiman, and his speech was a capital success. The crowd thoroughly enjoyed the big man's mellifluous manner of speaking, his folksy humour, and his generous praise of their country. Most of all they liked his message that there was nothing to fear from commercial union. It was, Butterworth repeated, "purely a business proposition."[30]

The Dufferin Lake picnic was a smashing success, and it was only the beginning of a spectacular week for the movement. That same night, Wiman and Butterworth got an extraordinary reception in nearby Orangeville. Thousands lined the streets and cheered as their entourage was driven into town (in a carriage pulled by four white horses, no less) to be greeted by the mayor and a committee of local citizens. By torchlight they were led to the lacrosse grounds, all to the strains of a brass band, and rousing speeches were made beneath a night sky that was illuminated by crowd-pleasing fireworks. The *Globe* reporter, taken aback by the enthusiasm of the crowd, considered the meeting a greater success than the Dufferin Lake picnic. At ten o'clock the next morning the group departed Orangeville by train, headed for a similarly boisterous meeting in the village of Drayton. The requisite brass band was there to greet them on the platform, and Goldwin Smith made an appearance at the event. He was in surprisingly good form, praising Canadian nationalism and insisting that commercial union had nothing to do with annexation or party lines. It was about free trade, and free trade alone. "This is what we mean," Smith declared, "and this is all we mean. With politics or party we have nothing to do." Butterworth followed, making a speech that produced "such a wildfire effect"—to hear the *Globe* tell it, at least—"that the enthusiasm was shared by every man, woman and child present."[31] The meeting ended in loud cheers for the speakers, for free trade, and of course for the Queen.

Two days later Wiman and Butterworth were in Port Hope, the guests of the local Farmers' Institute, and the same speeches were repeated to the same effect. The audience was moved to pass a resolution favouring commercial union as a purely economic policy. Then, realizing that this did not address the question of politics, it felt compelled to pass another resolution, this one announcing that "commercial union is our politics."[32]

Perhaps C.U. was set to become a staple of Liberal politics, too. An important organizer for the federal party in Ontario, W.T.R. Preston, was conspicuously on the platform at the Port Hope meeting. On July 5 the *Globe* reported excitedly that "the feeling in favour of Commercial Reciprocity grows and spreads with extraordinary rapidity." And on July 8, obviously moved by all that had happened in the last few weeks, Sir Richard Cartwright picked up his pen and worriedly advised Wilfrid Laurier that the Liberal Party had better face the music.

The Question of the Hour

Laurier was in a tough spot. Commercial union appeared to be making great headway in Ontario, but it was hard for Laurier, who lacked an intuitive feel for Ontario politics, to be sure of its strength. Sir Richard's views had to be taken seriously, if only because many grumbling English Canadian Liberals regarded him as the proper leader of the party. The Liberal press had largely embraced commercial union, and the editor of the *Globe*, John Cameron, was privately nudging him toward a more daring trade policy. Topping it all off, two important Liberal newspapers at opposite ends of the country, the Manitoba *Free Press* and the Halifax *Chronicle*, had recently jumped on the commercial union bandwagon.

On the other hand, the bold course was rarely the correct one in Canadian politics. There were compelling reasons not to do anything rash. First, the Tories were going to raise patriotic bloody hell if the Liberal Party embraced commercial union. They would rally around the National Policy and claim that the apocalypse—meaning the annexation of Canada—was at hand. The next election would revolve around it, and it would be an ugly and divisive election. Second, within the Liberal Party itself there was no consensus on the issue. Would the party as a whole accept commercial union? Edward Blake had never accepted the policy and he was still, presumably, returning at some point to reclaim the leadership. The party would be in a terrible mess if Blake returned to discover, to his horror, that in his absence it had adopted commercial union.

Nobody knew what Laurier was thinking. He had never cared very much about economics, and the Liberals had never bothered to seek out his views on the subject. In fact Laurier was still making up his mind. He had a natural sympathy for free trade, and felt that some kind of deal with the United States would be good for Canada. It was not the economic merit of commercial union that intrigued him, however, but its potential as an election winner. Laurier was looking for a bold new policy that would divert attention from the divisive race-and-religion issue, put the Tories on the defensive, give the Liberal rank and file something exciting to fight for, and help them to get over the discouraging retirement of Edward Blake.

Still, it would be best to feel out the party before committing to anything. On July 11 Laurier issued an internal circular that, without giving any hint of his own feelings, asked his fellow Liberals for their thoughts on commercial union. It was a smart move, and the results were interesting. Blake did not like it, though he was then vacationing in Europe and seemed reluctant to speak too strongly on the question. James Young, a level-headed party elder who edited the small-town Galt *Reformer*, warned that C.U. was "an anti-national and Americanizing policy." Young published several eloquent letters on "Our National Future" in the *Reformer*, arguing that the Dominion could not withstand the economic and cultural pressures that would stem from commercial union.[33] Alexander Mackenzie, the former Liberal leader and prime minister, felt that the policy would sever the British connection. "We are to raise a barrier against English trade and so commence a downgrade political life," he protested to Cartwright. "My feelings revolt at the proposal."[34]

These opinions were exceptions to the general rule. Most Liberals who responded to the circular were surprisingly gung-ho for commercial union. The party was obviously yearning for a change from the caution and indecision of the Blake years. Laurier soon reported to Cartwright and Edgar that he was getting almost universally positive feedback from Quebec and the Maritimes. A few letters came in from western Canada, also happy to see the policy under consideration. And in Ontario, where there was the most popular feeling for the scheme, the vast majority of respondents urged Laurier to take the plunge. "In my humble opinion the Liberals have nothing to lose and everything to gain by adopting Commercial Union as the plank in their platform," wrote one Thomas McInnes of Toronto. "If prudently handled I can see no reason why it will not do for them what the national policy cry did for the Conservatives in 1878."[35]

Laurier wanted more time, but he was being pressed to make a decision. On August 2 he was scheduled to speak at a political picnic in Somerset, Quebec, in his first policy speech since becoming the Liberal leader. It was a much-anticipated event, though there were some snickers in the Conservative newspapers that Laurier had chosen for this early test a cautious and obscure venue—small, rural, friendly, and French—rather than a big city in Ontario. Was he afraid, journalists wondered in print, to step in front of an English Canadian audience? And what, if anything, would he have to say about commercial union? Surely the Liberal leader would be compelled by the fast march of Canadian public opinion to make some statement on that controversial subject.

If the Somerset speech was an indication of anything, it was the fact that Laurier did not succumb easily to pressure. His speech was long on pleasant-sounding patriotic sentiments and short on specific policy proposals. He took plenty of potshots at the Macdonald government and devoted considerable time to the subject of national unity. But there was little mention of commercial union, and what he did say was cryptic. "For my part, gentlemen," Laurier carefully remarked, "I am not prepared to say that the advocates and adepts of Commercial Union have as yet very clearly defined their views." Perhaps in time it would be possible to more clearly discern the potential costs and benefits of the proposal. At the moment, however, the Liberal leader would only venture to say, "What lies at the bottom of the idea, what we see clearest in it ... is the conviction that any kind of reciprocity with the people of the United States would be to the advantage of Canada."[36]

That was good enough, for the time being. Laurier had shrewdly kept his options open, and most Liberals were supportive of his cautious approach. But as summer turned to fall, the pressure kept building for the party to come out for commercial union or risk falling out of step with popular opinion. The *Globe* and other leading Liberal newspapers kept beating the drum, as did Ned Farrer at the independent *Mail*. Erastus Wiman, Ben Butterworth, and Goldwin Smith were out stumping in both countries and attracting good crowds wherever they went. At a major interprovincial conference held in Quebec City in late October, five provincial premiers passed a resolution endorsing "unrestricted reciprocity" with the United States. (Wiman was partly responsible for that, having hustled publicly and privately around Quebec City to get the subject on the conference agenda.)[37] Finally, Sir Richard Cartwright, the financial expert of the Liberal Party and the virtual co-leader in the eyes of many English Canadians, forced his leader's hand by speaking out publicly in favour of the movement.

The Cartwright speech took place on October 12 in the small town of Ingersoll, Ontario, in his home riding of South Oxford. It was a typical Blue Ruin Knight speech, burdened with depressing statistics and a gloomy forecast of the future unless, of course, commercial union was adopted without delay.[38] It was a major event not for the size of the crowd or the quality of the speech, but for the precedent it set. Sir Richard insisted that he was speaking only for himself. He was not committing the Liberal Party to commercial union. But he knew better than that. His voice carried a lot of weight, and he was certainly, perhaps deliberately, making it harder for Laurier to say no to the policy when the time came to make a final decision.

The New Departure

One leading Liberal who was not impressed with the Cartwright speech was J.D. Edgar, the Ontario organizer who was fast becoming a confidant to his French Canadian leader. Two days after the Cartwright speech he wrote Laurier that it "pleases some but annoys others ... however it is a good 'trial balloon' and we will see better how the wind blows."[39] Edgar also reported that he had just met with Erastus Wiman. That was interesting, because shortly after that meeting, Edgar and Wiman exchanged a series of open letters that would have a profound effect on the debate.[40]

In his letters Edgar criticized the entangling nature of commercial union—especially the necessity of having a common tariff with the United States against all other countries—and suggested that "unrestricted reciprocity" was a more moderate alternative. This was a proposal for complete free trade with the United States, but with the retention of customs houses along the border and the continuing right of each country to set its own tariffs against other countries. It was, in effect, a watered-down version of commercial union. Wiman was not comfortable with it. He knew that unrestricted reciprocity would not go over well in the United States because it would allow British imports to enter Canada at a low tariff rate, then sneak into the United States from Canada tariff-free and compete directly against the products of domestic American manufacturers.

Still, Wiman grudgingly accepted that unrestricted reciprocity might work as an alternative to commercial union. It seemed to be a less radical and less dangerous policy. It allowed Canada to keep control of its own tariff rates, rather than having to set them in lockstep with the United States, and that was certainly appealing. Even Cartwright had admitted to Laurier that most Liberals were "in mortal terror" of having their patriotism questioned by the Tories, and that was sure to happen if they adopted commercial union and were seen to be setting the country's tariff rates in accordance with the wishes of the United States Congress.[41]

Laurier remained undecided. In mid-December he expressed his misgivings in a thoughtful private letter to J.D. Edgar.

> I am afraid this plan of unrestricted reciprocity would be coupled with very many disadvantages. I think it would not do to commit ourselves to any distinct plan in advance. My opinion is that we should first assert the principle that the most unlimited reciprocity, would be for the advantage of both nations, and then let the idea be carried out by treaty negotiations. We must in the discussion keep ourselves in generalities. The moment we attempt to particularize, we will be met by objections upon objections. The only thing we should unreservedly commit ourselves to, should be reciprocity, limited if nothing better can be obtained, unlimited if possible.[42]

That was smart thinking, but a policy of having no policy was not going to be acceptable much longer to the Liberal rank and file. The new year dawned, the next session of Parliament loomed, and the leading figures in the party weighed the risks and possible benefits of the decision that they had to make. Sir Richard Cartwright had been tormented by second thoughts since coming out for commercial union back in October. On January 2 he wrote Laurier to inform him of a change of heart. "I do not think there is any choice left," he declared. "We <u>must</u> make a new departure and there is nothing which will fill the bill half as well as unrestricted reciprocity."[43] Three weeks later, having mulled the situation a little longer, he had regained his old confidence. "I am ready to tackle the question," he assured Laurier. He wanted to introduce a resolution favouring unrestricted reciprocity, one that would trigger a high-profile debate, in the next session of Parliament.[44]

The final decision was not made until February 22, the day the new session opened in Ottawa. That evening the leading Liberals gathered for a private meeting. There was a clear sentiment in favour of adopting a new trade policy, and the only real question was whether it would be commercial union or unrestricted reciprocity. Laurier was leaning toward the former, but Cartwright and Edgar favoured the latter, and in the end unrestricted reciprocity won out. At a meeting of the full Liberal caucus three days later, the decision to embrace the new policy was made official. It was an important moment in the history of the party and the country, and everyone knew it.

The Great Free Trade Debate

As soon as the Liberals declared for unrestricted reciprocity, a major debate in the House of Commons became inevitable. Here was precisely the situation that the chamber had been designed for: two warring parties, each seeking to win over the Canadian public, were about to engage each other in debate on a matter of profound national interest. The Liberals gave notice that they intended to introduce a motion pressing the government to adopt unrestricted reciprocity. The prime minister, recognizing the importance of the motion, cleared the schedule of the House to allow a thorough debate. On March 14, at about four o'clock in the afternoon, Sir Richard Cartwright rose before a packed House to deliver the most important speech of his life.

It was an ideal setting for a great national debate. The House of Commons looks cavernous in the grainy photographs of the era, but actually it was surprisingly intimate. Beneath its magnificent arched pillars and massive Gothic windows, the Commons floor was just eighty-eight feet long and forty-seven feet wide. It had been built to hold just 130 members, not the current 215, and because the government and opposition benches faced each other across the width of the chamber rather than the length, it was a rather cramped-looking setting. Only fifteen feet of plush green carpet separated the two sides. The members were not seated in "benches," actually, but in two-seat desks that were seven rows deep on each side, gradually raked from the front to the back. It was a cozy, slightly claustrophobic arrangement, made all the more so by the crowded public galleries on all four sides.

Cartwright knew the House as well as almost anyone, and there was no doubt that he was the perfect speaker for the occasion. He had an imposing physical presence, and his voice was loud and commanding; there was no chance of falling asleep in the middle of a Cartwright speech. His mastery of the language was admitted even by Joseph Pope, Macdonald's loyal secretary, who felt that Cartwright was the only member of the House "who could afford to have his words taken down and printed exactly as he spoke them."[45] His speeches were a reflection of the man and the politician that Sir Richard was: intelligent and carefully reasoned, but humourless, merciless, and relentless. His speeches could be devastating, but they were never much fun to listen to.

Cartwright peered over his spectacles at the government side, where Macdonald sat in his usual relaxed pose. For years Sir Richard had endured the smirks and taunts of the prime minister. Now, he sensed, the tide was about to turn. Everything depended on making a case for unrestricted reciprocity that would put the Conservatives on the defensive and convince Canadians that their future was most secure in Liberal hands. "I rise on this occasion," Cartwright began solemnly, "to address this House, under a sense of grave and weighty responsibility."[46] (The Tories might have jibed that Sir Richard lived his entire life under a sense of grave and weighty responsibility.) From there he launched into a classic Blue Ruin Knight speech. All the depressing statistics were trotted out. All the gloomy predictors of the future were lamented. Population growth had stagnated under the National Policy. Taxes had tripled, and so had the national debt. Foreign trade had actually dropped. Most distressing was the mass emigration; it seemed to Cartwright that there was not a single family in the Dominion that did not have a loved one living in the United States. What kind of National Policy was it, he asked the House, when "those who are our own flesh and blood, our own kinsmen, have been obliged for lack of opportunity to leave Canada and seek a home elsewhere? I say that this is proof positive that we are in a state of retrogression."

The themes that followed were familiar to anyone who knew his speech from the previous October or, for that matter, any speech by

Erastus Wiman in the past year. The great advantage of free trade lay in opening the huge and prosperous American market to Canadian resource producers, who clamoured for access to the "very best customers on earth." Cartwright also insisted that manufacturers—those with competitive products and efficient production methods, anyway—would benefit. "All manufacturers who deserve to flourish in Canada by reason of their pluck, and capital, and energy," he declared, "will prosper likewise enormously if that great market be opened to them ... Give us free and unrestricted intercourse with the United States, and by that act you enormously increase the whole income of the vast majority of the people of Canada."

The most emotional part of the speech dealt with the question of patriotism, where Sir Richard knew that the Conservatives planned to focus most of their attacks. First, he informed his opponents, unrestricted reciprocity was not the slightest bit disloyal to Great Britain. The Tories were hardly in a position to make such a claim; their own National Policy imposed tariffs on British manufactures that were almost as high as those currently placed on goods from the United States! At any rate, the interests of the Canadian people, not the interests of a few British manufacturers, had to come first. And since unrestricted reciprocity was bound to improve the relations of the United States and Canada, thereby reducing friction between the United States and Great Britain, would it not be performing a great service for the Empire as a whole?

Cartwright next dealt with the predictable accusation that supporters of free trade were secretly hoping to hand Canada to the United States. The charge disgusted him, and it showed; this was the most combative and unapologetic portion of the entire speech.

> I am no annexationist and I do not propose to become one. I have no desire to see our country merged in the United States, and I can tell the House that after conferences with a good many distinguished Americans, I am well advised they do not particularly desire to add to their heavy responsibilities by seeing us politically incorporated with

> them. I have always held and declared that I regard annexation as undesirable. I have no more wish to see my country merge her existence in that of the great state to the south of us ... than I would have to merge my own individual existence in that of another man's, because I admire his abilities or envy his great estate.

Cartwright had no respect for the manufacturers who equated support for the tariff that protected them with loyalty to Canada or Great Britain. "I have the greatest possible respect for genuine loyalty and for genuine loyalties wherever I meet them," he assured the House, but "I must say that I have not much respect for 35 per cent tariff protection loyalty, or for 35 per cent tariff protection loyalists." Who were these people to claim the mantle of Canadian patriotism for themselves? The supporters of unrestricted reciprocity wanted only the best for their country. They were willing to take a risk to bring hope and prosperity to its people. "We are in a new world," he concluded, "and we own half a continent in it. It may be that there is no precedent to fit our case. My proposal is new and so is our situation, and, Sir, I have to say if there is no precedent to fit, it is our business to make one."

The speech was four hours in length, and when Cartwright sat down his fellow Liberals gave him a thunderous ovation. It was the greatest defence of free trade with the United States that the House of Commons would hear for many years, perhaps the best that it would ever hear.

Who would reply from the Conservative Party? All eyes turned to the government benches. But Sir Charles Tupper, who would normally have responded as minister of finance, was absent from the House because of a sudden bout of poor health. Hector Langevin, the most important minister from Quebec, remained in his chair. So did John Thompson of Nova Scotia, though he was quite capable of giving a stout reply. None of the senior ministers stirred.

The task of answering Cartwright therefore fell upon Thomas White, the minister of the interior and superintendent-general of Indian affairs. He acquitted himself as well as could be expected, and it soon became obvious what the Conservative line of attack was going to be. White taunted the Liberals for their apparent change of heart, reminding Cartwright that he had personally endorsed commercial union only a few months earlier. He dismissed the differences between C.U. and U.R. (unrestricted reciprocity) and argued that the Liberals were merely using a different name for commercial union. He claimed that their party had been hijacked by Erastus Wiman, the evil genius behind the movement, and concluded by asserting that commercial union would ruin the economy and lead to the annexation of Canada, no matter what the Liberals might say.

And so the battle was joined. The Great Free Trade Debate of 1888 would last for three full weeks, and by the time it was over every conceivable aspect of the subject had been exhausted. (Probably it had been exhausted before that; near the end of March, newspapers on both sides called for an end to the debate on the grounds of excessive boredom.)[47] Seventy-one members of the House took part, including Laurier and the other heavyweights on the Liberal side. But the most prominent Conservatives were missing. The most conspicuous silence was that of the prime minister himself. He was present in the House throughout, usually leaning back in his chair with his feet on his desk, but he hardly uttered a word and never made a speech. Macdonald was not going to dignify the new Liberal policy by awarding it his personal attention. He preferred to let it be debated to death by lesser lights in the House, knowing that the press would eventually tire of the subject. It was not a heroic tactic, but it was clever.

The vote finally came on April 9, and the Tories triumphed on an amendment to the original motion with an easy 124–67 majority. Everyone had expected that the motion would be defeated; the real question was whether the Liberals had made their case successfully with those Canadians (and, perhaps, Americans) who had followed the debate in the newspapers. Erastus Wiman, for one, was encouraged. He embarked on another speaking tour, heading as far west as Chicago and Winnipeg and helpfully confining himself to an endorsement of unrestricted reciprocity rather than commercial union. He also wrote Laurier to congratulate him, to invite him to spend a few days at his Staten Island mansion, and to report "a steady growth of sentiment in the commercial community here in favor of closer trade relations with Canada." As for the Great Free Trade Debate, Wiman told Laurier, the outcome was "surprisingly good in the view of those who understand the peculiarities of the question."[48]

Laurier and the Liberal Party had tried mightily to sell unrestricted reciprocity as a necessary, lucrative, and wholly patriotic policy. Macdonald and the Liberal-Conservative Party had tried—without Macdonald's direct participation—to demonize it as indistinguishable from commercial union, which was the same thing as annexation to the United States, which meant the end of the world for all loyal and self-respecting Canadian citizens. It remained to be seen which argument had won over the Canadian electorate.

There was time, of course, for further debate. The next general election might be three or even four years away—a long time for the Liberal Party to keep people interested in its "new departure" and "business proposition." It was even possible, though it did not seem likely, that the trade question might not be the dominant issue of the next election. Both parties were now gearing up for a campaign between unrestricted reciprocity and the National Policy, there was no doubt about that. But it was simply too early to tell what would happen when the election was finally called.

FOUR

The Bastard Nationality

Wilfrid Laurier should have been happy with the performance of the Liberal Party following the debate on unrestricted reciprocity. It had been long and hard fought. It had sometimes gotten ugly, and in the end it had been lost. But there had been positive indications for the Liberals. They had presented their new policy to the voters and kept it in the spotlight for almost a month. They had met the Conservative accusation that unrestricted reciprocity meant commercial union—which in turn meant annexation—fully and forcefully, without apologies. That was an achievement, given the "mortal terror" that Sir Richard Cartwright had sensed in the ranks before the debate.[1] Most of all, the Liberals had managed to stay *united*. Considering that they had been so dispirited the year before, it should have been heartening for Laurier to see his supporters rallying around their new policy and, no less importantly, their new leader.

But Laurier wasn't feeling heartened at all. In late March 1888, even as the debate raged, he was finding the leadership an increasingly heavy burden. For several months, in fact, he'd been looking for a graceful way to resign. Although few knew it—even among party members—Laurier had tried to quit in January. He had confided his plans to a few colleagues and written to Blake, then travelling through Italy, all but begging him to return. His colleagues had been dismayed, to say the least, and Blake had politely but firmly refused. Now, in late March, Laurier felt compelled to try again to divest himself of the leadership.

He wrote again to Blake, reminding him that the Liberals loved him best and longed to have him back. He claimed, again, that he had never wanted to assume the leadership in the first place. ("I have no taste for the position," Laurier insisted, "I find no pleasure in it.") He brought up the subject of his personal finances, which the duties of the leadership had forced him to neglect. Debts had accumulated, and unless he applied himself vigorously to his practice, Laurier grimly predicted, "I will have to face, at no distant date, serious embarrassment."[2] Apparently, though, he held out little hope that Blake would respond positively to his plea. In fact, two days before writing Blake at all, Laurier sent a strictly confidential letter to J.D. Edgar, serving notice that he wished to resign and adding, "Since Blake will not resume the leadership, Cartwright is the man and ought to be put in the position."[3]

Parliament rose in late May. By then Laurier had drawn up a letter of resignation addressed to the chairman of the Liberal caucus. But if he sent it, nothing came of it. The Liberal Party carried on as usual through the summer. Blake returned from Europe after a holiday that had lasted almost a year and spent the summer at his beloved cottage in Quebec. Wilfrid and Zoe took a ship from Quebec to pay Edward and Margaret Blake a visit, and in that idyllic setting, the two men had a series of long conversations about politics, the party, and inevitably, the leadership. Laurier found his old friend infuriating. Blake was in better health, and he had obviously regained his interest in Canadian political affairs, but he still could not be persuaded to come back and lead the party.

Laurier accepted his fate, but it was clear from his persistent efforts to woo Blake that he was unhappy in his position. Why? His finances were bad, but that could hardly be the reason for surrendering something as important as the Liberal leadership. A weak constitution was not, for once, the problem; Laurier had admitted to Blake that "my health is at present very good."[4] Nor had he been discouraged by the performance of the Liberal Party in the House of Commons. His followers were enthusiastically in favour of unrestricted reciprocity, and Laurier, at any rate, had never been one to worry about the Conservative "loyalty cry" or its possible impact in the next election. The trade question was not the one that frightened him.

What he did fear was the re-emergence of race and religion as a divisive force in Canadian politics. Though he had made the conciliation of Canada's "two founding nations" the central aim of his political career, Laurier had little faith that English Canadian Protestants would ever accept the idea of a prime minister from Quebec. He was convinced that even in the best of times the Liberal Party was disadvantaged by his leadership, and prejudice that ran as deep as it did in Canada could not be suppressed forever. It was always lurking below the surface, ready to be awakened by even the most insignificant provocation. Laurier believed that only an English-speaking Protestant leader from Ontario could keep this monster at bay in a crisis. He lamented it, but he was sure it was the truth. "A French Canadian," Laurier later mused to Blake, "will not get a cheerful support in the English provinces."[5]

Still, he was the Liberal leader for the foreseeable future. He would have to strive for the support, cheerful or not, of the English provinces, particularly Ontario. That was a tall order. In his entire political career Laurier had made only one important speech to an Ontario audience, in December 1886, when he had ventured to Toronto to speak in support of Blake. Laurier had been deeply unpopular in Ontario at that time, because of his declaration in support of the rebels in the North-West Rebellion. The Liberals had actually worried for Laurier's safety and had arranged for a bodyguard of young Liberals to surround him on his arrival at the station. Laurier's speech, given at the Horticultural Pavilion before an unruly crowd, had not gone smoothly. He was heckled—this was the occasion when smart-mouthed Tories hollered "Where's your musket?"—and though he persevered with his message of tolerance and earned grudging respect from the crowd, the episode had been a rough initiation to Ontario politics.

Now, in the summer of 1888, Laurier decided that it was better to avoid Toronto altogether and speak instead at rural venues where unrestricted reciprocity was popular. That wasn't very courageous, but it was prudent. Yet Laurier didn't know what to say even to these rural audiences. He wrote to Edgar seeking advice: "Reciprocity, of course, is to be the main subject. Are there however any other questions which I could refer to. In the peculiar position which I occupy, French, Catholic, is there anything which grates upon the feelings of some of your people, & should I allude to this. I always endeavour beforehand, to understand exactly the views, the feelings, the passions & prejudices of those whom I am to address."[6]

Edgar agreed that Laurier should emphasize the trade platform. Also, he replied, "let it be seen that you are national & not provincial, Canadian not French, a believer in Confederation not a secessionist, loyal, of course, full of toleration for all religions." To this lengthy list Edgar helpfully added, "Patriotic generalizations, which you can make so eloquent, will take well."[7]

Laurier did his best. He addressed a dozen small-town meetings in Ontario during the muggy month of August, beginning with Oakville, just west of Toronto. The Liberals boasted that the tour was a huge success, but the crowds weren't really that enthusiastic. Laurier's manner was formal and hesitant. He insisted on telling his audiences that he wished Blake would take his place, and seemed almost apologetic when reminding them that even though he was a French Canadian, his first loyalty was to the whole of Canada. He criticized the Conservative record, sang the praises of unrestricted reciprocity, and even attended a couple of Protestant church functions. It was a worthy effort. But there was still a great distance between himself and the curious audiences that came to see him. Laurier was simply not one of them, and he felt that keenly, and so did they. Only once did he impress, when a small-town Protestant clergyman made an ugly slur against Roman Catholics. Laurier, visibly irritated, issued an icy reply that shamed the man into silence. The surprised crowd cheered, prompting the Liberal journalist John Willison to recall, "I had the impudence to tell the leader that he should engage the belligerent divine to attend and interrupt at subsequent meetings."[8]

Laurier returned home to Arthabaskaville in early September. He was lucky to get out of Ontario when he did, because as summer turned to fall, the political mood in the province took a sharp turn for the worse. The race-and-religion monster had awakened, just as Laurier had feared that it inevitably would. In June 1888 the premier of Quebec, Honoré Mercier, had introduced into the provincial legislature "An Act respecting the settlement of the Jesuits' Estates." It had breezed through both chambers in Quebec City without dissent, and became law on July 12. The Jesuits' Estates Act was destined to throw many English Canadian Protestants into emotional uproar, thoroughly poison the political atmosphere, and endanger the unity of Canada itself.

The act itself was a matter-of-fact document that compensated the Society of Jesus of the Roman Catholic Church—the Jesuits—for lands confiscated from them by the government of Quebec nearly a century earlier. Four hundred thousand dollars of provincial funds were divided among the Jesuits, the Catholic Laval University, and the ten Catholic dioceses of Quebec. Also, in proportion to the one-seventh of Quebecers who were Protestant, an additional sixty thousand dollars was allocated to Protestant separate schools across the province. It was, all in all, a fair settlement. All the interested parties received something, a long-festering problem was laid to rest, and the amount of money involved was modest. The Jesuits' Estates Act had nothing to do with the other provinces and there was no reason—no *rational* reason, anyway—why anyone outside Quebec would be terribly concerned about it. The reaction it provoked among many English Canadian Protestants, unfortunately, was hardly rational.

One reason for the inflamed response was that the settlement was the work of Mercier, a French Canadian nationalist who was thoroughly distrusted in English Canada. The proud and charismatic premier possessed an impeccable *Canadien* pedigree, his family having settled in Quebec in 1647, in the early days of New France. In person he was impressive: handsome and broad shouldered, with startling grey eyes and a bushy black moustache. Since his school days at a Jesuit college he had always been a natural leader, a man who easily excelled at everything he did but still, somehow, earned the affection (rather than the jealousy) of his peers. After considering the priesthood, Mercier had become a successful lawyer, journalist, and politician. He was a Liberal in name, but his Quebec nationalism trumped his loyalty to the party. He was not necessarily hostile to the English Protestant minority in his province, but he believed that his people had to stop thinking as Tories or Liberals. They must unite, he argued, to defend their French-speaking, Roman Catholic society against intolerant English Canadian Protestants.

Mercier rose to power in Quebec after the hanging of Louis Riel in 1885. As he saw it, the execution of Riel—a French-speaking Roman Catholic who had only been trying to defend the Métis way of life—was a horrific act sanctioned by Macdonald purely to appease bloodthirsty English Canadian Orangemen. In the provincial election of October 1886—in which Mercier "dragged Riel's corpse" across Quebec, in the bitter words of Macdonald[9]—he persuaded disaffected voters to support his brand of confident French Canadian nationalism. The provincial Conservatives lost their hold on power, and in January 1887 Honoré Mercier took over as premier.

Mercier was an atypical Liberal in that he was deferential to the Catholic Church. He realized that it was pointless to cross swords with the powerful clergy in the province, a tactic that had doomed the Liberals to perennial opposition in the past. Instead he made a determined effort to prove that he was a defender of the Catholic faith. He even tried, with some success, to court the ultramontanes, an uncompromising right-wing faction within the Church that stressed the infallibility of the Pope, opposed the modernization of doctrines of the Catholic faith that "Catholic liberals" proposed, and flatly rejected the principle of separation of church and state. Mercier also wanted to make peace with the Jesuits, who had long demanded compensation for the seizure of their estates. It was a delicate business, because the Jesuits and the bishops of Quebec had never agreed on how compensation should be distributed among them. To resolve the impasse, Mercier asked Pope Leo XIII himself to arbitrate. That was clever, because whatever His Holiness decided would surely be accepted by both sides. The Pope did arbitrate, and to underline the role he had played, Mercier published twenty-one pages of their correspondence in a lengthy preamble to the Jesuits' Estates Act.

Macdonald suspected that Mercier had concocted the act, especially its preamble, deliberately to provoke a response in English Canada. The fact that the Society of Jesus was being compensated for its lost estates was bothersome enough to most Protestants. They regarded the Jesuits as the Pope's fanatical foot soldiers, priests who were loyal to no country or sovereign and who would resort to any means necessary to exterminate the Protestant faith. The fact that the Pope had been called in to arbitrate the settlement—in effect, to determine how Quebec tax dollars would be spent—was even more offensive. Queen Victoria, not Pope Leo XIII, was the sovereign of Canada! Who did Mercier think he was, encouraging this kind of meddling in Canadian affairs? It was a slippery slope that many English Canadian Protestants were determined not to slide down. Something must be done. The Jesuits' Estates Act must be disallowed.

The federal government certainly had the authority to intervene. The prime minister was an experienced practitioner of the constitutional power of disallowance, which permitted his government to strike down provincial legislation contrary to the national interest. He had used this power regularly since Confederation, treating the provinces like naughty children who required frequent discipline. Surely, it was said in Protestant circles, Macdonald would disallow this petulant Quebec legislation. The agitation for disallowance, with its undercurrent of racial and religious intolerance, was most fervent in Ontario but also evident in Manitoba, the Maritime provinces, and even Quebec itself. The most heated opposition to the act came, not surprisingly, from the Orange Order. For Orangemen, dedicated to the defence of Protestantism against the sinister conspiracies of Catholicism, the issue was tailor-made to arouse their collective sense of righteous indignation. In September 1888 the *Sentinel*, the official newspaper of the order, threw down the gauntlet and demanded that the act be disallowed.

The opposition quickly grew. In October the Presbyterian Church of Montreal expressed its strenuous objection to the act, taking the opportunity to denounce the Jesuits as an "enemy of civil and religious liberty."[10] That same month, a new organization, the Evangelical Alliance, was formed in Montreal and joined the chorus. The Alliance pointed out that revenues from the Jesuits' estates had previously been funnelled into Catholic and Protestant schooling; thanks to the act, this source of revenue for the Protestant schools would dry up. As fall turned to winter the prime minister was receiving a growing number of demands that he strike down the act.

Macdonald understood that the act was objectionable to many English Canadian Protestants—the preamble with the correspondence with the Pope had been a needlessly inflammatory touch—but it was, in his judgment, well within the purview of the Quebec government to settle the matter. It was a purely provincial concern that had nothing to do with the rest of the country, and practically speaking it was of very little significance. To disallow the act would create a *nationaliste* furor in Quebec, drive voters into the arms of Honoré Mercier, and injure the federal Conservative Party. Even Catholics in English Canada would be offended, not because they especially cared about the act, but because if Macdonald disallowed it, he would be caving in to Protestant bigotry. Those Catholic votes tended to go Conservative in many close Ontario and Maritime constituencies, and the Old Man was not about to throw them away.

Mercier already knew Macdonald's position. In the early fall of 1888 the premier visited Ottawa to see the prime minister on unrelated business. They did not know each other well, having met only once before, and there was no easy banter between them. Mercier, dressed formally in a frock coat, exchanged stiff pleasantries with his host as they awkwardly waited for the cabinet to assemble for their meeting. While they were at last walking down the corridor toward the chamber, Mercier asked casually, "Sir John, I wish you would tell us whether you are going to disallow our Jesuits' Estates Act or not." The prime minister's eyes brightened at this cheekiness. He replied, "Do you take me for a damn fool?"[11] Months later, in January 1889, the Macdonald government announced publicly that the power of disallowance would not be used against the Jesuits' Estates Act.

The announcement only aggravated the people who had been riled by the act. The chorus of opposition broadened to include one of the most influential newspapers in Canada, the Toronto *Mail*, which took up the anti-Jesuit cause with enthusiasm. The *Mail* was a rarity in Canada, a genuinely independent paper, and it was competing with the Toronto *Globe* for circulation across southern Ontario. Its mischievous editorial writer, Edward Farrer, had been booming commercial union for the last two years. Now he embarked on a crusade of virulent opposition to the Jesuits' Estates Act, the Catholic Church, and more broadly, French Canadian nationalism. It was rumoured that Farrer, of Irish Catholic background, had once trained to be a priest but had fallen out with the Church and harboured a grudge against it ever since. Certainly he was familiar with Catholic doctrine, and that gave an air of authority to his attacks against the Jesuits. He was assisted by Goldwin Smith, a fellow commercial unionist and Catholic-basher, who also took to writing anti-Jesuit editorials for the *Mail*. It proved to be a popular cause. It was so good for business, in fact, that the normally more moderate Toronto *Globe*, feeling the pinch, felt compelled to get on the bandwagon and oppose the act as well. That was embarrassing to Laurier and the Liberal Party, and an indication of just how overpowering the anti-French, anti-Catholic sentiment in the largest city in English Canada really was.

The *Mail* shrewdly played on the frustrations of Ontario Protestants who felt that the politicians were not listening to them. Its editorials implied that Macdonald, who was easily caricatured as a compromiser rather than a man of principle, had let them down. No one was more fond of exercising the power of disallowance, the *Mail* suggested, but now, faced with the Jesuits' Estates Act, he had suddenly become the champion of "provincial rights." The early announcement of his decision, six months before the time to disallow the act expired, was particularly galling. For Ontario Protestants, long accustomed to watching the Old Man perform acrobatics to woo votes from French Canadians, the decision was further proof that the Conservative government in Ottawa could no longer be trusted to represent the interests of the country's English Canadian Protestant majority.

Even within the Conservative Party there were some rumbles of discontent. Rank-and-file members pointed out that the government had used disallowance against less offensive acts in the past. Orange Lodges mailed Macdonald resolutions recommending forceful action against the Mercier government. Some of these messages sounded like threats. In private correspondence and public newspaper accounts, there were ominous indications that the Conservatives might abandon their own leader over this issue. Few were more explicit than the Orangemen of Ottawa, who hinted darkly that they might "break up old associations and friendships, whether political or otherwise," if the Jesuits' Estates Act was not disallowed.[12]

Macdonald surveyed this disquieting situation with his usual calm. He had seen it all in his forty-five years in politics, and he knew his course was right. Publicly, he used the Toronto *Empire* to defend his inaction as a sensible response to a perfectly legal and largely insignificant piece of legislation. Privately, he reminded his caucus that the Catholic vote, which they had assiduously cultivated over the years, was essential to the government's success in many closely fought Ontario constituencies. Try as he might, however, Macdonald was unable to prevent the growing tumult from reaching the floor of the House of Commons. On March 1 he was notified that Col. William O'Brien, the Conservative member from Muskoka and Parry Sound, planned to introduce a motion for the disallowance of the act. All efforts to dissuade him, including an urgent party caucus held on March 15, failed.

This was a dangerous development. The O'Brien motion forced the question, with all its poisonous implications, onto the parliamentary agenda. Members would have to submit to a recorded vote on disallowance, and that vote had the potential to expose divisions within both parties along French and English lines.

O'Brien himself was not the problem; he had held his seat for ten years, but he was not a major figure in the party. His collaborator on the motion for disallowance, however, had a substantial following. This was D'Alton McCarthy, the member for Simcoe North in Ontario, and one of the most remarkable and infuriating politicians in all of Canadian history. McCarthy believed that the Jesuits' Estates Act was a serious threat to the future of the country. In the course of opposing it during the spring of 1889, he was destined to become an even more serious threat himself.

The Man and His Cause

By all accounts he was a man of flawless integrity and tremendous natural ability. Even the Liberal journalist John Willison would admit years later that D'Alton McCarthy was "an admirable figure in Canadian politics.

He was singularly courageous and incorruptible."[13] McCarthy came originally from Ulster, the most staunchly Protestant part of Ireland, but he had lived most of his life in Canada. He was a lawyer by trade, a very good one, with a thriving practice in Barrie, just northwest of Toronto. There he maintained an impressive rural residence, in keeping with his status as a leading citizen, as well as a farm that he lovingly tended with his own hands. He was always lean and fit, a testament to his love of sports (particularly horseback riding), and his physical prowess was matched by his intelligence, sophistication, and civility. McCarthy was no beer-swilling boor. But his dignified demeanour only made him more dangerous, because it provided an aura of respectability to political views that were intolerant and inflammatory.

McCarthy was a fervent Canadian nationalist. He never tired of talking about the destiny of the Dominion, which was, as he saw it, to become one of the leading nations of the British Empire. That was fair enough. Many English Canadians shared this view, and there was nothing particularly dangerous or controversial about it. Where McCarthy was out of step with more moderate-minded Canadians was in his conception of the linguistic complexion of this future Dominion. A nation, he believed, could not thrive unless there was a "community of language" among its people. How else could they understand or truly respect one another? How could they share the same sense of national identity? It was a ludicrous notion that Canada could achieve greatness as long as it was divided between English and French. For Canadians to be truly unified, he reasoned, the French language must be extinguished throughout the country.

That was, of course, an impossibility. Sir John A. Macdonald knew it and so did the vast majority of late nineteenth-century Canadian politicians. The country had been built on a foundation of tolerance and mutual respect between its "two founding nations," French and English. As unsteady as that foundation might be, as badly as it might creak and groan under the strain of constant compromise and accommodation, it was the only one that could support the structure of Confederation. The country would never be purely English speaking, not without forcing some terrible confrontation, perhaps even civil war, between French and English. McCarthy advocated legal measures to promote English, such as banning French in federal and provincial legislatures and public schools. But if French Canadians resisted these measures, what then? Perhaps the outposts of French Canada—the declining Métis of the North-West, for example, or the minority French-speaking populations of eastern Ontario and New Brunswick—could be bullied into adopting the English language. But it was hard to believe that French could be extinguished in Quebec without the occurrence of, as Governor Guy Carleton had put it in the 1770s, "a catastrophe shocking to think of."[14]

McCarthy stood firm. He knew that many Ontario Protestants, angry about the passage of the Jesuits' Estates Act and tired of the endless appeals for tolerance made by politicians like Sir John A. Macdonald, agreed with him. The O'Brien motion for disallowance was a way to bring the question of Canada's future—as McCarthy put it to Macdonald, "whether we are to be French or English"[15]—before Parliament. A vote in support of the motion was sure to cause problems for the Conservative Party, but for McCarthy, the cause of a common language was more important. It was time for English Canadians to stop pandering to Quebec and make a stand.

As the date set for the debate on the Jesuits' Estates Act neared, the atmosphere in all parts of the Dominion grew increasingly uneasy. The politicians, especially, worried that harsh words spoken during the debate would do irreparable harm to national unity. In Ontario many Conservative members of Parliament knew that voting against disallowance, in accordance with the prime minister's wishes, would be met with outrage in their own constituencies. Still, the rank and file would not desert Macdonald. One of them, George Dickinson, one day left a meeting with the Old Man just as Joseph Pope was walking into the room. "Dickinson is a plucky fellow," a pained Macdonald told Pope after Dickinson left. "He has come in now to tell me that he was elected to support me, and he is going to do it, though he knows full well that in voting with the Government in this matter he is committing political suicide."[16]

When Colonel O'Brien rose in the House of Commons on the afternoon of March 26 to introduce his motion, the galleries above the chamber were packed with observers, and an unusually large number of the members themselves had taken their seats. The atmosphere was exceedingly tense. O'Brien informed the House that he was reluctant to raise a subject that was "so likely to give rise to angry feelings, and possibly to acrimonious discussion."[17] But raise it he did, in uncompromising fashion, insisting on the fearless use of disallowance against the Jesuits' Estates Act. He made three essential arguments in support of his motion. First, the Mercier government had no right to award public funds to a religious organization because it violated the fundamental principle of separation of church and state. Second, giving the Pope authority to dictate the allotment of public funds in Canada was a grotesque violation of the sovereignty of Queen Victoria. Third, the Jesuits themselves were an evil and destructive force, an "alien, secret, and politico-religious body" whose insidious activities were "fraught with danger to the civil and religious liberties of the people of Canada."

O'Brien did not mince words, and no doubt many of the more moderate members of the House winced as his speech continued. Most of his time was devoted to damning the Jesuits. He pointed out that even the Catholic Church had banned them in the past, and that there was a good reason why their estates had been confiscated in the first place. They were no less dangerous today, no less fanatical in their desire to press the Catholic religion upon the people of Canada, than they had been in centuries past. "Sir, a Jesuit is a being abnormal in his conditions," O'Brien assured a silent House. "He has no family ties, no home nor country. He is subject absolutely to the will of his superior." The order would stop at nothing to undermine the foundations of Canadian society, to "inculcate principles repugnant, not only to our civilization, but to every principle that unites communities in every condition of life." For this reason the majority of Canadians wanted disallowance, O'Brien concluded. He added darkly that if the House of Commons did not reflect their wishes, he would be glad to see the matter settled by the "jury of the people."

O'Brien had advanced his argument in extreme terms. He could have made the case for disallowance using the first two arguments cited in his motion: that the act violated the separation of church and state and wrongly injected the Pope into the political business of the Dominion. Instead he had railed angrily against the Jesuits, doing his best to aggravate the latent prejudices of his English Canadian Protestant constituents. A strong response was called for. Onlookers might have guessed that Macdonald or the minister of justice, Sir John Thompson, would rise to defend the government's position. Neither did. Instead John C. Rykert, an unremarkable Ontario Tory, stood first to speak against the O'Brien motion. He delivered a decent speech, and he was followed by lesser lights from both parties, on both sides of the subject. Not one member of the Macdonald cabinet, however, spoke against the O'Brien motion on the first day of the debate.

D'Alton McCarthy was greatly offended by this apparent snub, and his frustration showed when he stood to deliver his own much-anticipated speech the next day. He began by dwelling upon the lack of a response from even one cabinet minister, muttering that this was "hardly giving us fair play," and somewhat lost his customary composure. McCarthy then went to the heart of the matter, giving two carefully reasoned arguments for disallowance. The first, adding to those made in the O'Brien motion, was that the Jesuits' Estates Act was ultra vires, that is to say, beyond the jurisdiction of the Quebec government. The province did not have the legal right to make the Pope the arbiter of how tax dollars were spent. McCarthy went to enormous lengths to prove that this violated centuries of British and Canadian legal precedent, and provocatively asked the House, "Can humiliation go much further, if we are indeed a free people?"

That inflammatory remark prompted laughter and derisive comments from several members. McCarthy was annoyed, but not deterred. After elaborating further upon his contention that the act was unconstitutional, he moved to his second argument: that even if the act *was* constitutional, it still must be disallowed on the grounds of national unity. The point of disallowance, McCarthy contended, was to prevent a single province from passing legislation that would be intolerable to the others, and therefore damaging to the country as a whole. If the federal government did not have the courage to act against this kind of renegade behaviour, where would it end? "We can easily see, sir," he predicted, "that before long these provinces, instead of coming nearer together, will go further and further apart. We can see that the only way of making a united Canada and building up a national life and national sentiment, is by seeing that the laws of one Province are not offensive to the laws and institutions, and, it may be, the feelings of another."

That was the most memorable line in what was, by McCarthy's standards, a mediocre speech. He had been irritated from the beginning, and his demeanour had not improved as he had been repeatedly interrupted by members from both sides of the House. The hostility of the majority of them was obvious, and his complaint about not getting fair treatment from the government had not helped his cause. His three-hour-long speech had dwelled too long on the history of the Jesuits and on the debatable argument that Mercier had surrendered his province's sovereignty to the Pope. McCarthy had, however, succeeded in taking the controversy over the Jesuits' Estates Act into much broader territory, away from the religious question and toward a more fundamental debate about the language question, and about just what kind of country the Dominion of Canada ought to be.

That was the most dangerous aspect of McCarthy's position. Though he did not elaborate, he was contending that the provincial government of Quebec did not have the right to pass laws that the English-speaking provincial governments disagreed with. This line of reasoning implied that the wishes of the other provinces might prevail over other Quebec policies. They might object to the practice of French civil law or even the use of the French language. McCarthy did not go that far, not yet. Yet he had unmistakably implied that French Canadians must live in accordance with the sensibilities of English Canadians, and that was a dangerous argument for a member of Parliament to make in the name of "building up a national life and national sentiment."

Now Sir John Thompson, the minister of justice, rose to respond for the government. He knew that this would be one of the most important speeches of his political career, and as an adult convert to Catholicism, he also knew what it was like to suffer the slings and arrows of bigoted Ontario Protestants. Since his conversion, which had been a necessary precondition of his marriage, he had been denounced as "the Pervert" by Orangemen in Ontario. He did not particularly care what they thought of him, but he did care about the potential consequences of the irresponsible appeal that he had just heard delivered on the floor of the House of Commons. He was conscious that, politically speaking, it would be unwise to attack McCarthy too harshly, lest he be further alienated from the Conservative Party. But Thompson had never been an especially savvy politician. He was first and foremost an exceedingly decent and tolerant man, and he knew that a threat like the one posed by D'Alton McCarthy could not be handled lightly.

Thompson's speech was devastating. He had spent long hours preparing it, and his superior knowledge of the legal precedents of the case was evident. McCarthy had cited numerous British laws that had been designed to curb Roman Catholicism and prevent the Pope from usurping the Queen's sovereignty. Thompson pointed out that these laws were ancient relics, hundreds of years old, and relevant only as examples of the shameful intolerance that had once animated the British Parliament. None had been enforced for centuries; in most cases they had never been enforced at all. Even if they had been, Sir John pointed out, the Jesuits' Estates Act did not in any way assert the sovereignty of the Pope over Canadian affairs. He was simply the best arbiter of this particular question, the one person upon whom both parties could agree, and he had acted as an arbiter and not as a sovereign power. The responsibility of awarding the compensation as the Pope had recommended had rested entirely with the Quebec government. The preamble had been obnoxious, but no legislation in the history of British North America had been disallowed because it had an annoying preamble.

The most important principle that Thompson expounded was not a legal principle. It was his firm conviction that Canada could not be governed "on the fashion of 300 years ago." Canadians had to be motivated by something greater than the prejudices of the past. They had to look to the future and to keep embracing the tolerant approach that allowed them, despite their differences, to live together peacefully and still work toward a truly Canadian nationality. It was the only way to go forward, and it was the only noble and honourable way.

When Thompson finished, there was a general sense that something special had just occurred. His fellow members rose and applauded. Even the reporter for the Toronto *Mail*, that fierce proponent of disallowance, remarked that it was the greatest parliamentary speech since Confederation. Edward Blake (back in the House after his long absence) crossed the floor and shook Thompson's hand, their party differences notwithstanding. The minister of justice had crushed D'Alton McCarthy's argument both in letter and in spirit, and a grateful House acknowledged the achievement.

The debate carried on into the next evening, March 28, but there were only two speeches left that really mattered. The first was made by Laurier, who announced that his party would support the position of the government. He was troubled by the agitation in Ontario, and relieved that the House would refuse to stand upon such "very narrow, very unsafe, and very dangerous ground." When he mentioned that

McCarthy would prefer to see a single race in Canada, McCarthy interrupted with a cry of "Hear, hear!" and Laurier replied with one of his great ringing phrases. "There can be more than one race," he told the House, "but there shall be but one nation."

Aside from that line, unfortunately, Laurier was not at his best. Most of his speech was fiercely partisan, devoted to dredging up old grievances with the Conservative government and perhaps overcompensating for the fact that, on this one issue, the two parties actually agreed.

It was very late by the time that the prime minister rose to answer the leader of the Opposition. Macdonald was in a good mood. The debate had gone so well, he noted, that he could easily forgive the needless potshots that Laurier had taken at his "double-faced" government. "I pardon my honourable friend in that regard," he said with a grin. "He is a young man ... the honourable gentleman has forgotten the history of his country." He took a few partisan jabs of his own, reminding the House that the Reform Party of Ontario had once been animated by the most wicked prejudices against the French language and the Roman Catholic faith. He recalled the argument of one of these old Reformers ("a very honest and respectable man, strange to say," he quipped) in a debate of the Canadian legislature prior to Confederation. "Mr. Speaker," the Reformer had said simply, "I don't like them there Jesuits." And that, as Macdonald saw it, was the gist of the call for disallowance. It was about prejudice, and that was all it was about. To disallow the Jesuits' Estates Act would be short-sighted and disastrous. It would merely make Mercier the "champion of his church" and spark a "racial and religious war." Anyone who understood the nature of Canada could not help but know that. With that, Sir John A. sat back down.

Sir Richard Cartwright spoke briefly, responding to a couple of remarks from the prime minister, and the debate was over. The outcome had never been seriously in doubt. The House of Commons had risen to the challenge of defining a broader vision of Canada than the narrow one promoted by D'Alton McCarthy. Cartwright, observing that even the stricken and paralyzed former prime minister Alexander Mackenzie had come to the House to cast his vote, had the final word. "If I had any doubt as to the correctness of my conviction," he declared, "I would find it in ... my venerated friend coming here to record his vote against a proposition which would set man against man and kindle the flames of religious bigotry from one end of this Dominion to the other."

The vote on the O'Brien motion finally came at a quarter to two in the morning on March 29, after three long and emotionally exhausting evenings of debate. The House was virtually full despite the late hour, with more members in their places than anyone could remember having seen in years. McCarthy himself thought that it was the largest turnout in the history of Parliament. When the division was taken, 13 members supported the motion; 188 members opposed it. It was an overwhelming victory, a rare common effort between Liberals and Conservatives. It was also an inspiring defence of the principles of tolerance and moderation that had guided the country since Confederation.

Macdonald was obviously relieved. After lending his lungs to the traditional rendition of "God Save the Queen," he strolled out to the lobby and called to one of the few Liberals who had supported the motion. "Hello, Sutherland," he hollered cheerfully, "you belonged to the devil's dozen tonight, eh?"[18]

Facing the Monster

Macdonald had expected that this decisive vote would bring an end to the campaign for disallowance, but he was wrong. Many Ontario Protestants were furious that so few politicians had supported them, and their sense of betrayal was evident in the headlines of pro-disallowance newspapers across the province. There was dark muttering that the whole issue could no longer be trusted to the no-good politicians, except, of course, D'Alton McCarthy. His speech to the House had been easily the most memorable of the "Noble Thirteen," as friends and supporters took to calling the backers of the O'Brien motion, and he remained the darling of the agitation in Ontario. As Macdonald had feared, Thompson's speech had been too good. It had only infuriated McCarthy, whom David Creighton, the editor of the *Empire*, reported was so disillusioned that he was thinking of resigning his seat in Parliament in protest. He did not do that, but early in April he did quit the presidency of the Liberal-Conservative Union, a position of influence within the party.

Macdonald was alarmed. He had hoped that McCarthy would accept the outcome and stop pressing his campaign. This resignation signalled otherwise. Something must be done. Creighton urged a gentle approach, noting that McCarthy was "feeling very very sore ... in his present temper he ought to be soothed rather than irritated."[19] Macdonald agreed. On April 14 he wrote to his wayward friend, urging him to stop his campaign for the good of the party. But McCarthy was defiant. The majority of English Canadians were with him, he believed, and Macdonald had better stop pandering to the Catholic vote or risk the extinction of the Conservative Party.

Following his heart, McCarthy delivered a rousing speech on April 22 at a large gathering in honour of the "Noble Thirteen" at the Granite Rink in Toronto. Thousands were in attendance. There were other speakers, John Charlton of the Liberal Party being the most prominent, but the night belonged to McCarthy. The crowd hung on every word as he spoke for two hours, reiterating his argument for disallowance and, more broadly, explaining that a common language was the essential ingredient of the nation. He did not attend the "Great Anti-Jesuit Convention," a brainchild of hard-line Protestant clergymen, that was held in Toronto on June 11 and 12. That meeting was too intolerant even for McCarthy; he was committed to his cause, but he did not want to make more trouble for the Conservative Party if it could be avoided.

Then came the thundering remarks of Honoré Mercier at the Feast of St. Jean Baptiste celebrations in Quebec City two weeks later. In front of an open-air audience of thousands, the premier urged French Canadians to embrace their own strident nationalism. "The province of

Quebec is Catholic and French, and it will remain Catholic and French," he proclaimed. "We solemnly declare that we will never renounce the rights that are guaranteed us ... Let our rallying cry in the future be these words that will be our strength: Let us cease our fratricidal fighting, let us unite!"[20]

McCarthy could not let these provocations go unanswered. He was incensed by such an unabashed display of French Canadian aggression—one Mercier supporter at the Feast of St. Jean Baptiste had even urged the Quebec militia to prepare to repel English invaders—and he made up his mind to issue a stern rebuttal. On the Glorious Twelfth of July, the most revered holiday of the year for the Orange Order, McCarthy addressed the Orangemen of Stayner, in his constituency of Simcoe North.[21] It was his most belligerent speech yet. The Jesuits' Estates Act was touched upon, but it was no longer the real issue. The larger question was the threat to Canada represented by French Canadian nationalism. "This bastard nationality," McCarthy warned, "begins and ends with the French race—which begins and ends with those who profess the Roman Catholic faith—now threatens the dismemberment of the Dominion of Canada."[22]

The Orangemen cheered lustily as McCarthy went on to outline his vision of the Canadian future. The time had come, in his view, to end the nonsense that had prevailed since the Conquest. French Canadians must accept that Canada was a British country, and that the English language must become the language of the entire population of Canada. That was right and inevitable, and if French Canadians did not submit to the will of the majority, the consequences would be severe. "Now is the time, when the ballot box will decide this great question before the people," he predicted. "And if that does not supply the remedy in this generation, bayonets will supply it in the next."[23] That was a frightening prophecy. McCarthy retreated from the spotlight after uttering these ominous words, but only briefly. In August he would deliver two more incendiary speeches while on a visit to the West, at Portage La Prairie and

Calgary, where he again hinted darkly that an English-French confrontation might be inevitable.

Thanks in part to D'Alton McCarthy, public opposition to the Jesuits' Estates Act continued well beyond August 8, the final day that the Macdonald government could have disallowed it. By then the agitation had morphed into something larger and more dangerous. It was no longer targeted merely against disallowance. Now it seemed to be against the continued existence of French Canada itself. Macdonald had kept his Conservatives from falling under the spell of McCarthy, and that was important. He saw no sense in doing more in the summer of 1889. There was little point in drumming McCarthy out of the party; too many followers would go with him. Nor was there any need for public speeches, which would only aggravate one side or the other. Macdonald settled on a strategy of waiting patiently, as he had often done in the past. He would depend on the passage of time to sap the movement's strength. It was his way, and his way usually worked.

Wilfrid Laurier thought differently. He was convinced that a strong statement was needed against McCarthy, the Equal Rights Association, and anyone else who was out on the stump bashing French Canada. There had been a Liberal gathering in Toronto on June 29 but the featured speaker, Sir Richard Cartwright, had delivered a hesitant and poorly received speech. "Sir Richard was not in good form," E.W. Thomson, a *Globe* journalist, wrote to Laurier. Cartwright had been unsure of what to say about the Jesuits' Estates controversy, and his tone had been much too gloomy for the occasion. "After all," Thomson hinted, "the people love best a *human* man for a leader, one that looks pleasant and talks in a cheery way." Just in case Laurier had missed his point, Thomson added, "It was a mistake that you did not come."[24]

Laurier was already thinking of going to Toronto. The idea of speaking out against McCarthy deep in the heartland of English Canada appealed to him. It would be a bold step, at a time when no one else—not even the prime minister—seemed willing to publicly confront the leaders of this pernicious and intolerant movement. Several prominent Liberals agreed. David Mills, for example, cursed his party for lacking the courage to make a stand. "People everywhere say We thought you were right," Mills reported, "but how is it you are afraid to come out boldly and defend yourselves?"[25] Still, appearing in Toronto was risky. J.D. Edgar urged Laurier to speak somewhere else in Ontario. "Toronto is not the place," he warned. "There would certainly be a *rough* meeting over the Jesuit question ... I think a bad reception would have a bad effect."[26]

Laurier preferred the advice that he was getting from the *Globe* staff. Thomson was trying hard to stiffen his resolve, proposing the slogan "Be Bold, Be Bold, Be Bold."[27] He insisted that Ontario Liberals would rally enthusiastically around him if Laurier came to Toronto and took a firm stand. In August John Willison, the *Globe*'s chief editorial writer, visited the Lauriers at their little red brick house in Arthabaskaville. Willison found Zoe to be a gracious host in a warm and happy home surrounded by lush lawns and leafy trees, and bustling inside with family members and guests. A bust of Blake and a portrait of Mackenzie watched over the two men as they discussed the potential Toronto visit. Laurier worried that the crowd would turn on him. Willison assured him that it would go well. He was convincing, too, because he returned home with instructions to organize a massive rally, under the auspices of the Young Men's Liberal Club of Toronto, for Laurier and Premier Oliver Mowat to address jointly that fall.

It was all arranged for September 30, 1889. The Horticultural Pavilion was one of the largest buildings in the city, a unique three-tiered glass and iron structure that had massive windows all around and featured, directly in front, a towering, cascading fountain. The pavilion was crammed that night with five thousand Torontonians, at least by the *Globe*'s partisan estimate. A brass band began playing at seven, welcoming the audience (which included hundreds of ladies, it was duly noted) as it poured into the hall. The walls had been decorated with streamers and a rather excessive number of Union Jacks, kept fluttering by special gas jets. Above the main stage hung a large banner reading, "Welcome to Our Leaders, Laurier and Mowat." An impressive gathering of Liberals, including the entire Ontario cabinet, shared the platform with the featured speakers. By eight o'clock there was standing room only, and when Laurier stepped onto the platform a reassuring cheer went up. John Willison made a few remarks of introduction, urging that "fair and honest consideration" be shown the guest of honour. Then Wilfrid Laurier was left alone to win over his sceptical audience.

He cut a lonely figure on the platform, pale, frail, and perspiring, a single French Canadian in front of thousands of English Canadians who, he knew, had little sympathy for what he was about to say. His speech, however, was courageous from the beginning. It was never easy to find common ground on painful questions, Laurier admitted, and he could not deny that there was distrust between the peoples of Ontario and Quebec. Some Ontarians would stamp out the French language across Canada if they had their way, and some Quebecers would prefer to live in a purely French-speaking province. But he had no respect for either of these extremes. "We live under Confederation," Laurier reminded his audience, "and it is our duty to stand by Confederation, to be loyal to Confederation." That great pact had not been based upon the humiliation of either of its founding peoples, "but that though every nationality might retain its individuality ... all would be actuated by one aspiration and would endeavour to form one nation."[28]

It was wrong for any English Canadian to deny him, as a French Canadian, the right to speak the language that he had learned at his mother's knee. It was just as wrong for anyone to claim that the Jesuits' Estates Act had been concocted by the Mercier government as a deliberate threat to Protestantism, or to the country as a whole. It was merely the settlement of an old and delicate historical question. And it was absolutely false that the province's sovereignty had been surrendered to the Pope. Any government in Canada that did that, Laurier insisted, would be committing treason. He had no time for religious extremists who would use the act as a tool to inflame the people, no matter where they might reside in the Dominion. To the charge that he lacked the toughness to battle his own church when necessary, Laurier declared firmly, "I shall be asked—we are asked every day—what will you do if the Ultramontanes of the Province of Quebec make an attempt against our liberties and free institutions? Why, Sir, we shall do as in the past. We shall fight them."[29]

He was speaking boldly, and the audience complimented his courage by listening, for the most part, in attentive silence. When he mentioned D'Alton McCarthy, however, a defiant cheer reverberated through the pavilion. Laurier was temporarily forced to stop speaking. There was nothing he could do but stand there, waiting helplessly as the steady, rhythmic applause for McCarthy continued for what seemed like an eternity. Five minutes passed before Laurier could resume his speech, and when he finished he was under no illusion that this English Canadian crowd had been won over. Oliver Mowat then gave a speech, but it was not the one—filled with glowing praise for Laurier—that he had been planning to deliver. Mowat was a canny politician. He could sense the crowd's hostility to Laurier, and he was not one to go sticking pins in tigers. He confined himself to reciting Liberal platitudes so obvious, and so boring, that some audience members laughed out loud.

The meeting ended without incident, and the reviews in the Toronto newspapers the next day were surprisingly positive. Laurier himself was pleased with the effort, and at a private luncheon held in his honour by the Reform Club of Toronto, Mowat decided to give the flattering speech that he had kept under wraps the night before. Laurier was sitting beside Willison. As Mowat spoke he whispered, "Damn him. Why didn't he say that last night?"[30] That the premier had thought it unwise to rally publicly behind Laurier did not bode well for the party's prospects in Ontario. But Willison, for one, was encouraged by what he had seen of his leader over the summer of 1889. In the *Globe* he had written that

Laurier was "very, very firm; a calm, strong, steadfast man who will not be turned from his purpose while a hope of achievement remains ... This man would be a giant in some great national crisis."[31]

It was too early to tell whether a great national crisis had been averted, but it was clear that both Macdonald and Laurier had done their best to limit the damage caused by the Jesuits' Estates Act controversy. The prime minister had employed all his powers of patience and persuasion to shepherd his party through the debate on the O'Brien motion. He had even given a formal speech himself, which he rarely did, and he had thus far prevented a faction of the Conservative Party from defecting under the demagogic leadership of D'Alton McCarthy. Laurier had not faced the problem of a McCarthy in his ranks (the self-righteous John Charlton excepted), but as a French Canadian Roman Catholic, he had been affected profoundly by the intolerance of so many English Canadian Protestants. The precariousness of his position had never been more evident—he still did not believe that a French Canadian leader could win a federal election—but at least he had confronted the race-and-religion question directly. He was now more firmly in charge of the Liberal Party, and more ready to lead it into the next campaign.

As the new year dawned, neither Macdonald nor Laurier could know that just thirteen months would pass before that bitter fight was joined. If the two leaders had their way, racial and religious prejudice would not figure in the campaign. The primal passions that it evoked were too dangerous for both parties to control. That did not mean, however, that race and religion would not intrude into the election debate. And what else was in store? What other issues were destined to rise to the forefront before the election of 1891? Neither Macdonald nor Laurier, for all their political skill and foresight, had yet framed them. They could only watch and wait and hope for the best.

FIVE

The Gathering Storm

In January 1890 only a brave soul would dare to predict the future in the unsettled realm of Canadian politics. There were two vital but maddeningly unanswered questions. First, when was the next election coming? The rule of thumb for majority governments was to govern for four years before going to the people, and that would place the next election sometime in 1891. However, the prime minister had discretion over when the writ would drop, and this could happen whenever a Conservative victory seemed probable. Second, what was the election going to be about? Two years ago it would have been a good bet to put money on the trade question. But a lot had changed in the last two years, and the question that both parties dared not confront—the dreaded race-and-religion question—now seemed more likely to overwhelm them in the next election.

This would certainly be the case if D'Alton McCarthy had his way. On January 16, he made good on an earlier pledge to introduce a private member's bill in the House of Commons that would abolish French as one of two official languages of the North-West Territories. This was a popular measure in the Territories themselves, where the overwhelmingly English-speaking majority was annoyed that the Territorial council, judicial system, and school system were all obliged to accommodate the use of French. Only a few thousand people, the dwindling number of French speakers of the region, would be affected by the bill. But it was obviously intended to have more far-reaching consequences than that. The point was to ensure that the North-West would not become a second Quebec, and beyond that, to set a precedent that would be applied across the rest of the country. In case anyone had missed his point, McCarthy included a preamble in his bill that stated that the creation of a "community of language," English, of course, was the only way to unify the Dominion.[1]

In a sense it was the Jesuits' Estates Act controversy all over again, but this time the implications were more dangerous. The Jesuits' Estates Act had not affected the lives of ordinary Canadians. This was different. Nothing—nothing—was more fundamental to the survival of a language than its use in the school system. The Territorial council was attempting to remove the right of French Canadians to educate their children in their own language, and if they succeeded, French would almost certainly be extinguished in the region within one or two generations. If this principle was applied to the provinces, even to Quebec itself, the effect would be more than merely symbolic. It threatened a fundamental right. McCarthy's bill was, for all practical purposes, a declaration of war against the French language.

The North-West Schools Question would have to be settled in Parliament, because the federal government retained extensive legal control over the Territories. Through the North-West Territories Act of 1875 and other legislation, it was obliged to defend the Roman Catholic separate school system as well as the use of French in the assembly and the courts. Doing so would be tricky, however, because popular sentiment in the Territories itself was generally in favour of abolishing the use of the language. Sir John A. Macdonald knew that he had to act, but in a way that would not aggravate the English-speaking majority of the Territorial council and spur it toward even more draconian action.

The prime minister was also keenly aware that bringing up the issue in the House of Commons, though necessary, was dangerous. Its members would be under pressure to echo the bigoted views of some of their constituents—indeed, there were members who held such views themselves—and as with the Jesuits' Estates debate, there was a grave risk that the House, and the two parties, might become divided along English and French lines. Macdonald shuddered to think of the consequences in the next federal election if the parties could no longer fill their traditional role as brakes on the emergence of open ethnic conflict. It was imperative that the House of Commons rise to the occasion and prevent this from happening.

D'Alton McCarthy delivered one of the great speeches of his life. And as had happened during the Jesuits' Estates debate, virtually the whole House rallied against him. Macdonald, so often inclined to sit back, rose and condemned his friend and fellow Conservative for dragging the country into this painful debate about a community of language that would never come to be. Justice Minister John Thompson delivered another cool and carefully reasoned attack on the spirit and letter of the proposed bill. From the other side of the House, all the important voices were heard as though in a single chorus. Sir Richard Cartwright took the matter personally; he denounced not just the bill in question but McCarthy himself. Edward Blake, finally back in the House but sitting in self-imposed exile on the backbenches, roused himself to deliver a speech that displayed all the brilliance and greatness of his too-often tortured mind.

Wilfrid Laurier rose to the occasion as well. He sensed the anxiety in the air, the danger that was clearly present. He did not mince words. "I denounce this policy as anti-Canadian," he thundered. "I denounce it as fatal to the hope we at one time entertained, and which I, for one, am not disposed to give up, of forming a nation on this continent. I denounce it as a crime, a national crime."[2] He called instead for respect and tolerance, and the House of Commons courageously and wholeheartedly agreed.

It was Thompson, with his great legal mind, who developed the compromise that eventually resolved the debate. The Territorial council could decide to function in English if it chose, in keeping with the principle of local autonomy. But all of its ordinances must be printed in French, all judicial proceedings must be made accessible in French, and most important, the separate schools must remain in place. This amendment to the McCarthy bill passed with nearly a one-hundred vote majority, 149–50, and it was one of the finest moments of the Canadian Parliament.

The Dragon's Teeth

Those Canadians who were fighting for an all-English nation were not so easily defeated. In March 1890, only a month after the two parties had parried the dangers represented by the North-West Schools Question, they faced the even more threatening Manitoba Schools Question.

In many respects the circumstances were similar, and the principle was the same. Manitoba had been established as a province in 1870, at a time when its population was just about evenly divided between English and French Canadians. The Manitoba Act reflected this fact by creating an essentially bilingual province and instituting a publicly funded separate school system. The schools were divided along religious rather than linguistic lines, but as was the case in most of Canada, in Manitoba most Protestants spoke English and most Catholics spoke French, so language and religion in the schools were closely entwined. It had been a happy arrangement for the province, perhaps even—for those who might dream of a genuinely bilingual country—a model that the rest of the country might one day follow.

Since 1870, however, the population of Manitoba had become 90 percent English speaking and Protestant, mainly the result of immigration from Ontario, and many of the new arrivals had little interest in paying taxes so that a small minority, the French-speaking Catholics, could continue to send their children to separate schools. Given the prevailing attitudes of the period, it was hardly surprising that the English majority wanted to impose on the province the community of language championed by McCarthy. And this is what the provincial Liberal government, under Premier Thomas Greenway, was attempting to do through the Manitoba Schools Act. If allowed to take effect, the act would abolish public funding of Catholic (thus mostly French-speaking) separate schools.

That was a big if. Once again, the federal power to disallow legislation deemed harmful to the national interest came into play. Because education was a provincial responsibility, however, it was not clear under the terms of the British North America Act that the legislature of Manitoba had overstepped its constitutional authority. If it had not, it would set a risky precedent for the federal government to meddle so brazenly in the affairs of a province. If Ottawa could override the will of the people and the legislature of Manitoba, what was to stop it from doing the same in any of the other provinces? The doctrine of "provincial rights" also had to be respected. This was especially important to French Canadians, who expected the federal government to give Quebec wide leeway to protect its distinct language and society as it saw fit.

Macdonald was worried. Nothing good could possibly come out of the Manitoba Schools Question. The act was already provoking bitter feelings across the country, and these emotions would play a part in the Ontario provincial election that Premier Oliver Mowat had called for June. Mowat was the most successful Liberal politician in the country and an enemy of Macdonald, but the two men agreed that French-English relations had to be built on a foundation of tolerance and mutual respect. Though his province was mainly English and Protestant, Mowat was a champion of the separate school system in Ontario and a consistent friend to French and Catholic interests. Now, after passage of the Manitoba Schools Act, he was facing a provincial Conservative Party that was campaigning against separate schools. Its main gripe was over religion and not language, but the one could hardly be separated from the other, and if the Conservatives won, they might also embrace the community of language of D'Alton McCarthy and cause irreparable damage to national unity.

Under these circumstances it was not surprising that Macdonald was ambivalent about the outcome of the Ontario election. There had never been a more loyal Tory, but the prime minister could not bear to see the provincial Conservatives pandering to anti-French, anti-Catholic sentiment to get themselves elected. Therefore he kept his federal party clear of the election, avoiding even the slightest indication of sympathy with the Ontario Tories, and privately he wrote to Sir Charles Tupper that he hoped Mowat and the Liberals would win. They did, in another triumph of tolerance that echoed the one so recently achieved in the federal Parliament. Mowat was returned with a comfortable, though reduced, majority, and the frightening prospect of an Ontario Schools Question faded away.

There was still, of course, the Manitoba Schools Question to confront. Macdonald was furious with McCarthy for helping to bring about this crisis. "McCarthy has sown the Dragon's teeth," Sir John gloomily reported to a confidant. "I fear they may grow up to be armed men." A note of pessimism, so uncommon to the Old Man, pervaded his thoughts. "Canada, as just punishment for her ingratitude for her blessings, is about to undergo a time of trouble. The demon of religious animosity, which I hoped had been buried ... has been revived. God only knows what the results may be."[3] For the time being his government challenged the bill's constitutionality and referred the matter to the courts. That would buy him time. It was not for nothing that Macdonald was sometimes called Old Tomorrow.

Some American Foolishness

With the Manitoba Schools Question submitted to judicial review, thus essentially calling a political time out, the agitation surrounding the race-and-religion question subsided in the summer of 1890. In its place the trade question, which had the potential to be nearly as divisive, was re-emerging as the leading political issue in Canada. It had been a long road back to the public spotlight for unrestricted reciprocity, which the Liberals had been struggling for almost two years to keep in the headlines. There had been nothing new to say after the Great Free Trade Debate of 1888, and no prospect of a showdown between unrestricted reciprocity and the National Policy until the next election rolled around. The furor over the Jesuits' Estates Act had pushed trade out of the public mind and there it had lain dormant, in a kind of political hibernation, for the better part of the last two years.

On the rare occasions when the trade question grabbed headlines, it had been, from the Liberal point of view, for entirely the wrong reasons. In the summer of 1888 the United States Senate had debated the Bayard-Chamberlain Treaty, a sensible settlement of a festering dispute with Great Britain that revolved around intrusions by American fishing vessels into Canadian waters. In the U.S. system the Senate must approve foreign treaties with a two-thirds majority, and unfortunately for President Grover Cleveland, the Republican-controlled Senate was not about to hand the Democrats a diplomatic triumph in the middle of an election year. The Senate debate over the treaty, which in the end was defeated, was notable for its general ugliness. It also happened to give Republican senators an opportunity to bash the Macdonald government (which had pushed strongly for the treaty) and to make some moronic speeches about the desirability and practicality of annexing Canada to the United States.

Senator George Hoar of Massachusetts, an influential Republican, kicked off this impromptu celebration of America's manifest destiny. Hoar was considered something of an expert on Canada, as he represented a northeastern state and had recently been made chairman of a Senate committee on relations with Canada. His "expert opinion" was that the fisheries mess could be resolved in one simple stroke. All that was needed was for the Dominion to become part of the United States. Why couldn't the slow-witted Canadians understand that? Senator Henry Blair of New Hampshire, another Republican, felt that Hoar was not going far enough. Blair, one of a dwindling number of blowhards who mused publicly about taking Canada by force, introduced a resolution advising President Cleveland to begin immediate negotiations with Great Britain for the entry of Canada, or some of its provinces, into the United States.

It got worse. Next to join the chorus was Senator John Sherman, a Republican from Ohio who was a good friend of Erastus Wiman. He had expressed cautious interest in commercial union since the spring of 1887. Now, condemning the fisheries treaty on the Senate floor, Sherman revealed his true feelings. Commercial union, he announced, was worth supporting only if it would help bring about the annexation of Canada. Just to be sure that everybody got his drift, Sherman added, "I want Canada to be part of the United States."[4] Later in the summer he informed the Senate that he had revised his views: commercial union must be rejected by the United States because, he judged, it was more likely to hurt rather than help the cause of annexation. America's interests would best be served by frustrating Canadian attempts to negotiate free trade and thus starving them out, making them so desperate for access to the American market that they would surrender their political sovereignty to achieve it.

Canadians, egged on by their own indignant newspapers, were outraged by all this talk of annexation. It was particularly distressing to hear it from John Sherman, who was supposed to be a friend of Canada and a backer of commercial union. The Conservatives rejoiced. They had warned from the beginning that the Republicans were interested in commercial union only because they assumed that it would help them add Canada to their Republic. Now, they crowed, all had been revealed. And it got worse still. Many American newspapers were thrilled by the position taken by Sherman, and in the fall of 1888 they published various speculative stories about the complexion of a political union between Canada and the United States. Most infamous was the front-page headline in the New York *World*, "When Canada Comes In," which accompanied a fanciful map of North America that carved the Dominion into twenty-eight new U.S. states, all named according to American sensibilities. The *World* wondered, with breathtaking Yankee crassness, "How much is it worth in cash?"[5]

That was guaranteed to offend Canadians, and that was not all. The *World* story also quoted notable American politicians who supported annexation. Among them were two more supposed friends of Wiman and the commercial union movement, Robert Hitt of Illinois and—most egregiously of all—Benjamin Butterworth of Ohio. Hitt, who had introduced a C.U. resolution in the House of Representatives in the spring of 1888, confirmed the conspiracy theories circulated among Conservatives by casually remarking that commercial union was merely "a stepping stone to political union." Butterworth, according to the *World*, took one look at their map and exclaimed "Beautiful! Beautiful!"[6] Shortly after this story came out, Butterworth introduced a joint resolution in the House that was much like the earlier Blair bill, again authorizing the president "to negotiate with reference to the unity and assimilation with the United States of the Dominion of Canada, or one or more of the provinces thereof."[7]

This was shocking stuff coming from the American politician who had been most passionately in favour of commercial union, and who had insisted to Canadian audiences that it was all "purely a business proposition." It was a total betrayal of Erastus Wiman, who was publicly humiliated for having consorted with self-confessed annexationists (the Toronto *Empire* referred to Wiman as one of the "children of Satan"[8]). It was also bad news for the Liberals. Obtaining unrestricted reciprocity was going to be a severe challenge if the U.S. Senate was interested only in trade schemes that led to annexation. Some leading Liberals wanted to drop the policy, among them a panicked J.D. Edgar, who advised Laurier to distance the party at least temporarily from its own trade platform.

Laurier, showing some gumption, refused to allow the foolishness of a few silly American politicians to dictate the actions of the Liberal Party. Abandoning unrestricted reciprocity now would only give credence to the Tory accusation that the policy was synonymous with annexation. Besides, there was nothing to replace it. Laurier was confident that he could ride out the storm and sent a letter to his followers, trying to stiffen their resolve with an uncompromising declaration of personal support for the party's trade policy. It worked. The Liberals rallied around Laurier and unrestricted reciprocity as 1888 came to an end. One rank-and-file member, capturing the general sentiment of the party, wrote Laurier to commend his "pluck and spirit" and concurred that "the time to fight most unflinchingly is just when the battle seems most doubtful."[9]

Unrestricted reciprocity had been given a reprieve. But Laurier and the Liberals were not much inclined to beat the drum for it either, not until the annexation scandal was forgotten and the times were more favourable. During the parliamentary session of 1889 they introduced another resolution in favour of U.R., but the ensuing debate featured few prominent speakers and attracted little attention. The resolution was defeated easily by the Conservatives, who enjoyed reminding the House that the only American politicians who seemed to favour the policy were admitted annexationists. The Jesuits' Estates Act controversy overshadowed the trade question completely, and it continued to dominate Canadian politics for the rest of the year. Even an earnest and energetic speaking campaign by Erastus Wiman, culminating on Halloween night in a huge Toronto rally sponsored by the Liberals, failed to re-inspire popular support for the cause of free trade.

Wiman, characteristically, refused to be discouraged. Over the winter he was his usual busy self, holding several high-profile speaking engagements in which he boomed free trade and condemned annexation. He also bustled about Washington trying to attract U.S. politicians to his cause and, as he put it, "rehabilitate" those who had already come out in favour of annexation. He reportedly rented a house in Washington so that he could spend more time lobbying Congress for unrestricted reciprocity. He also persuaded Ben Butterworth to introduce a resolution in its favour—an exercise of perhaps dubious sincerity, given that Butterworth had come out for annexation the year before—but the House of Representatives, as had been the case with earlier bills on the subject, could not even be bothered to bring it to a vote.[10]

American indifference to unrestricted reciprocity was made obvious when Wiman testified, in December 1889, before Senator Hoar's Senate Committee on Relations with Canada. He spent three hours painstakingly making the case for commercial union, but came away with the frustrated feeling that the committee had hardly listened to him and that its members were interested only in annexation. He was right. The Toronto *Globe*, smelling a rat, did some digging. In January 1890 it triumphantly broke the story that Edward Farrer, editor of the rival *Mail*, had been secretly advising committee members that the best way to force Canada into annexation was to give a cold shoulder to its hopes for a free trade agreement. The flagship Tory paper, the Toronto *Empire*, also covered the story. In its eagerness to condemn Farrer, it accidentally (and amusingly) portrayed Erastus Wiman, normally its mortal enemy, as a great Canadian patriot.

The Revival of the Trade Question

Wiman had been stymied by Farrer in Washington, but early in 1890 he was enjoying considerable success in his relations with Laurier and the Liberal Party. He had been trying to ingratiate himself with Laurier for the past three years but things had often been strained, largely because

Wiman was the sort of person who simply could not follow a party line. John Willison, the Liberal journalist, expressed his frustration with Wiman in a scathing private letter to Laurier.

> You ask me what I mean by saying that Mr Wiman hurts us at Washington. I mean that he has no tact, no judgment, no discretion, that although a good fellow, he is vile with egotism ... In his mania for advertising himself he overturns the best plans that are laid at Washington and hurts the movement in the House and Senate. Such men as Blaine and Hitt and Carlisle and Mills will not be led by Wiman. These men resent his posturing and assumptions to leadership. He goes to Washington and rants of (almost?) political union ... Who made him the official mouthpiece of any party in Canada?[11]

The leading Liberal politicians had probably all concurred with that assessment at one point, but Wiman had gradually won them over by expending an incredible amount of energy to champion free trade. He had undertaken more promotional speaking tours, issued more pamphlets, and published more articles than anyone else, and he appeared to have finally accepted unrestricted reciprocity as a suitable alternative to his first love, commercial union. This was a relief to the Liberals, who were keen to start pressing the trade question again. Early in 1890 Wiman informed a friend that he was "in constant correspondence with Mr Laurier and Mr Richard," and it was with the latter, Sir Richard Cartwright, that he enjoyed the closest working relationship.[12]

Cartwright was, perhaps uncharacteristically, in the mood to take some risks. At the end of 1889 he had complained to Laurier that the Liberal Party really had no idea what U.S. politicians thought of unrestricted reciprocity, and shortly after that he decided to conduct some research himself. Wiman suggested that Cartwright come to New York and make a public speech, and on February 21 they shared the head table at a banquet of the New York Board of Trade and Transportation. Sir Richard gave a capital speech, focusing on the theme of "so near, and yet so far" and explaining that while Canadians did not want annexation, they did yearn for unrestricted reciprocity. It was a happy and successful evening.[13]

The New York speech was not, however, the most controversial part of the trip. Wiman secretly arranged for Cartwright to visit Washington as well, and there he seems to have met behind closed doors with prominent politicians including the powerful secretary of state, James Blaine. No one knew what was discussed. No one even knew for certain that the meetings had taken place. The Canadian press got wind of them, however, and the Conservative newspapers in particular had no shortage of conspiracy theories with which to titillate their readers. David Creighton, the editor of the Toronto *Empire*, had this to say to Macdonald just before breaking the story in his newspaper: "I am convinced that the annexationist traitors are all in league, and if we convince the public that they are intriguing at Washington, we will not only kill the Mail, but also smash Sir Richard and the wing of the Grits which follows him."[14]

The hoped-for smashing of Sir Richard did not take place, since there was no hard information about what he might have said or done. Perhaps emboldened by his trip, Cartwright decided upon his return that the Toronto *Globe*, still the flagship newspaper of the Liberal Party, required the services of a "vigorous and slashing writer" who could boom the issue of unrestricted reciprocity over the summer of 1890.[15] Laurier and the other Liberals agreed, but were less than thrilled about Cartwright's choice of journalist—Edward Farrer.

What was Sir Richard thinking? Just six months earlier Farrer had been advising a committee of U.S. senators to deny free trade to Canada so that they could force the country into annexation. That did not necessarily mean that Farrer was an annexationist himself, but it was a pretty good indication that he was capable of embarrassing the Liberal Party. Still, Cartwright believed, Farrer was worth the risk. He was unrivalled as an editorial writer. Stealing him from the *Mail* would cripple that newspaper while giving an immense boost to the *Globe*. The other Liberals agreed, but only on condition that John Willison, a more reliable fellow, be made the nominal editor so that somebody could keep an eye on Farrer. The new arrangement was an immediate success. Laurier instructed Willison to "compel the people of the Dominion to think of nothing else" but unrestricted reciprocity, and the new *Globe* editors threw themselves into the effort.[16] J.D. Edgar, who as the primary organizer in Ontario had his ear close to the ground, was convinced that the trade question was gaining popularity and thus improving Liberal prospects for the next election.

The *Globe* was doing a fine job of promotion, but could hardly take sole credit for this change in the mood of the Canadian electorate. The main reason for revived interest in free trade was the McKinley Tariff, an onerous piece of legislation that was slowly working its way through Congress. Once passed, the tariff on virtually all Canadian products coming into the U.S. would be dramatically increased, almost to the point of shutting down trade between the two countries. This prospect caused both anger and panic among Canadians whose livelihood depended on access to the American market. Suddenly there was pressure on the Conservatives to reach some kind of agreement with the United States, but Macdonald seemed neither willing nor able to obtain one. The Liberals were the champions of free trade, not the Conservatives, and to many Canadians they seemed to have a better chance of negotiating a deal if given the chance. That, in a nutshell, is why the party found itself surging in popularity during the summer of 1890.

The Boodlers Get Caught

In addition to the revival of popular interest in the trade question, Sir John A. Macdonald soon found himself dealing with an unexpected political problem. On November 19 the Quebec City newspaper *Le Canadien* published a scandalous accusation against Minister of Public Works Hector Langevin, one of the most trusted men in Macdonald's cabinet. Since April, the newspaper, one of the most influential French-language dailies, had been implying that there was corruption in the Public Works Department. Now, for the first time, it named an important name. Langevin was personally corrupt, it alleged, having pocketed kickbacks from government contracts that his department had awarded to the construction firm of Larkin, Connolly, and Company. One of its employees, a contractor named Robert McGreevy, happened to be the brother of Thomas McGreevy, who was a Tory member of Parliament, as well as the brother-in-law of Langevin himself. For years, *Le Canadien* charged, this unholy trio had circumvented the rules regulating the awarding of government contracts and made themselves enormous sums of money at taxpayers' expense.[17]

This was a serious charge. Canadians had notoriously low expectations of their politicians, but they did expect them to follow the rules when awarding government contracts. It was one thing to award them to the supporters of your party. Every government did that, and it was more or less accepted practice. But it was another thing entirely to line your pockets with kickbacks from those supporters in exchange for doling out those contracts. That was both criminal and a gross violation of public trust. Nor were the accused individuals of trifling importance. Langevin was an important minister, Macdonald's trusted Quebec lieutenant, and even his possible successor. If the charges of *Le Canadien* were true—which in fact they were, for the most part—the scandal had the potential to bring down the government.

Much of the blame for this sorry state of affairs rested with Macdonald himself. He had built the Conservative Party into a patronage-dispensing machine, and it was not surprising that some of his followers had abused the practice. It was the prime minister's inclination to let his ministers run their own departments, but in Langevin's case, he had been too trusting. There had been warning signs. Mackenzie Bowell, a man whose entire political philosophy was "consult your friends first," had told Macdonald that Langevin had gone too far. The editor of *Le*

Canadien, Israël Tarte, had even privately shown Sir John evidence of Langevin's behaviour, but he had refused to believe it.

That would prove to be a serious mistake. Tarte, a small, dapper man with a neat black goatee, was a loyal Conservative and an influential figure in the Quebec wing of the party. He had first risen to prominence as a "Langevin man," his newspaper serving for many years as the unofficial mouthpiece of the minister of public works, and Macdonald probably felt sure that Tarte would ultimately bury the evidence against him for the good of the Conservative Party. But Tarte's loyalties were more complicated than that. He had lost faith in Langevin, finding him a mediocre leader and gradually coming to prefer Chapleau as the head of the party in Quebec. He was on unfriendly terms with Thomas McGreevy, with whom he had clashed frequently in the past. And Tarte was a man of strong moral conviction, in his own way, and the corrupt behaviour that he had uncovered genuinely offended him.

He was also, finally, a journalist, and this was a hard story to ignore. He had a reliable first-hand source in the person of Robert McGreevy, who had first brought the corruption in the Public Works Department to light in a destructive attempt to settle an unknown personal score against his brother. The affair had become personal for Tarte in May 1890 when Thomas McGreevy, upon seeing the first incriminating documents in the pages of *Le Canadien*, had sued him for libel to the tune of fifty thousand dollars. That decision ensured that the scandal would go public. It also pushed Tarte, gradually, into the arms of the Liberals. Laurier himself, seeing the political gains to be made, took on the case. The court action was delayed and then held over until after the next session of Parliament, but that was hardly good news for the Conservatives. It simply meant that there would be more time for gossips to embellish the rumours and that the affair would cast a shadow over the party for the foreseeable future.

Macdonald had to take all of this into account as he reviewed his political options. A snap election, held before the worst of the McGreevy-Langevin scandal was exposed, might work to the Conservatives' advantage. J.W. Bengough, the great political satirist, made the case in a *Grip* cartoon that appeared on November 29, 1890. It depicted a gathering storm, a swirling funnel cloud bearing down on Macdonald and Langevin. The latter was hollering into the wind, "It's coming this way, Sir John, but if we can manage to reach the general election before it strikes—that's our only hope!"[18] The decision to call an election rested solely with the prime minister, however, and as 1890 expired there was no telling what was going on in the depths of that remarkable and inscrutable mind.

The Pending Decision

Macdonald, as he had done all his life, was still taking on too much. He was now almost seventy-six years old and yet he still handled all his usual responsibilities as prime minister, and more. There was, first of all, the immense correspondence to attend to. There were many complex and intractable matters of state to deal with, such as the North Atlantic fisheries dispute that still aggravated relations with the United States. There was the routine Conservative party business, such as the endless requests for patronage appointments, which Macdonald preferred to handle personally. Since April 1889, he had also been serving as minister of railways and canals, a large and time-consuming portfolio that he had taken on when no one else seemed suitable for the position. Even with the assistance of Joseph Pope, this was an enormous workload for a man in his mid-seventies.

Pope was worried about him. Macdonald had aged in the last four years. His mind was as sharp as ever, but his body was slowing down, and after long, exhausting days his face took on an ashen complexion that Pope found alarming. The indomitable good cheer was still there, but so too were occasional feelings of melancholy that had not been apparent before. Most of his old friends were dead. One day, walking with Pope through the Senate lobby, Macdonald gestured with his cane to a row of portraits of former Speakers. He had known all of them, and nearly all were now gone. "Whenever I come this way," Pope recalled him saying, "I feel as if I were walking through a churchyard!"[19] The most crushing blow had been the death of his sister Louisa, his last surviving sibling, in the fall of 1888. She had been like him in many ways—had even looked a little like him, an unlucky twist of fate that she had borne cheerfully—and they had always been close. Thankfully Macdonald still had Agnes, and their daughter, Mary, and relatives who visited Earnscliffe from time to time. Still, it seemed to Pope, age was catching up to the Old Man.

The deteriorating political situation worried Macdonald, for there was almost too much to stay on top of. The race-and-religion question had subsided, but the court would eventually rule on the constitutionality of the Manitoba Schools Act, and its decision was sure to aggravate all sides. There was the McKinley Tariff, which was demonstrating the tremendous importance of access to the U.S. market and giving a boost to the free-trading Liberals. Finally there was the McGreevy scandal, a disaster waiting to happen. It was a gathering storm indeed.

Under the circumstances, it would have been natural for the prime minister to show signs of stress and weakness. To his surprise and relief, Joseph Pope found that the opposite was true as the new year dawned. Despite all the troubles that the party and the country were facing, Sir John had been feeling better of late. The previous summer he had managed to get away for a long-desired vacation at Rivière-du-Loup, Quebec, and the time there had recharged his batteries. The autumn had been filled with visits to each of the Maritime provinces, a tour that involved public events and allowed him to get some inkling of the political atmosphere there. Macdonald had always liked being out on the stump, and this sojourn too seemed to invigorate him. Pope told him so at one point, and the Old Man cheerfully replied that he was feeling "tolerably well for an old chap."[20]

The Scandalous Discovery

In November 1890 the prime minister was given another reason to be in good humour, a reason that Pope knew nothing about. No one knew about it, in fact, save for a half-dozen individuals who had been entrusted with the secret. It originated with Christopher Clark, a young Toronto journalist and accountant, and an ordinary fellow in every respect but for the extremity of his political views. By his own admission Clark was a lifelong "fanatical Conservative," one convinced enough of the evils of the Liberal Party that he "scarcely regarded Sir Richard Cartwright as good enough to live."[21] That was important, for it undoubtedly affected his conduct on a mid-November day when he looked up from his work at the Hunter, Rose & Co. print shop and noticed Edward Farrer stroll into the office and hand a sheaf of handwritten pages to the manager on duty. At first glance there was nothing odd about that. Ned Farrer was a prolific author, and Hunter, Rose handled a lot of pamphlet-sized publications. But Clark sensed that something was amiss. This job was being handled in a hush-hush manner, as though a secret was being protected. After being called upon to set the type, giving him a chance to look over the handwritten text, he discovered why. The pamphlet was full of advice to unnamed and highly placed Americans, it appeared, on how best to force Canada into annexation to the United States. Edward Farrer, chief editorial writer of the Toronto *Globe*, the greatest Liberal newspaper in the Dominion, was committing treason!

Clark was beside himself. He was not sure what to do, but knew the composition was Farrer's, as he knew his handwriting, and believed that the sinister intentions of the document had to be exposed. He had some Conservative Party connections, and first contacted Sir Charles Hibbert Tupper, the son of Sir Charles Tupper and current minister of fisheries. Charlie Tupper was an able, trustworthy fellow, and as a cabinet minister he would have access to the prime minister. Clark had no physical evidence to give him as yet; so far it had been too closely guarded. Still, he passed along word of his scandalous find. Tupper reported the news to Macdonald in Ottawa, and the prime minister dispatched Percy Sherwood, chief of the Dominion Police, to investigate. Upon his arrival in Toronto, Sherwood called at Heydon Villa, the imposing mansion of the local police magistrate, Lt. Col. George Taylor Denison. This was the man who would, years later, put to paper the only lasting record of the whole affair.

This was the conspiracy that the lieutenant colonel had waited for all his life. A gaunt, imperious character with a dignified white moustache, Denison was the product of a Loyalist military family known as the "Fighting Denisons." He was a cavalry officer—the most dashing kind of soldier—who had defended Canada against the Fenian raids in 1866 and the North-West Rebellion in 1885. He believed intensely in the British Empire and saw no contradiction in being both a Canadian nationalist and a British imperialist. Now in his early fifties, Denison was still lean and physically fit, still ready to mount a charge against his enemies and always on guard against possible threats to his country. Throughout his career, most of which he had spent dispensing justice to criminals from his magistrate's bench, he had been quietly frustrated, there being no one to fight. But he had kept a close eye on the United States, a nation that he instinctively distrusted and suspected of harbouring sinister motives. The Americans had tried to obtain Canada by invasion in the past, after all, in 1775 and 1812. Other Canadians might laugh at the thought that they might try again, or that they might use other nefarious means to coerce their quarry into annexation. Denison did not laugh. He was deadly serious about protecting his country.

At Heydon Villa, a residence adorned with portraits of glorious Denison ancestors and glass cases displaying antique weapons, Denison conferred with Sherwood about the appropriate course of action. It was agreed that Clark must immediately make a sworn statement as to the authenticity of the pamphlet and that he should endeavour to acquire as much of it as he could get his hands on. (Clark had by this time succeeded in stealing two or three pages of galley slips.) He was instructed now to seize any opportunity that arose to obtain more of the document. When Clark got back to the office, the pamphlet had already been printed and no copies were on hand, but the type was still set. At the dinner hour the printer left the office briefly, and Clark hurriedly took a roller and inked a rough copy of about two-thirds of the pamphlet. This was brought to Denison, who, no less than Clark, was appalled by its contents. As a police magistrate he ought to have retained it as evidence of treason, a crime then punishable by death. Instead, fatefully, Denison conveyed it to Macdonald, no doubt confident in the belief that Canada was in danger and the prime minister must be notified.

Macdonald read the proofs and took stock of the situation. This was, on the one hand, a marvellous stroke of luck for his Conservatives. The prime minister's suspicion that unrestricted reciprocity represented the thin edge of the wedge toward annexation had been confirmed. Here, in black and white, was indubitable proof that Farrer not only favoured annexation but was now channelling advice to mysterious American friends to help bring it about. The enemy had truly been delivered into the Old Man's hands.

True to form, however, he paused before committing himself to a course of action. What would be the consequences of making the pamphlet public, as he would have to do to gain political advantage from it? This was a private document, one obviously not meant for publication, and in an age of letters it was gravely inappropriate to publish such material without permission. There might be a backlash of public opinion against the Conservatives for having stooped so low, or at the very least, the authenticity of the document might be called into question. It would be a risky move.

For the time being, Macdonald chose not to play his hand. There was little point in doing so, anyway, until he decided to call a general election. About when that might be, or whether the Farrer pamphlet would be revealed during the campaign, the prime minister remained inscrutable. He did give a hint of his intentions, however, when he made a clandestine visit to Denison at his Toronto office in early January 1891. The two met that day at around twelve o'clock, when most people in the building would be at lunch and the chances of Macdonald being spotted—perhaps leading to awkward questions—would be at a minimum. They discussed the great secret between them. Macdonald hoped to get further documentation; Denison promised to do his best to acquire it. Then Macdonald, in a coy fashion, asked him whether he thought it would be wiser to call an election immediately or to wait for another year.

Denison literally jumped out of his chair. "What, Sir John," he exclaimed, "in the face of all you know and all I know, how can you hesitate an instant? You must bring the elections on at once." He warned, ominously, "If you wait till your enemies are ready, and the pipes are laid to distribute the money which will in time be given from the States, you will incur great danger, and no one can tell where the trouble will end."

Macdonald flashed Denison a mischievous grin. "Keep all your muscles braced up, and your nerves all prepared," he replied cheerfully, "so that if the House is suddenly dissolved in about three weeks you will not receive a nervous shock, but keep absolutely silent."[22] Then, without another word being exchanged between them, the prime minister took his leave of Denison, his head wagging to and fro in the familiar way as he strolled out of the office.

PART 2
The Campaign

SIX

The Call to Arms

In a roundabout way it was the little colony of Newfoundland that, by seeking its own trade deal with the United States, finally compelled Sir John A. Macdonald to call an election in February 1891.

The story went like this. In the fall of 1890 it seemed, as usual, that there was no possibility of the Canadian and American governments getting together for trade talks. The Macdonald government and the Harrison administration were equally committed to maintaining high tariffs along the border, and that was that. The last time an agreement had been reached was in January 1888, when the British government (acting for Canada) and the Cleveland administration had painstakingly carved out a fisheries treaty, only to see it defeated in the U.S. Senate. Neither the British nor the Canadians wanted to go through that again, even though the fisheries dispute was still unresolved and there was increasing pressure on the Conservatives to get Canada exempted from the crushing McKinley Tariff. The Harrison administration, for its part, had not shown the slightest interest in talking trade with Canada.

So things had stood until November 1890, when the Macdonald government was informed that Newfoundland was on the verge of negotiating its own trade deal with the United States. This was disturbing news to Macdonald. He suspected that the Harrison administration was not really interested in its talks with Newfoundland, but was playing Newfoundland and Canada against one another so that each would battle for the better deal with the United States, thereby undermining the unity of British North America. It was all part of the broader strategy, Macdonald was sure, of isolating Canada from the rest of the British Empire and softening it up for annexation. He also suspected that it was not President Harrison who was pulling the strings, but James Blaine, his popular and powerful secretary of state.

Macdonald did not like Blaine, or, perhaps more accurately, he did not trust him. Blaine had been an enormously influential politician for thirty years, having served as a congressman and senator from Maine, as Speaker of the House, and twice as secretary of state. He was the hero of the Republican Party, a charismatic man with fanatical legions of "Blaine men" who desperately wanted to put him in the White House. He had been their candidate in the presidential election of 1884, and had lost a narrow and disputed contest to Grover Cleveland. (Had a few hundred votes gone the other way in the state of New York, Blaine would have won the election.) He had not run again, instead throwing his support behind the affable but unexceptional Benjamin Harrison. After his victory in 1888 Harrison had rewarded Blaine with the position of secretary of state, and Blaine was widely regarded as the real driving force in the Harrison administration.

"Blaine from Maine" had never been much of a friend to Canada. He was an unflinching champion of the protective tariff. He had a habit of bemoaning Canadian fishing regulations. And, most alarmingly, he was an annexationist. Many Canadians suspected that Blaine had supported the McKinley Tariff to cause them such hardship that they would plead for political union just to regain access to the U.S. market.

That was, in fact, the truth. Later in 1891 Blaine revealed his intentions to Harrison, writing privately, "The fact is we do not want any intercourse with Canada, except through the medium of a tariff, and she will find that she has a hard row to hoe and will ultimately I believe seek admission to the Union."[1]

Macdonald correctly suspected the worst of Blaine, and was determined not to let him drive a wedge between the Dominion and Newfoundland. He expressed concern to the British government (diplomatic business still had to go through its Colonial Office), and the British high commissioner in Washington, Julian Pauncefote, dutifully sounded out Blaine about the prospect of trade talks with the Dominion. The secretary of state replied, surprisingly, that he was willing to consider a wide-ranging agreement between Canada and the United States. He would not agree to a formal commission, however, until he was convinced, through private talks, that there was a good chance of actually reaching an agreement. Further, these talks could not be held until March of 1891, when the present session of Congress concluded.

Macdonald smelled a rat. A formal commission would be a good thing: it would give the proposed talks prestige and leave no doubt that both countries were serious. But Blaine was offering much less than that. He was proposing talks that were strictly off the record, so that he could later deny anything he might have said, or even deny that talks had taken place. Macdonald suspected that Blaine would do just that, pretending to negotiate in good faith only to embarrass his Conservatives at an inopportune moment by denying that negotiations were taking place between the two countries.

That would be devious, but it was certainly possible. Macdonald believed that the secretary of state was capable of doing just about anything that would help to bring about the annexation of Canada. Still, Sir John mused, perhaps he could turn Blaine's duplicity to his own advantage. Sincere or not, the United States *had* expressed interest in a new trade agreement. That conceivably included partial reciprocity, meaning free trade in natural products, where Canadians excelled, but not in manufactured goods, where the Americans had the advantage. Partial reciprocity would be good for Canada and even better for the Conservative Party, because it would instantly make the Liberal trade policy obsolete. Why would voters want to take a risk on unrestricted reciprocity if they could get partial reciprocity from the Conservatives? The reality, Macdonald knew, was that James Blaine was not the slightest bit interested in negotiating with Canada. But if the prime minister could finesse the issue, if he could make it *seem* that a deal for partial reciprocity was imminent, the Liberals would be completely outmanoeuvred. Blaine, in fact, might have been too clever by half. He might actually have dealt the prime minister a winning hand.

So Macdonald agreed to informal trade talks with the United States starting after March 4, 1891. They were supposed to be secret, but rumours soon began to appear in Canadian newspapers. On January 14, the Toronto *Mail* claimed that the British had been pressing the Macdonald government to mend its differences with the United States through a wide-ranging trade agreement. The *Mail* had obtained this information, it added mysteriously, "on authority which leaves little reason to doubt that the rumour is true." This was damaging to Macdonald, because it made it appear that the Americans wanted to open up their border, only to have the prime minister standing obstinately in their way. Two days later the Toronto *Empire*, the official organ of the Conservatives, issued an emphatic reply.

> Ottawa, Jan 15—The Toronto Mail, in its issue of yesterday, says: *It is reported from Ottawa, on authority which leaves little reason to doubt that the rumor is true, that the Imperial Government is urging the Dominion Ministers to unite in a proposition to arrange all matters in dispute between Canada and the United States on the basis of a wide measure of commercial reciprocity.*
>
> THE EMPIRE is authorized to give this statement an unqualified denial. Not only is it not true, but, on the contrary, it is learned from the very best sources that the Canadian Government has recently

> been approached by the United States government with a view to the development of trade relations between the two countries, and that our Government has requested the advice of her majesty's government on the subject.

Clearly this statement had been authorized by the Macdonald government, and if it was true, it was a disastrous development for the Liberal Party. The Americans had come asking for freer trade with Canada, to be negotiated with the Conservatives? All Canadians knew that Macdonald would never agree to unrestricted reciprocity, so the Harrison administration must have had a change of heart about partial reciprocity. Now Canadian wheat, barley, apples, horses, coal, iron, nickel, and every other natural product that the country produced for export might soon be put back on the free list! It seemed improbable, but there it was in the *Empire*. And if the Conservatives were on the verge of obtaining partial reciprocity, the limited sort of free trade that Canada most urgently needed, the Liberals were now sitting in a hopeless position.

Over the next two weeks the Conservative newspapers crowed. The Old Man had once again shown himself to be the grand master of Canadian politics. He had outfoxed his opponents, stealing their thunder on the trade question and ensuring the survival of his government in a single stroke. All that was left for him to do was call an election, watch the Liberals flounder, and wait for the triumphant result on election night. It seemed too good to be true. Because it was.

Calling Macdonald's Bluff

Two weeks after the Conservatives implied that the United States had come cap in hand to Canada in search of a trade deal, a surprised congressman asked James Blaine to confirm or deny the *Empire*'s story. Blaine replied with a curt statement that appeared on January 29 in newspapers throughout North America: "I authorize you to contradict the rumors you refer to. There are no negotiations whatever on foot for a reciprocity treaty with Canada, and you may be sure, no such scheme for reciprocity with the Dominion, confined to natural products, will be entertained by this Government. We know nothing of Sir Charles Tupper coming to Washington."

Blaine had done exactly what Macdonald had feared he would do. Not only had he denied that negotiations were "on foot," he had also made it crystal clear that Canada had no chance of getting partial reciprocity from the United States. Moreover, the irked tone of the denial suggested that it was Macdonald, not Blaine, who had come looking for trade talks in the first place.

This was a disaster for Macdonald. Blaine had made a mockery of his claim to be negotiating partial reciprocity, destroying the credibility of the Conservatives on the trade question. Canadians who were desperate for relief from the McKinley Tariff—especially farmers, who made up the majority of voters—might well conclude that if they voted for the government, all they could look forward to was tariffs, tariffs, and more tariffs. Yet Blaine had been silent about unrestricted reciprocity. Could a deal be negotiated on those lines? If so, those Canadians who could live with the risks of free trade, so long as natural products were returned to the free list, were probably going to vote Liberal in the next election.

Why had Blaine seemingly gone out of his way to make trouble for Macdonald? First, he was annoyed by the implication that the Harrison administration had pursued talks with Canada in the first place. That was a half-truth, at best. In reality, Blaine had been approached by the British legation in Washington at the instigation of the Canadian government. Only then had he suggested secret talks, and here was another reason for his irritation: secret talks were supposed to be kept secret. Instead, the Toronto *Empire* had confirmed their existence to help the Conservatives score political points in an expected election campaign. Macdonald would protest that it was the *substance* of the talks, not the fact of their existence, that was to have been kept secret. But that was splitting hairs. Blaine obviously had not wanted anything said about the proposed talks, and the prime minister's indiscretion partially accounted for the vehemence of the secretary of state's harsh statement.

Even so, it seemed that something else was going on. Was Blaine trying to assist the Liberals? Was someone whispering in his ear? The answer, the Tories soon alleged, was yes. Citing American newspapers as its source, the *Empire* reported that just before issuing his denial, Blaine had met at his residence with a representative of the Liberals. This secret agent's advice had been to put the screws to the Conservatives by denying everything stated in the *Empire* about the proposed trade talks. The representative in question, the individual who had undermined the relations of the Canadian government with a foreign power, was Edward Farrer, lead editorial writer of the Toronto *Globe*.

The Conservatives could hardly believe the gall of the Liberals. David Creighton, editor of the *Empire*, dispatched a reporter to the *Globe* office to confirm that Farrer had been to Washington. John Willison was sitting at his desk when the reporter arrived.

"I have come to ask you, Mr. Willison," the reporter began, "if there is any truth in this dispatch in regard to Mr. Farrer's visit to Washington?"

"It is a fact," the *Globe* editor replied coolly, "that Mr. Farrer is in Washington."

"Can you tell me if he has had any interviews with Secretary Blaine or any of the congressional representatives, as mentioned in the dispatch?"

"Mr. Farrer is in Washington on the Globe's business. I take the position that Mr. Farrer is a member of the Globe's staff and his business there is the Globe business."

This tight-lipped exchange was repeated word for word in the *Empire*. "That was all Editor Willison would say," it observed with satisfaction, "but it was quite enough."[2]

That much was correct. Farrer had been to Washington, he had conferred with Blaine, and then Blaine had issued his denial. What that meant for the two parties was more ambiguous. Would Canadians be swayed by the argument of the *Empire* and other Tory organs that

Farrer's actions constituted treasonous behaviour? Or would they take more notice of the fact that the Conservatives had annoyed the Harrison administration and apparently bungled their chances of getting partial reciprocity?

Sir John A. Macdonald, having been surprised by the daring of the Liberals in calling his bluff, quickly took stock of the situation. His plan to outfox them on the trade question had backfired. In the face of Blaine's repudiation, it would be exceedingly difficult for him to convince the voters that his Conservatives were going to negotiate partial reciprocity. The most logical alternative was to call an election and run on the National Policy. That had been a winning strategy in the past, but Macdonald knew that it would be harder this time, in the current economic climate, to sell the Canadian people a policy of more high tariffs.

Perhaps even more important than the weakness of the Conservative position on the trade question was the condition of the Conservative party itself. Macdonald knew better than anyone that elections were not won merely with sound arguments. Nor could they be won simply by controlling the electoral machinery of the country, as his Tories already did (though that, of course, helped). Elections were won by the countless local party supporters who canvassed constituencies, put up broadsides, organized meetings, nominated candidates, raised campaign funds, and turned out the vote on election day. Before dropping the writ, it was critical that Sir John take into account the strength of the party on the ground.

The West

If there was one thing that Macdonald could rely on, it was that western Canada was still safe Conservative territory. The Tories had won fourteen of fifteen constituencies there in the election of 1887, and if anything their political position had improved since then. In British Columbia, the staunchest Tory bastion in the Dominion, several members of Parliament doubted that they would even face Liberal opponents. Even if they did, there seemed to be little to worry about, for the agitation for unrestricted reciprocity had not made much of an impression on British Columbians. The newspapers there were also heavily Conservative. Both daily papers in Vancouver were Tory organs—an unusual situation—and in Victoria the *Colonist* was more than a match for the upstart *Times*, one of the few British Columbian dailies to support the Liberal Party.

The odds were even more lopsided in favour of the Conservatives in the four vast constituencies of the North-West Territories, where patronage was a major factor. Federal employees wielded great authority in the Territories, with the North-West Mounted Police and the Indian agents of the Department of the Interior being the most numerous and visible. Those employees owed their jobs to Macdonald, and they would use all their prestige and authority to secure the constituencies in which they worked. The use of the open ballot in the Territories would make their jobs easier, since they would be able to keep track of which voters were loyal and disloyal on election day. The re-election of four Tories in the North-West Territories, then, seemed assured.

Manitoba was the only doubtful territory for the Tories in western Canada, even though they enjoyed their usual institutional advantages. Federal patronage was in their hands there, as it was everywhere else. The press was on their side, too, especially since the Canadian Pacific Railway had gained a controlling interest in what had been the most important Liberal organ in the province, the Manitoba *Free Press*. Its content was now watched over by William Van Horne, the general manager of the C.P.R. and a powerful ally of the prime minister. A massive and imposing man with a full black beard, Van Horne had been the driving force behind the construction of the railway. Though his demeanour—always positive and energetic—resembled that of Erastus Wiman, he was Wiman's superior in physical and mental prowess, not to mention the range of his accomplishments. Once asked the secret of his success, legend has it, Van Horne matter-of-factly replied, "I eat all

I can, I drink all I can, I smoke all I can, and I don't give a damn for anything." On the frontier of western Canada, it was good to have a man like that on your side.

Van Horne notwithstanding, the alliance of the Canadian Pacific Railway with the Conservative Party was not an unmitigated blessing. Farmers resented the imperious air of the company. They also resented its high freight rates and the twenty-year monopoly on railway traffic that it had been guaranteed by the Macdonald government. Repeatedly the Manitoba government had tried to build local railway lines that would feed directly to the United States, circumventing the C.P.R. monopoly, and every time the prime minister disallowed the legislation. That burned Manitobans and contributed in 1888 to the election of a Liberal provincial government. Now Premier Thomas Greenway would throw his weight behind the federal Liberal Party, and as the instigator of the Manitoba Schools Question, an attempt to end public funding for Catholic schools in the province, Greenway might command the allegiance of militant Protestants who normally would have supported the Conservatives. That might be enough to swing two or three of the five Manitoba constituencies to the Liberals.

The East

Traditionally, the Maritime provinces had the deepest attachment to the British Empire. That was good news for the Conservatives. There had also been considerable, if erratic, industrial development in the region on account of the stimulus provided by the National Policy. Even so, the economy of the Maritimes had been in decline for years. This was partly a result of technological change—the gradual end of the era of "wood, wind, and sail" that had long defined the Maritime economy—but the National Policy's restrictions on trade between the Maritime provinces and their natural trading partners, the New England states, was also a factor. As a result, the promise of unrestricted reciprocity was playing pretty well in the region.

The provincial legislatures of Nova Scotia and New Brunswick were controlled by the Liberals, as they had been in 1887, and so the election-winning machinery of these governments would be placed at Laurier's disposal. Premier William Fielding of Nova Scotia and his mischief-making attorney general, James Longley, were especially keen to see the Macdonald government defeated. The problems that the Tories might have in both provinces were evident from the reports of Sir John Thompson of Nova Scotia and George Foster of New Brunswick, the most prominent federal cabinet ministers from the Maritime region. Neither was confident of carrying his own constituency, and that was alarming. If these cabinet ministers were facing uphill fights for re-election, lesser Tory candidates would be sure to struggle as well.

Prince Edward Island, which was a very different place from either Nova Scotia or New Brunswick, would be a tough nut to crack. Because it was so small, the Island had only three "double constituencies"—King's, Queen's, and Prince—each with a pair of members of Parliament. (In a double constituency, electors cast votes for two among the competing candidates, and the two with the most votes were both elected.) Its government, led by Premier Neil McLeod, was Conservative, but in the election of 1887 its influence had not been enough to win a single seat for the federal party. This time around the issue of overriding importance to most Islanders was the construction of a tunnel to the mainland. It was a difficult issue for the Macdonald government to handle. In the rest of the country, the tunnel was regarded as a lunatic pet project of the Islanders, a prohibitively expensive public works project that was about as realistic as a highway to the moon. But the island was all but cut off from the mainland in winter, and its economy suffered as a result, so the tunnel was a political litmus test for all federal candidates. Were they "Tunnel Men" or not? Liberal members on the Island could cite their Opposition status as the reason for their inability to get the project going. Conservative candidates, whose governing party had done nothing to advance the project, had no excuse.

Anticipating difficulties in all three Maritime provinces, Macdonald had already recalled mighty Sir Charles Tupper from London, England, where he was serving as the Canadian high commissioner. As a public servant Tupper was supposed to be above the fray of partisan politics, and his active participation in an election campaign would be a severe breach of protocol. That, Macdonald shrugged, was too bad. On January 21 he had urgently wired Tupper: "Immediate dissolution almost certain. Your presence ... in Maritime Provinces essential to encourage our friends. Please come. Answer."[3] That was all the War Horse needed to hear. Even before James Blaine had issued his repudiation of the planned trade talks, Tupper had set out across the Atlantic aboard the White Star liner *Teutonic* in order to take part in the fight to come.

Ontario

Macdonald had never taken Ontario, the greatest electoral prize, for granted. Its ninety-two seats had been competitive in every election since Confederation, and even when the Liberals had lost badly elsewhere in Canada they had retained a substantial foothold in Ontario. In 1887 the Conservatives had won fifty-five seats in the province, a seemingly comfortable majority. Yet the popular vote had been close, and twenty-six constituencies had been decided by fewer than a hundred votes. The Conservatives had barely won some races that should not have been close; John Carling, the famous brewer and minister of agriculture, had been re-elected in London by thirty-nine votes, and Macdonald himself had recaptured Kingston by a mere seventeen. Narrowest of all was the race in Haldimand, in the Niagara region, where the Tories had won by *one vote* out of thirty-five hundred cast.

With so many close results in mind, Macdonald was well aware that even a slight shift in the mood of the electorate could produce a very different result. That was why the unsettled state of Ontario politics was worrying him. For two years now the race-and-religion question, sparked by Quebec's passage of the Jesuits' Estates Act, had roiled the province. Macdonald had let the legislation pass over the bitter objections of Ontario Protestants, and since then he had been using all of his powers of persuasion to bring the church, the Orange Order, and every other unhappy Ontario Protestant voter back inside the big tent of the Conservative Party.

That had been a hard business for Macdonald, and there was no telling how much of the Protestant vote he might lose in the province. It was unlikely that the most militant Protestants would bolt to the Liberal Party—not with a French Canadian Roman Catholic for a leader—but there was a chance that they might not vote at all, or throw their ballots to candidates of the Equal Rights Association. The influence of that bigoted body in the coming campaign was difficult to determine. It was unlikely that the E.R.A. would run its own candidates in many Ontario constituencies. But it certainly would apply pressure on Conservative candidates to support its anti-Catholic platform, and it would remind Protestant voters to reject Conservative members of Parliament who had supported the prime minister's decision to allow the Jesuits' Estates Act.

The impossibility of the Canadian political system was further evident in the fact that the Catholic vote in Ontario, traditionally pretty solid for the Tories, might also have become disaffected on account of the Jesuits' Estates controversy. This would not be the fault of Sir John, who had allowed the act to pass and done his best to damp down the Protestant furor that had resulted. It would be the fault of other Tory politicians who had aggravated the furor but succeeded merely in alienating the Catholic community that made up about 17 percent of the population of Ontario. William Meredith, the provincial Conservative leader, had not helped the federal party when he waged an anti-Catholic campaign in the provincial election of June 1890. Other blowhards, such as Sam Hughes, a prominent Tory journalist and candidate in the constituency of Victoria North, had also been attacking Roman Catholicism and thereby bringing discredit—and tougher prospects of re-election—upon fellow party members.

Most damaging to the Conservatives had been the agitation of D'Alton McCarthy. Sir John had done everything possible to rein him in, but McCarthy had been determined to seize upon the Jesuits' Estates Act as a convenient pretext for his national crusade for a "community of language." It was possible that his crusade would win the Conservative Party some militant votes in Ontario (though most of them probably would end up in the Tory column anyway). It was more likely that McCarthy would cost the Tories a large percentage of the Catholic vote, which traditionally had made the difference in many close constituencies. McCarthy was running as a Conservative in Simcoe North, and his continued attachment to the party was embarrassing. Still, Macdonald judged, it was better to keep him onside than to have him leave the party altogether and take up the leadership of the Equal Rights Association.

Even without McCarthy, without the race-and-religion question, Macdonald knew that the Conservative Party would be vulnerable in Ontario because of the trade question. Unrestricted reciprocity was more popular there than anywhere else in the country. In the urban areas the Tories would probably hold their support, owing to the more positive and direct impact of the National Policy upon the manufacturers and workers who lived there, but in the many rural constituencies the appeal of Sir Richard Cartwright and his free trade nostrums was undeniable. The Liberals had been stumping this ground more actively than the Conservatives, and so much face-to-face contact with so many voters was bound to have its effect. Perhaps, Macdonald could hope, the loyalty cry would bring wayward Ontario farmers back into the fold. Perhaps the institutional benefits of the Franchise Act of 1885, which had given the federal government control of the voters lists, plus the generous assistance of the Ontario manufacturers, would be sufficient to offset the advantage that the Liberals believed they enjoyed on the trade question. But then again, perhaps not.

Quebec

Nowhere did Conservative prospects seem more uncertain than in Quebec. It was not just one thing. Every conceivable difficulty seemed to be converging upon the party in the province where it had once seemed invincible.

Party organization had deteriorated in recent years. The endless jockeying for position between the leading Quebec Conservatives—Langevin, Chapleau, and Caron—had badly divided the party. Each had his own following and his own turf, and no one was able to assume the overall direction of affairs for the whole of Quebec. This was exasperating for Macdonald, who had tried for years to play referee but had never found a permanent solution to their constant power struggle. He had supported Langevin most prominently—a decision that appeared to have backfired, with the McGreevy scandal looming on the horizon—and as a consequence of that, Chapleau and Caron had been relegated to junior portfolios in the federal cabinet.

That had been terribly frustrating for Chapleau, who was widely acknowledged as the most capable and popular Conservative in Quebec. He had given up the premiership of the province in order to become its representative at the federal level and, if all went well, perhaps even the first French Canadian prime minister. He could have seized the moment and rallied Quebec around him in 1885 if he had chosen to oppose the hanging of Louis Riel. Instead—and despite his personal objection to the hanging—Chapleau had stayed loyal to Macdonald, because the alternative had been to create a purely French party that would clash with its English equivalent and cause long-term disaster for the country. For nearly a decade he had waited to take over the party in Quebec, toiling meanwhile in the insignificant cabinet post of secretary of state. (The Toronto *Globe* snidely referred to it as the "chief comptrollership of the red tape and sealing wax.")[4] Langevin had always stood in the way, and he was in the way still, despite everything that had happened to diminish his status.

Chapleau had painted a grim picture for Macdonald in recent months. In August 1890 he had written a bitter, despairing letter outlining the political situation in Quebec.

> You asked me to "work out some scheme for the organization of my district for the next general elections." I must say that I have often put the question to myself since the last six months how could our Quebec elections be secured ... and I must confess that I have not yet found a satisfactory solution to the problem, nay, I am afraid there is none. The situation is hopeless ...
>
> There is no political authority in our province, in federal matters, and the necessary discipline in the respective political districts of the Province has been destroyed by the leaders of our party itself.

According to Chapleau not even the Roman Catholic Church, so thoroughly loyal to the Conservative Party in elections past, could necessarily be counted upon: "The different bishops of the Province must be seen and a common action determined upon to control the lower clergy which is lost to us in a greater measure than we are ready to admit. A large proportion of the clergy look to annexation as the dawn of an era of greater liberty and comfort to them."[5]

This was unfortunate news, because in the campaign to come the race-and-religion question was, as usual, likely to have a greater impact in Quebec than in the English-speaking provinces. Premier Honoré Mercier, who still maddeningly controlled the province after his triumphant re-election in June 1890, would make sure that neither the "corpse of Riel" nor English Canadian opposition to the passage of the Jesuits' Estates Act would be soon forgotten. Then, of course, there was Wilfrid Laurier. Never before had a French Canadian Roman Catholic led a federal party into an election, and the pull of sentiment—the desire to vote for the hometown boy—ought not to be underestimated. It was not just his background that was appealing, either. Macdonald did not know Laurier well, but he recognized that he was a much stronger opponent than the indecisive, hand-wringing Edward Blake. How the Liberal leader performed in the campaign might well determine the outcome in Quebec where, like Ontario, a great many constituencies would be closely fought and a small change in the popular vote might give a slew of vulnerable Conservative seats to the Opposition. If that happened, the prospect of re-election would be grim for the prime minister.

Macdonald did not take long to chew over the information that his intelligence network—the vast correspondence that flowed to and from his desk—had furnished him. On February 2, as rumours swirled around Ottawa, he quietly notified Governor General Lord Stanley of his wish to dissolve Parliament and enter into an election campaign. His request was duly granted. A notice appeared in the Conservative newspapers the next morning that official nominations would take place on Thursday, February 26, and the election would be held on Thursday, March 5. The Tory explanation for the dissolution, received with derision by the Grit press, was that the government was on the cusp of negotiations for partial reciprocity with the United States, and wished to have a fresh mandate from the people before proceeding. It took nerve to call an election for a reason as transparently phony as that. Macdonald had called the election now to give his party the best odds of winning, and that was that.

Now there were campaign logistics to consider. For the moment Sir John would remain in Ottawa, conducting business both at Earnscliffe and his office in the East Block of Parliament. Cabinet meetings had to be held before ministers departed to direct the campaign in their respective territories, and for Macdonald there was still the Department of Railways and Canals to run (even during campaigns the business of government had to be attended to, a significant disadvantage for ministers). After wrapping up matters in Ottawa he would, as usual, move to Toronto and direct the campaign from there. Agnes would remain at Earnscliffe, however much she might wish to be at his side. Her absence from the campaign trail would not affect his judgment, for Sir John had never allowed Agnes to play the role of political advisor. But it would mean for him that the weeks to come would be solitary ones, totally absorbed by the needs of the party. Joseph Pope would be his only constant companion.

Pope was concerned as always for the health of the prime minister, knowing that he would be "insensibly drawn into the conflict" and would have difficulty refusing the incessant demands of the party.[6] On the eve of the campaign, however, he noticed that Macdonald was in good spirits. Indeed, he seemed to be energized now that his course was clear. Resting at home at Earnscliffe on the evening of February 2, after his consultation with the Governor General, the Old Man decided to get started on the party platform. He disappeared into his study and was there still, holed away in his rambling manor overlooking the Ottawa River, as the lamps burned low and long into the night.

The Liberal Response

Three days earlier, in the early-morning hours of January 31, 1891, Wilfrid Laurier gazed wearily out the window of the overnight train that was speeding toward Toronto's Union Station. There was nothing to see outside, but he found it impossible to sleep. It had been a jarring ride from Montreal, following on a similarly jarring overnight train from New York, and with no scenery to distract him there was at least time to think. Laurier had crucial decisions to make, for the election was imminent and the Liberal Party had to be hurriedly readied for the contest. Plus, he had a fire to put out in Toronto, a potential disaster, which absolutely had to be dealt with before the campaign began in earnest.

His trip had been brief and somewhat calamitous. He had been to New York City to attend the annual dinner of its Board of Trade and Transportation on January 29 and to give a speech titled "The Future of Half a Continent" before a distinguished American crowd. He had been scheduled to speak late that evening, but at ten o'clock the U.S. secretary of the treasury, William Windom, finished speaking and then died of a heart attack in front of his horrified audience. There was nothing for Laurier to do after that but go back to his hotel, wait out the next day, and then return to Montreal. With election talk swirling and the probable line of attack against the Liberals being that they were too cozy with the Yankees, the optics of the Liberal leader scurrying home from the United States were, well, regrettable. But that could not be helped. Laurier had too many things to put straight now to worry about appearances.

His first order of business was to make sure that the party was placed immediately on the best possible campaign footing. There was no denying that the election call was coming sooner than expected, and that to some extent the Liberals had been caught flat-footed. After all, the government was not even four years into its term. There was no pressing reason for an election, and Sir John A. Macdonald had pledged not to call one until after the next parliamentary session and after the 1891 census had been completed. The latter business was important. It had been ten years since the previous census, and without waiting for a new one, the election would be held using constituency boundaries that were perilously out of date. (This was not good for the Liberals, since the boundaries had last been redrawn by the Conservative Party through legislation that was referred to in Liberal circles as "the Great Gerrymander of 1882." This act, in concert with the Franchise Act of 1885, had been intended by Macdonald to give the Conservatives the advantage in future federal elections.)

A more immediate problem would be the disenfranchisement of tens of thousands of first-time voters who would not appear on the old lists, which had not been updated in two years. For this reason alone, calling an election so precipitously was arguably unfair and irresponsible. Many Liberals had honestly believed that Macdonald would not break his pledge, but really, they should have known better than to trust the Old Man on such a vital matter. There would be much Liberal complaining about the unfairness of the call in the early days of the campaign, but it would go for naught. They would have to build on the preparations already made, and those varied considerably across the country.

The outlook was most discouraging for the Liberals in western Canada, where they had always been weak on the ground. Few leading Liberals had even set foot in the region—Laurier himself had never been west of Ontario—and the news he was soon to receive from Manitoba was very discouraging. "The people of this province are, I am convinced, practically unanimous in favour of free trade with the United States," one Winnipeg supporter reported. Alas, he added, "this unanimity may not, probably will not, find expression at the polls as we are finding great trouble in putting candidates in the field."[7] The best that could be hoped for was a gain of three or four Manitoba seats, and even that seemed wildly optimistic. The Tories might not be beloved in western Canada, but they were in control of government patronage as well as most of the daily newspapers. Those conditions made the situation almost hopeless for the Liberals.

There was better news from the other end of the country. In December, Laurier had been to the Maritimes on a highly publicized speaking tour, appearing in the major cities with the leading provincial party captains, and the big crowds and hearty receptions had been encouraging. In Prince Edward Island, where all six seats were in Liberal hands, the campaign would be directed by the capable Louis Davies, the former premier and current member of Parliament for Queen's County. In New Brunswick the task fell to Charles Weldon, long-time M.P. for the City and County of Saint John. He had failed to anticipate the election call, but could probably depend on some aid from Liberal Premier Andrew Blair. Overall, the prospect of picking up a few seats in New Brunswick seemed fairly bright.

In Nova Scotia, where the most seats were at stake in the Maritime provinces, the party leaders were in excellent spirits. The long-standing Liberal premier, W.S. Fielding, would direct the campaign in the eastern part of the province, and his attorney general, J.W. Longley, would do the same in the west. Longley, who had been with Laurier at the dinner in New York and was stopping off to confer with politicians in Washington before returning home, was flushed with confidence. The Conservative Party was in poor shape, he would shortly report to his chief, having less money to throw at the voters of Nova Scotia than in previous campaigns. Sir Charles Tupper was coming back, but his influence would be minimal. As Longley confidently put it, "It will not change 20 votes in the Province."[8] He predicted that the Liberal Party would win a majority of seats in Nova Scotia, as long as more campaign funds could be brought in to level the playing field with the Conservatives. Longley himself was working on that.

In Quebec, of course, Laurier could be his own judge. He liked his chances, for a number of reasons. First, there was the fact that he was the first French Canadian to lead a federal party into an election campaign. It was hard to tell how much that would count for, exactly, but it certainly was not going to hurt him. He planned to drive home this unprecedented advantage by focusing his personal campaign in Quebec, stumping there extensively and leaving the English-speaking provinces largely, though not entirely, to regional lieutenants. Second, he knew that the Tories were hurting in Quebec. The ghost of Riel still haunted the province. The conflicts between Langevin, Chapleau, and Caron, and the headaches they had created for their party, were not exactly a secret. This was all good news for the Liberal Party. Then there was the fallout from the anti-French crusade of D'Alton McCarthy, which might gain Laurier votes from disgusted French Canadians who had until now been loyal to Macdonald.

Another important asset was the talented Israël Tarte, formerly a Tory organizer and journalist and now essentially a Liberal ally. Tarte, who was running as a nominal Conservative in Montmorency but with obvious Liberal aid, was in a perfect position to do serious damage to the government. In the pages of *Le Canadien* he would continue to leak the details of the McGreevy scandal, and considering the importance of Sir Hector Langevin in Quebec and the severity of the accusations against him, that one issue might well come to overshadow all others in the province. Meanwhile the Liberals could count on the support of Premier Honoré Mercier, who had just postponed a trip to Europe in order to throw himself into the fray. His steely grey eyes and thunderous oratory would be a great asset on the campaign trail. There was a chance, however, that his nationalist rhetoric might create embarrassment for Laurier in Ontario, where the election might be won or lost.

Laurier had never been sure that he could lead the Liberals to victory in English Canada, and particularly in Ontario. In May 1890 he had written sadly to Edward Blake, "Apart from my personal shortcomings, it is now more & more manifest to me that I can never successfully lead the party ... a French Canadian will not get a cheerful support in the English provinces."[9] Certainly it looked like an uphill fight. The province was an overwhelmingly Protestant society, the heartland of the "No Popery!" cry, and home of the Orange Order and the Equal Rights Association. There were residents of some rural constituencies who had never even *seen* a Roman Catholic, and who routinely swore an Orange oath to oppose Roman Catholicism in all its sinister forms. How could Laurier carry an election in a province like that?

Still, all hope was not lost in Ontario. The leader was not everything. J.D. Edgar and W.T.R. Preston were capable organizers, and even with the surprise election call, the Ontario wing was more battle-ready than it had been last time. The Liberal government had successfully tested its mettle in the provincial election of 1890, and the formidable and finely tuned "Mowat machine" could now be put to work for the federal party. Sir Richard Cartwright, leading the campaign in Ontario, had anticipated the snap election and made the necessary moves to combat it. He had conducted a speaking tour of the province in November, talking up unrestricted reciprocity to excellent effect, and had instructed Preston to sound the alarm and press the constituency associations to hold meetings and recruit candidates. A public convention of the

Ontario wing of the party had also been planned for mid-February, largely at the direction of Cartwright. As for campaign funds, there were never enough, but Edgar had constructed a more reliable system of party financing in recent years, and that was a big improvement. The party would still be outmatched in the "ground game," but not as badly as it had been in the election of 1887.

The greatest thing that the Liberals had going for them in Ontario was, of course, unrestricted reciprocity. The Toronto *Globe*, assisted by the pen of Edward Farrer, had promoted the policy throughout the summer and fall, and the Liberal press across the province had followed its lead. Cartwright had done the same on his tour and so had John Charlton, the colourful M.P. for North Norfolk, on a swing through southwestern constituencies. There was a confident feeling in the Liberal Party that after so many years of painful defeat they had finally discovered a winning formula. The trick would be to present unrestricted reciprocity as a sound and patriotic policy, and to avoid having anyone associated with the Liberal Party say something foolish that could be used to make the voters think otherwise.

Loose Cannons

Unfortunately for the Liberals, a few of their well-meaning friends had a tendency to cause them embarrassment. Goldwin Smith, the chief annexationist of the Dominion, was at the top of that list. The professor had been confining himself to remarks about the trade question, leaving the greater "Canadian question" to the side, but it was obvious that he supported unrestricted reciprocity purely because he thought that it would lead to political union. It was dangerous to have somebody like that speaking freely throughout the campaign, but Smith was fiercely independent; no one could possibly persuade him to consider the effect of his public remarks on the fortunes of the Liberals. On the eve of the campaign, for example, he intended to deliver a speech on loyalty that was designed to irritate Canadians who treasured the British connection.

There was a good chance that Smith was going to create headaches for the Liberals.

Edward Farrer also had the capacity to make trouble for the party, even though he was formally hitched to the Liberal team as the editorial writer of the Toronto *Globe*. His foray to Washington had demonstrated both his resourcefulness and his recklessness, and his chummy relationships with leading American politicians were a double-edged sword. Those trips provided the Liberals with insight into the political scene in Washington—perhaps even a bit of influence—but they also raised questions about Farrer, and what exactly he had been telling those politicians behind closed doors. Had he not been exposed only a year ago, urging his powerful American friends to cold-shoulder the Dominion into annexation? Laurier, himself just returned from the United States, would have to fight hard to correct the impression that he was too friendly with the Yankees. He could only hope that Farrer would stay out of trouble on that front.

Erastus Wiman was another potential source of embarrassment. The gregarious "Canadian-American" was earnestly trying to assist the cause. His promotional talents had been a significant asset to the Liberal Party, which he had been supporting in a more partisan manner, and lately he had been doing his usual good work—speeches, articles, pamphlets, letters to leading U.S. politicians—to help Liberal fortunes. He also seemed to be aware that his presence in Canada might cause trouble, given the visceral emotions that he tended to evoke from the Conservatives. He had apparently decided to assist his Liberal friends by remaining in the United States and lobbying Congress, which would be useful, since a friendly Congress would strengthen the Liberal argument that if elected, they would actually be able to make unrestricted reciprocity a reality.

But Wiman still found ways to make life for the Liberals awkward. He tended, for example, to give the impression in his public remarks that Sir Richard Cartwright, rather than Laurier, was the leader of the party. Perhaps this was an innocent misreading of the situation—Wiman had far closer relations with Cartwright than with Laurier, after all—but it was unhelpful, to say the least. It made Laurier look weak and encouraged division within the party. Wiman also could have tried a little harder to shoot down rumours that he was thinking about taking over the leadership himself. The Ottawa *Journal* had made this suggestion in July 1890, and though Wiman laughed it off, he seemed to accept the premise that the leadership was his for the taking.

This played into the hands of the Conservatives, who were convinced that Wiman was a kind of sinister master puppeteer, secretly pulling the strings of the Liberal Party. Walter Montague, the Conservative member for Haldimand, typified this sentiment when he wrote Macdonald, "I think nothing ought to be more disgusting to the true Canadians in the Grit ranks than to see their party movements practically controlled in another country."[10] George Johnson, the Dominion statistician and an advisor to several leading Tories, circulated a memorandum that depicted "Czar Wiman," dictator of the "so-called Liberal Party of Canada," issuing commands that were "slavishly obeyed" by Laurier and Cartwright.[11] Such inflammatory imagery strained believability, to say the least, but there was political value in it, and the Johnson memo soon showed up as an editorial in the Montreal *Gazette*.

Wiman also worried some Liberals because he had never put an end to persistent rumours that he was a closet annexationist. Although he had published several articles in the popular *North American Review* that were intended to disabuse American readers of the impression that Canadians were interested in joining the United States, he had a habit of asking eyebrow-raising rhetorical questions to make his points, such as, "Has not the time for the capture of Canada come?"[12] The answer was no, if one actually read the article, but if the question itself was quoted out of context it was almost too easy for the Tories to use it against him. The titles of the articles, too, had become embarrassing. In June 1889 he asked, "What is the Destiny of Canada?" That was not that bad. In

August 1890, however, the topic was "The Capture of Canada." (The "capture" in question was increased commerce with Canada, but that distinction was lost on sceptical Canadians.) Finally, only weeks before the election was called, Wiman had asked readers, "Can We Coerce Canada?" Again the answer was no, if one bothered to read the article. But most Canadians would not, least of all Macdonald and the Tories. They cited it as the latest damning evidence that Wiman was a traitorous annexationist.

Only one man seemed to enrage the Tory press more thoroughly than Wiman, and that was Sir Richard Cartwright. There was something about the Blue Ruin Knight that got under their skin. Perhaps it was because he had once been a Tory himself, back in the 1860s, before switching to the Liberals out of disgust for Macdonald's dubious methods. (The Tories claimed that Cartwright had left the party because he had been denied the plum post of finance minister.) Perhaps it was because of his relentless attacks on the National Policy, which were backed by facts and figures that undermined the cheerful economic forecasts of the government. Perhaps it was because Sir Richard, more than even Laurier, had led the Liberal Party into battle on behalf of unrestricted reciprocity. Perhaps, finally, it was because he was such a bitter politician. As the Toronto *Empire* harshly remarked, "No man in public life has done so much to degrade the standard of political strife in Canada as Sir Richard Cartwright."[13]

There was one thing that the Conservatives did like about Cartwright, however: he was a loose cannon. No other leading Liberal had his legendary capacity to make comments and take actions that could so disastrously embarrass the party, especially when it came to Canadian-American relations. Cartwright, to the great delight of the Conservatives, never seemed to appreciate the patriotism of most ordinary Canadians. His periodic visits to the United States, topped off with speeches that were regarded by Canadian nationalists as pathetic attempts to curry favour with the Yankees, were a case in point. On the night of

January 30, even as Laurier was boarding his train to Toronto, Sir Richard was the featured speaker at a banquet of the Boston Merchants' Association. There, before an influential American audience, he uttered words that the Conservatives would quote endlessly throughout the election campaign.

The lead line in the Boston *Globe*'s coverage of the banquet the next morning conveyed the patronizing tone of the rest: "Big boy Boston clasped his big sister Canada around the waist, and both shouted for 'unrestricted reciprocity' at the top of their lung power." The description of the banquet hall, which had been decorated to the Yankee taste with electric lights, countless American flags, and a statuette of a golden eagle, also seemed inconsistent with the welcome that might be accorded a Canadian statesman. But to Canadian sensibilities, the most objectionable remarks were not those of the *Globe*, but those of Cartwright himself. Quoted selectively, he had stepped beyond what most of his countrymen deemed the limit of friendliness toward the Americans.

> Sir, I have no wish to mislead you. The trade of the United States is certainly worth more to us collectively than ours is to you. That is a manifest truth.
>
> Briefly, sir, if this project can be carried out, it will mean for you the addition of half a continent for commercial purposes, and the creation of a complete new tier of Northern States, with an enormous area of unoccupied fertile land, with very great mineral resources, with a present population of some 5,000,000 ... with essentially in character the same as your own, with much the same habits, customs and prejudices even.[14]

Laurier, his train hurtling toward Toronto, had not yet read these remarks, though he was certainly aware that Cartwright was speaking in Boston. When he picked up a newspaper in the morning, however, he was not going to be thrilled. That line about the "new tier of Northern States," in particular, would be fodder for every Conservative organ in the country. But what could he do about it? Cartwright was essentially the leader of the federal party in Ontario, and he would have a more direct role in managing the campaign there than would Laurier. His devotion to free trade was appreciated by farmers, and their votes would be decisive in the majority of Ontario's ninety-two constituencies. Laurier knew that Cartwright was indispensable, and he could only pray that his Ontario lieutenant would refrain from making any more "Northern states" comments.

Even at his most indiscreet, however, Cartwright could not cause anything like the catastrophic injury that might be done to the Liberals by the man who had forced Laurier to drag himself aboard the overnight train to Toronto.

The Ticking Bomb

The leading Liberals were worried about Edward Blake. Since his return to the House of Commons in January 1890 he had been a ghost from the past, an unsettling spectre on the backbenches. No one knew what Blake was thinking as he sat at the back of the House, peering down at his old protégé Laurier and at Laurier's new parliamentary deskmate, Cartwright. They wondered whether he was really content to watch them direct the affairs of the party. Was he not wishing, somewhere within that brilliant and tortured mind, to be called to resume the leadership, regardless of what he might say in public or in private? And could he remain silent while the Liberals campaigned for unrestricted reciprocity, a policy that he opposed?

Cartwright believed that Blake had a duty to support the platform out of loyalty to the party, even if he had reservations about it. He had not invited Blake to the upcoming Ontario convention, a fateful decision that reflected his uncertainty about where Blake stood. "He had most decidedly better not attend," Sir Richard had told Laurier. "He can do us very little good but ... he may do much harm." It would be better for everybody, in fact, if Blake spent the next parliamentary session in Europe. "He did us nothing but injury last Session and he cannot control himself," Cartwright confided to Laurier. "'Tis a great pity but so it is."[15]

Blake was a smart man, and he was aware of these rumblings as he contemplated his future early in 1891. He resented that Laurier and Cartwright were treating him like some sort of wayward child and that they seemed interested only in shutting him up. He was particularly hurt that Cartwright had excluded him from the convention. When the Liberal association of his West Durham constituency asked him in mid-January if he planned to run again, he came to a crossroads in his political life. He liked these men who had supported his candidacy in the past and who had worked so hard to ensure his election. He could not lie to them about his views on unrestricted reciprocity. He could not lie to himself. Nor, he decided, could he lie to the Canadian people. Blake decided to write a letter—a letter filled with shocking revelations of his views—to his faithful supporters, explaining why he could not in good conscience stand as a Liberal candidate. A copy went to the West Durham constituency association in Bowmanville. More ominously, another was dispatched to the office of the Toronto *Globe*, with clear instructions that it be published in the newspaper the next morning.

It was just before midnight on January 28 when John Willison, still working at his editor's desk at the *Globe* office, received the letter from Blake. He read it with horrified astonishment. Its contents, if released to the public, would cause disaster for the Liberal Party. He showed the letter to a confidant, who concurred that they could not publish it in the *Globe*, especially not with an election looming. Yet Willison knew that refusing to publish the letter might make the situation worse. Blake would be outraged, and might simply send it on to the Toronto *Mail*, which would delight in splashing the contents across its front page. That would not do either. Willison therefore found himself in a hopeless position.

He scrambled to buy some time for himself and the party. It occurred to him that the executive board of the *Globe* ought to be consulted.

He could hardly rouse the board members from their beds, of course. They would have to meet the next day, and in the meantime Blake's letter would stay in the *Globe* office, safely hidden from public view. The next morning, January 29, Willison explained in a hurried note to Blake that since his letter had been marked "personal," the *Globe* was unsure whether it had been meant for publication. This was lame, and Blake was annoyed. He sent a frosty note back to Willison, insisting that the letter be published straight away. The *Globe* board met that afternoon and nevertheless decided to delay publication for as long as possible.

Another night passed, this time with the letter set in type but not yet placed in the columns of the newspaper. The next morning, January 30, Willison visited Humewood and pleaded with Blake to reconsider. That went nowhere. Blake had spent a long time debating his course of action and he was resolved to see it through. Already he had been visited by the *Globe*'s president, Robert Jaffray; by W.T.R. Preston, the party organizer; and even by his own brother, Samuel Blake. None of them had swayed him. Willison, his options running out, begged Blake to give him time to consult with Laurier. He had not returned from his trip to New York, and how could the letter appear in the official newspaper of the Liberal Party without the leader's having read it? This was stalling and Blake knew it, but he agreed to allow Willison a little more time. An urgent telegram was wired to Laurier—"come at once"—who received it upon his arrival in Montreal. He read it with alarm, boarded a train for Toronto, and arrived at Union Station on the cold morning of January 31.

There was, first of all, a meeting of Liberal minds at Rossin House, the impressive hotel on the corner of King and York streets. Sir Richard Cartwright had also hurried to Toronto, having received his own telegram, and he and a rather ragged-looking Laurier conferred anxiously with Willison and Preston. Laurier then proceeded on his own to Humewood, in the northern part of the city, to have a confrontation with Blake. Preston and Cartwright waited at the hotel for his return, dreading the news that he would bring back with him. It seemed to them that Laurier was gone for an interminably long time. At least three hours had passed before he finally returned. He said simply, wearily, "He will say nothing till after the elections."[16]

For the rest of their lives, neither Blake nor Laurier would reveal to anyone what exactly they had said to each other in that meeting. It was clear, however, that Blake had insisted that Laurier cancel the convention of Ontario Liberals and that Laurier had given in to that demand. That would cause him much embarrassment—invitations had already gone out, after all—but it was a small price to pay if it soothed Blake enough to get him to withhold his damning letter. Even after their tumultuous meeting, however, Laurier was not sure that he could rely on his old friend to keep his opinions to himself. He wrote to Blake on February 2, even as Sir John A. Macdonald was advising the Governor General to call the election, with an emotional argument aimed at securing his silence.

> Now I have your manifesto. As you admit yourself, it will do harm all around, & now let me ask you, to what person or to what cause will it do any good? Not to you, not to me, not to the country, nor to the party, nor to the cause.
>
> Now, my dear Blake, listen to the voice of a true and sincere friend. You should never publish such a document.
>
> The weak point of your position is that while showing all the objections to every system & to every policy, you conclude with nothing at all. Now, if you have no policy of your own to offer, if you simply remain in the negative, why should you sever from your friends, and why should you strike them such a blow at such a moment?[17]

It was just enough to save the Liberals from losing the election of 1891 before it started. Laurier knew that he could not stop Blake from publishing his letter eventually. He had, he was fairly sure, persuaded him not to release it until after the votes had been counted. The Conservative press would surely notice his absence from the campaign trail—Blake would never be persuaded to make even a token appearance at any Liberal rally—and the *Empire* and the others would spread rumours of dissension in the ranks. But the letter would not appear, not for now at least, and that was the best that could be salvaged from this perilous and saddening turn of events.

"I cannot tell you what I have suffered and am suffering," Blake wrote Laurier on February 7, in a letter confirming that he would maintain his distressed silence during the campaign.[18] It must have hurt Laurier to know that it was the truth, and that his friend was agonizing over the situation. But Blake and his wounded feelings came second to a greater, more urgent priority. The Liberal Party of Canada now had to go out and win the election of 1891.

SEVEN

The Appeal to the People

Though he had decided to move to Toronto for the duration of the campaign, Sir John A. Macdonald was still holed up in his study in Earnscliffe, with no date set for his leaving. That was worrisome to his supporters, and his age and health came immediately to mind. Perhaps he was sick. Just before the holidays he had suffered a "sudden indisposition," as Joseph-Adolphe Chapleau had delicately phrased it, which had caused consternation within the party.[1] That had passed, thankfully, but every day Macdonald remained in Ottawa, new fears for his health arose. Already it had quietly been admitted that he would not be able to attend the big Toronto rally on February 6. Now his attendance at his own nomination meeting in Kingston the following evening was in jeopardy, and it would be alarming if he could not attend that, just two hours by train from Ottawa. His attendance had already been announced, and party organizers were pressing him hard, insisting, "We think it of great importance that you should be here tomorrow."[2]

If Macdonald was ill, nothing was being said publicly about it, aside, of course, from some crass speculation in the Liberal newspapers. The *Empire* was tight lipped, offering only that the prime minister was "detained in Ottawa," and other Conservative organs followed the same line.[3] But the vast correspondence that he was replying to during the first week of the campaign suggested that the Old Man was functioning well enough. In fact it was the correspondence that was most likely keeping him chained to his desk at Earnscliffe. Hundreds of letters and telegrams were streaming in, providing local updates and seeking instructions from the far corners of the Dominion. Deputations of party members were constantly seeking an audience as well. The Toronto *Mail* marvelled at the "influx of pilgrims who come to this Mecca to get the Old Man to straighten out the tangles in their constituencies."[4] His preference for keeping the reins in his own hands, so beneficial most of the time, was becoming a liability in the midst of a campaign in which he could not possibly direct the affairs of every single constituency.

That, apparently, was precisely what the Conservative Party expected him to do, judging by the constant flow of requests coming across his desk. It was not enough for him to merely spell out the party platform. It was essential that he intervene directly in the constituencies to ensure that the right candidate was chosen, the right policies put to the people, and the right promises made. The volume and variety of these requests were dizzying. They revealed not only the remarkable dependence of the party on its chief, a dependence that Sir John was guilty of cultivating, but also his unparalleled grasp of the local politics of more than two hundred constituencies.

Everybody needed something from Macdonald. From North Bruce, Ontario, a constituency that the party had retained by just over a hundred votes in 1887, came an urgent request from the member of Parliament, Alexander McNeill. The election there was not going to hinge on free trade, nor race and religion. It was all about roads. North Bruce was a rural constituency, situated on rugged terrain, and the condition of the roads had become a critical concern. McNeill urged the prime minister to take personal action. "Many of our friends have strongly urged me," he wrote, "to write you and ask if it wd. be possible for you to promise us a grant of $4000 or $5000, to be expended upon roads for these poor people."[5] Nor was this an unusual demand. In Fredericton, a new bridge was required, and in the Prince Edward Island constituencies, of course, there was no hope unless Macdonald gave his blessing to the almighty Tunnel. This was no way to run a national campaign, haphazardly dishing out promises of public works, but if he did not make these promises, Macdonald knew, these and other constituencies would be in doubt.

Grim reports were coming in from all over southwestern Ontario, where even the safest Conservative seats appeared to be in jeopardy. This was the case in Hamilton, a double constituency. Both members of Parliament were Tories, but despite the traditional attachment to Macdonald of the largely working-class electorate, the local party association was worried. Local brewing companies, apparently unappreciative of the benefits of the National Policy, were exerting "the most powerful influence" in favour of the Liberals.[6] The two glass factories in the city were also on the Grit side, and were expected to deliver the votes of three hundred employees. On the Tory side it was not even clear who was running. One local fellow, seeking to squeeze out one of the two sitting members, reminded Macdonald that "one little word from you" would ensure his own nomination.[7]

Some requests sounded more like demands. In West Durham, the constituency that Edward Blake had decided not to contest, there was the possibility of a Conservative gain. The Liberals were running a first-time candidate, and the presumed Conservative nominee, George Blackstock, had nearly defeated Blake in 1887. A local Tory furniture maker, however, was angling for the nomination. W.P. Purver wrote to Macdonald, "You know I can poll 100 votes more than any other man," and said that he was being pressed to run by his comrades.[8] He would not take up the torch, however, unless guaranteed a Senate appointment in case he was defeated. That was a little too much gall for Macdonald. Blackstock got the nod.

Other constituencies needed Macdonald to either find them a candidate or anoint one among several local party men who were competing for the nomination. This was bothersome work for Sir John, and he was fielding such requests from all over the country, even from constituencies in which there was already a Conservative member of Parliament. In Carleton, in the Ottawa region, the sitting M.P. did not want to run again, and the three other candidates were problematic, all of them Equal Rights supporters. In New Brunswick he had to issue a "peremptory command" to dispatch the right candidate to run in Queen's constituency.[9] And from Winnipeg came urgent reports that W.B. Scarth, a Scottish businessman and faithful Macdonald supporter who had been elected by the microscopic margin of eight votes in the last election, was unpopular and would be defeated. "Winnipeg is in a bad way at present," one Tory confided. "Scarth is dying to run and does not like plain honest advice."[10]

Macdonald knew these constituencies simply could not be lost. In Carleton the M.P. must be persuaded to run. In Winnipeg, a replacement candidate must be found. William Van Horne had discussed the situation with Sir Donald Smith, governor of the Hudson's Bay Company and member for Montreal West. "If he alone can carry Winnipeg you have only to say the word," Van Horne informed Macdonald.[11] Perhaps that was true. Smith had long represented the Manitoba riding of Selkirk, and he was wealthy and well respected. If he ran in Winnipeg, though, who would contest Montreal West? That problem was left unresolved for the time being.

From Quebec, in particular, Macdonald was deluged with all manner of requests. There was no central authority in the province to rely on; that much was obvious from the letters of Joseph Chapleau, who had asked for full control of party affairs there and been denied by the prime minister. Nor had a clear alternative plan been devised. "If I must go uninstructed," Chapleau complained, "I shall not take the responsibility of what may happen."[12] In Quebec City, infighting between the supporters of Sir Hector Langevin and Sir Adolphe Caron was paralyzing party machinery. The popularity of both men had suffered as well, to the point that neither could even be certain of carrying his own constituency. The Grit press gloated that Caron, despairing of re-election in Quebec County, had decided to run instead in Rimouski *and* Chicoutimi. Langevin was still contesting his own re-election in Three Rivers, but to hedge his bets he was also running in Richelieu. These were bad signs for the Conservatives.[13]

On top of everything else, Macdonald had to worry about winning Kingston. He had not always won there in the past. In 1878, otherwise a banner year for the party, he had been upset by Alexander Gunn, a local grocer. Only in 1887, after occupying a seat elsewhere in the meantime, had Macdonald gained the seat back. Gunn was popular, and the Conservatives had hoped to avoid facing him again. They were soon disappointed. In the first week of the campaign Macdonald received word from John McIntyre, an old friend and colleague, that Gunn had been recruited by the Liberals. "We shall now have to fight in earnest," he judged.[14] Another local Tory reported that Gunn was struggling with personal issues—his finances were in tatters and his daughters were suffering from consumption—and concluded, "Altogether he is not the Gunn of former years. I don't think there will be much trouble in electing if the work is systematically gone about."[15] Macdonald might feel sympathy for Gunn, but that was good news if it was true. He could not afford to devote time to his own constituency when so many others required his attention.

The First Broadside

On February 6, Sir John was still in Ottawa, sorting out this kaleidoscope of local political difficulties, when the Conservative Party held its campaign kick-off rally at Shaftesbury Hall in Toronto. His presence was sorely missed, but five of his cabinet ministers—Sir John Thompson (Justice), Sir Mackenzie Bowell (Customs), John Carling (Agriculture), George Eulas Foster (Finance), and Frank Smith (without portfolio)—were there in his stead. The hall had been done up in patriotic style, decorated by the Young Men's Liberal-Conservative Association with grand banners. "Hail to Our Chieftain," one implored. "Canada for the Canadians" struck a not-too-subtle anti-American tone, as did "Ottawa, not Washington, our Capital." Then there was the party's featured campaign slogan, "The Old Leader, the Old Flag, the Old Policy." Even the programs were patriotic, adorned with a picture of Macdonald, a Union Jack, and a reminder from the grateful Rolland Paper Company that "BUT FOR THE N.P.—This Grade of Paper would not have been manufactured in Canada." An orchestra played in the gallery, filling time while the audience filed in, and within half an hour of the doors opening "a mass of close-packed humanity was simmering in impatient expectation."[16]

Mackenzie Bowell, a slightly built older man with a perfectly groomed snow-white beard—his younger Tory colleagues called him Grandpa Bowell—was first to address the gathering. Bowell was not known for his charisma, and his speech was a long, cumbersome journey through heaps of statistics and incriminating quotations from Sir Richard Cartwright. He only managed to get the audience going with a reference to the hard-working prime minister—"wherever he is, he is not sleeping"—and it was with considerable relief that they welcomed the next speaker, Sir John Thompson. This, they knew, would be the most important speech of the evening.

Thompson, whose large frame and confident demeanour gave him an imposing platform presence, had a well-deserved reputation for being a fair and judicious speaker. He was not the type to go off on a rant. His scathing attack against the Liberals and unrestricted reciprocity was, therefore, endowed with more *gravitas* than a typical stump speech would have possessed. He was almost entirely preoccupied with the trade question, stressing the economic achievements of the National Policy and lamenting the unknown dangers inherent in the Liberal scheme. He poked fun at Sir Richard Cartwright, likening his efforts to win converts to unrestricted reciprocity to those of a man who went fishing with a shotgun, then couldn't understand why he hadn't caught any fish. Finally, he insisted that the government could still negotiate partial reciprocity with the United States, even if James Blaine had said otherwise. Thompson reminded the cheering crowd—in another sly dig at Cartwright—that "you will not find it necessary to send to the Government of the United States a Senator from the State of Ontario." The people loved that last line.

Foster, Carling, and Smith each took his turn. There were the mandatory cheers for the Queen, and the satisfied patrons streamed out, in an orderly fashion, at about eleven o'clock. The event had gone well, in particular because the trade question had remained paramount. On a couple of occasions, audience members who were angry about the Jesuits' Estates Act heckled Thompson, who as an adult convert to Roman Catholicism was considered suspect by ultra-Protestants. At one point, as he discussed the threat of annexation, a voice cried out, "What about the Jesuits?" "That gentleman wants to know about the Jesuits," Thompson replied coolly. "They are not in this race. They are not in this question at all." His firmness won the day, though he had to apply it once or twice more in the course of his speech. Race and religion, thanks to his dignity and calm, were not forced into the limelight.

The Toronto rally gave the Tories the jump on the Liberals, allowing them to start framing the campaign as they wanted it: not as a contest between the National Policy and unrestricted reciprocity, but as one between loyalty and disloyalty. Thompson (and Foster, who had simply ignored his own hecklers) had also done well to steer the audience away from the delicate question of race and religion. The gritty edge to their rhetoric, even that of the usually moderate-minded Thompson, was cheered in the Conservative press. Even the Toronto *Mail*, which was as impartial as any newspaper, could not resist indulging in dramatic military metaphors. "Active hostilities have commenced," its editors observed. "The air is full of the smoke of battle and the booming of great guns. The first broadside of the campaign was fired in Toronto last evening."

Canadians did not have to wait long for the second broadside. The next night, Saturday, February 7, the nomination meeting of Sir John A. Macdonald was held in Kingston. To the great disappointment of the audience, the Old Man could not attend. But Sir Charles Tupper arrived just in time from London, England, having disembarked from the *Teutonic* in New York and travelled by private train car to Montreal and then Ottawa in the past two days. His journey had been eventful. He was first needled by reporters about the propriety of a diplomat taking part in an election campaign, and then about a lawsuit just brought forward by an American woman who claimed that, while serving as his typist during negotiations in Washington, Tupper had impregnated her. He simply shrugged off the accusation. Disappointed reporters were left with little to report, and fortunately for Sir Charles, the story went no further for the rest of the campaign.[17]

When he arrived in Ottawa on February 6, Tupper found the following cheerful letter waiting for him:

> My Dear Sir Charles,
>
> Welcome! There is a meeting at Kingston—my constituency—to organize and nominate me. I have made so many appointments for tomorrow that I must not leave town. It is asking you a great deal, but I know your good nature. Will you go up to-morrow morning; you arrive about four? If you can't manage it, will you ask Charlie to go?
>
> Always yours,
>
> J.A. McD.[18]

Tupper wasted no time boarding a train for the Limestone City, and was in his usual form addressing a thousand-strong audience at

Macdonald's nomination meeting. It was a Tupper speech through and through, combative and denunciatory, with some heavy hammering on the loyalty question. It was widely and triumphantly reported in Conservative newspapers on Monday, February 9—the Canadian press generally did not publish Sunday editions, and even during campaigns the parties tended to take the day off—but it was not, by any stretch, the most dramatic item that appeared on their front pages that morning.

Veiled Treason

That Saturday night, when he was supposed to be speaking at his own nomination meeting, Sir John A. Macdonald put the final touches on his campaign manifesto. It was titled, simply, "An Address to the Electors of Canada," and when set in type it occupied about two columns of newsprint.[19] No time was lost in distributing the manifesto to the Conservative press across the country, which presented it to voters on Monday morning. The contents were kept secret until then. Not a single line was released to independent or Liberal newspapers, despite valiant efforts by some to secure an advance copy. No one tried harder than the Ottawa correspondent of the Toronto *Mail*, who wired his editors at two o'clock on Sunday morning to finally admit defeat. "Have tried to beg, borrow, or steal the Premier's address, but can accomplish nothing," he reported. "I can't even get an inkling of its drift. The utmost secrecy is preserved."[20]

The truth was that no one, even among Conservatives, had advance information about the manifesto. The Old Man had taken on this responsibility himself. There had been advice from within the party, certainly—no shortage of that. The general tone of the Conservative campaign was already pretty clear, as well, having been laid out by Sir John Thompson in Toronto and then reiterated by Tupper in Kingston. But the crucial intellectual task of the campaign—choosing and explaining the party's platform—was handled by the prime minister alone.

The manifesto began simply, explaining why the election had been called in the first place. "The momentous questions now engaging public attention," the opening line declared, had to be put to the electorate before definitive action could be taken. Most important was the trade question. "We propose to continue," Macdonald wrote, "in the work to which we have applied ourselves, of building up on this continent, under the flag of England, a great and powerful nation."

A brief history lesson followed. The National Policy had been invented to get Canada out of the terrible depression of the 1870s, a depression that the Liberals had utterly failed to rescue the country from while they were in power. The Conservatives had battled that depression with an indomitable can-do spirit. They had introduced the National Policy, boldly raising tariffs against the United States, refusing to keep the Canadian market open to a country that refused to open its market to Canada. Then, Sir John recalled proudly, with not a little exaggeration, "You all know what followed. Almost as if by magic, the whole face of the country underwent a change. Stagnation and apathy and gloom—ay, and want and misery too—gave place to activity and enterprise and prosperity. The miners of Nova Scotia took courage; the manufacturing industries in our great centres revived and multiplied; the farmer found a market for his produce, the artisan and labourer employment at good wages, and all Canada rejoiced under the quickening impulse of a new-found life."

Having brought the economy back to life, the Conservative government had then achieved the impossible with the construction of the Canadian Pacific Railway. Through it they had turned the dream of an ocean-to-ocean nation into an accomplished fact, and now, through subsidized steamship lines, the trade of Canada was being carried all the way to the West Indies, Europe, China, Japan, and even the remote sister colony of Australia. There had been other great public works, including steady improvements to the railways and canals that were the infrastructure of the country, and all this had been achieved without endangering the finances of the federal government. There was much to be proud of.

Through it all, what had been the attitude of the Liberals? They had opposed the Conservative government every step of the way. They had denounced the National Policy. They had sneered at the very idea of building the railway. They had opposed the settlement of western Canada. They had attempted to block every Conservative effort to improve the country in the last thirteen years, and now, having failed, they had adopted unrestricted reciprocity, which really meant commercial union, which was not even the idea of the Liberals themselves, but of Erastus Wiman. It was a terrible idea; it would have terrible consequences. It would force the federal government to impose direct taxation on the people, to make up for the loss of revenue from the abolished tariff. A direct tax would cost every Canadian family fifteen dollars per year, a painful burden. Even more ominous were the political implications of unrestricted reciprocity. "It would, in my opinion," Sir John wrote, "inevitably result in the annexation of this Dominion to the United States."

Here was the heart of the matter, the fundamental reason why the Liberal Party must be defeated. The existence of Canada itself was at stake. For one hundred and fifty years the English and French—that "gallant race"—had lived peacefully together, along with all the Scottish and Irish who had arrived under the "protecting aegis of the British Crown." Would that history now come to an end? "To you Canadians I appeal," wrote Sir John, "and I ask you what have you to gain by surrendering that which your fathers held most dear?" The British connection had allowed Canadians to govern themselves, to grow and prosper, and to remain safe from external threats. Now, he asked of all Canadians, "Shall we endanger our possession of the great heritage bequeathed to us by our fathers, and submit ourselves to direct taxation for the privilege of having our tariff fixed at Washington, with a prospect of ultimately becoming a portion of the American Union?"

There could be only one answer to a question like that, and the manifesto may well have ended there. But there was one last statement, a final appeal from the exhausted old man who had led the country for so long.

> As for myself, my course is clear. A British subject I was born—A British subject I will die. With my utmost effort, with my latest breath, will I oppose the "veiled treason" which attempts by sordid means and mercenary proffers to lure our people from their allegiance. During my long public service of nearly half a century, I have been true to my country and its best interests, and I appeal with equal confidence to the men who have trusted me in the past, and to the young hope of the country, with whom rests its destinies for the future, to give me their united and strenuous aid in this, my last effort, for the unity of the Empire and the preservation of our commercial and political freedom.
>
> I remain, gentlemen,
> Your faithful servant,
> John A. Macdonald.

This final passage was shocking. Sir John was not accusing Laurier, Cartwright, and the Liberals of pursuing a misguided policy. He was accusing them of committing "veiled treason"—an insidious phrase filled with dark hints of sinister conspiracy—for the explicit purpose of selling out their own country. He could hardly have made a more offensive or outrageous accusation. Worse, he had done it without offering proof of his charge, forcing the people to trust his word—for now, at least—that this was not just the final desperate dodge of a wily old politician.

Macdonald had proof of a sort, of course. He had the Farrer pamphlet, with its matter-of-fact talk of annexation and its advice to unknown Americans about pressuring Canada into submission. He had not mentioned it in his manifesto because he had not yet been able to canvass his fellow Conservatives about what ought to be done with it. The only individual whom he seems to have let in on the secret was Governor General Lord Stanley, and Stanley had not given him the

The iconic image of the election of 1891. Though it is most obviously an appeal to patriotic sentiment, "The Old Flag, The Old Policy, The Old Leader" also conveys the notion that the National Policy was a success. Note that Macdonald is hoisted by a farmer on one side, with green pastures behind, and by an industrial worker on the other, before a backdrop of puffing smokestacks. "The Old Flag" itself is a variation on the Red Ensign that served as the unofficial national flag in the late nineteenth century. (LAC C-006536)

Wilfrid Laurier in 1891, when he was still proving (to himself as much as to his fellow Canadians) that a French Canadian Roman Catholic could successfully lead a federal political party. (LAC 1966-094, C-051333)

Sir John A. Macdonald in 1890. The photograph shows the advanced age of the "Old Man," but in his expression one can still discern some of the jocular confidence that made the prime minister such a beloved and effective politician. (LAC 1937-307, C-000686)

Sir Charles Tupper, the indomitable "War Horse of Cumberland," whose legendary campaigning abilities were put to good use by Macdonald in 1891. (LAC1936-270, PA-027743)

The brilliant and honorable Sir John Thompson, the indispensable man in the Macdonald cabinet during the election of 1891. His untimely death in 1894 was a tragedy for the country. (LAC 1964-144, C-000698)

D'Alton McCarthy, who warned that bayonets might one day be needed to establish an English-only "community of language" in Canada, and whose crusade prior to the election of 1891 was denounced by both the Liberal and Conservative parties. (LAC 1951-010, C-003845)

A lot is going on in this Conservative cartoon, which accuses Laurier and Cartwright of "Laying Out the Grit Campaign" in Washington, scheming to sell out Canada to the United States. At right, Secretary of State James Blaine drives a hard bargain over a "Map of the Canadian States." Erastus Wiman sits calmly at his side, Edward Farrer holds a copy of the *Globe*, and President Benjamin Harrison, made to look ridiculous by his oversized top hat, looks on passively at the head of the table. The letter in Cartwright's pocket reads, "Senator for the State of Ontario," and the scroll in Blaine's hand says, "Annexation." (LAC 1983-33-1099, C-006539)

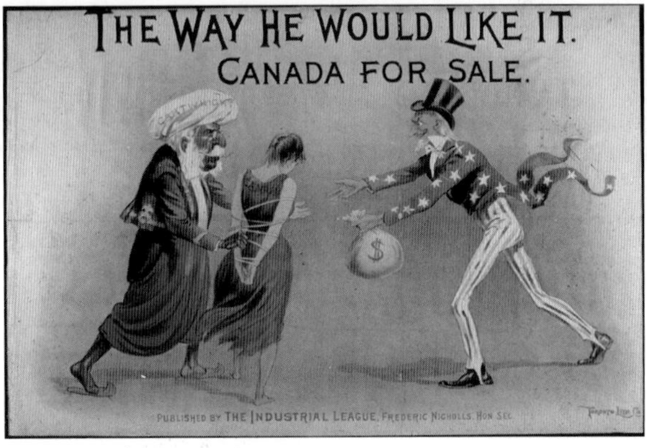

"Canada for Sale," the crudest cartoon of the campaign, depicts Cartwright as a dark-skinned slave trader and Canada as a bound young girl being sold into servitude to a sinister Uncle Sam. (LAC 1983-33-1103X, C-006533)

In this poster Macdonald holds a sign that reads "No Admittance" to Canada as Cartwright, Wiman, an unnamed "Heeler" carrying a bag of boodle, and a parade of "American competition" shuffle toward a wall representing the National Policy tariff. It says "Grit Party" on the donkey's rear end and "Senator for the State of Ontario" on the note in Cartwright's pocket. (LAC 1983-33-1108, C-006538)

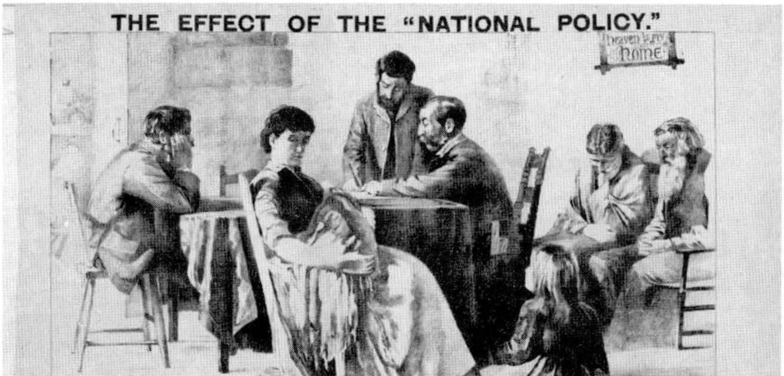

They tried hard, but the Liberals failed to produce a campaign poster in 1891 that had the poignancy of most Conservative material. "The Effect of the National Policy" is a good effort, depicting a family ruined by hard times, but the complicated scene and excessive text diminish its emotional impact. (LAC 1983-33-1094, C-095467)

Edward Blake, the tormented and ineffectual Liberal leader who shocked the party by choosing Laurier as his successor. It proved to be his shrewdest political decision. (LAC 1952-010, C-003833)

Sir Richard Cartwright in 1881, wearing a grave expression befitting his reputation as the "Blue Ruin Knight" of Canadian politics. (LAC 1936-270, PA 025546)

Honoré Mercier, the proud French Canadian nationalist whose Jesuits' Estates Act provoked a political crisis in 1888–89. (LAC accession no. 1963-157, PA-023361)

Another straightforward appeal to the heartstrings. The blurring of Canadian and British identity might feel alien to most Canadians of the twenty-first century, but it seemed natural to English-speaking Canadians of the Macdonald era. (LAC 1983-33-1083, C-111240)

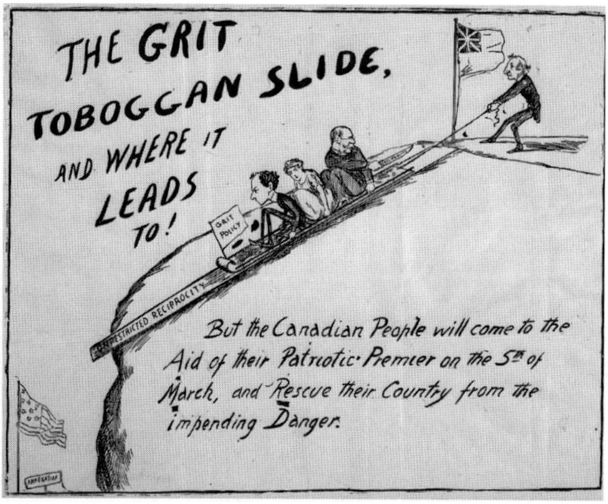

In "The Grit toboggan slide, and where it leads to!" the Old Man tugs at a toboggan (labelled "unrestricted reciprocity") carrying Laurier, Cartwright, and Miss Canada toward the abyss of "Annexation." (LAC, C-007369)

advice he was probably hoping to hear. His letter to Macdonald was restrained, but his distaste for the idea of using the pamphlet to attack the Liberals was clear. Only one passage contained "anything even approaching to treasonable language," Stanley concluded, adding, "Were I engaged in the election contest, I must say that I should not like to depend on this, as evidence of the annexationists being identical with the unrestricted reciprocity men." Having plainly expressed his opinion, he finished by dutifully observing, "Of course, however, you know best. I don't venture to express an opinion one way or the other, as to the policy of using this unpublished paper as a weapon of political war."[21]

Macdonald respected his opinion, and it is possible that Stanley had persuaded him to withhold the Farrer pamphlet. Even without using it, however, the Old Man had changed the tenor of the campaign by inserting that accusatory phrase, "veiled treason," into his manifesto. He had raised the stakes, and done so in the most inflammatory way possible. Once the blaze had been set, he knew, there might be no controlling it. Would the tactic work? And even if it did, could the damage that resulted be repaired? Sir John was taking a calculated risk, one that he believed he had to take. The only thing he could be sure of was that his supporters were going to absolutely love it.

The Conservative Offensive

On the morning of February 9 the Conservative press lavished praise on the "Address to the Electors of Canada." The charge of veiled treason was applauded, and in merciless editorials Tory editors called upon hidden reserves of righteous indignation to condemn the accused. All the leading regional party organs—among them the Halifax *Herald*, Saint John *Sun*, Montreal *Gazette* and *La Minerve*, Quebec *Mercury* and *Le Monde*, Toronto *Empire*, Ottawa *Citizen*, Hamilton *Spectator*, even the distant Manitoba *Free Press* and Victoria *Colonist*—indulged in verbal flag-waving and drum-beating on behalf of the Old Man. The attacks were not confined to the big dailies. Even the little Peterborough *Daily Review* got into the act with a poem composed for the occasion:

> Mr Wiman you're a sly man,
> But you can't bamboozle us.
> So stop your anti-British rant
> And don't make such a fuss.
>
> We were born beneath the Union Jack
> We'll die beneath its folds
> We would not sell that "meteor flag"
> For tons of Yankee gold.
>
> No Stars and Stripes for us, my man,
> No Presidential sway,
> We'll fight, if need be, for our Queen,
> And for our own John A.[22]

The Conservatives worked hard to make the most of the public stir created by the manifesto, and in the days following its release various regional lieutenants reinforced its message, holding big meetings and delivering hard-hitting speeches in their own districts. Sir Charles Tupper, having stopped for hurried conferences with party leaders in Ottawa and Montreal, embarked on a tour of the Maritimes with the force and fury of an Atlantic gale. He spoke in Moncton on the eleventh, in his hometown of Amherst, Nova Scotia, on the twelfth, then went south to Halifax, where he was to address a massive gathering along with his son Charles Hibbert Tupper and Sir John Thompson on the fourteenth.

Though the presence of the War Horse on the stump was the most dramatic boost to Conservative fortunes in the Maritimes, good news was also reaching Macdonald from other sources. George Foster reported from New Brunswick that "the finest nomination meeting ever held in St. John" had recently improved their prospects there.[23] Successful meetings were held in the three double constituencies of Prince Edward Island, where the Tory nominees, strongly supported by Premier Neil McLeod, embraced the overriding local issue—the Tunnel—as enthusiastically as they pledged their loyalty to the prime minister and the National Policy. In Prince they had a star candidate in Senator George Howlan, who had resigned his Senate seat to contest this election. The tunnel scheme was widely credited to him, boosting the credibility of the Conservatives on the issue, and there were high hopes that he might break the Liberal stranglehold on the Island.

In Quebec, where the fight had not been going smoothly, there was a cheerful report from an important source. Senator George Drummond, a spectacularly successful businessman and vice-president of the Bank of Montreal, was a fundraiser and organizer for the Quebec wing of the party. "Your admirable address rings like the blast of a trumpet," he wrote Macdonald on February 9. "We are organizing here fast ... the prominent grits are deserting." A meeting of Montreal manufacturers, a plum source of campaign funds, had been arranged—the next day the Manufacturers' Association would pronounce against the Liberals and unrestricted reciprocity—and pamphlets were being distributed. "No fear of the cities," Drummond assured the Old Man. "Everything looks well but of course," he added wryly, "I talk as downcast as possible."[24] It was easier to secure campaign funds, after all, if the situation appeared to be desperate.

The next night, February 10, a rally was held at the Château de Ramezay, a manor house that had stood on Notre Dame Street since the days of New France. The featured attraction was the oratory of Joseph-Adolphe Chapleau, and the theme of his address, following up on Macdonald's manifesto, was that unrestricted reciprocity would lead to annexation. Chapleau, still a striking man on the platform with his long hair and piercing eyes, observed that French Canadians had resisted American invasion in 1775 and 1812. How could they now allow Sir Richard Cartwright to steal their history from them? Perhaps Sir Richard had not disclosed his intentions, but it was revealing enough to see him acting "without official position, intriguing against his Government with American politicians." Chapleau hinted darkly that other plotters lurked in the wings, especially in Quebec. "If we have justifiable doubts on the aims of the Grits," he warned his audience, "we cannot ignore the secret hopes of the *rouges* of all shades."[25]

Due, in part, to the success of the Montreal rally, the Toronto *Mail* estimated that the Conservatives were now outpacing the Liberals in organization in Quebec, which was a pleasant surprise. Even the normally gloomy Chapleau reported to Macdonald that his troops were "confident and doing well."[26] Similar reports were coming in from all sides; the rank and file had clearly been inspired by Macdonald's manifesto. The Tory press was doing its part, hammering on the loyalty issue and publishing feature stories about the disastrous effect that unrestricted reciprocity would have on Canadian industries and, more poignantly, on working people. A good deal of credit for the party's surging confidence also went to the many constituency nomination meetings that had been held since the release of the manifesto. These feisty gatherings focused the energies of the local associations and allowed them to rally behind their candidates. There was some national direction to the campaign, of course, but the spadework was being done by thousands of Conservatives, toiling without fanfare in their own bailiwicks.

The loyalty theme was proving to be most effective in the Maritimes. Thompson, Tupper, and his able son Charles Hibbert were reunited in Halifax on Saturday, February 14, after conducting separate speaking tours in the preceding three days. Their energetic efforts were exalted by the party organs, especially the hyper-partisan Halifax *Herald*, which framed the election as a life-or-death struggle between the heroic Tories and the sinister "annexation party."[27] The *Herald* also printed excerpts from articles in American newspapers that would infuriate loyal readers. Most obnoxious among those quoted was the Boston *Republic*, which suggested that it was high time for the Canadian people to stop worshipping Queen Victoria, "an obese, beer-guzzling German woman who has no more claim on them than has the Ameer of Afghanistan."[28] That was pure gold for the *Herald*, which was doing its best to associate the Liberals with this kind of impudent Yankee slander.

At a spectacular event in Halifax on Saturday night, Thompson and the Tuppers entertained a crowd of about four thousand supporters that had been crammed into the militia drill shed, a cavernous structure adorned with red and blue bunting, Union Jack and Nova Scotia flags, and banners reading, "We Welcome Our Leader" and "God Save the Queen." The *Herald* overreached when it reported continuous deafening applause throughout the four-hour meeting, but not by much. The atmosphere was festive, to say the least, for the Conservative faithful. Sir Charles delivered the longest and most stirring address. He spoke for two hours and tore a terrible strip off Erastus Wiman, the odious "renegade Canadian," whom he portrayed as the evil genius behind the behaviour of the Liberal Party. When he finished his speech, a great roar filled the drill shed, and Tupper observed with satisfaction, "There's victory in that ringing cheer—the election is as good as won."[29]

It certainly seemed so. By raising the spectre of veiled treason and falling back on the loyalty cry, Macdonald and the Conservatives had raised the stakes and set Laurier and the Liberals on the defensive. How they responded was essential, for it would set the tone of debate for the rest of the campaign.

The Counterattack

Across Canada the Grits were outraged and indignant, but they were not particularly surprised. They had anticipated the flag-waving tone of the Tory campaign, and if the extremity of the charges made against them was a shock, the fact that Macdonald had made them was not. Now, as the "Address to the Electors of Canada" was circulated through the constituencies, the Liberals were being forced to make a hurried decision about the character of their own campaign. There were only two practical options. On the one hand, if they judged it would be too difficult to refute the charge of veiled treason, they could try to soften their message. They could retreat from unrestricted reciprocity, return to a more generic platform of seeking closer trade relations with the United States, and turn their attention to subjects like the McGreevy scandal. By doing so the Liberals could assuage fears that they were leading the country down a dangerous path and avoid further criticisms about the complications of unrestricted reciprocity. It was not very heroic, but it could work.

On the other hand, Laurier and the Liberals could collectively take a deep breath, stiffen their spines, and defend their platform as aggressively as the Conservatives had rallied round the National Policy. That meant tackling the charge of veiled treason head on: breaking it down, debunking it, ridiculing it, and finally destroying it. As they moved away from the National Policy nationalism of the Tories, the Liberals would also have to stake their future on a different brand of nationalism. They would have to make people believe in a confident continentalism, a welcoming of closer ties with the United States, while proudly maintaining Canada's economic and political sovereignty. It was not the safest course, perhaps, but it was the bravest. And that is what the Liberals chose to do as the campaign entered its second week.

The most thundering reply to the Conservative onslaught came, fittingly, from Sir Richard Cartwright. At a rally in Oshawa, a farming town a few miles east of Toronto, Cartwright made an appearance in support of the local candidate, James Davidson, who was running hard against the incumbent Conservative. It might have been just one of the countless small-town speeches that Sir Richard would deliver during the campaign, but because the Macdonald manifesto had been released that morning—and because the Grit press had not yet been able to respond to it—his remarks took on special significance.

Cartwright was in a fighting mood. He was the principal target of the charge of veiled treason, and he was outraged at the prime minister for making what Cartwright considered a vile personal attack. Contempt for the Old Man dripped from every word of his one-hour address. He mocked the reasons given for the dissolution of Parliament. He noted that the government had no chance of getting partial reciprocity with the United States (the supposed rationale for calling the election) and came armed with statistics to prove that their only alternative, the National Policy, had been a total failure. Most of all, Sir Richard stuck to his guns on the question of unrestricted reciprocity. It was an honest and patriotic policy, he insisted. There was no shame in advocating a trade platform that offered the best hope for the future of Canada.

Cartwright did not even shirk a question from a young man who asked if U.R. meant discrimination against British manufacturers. That was a delicate question, one that Liberals generally avoided answering directly. The answer from Sir Richard was a firm yes. The Liberal policy was a Canada-first policy, and if it were in the national interest, then yes, there would still be tariffs against Great Britain even as there was free trade with the United States. In fact, since free trade would improve Canadian-American relations and eliminate the chance of Anglo-American friction developing on that front, it would be to the advantage of the Empire. "I am prepared to prove," Sir Richard declared, "that it is to the interest of Great Britain as well as of Canada that we should regulate our own commercial affairs with a view to maintaining Canadian interests, as we should have done long ago."[30]

If Cartwright was leading the charge in English Canada, the premier of Quebec, Honoré Mercier, was doing the same for the Liberals in French Canada. He had gone all in from the outset of the campaign, placing his personal popularity and prestige, not to mention the services of his powerful political machine, at the disposal of the federal Liberal Party. On the evening of February 9, hours after the release of the Macdonald manifesto, Mercier gave a major address in Montreal that spelled out the terms of his participation in the campaign. There was no doubt that he was, as the Montreal *Witness* put it, "Hand in Glove with Mr Laurier—A FIRM LIBERAL ALLIANCE."[31] Mercier was getting something in return, too. Laurier, he told an audience of five thousand, had agreed to support every plank of the autonomous "provincial rights" platform that the Quebec government had been pushing since the Interprovincial Conference of 1887. That was an important concession, because the strict enforcement of provincial rights would weaken the federal government and secure a more autonomous place for Quebec within Confederation.

Had Laurier really agreed to this? The federal party supported the doctrine of provincial rights generally, but Mercier's long list included specific policies designed to tie the hands of the federal government in its dealings with the provinces. It was, as the Conservative press depicted it the next day, an extension of the destabilizing Mercier policy of "the provinces against the Dominion."[32] At the Montreal meeting the premier brandished a terse telegram from Laurier, confirming his acceptance of the provincial rights platform as the basis of their new alliance. But Laurier was not in attendance, despite published reports that he would share the stage with Mercier as a demonstration of solidarity. The Liberal press lamely reported that poor weather had detained him, even though he had arrived in Montreal well in advance of the rally. What was really going on? Where was Laurier?

During all the excitement over the Macdonald manifesto, the Liberal leader had been somewhat forgotten. In a way that was not surprising, since the prime minister had ignored him in the document—there was just one mention of him, in the same breath as Cartwright. As well, Laurier had purposely kept a low profile in the first week of the campaign. On February 5, he briefly visited Toronto to meet party organizers, then was quickly back to Montreal, where he spent most of his time behind the scenes at the party headquarters at St. Lawrence Hall. His movements were duly noted in the press, but there really was not much to report. Laurier said practically nothing to reporters and he made no speeches that could be quoted or editorialized about. To this point, he almost seemed content to allow Cartwright and Mercier to lead the party.

Those who knew Laurier well were not surprised. He was, by nature, a wait-and-see kind of politician. His natural caution was now being magnified by the fact that this was his first national campaign as Liberal leader. Outside of Quebec City and to a lesser extent Montreal, he did not have the friendly, easy relationships with local candidates and organizers that Macdonald had cultivated for decades on the Conservative side. Liberals were still getting to know him as their chief, and he was still getting to know them. Thus he was holding numerous face-to-face meetings with his supporters, the unglamorous foot soldiers who would be knocking on doors for him, before thrusting himself into the spotlight with a major public meeting. His excuse for missing the Montreal rally had been a weak one, indeed. But he was about to remedy that in grand style.

Laurier broke his silence on February 11, in Quebec City, before an impressive and enthusiastic crowd at Jacques Cartier Hall. Every detail had been arranged to add drama to the occasion, right from the moment his sleigh departed the St. Louis Hotel at seven o'clock that evening. The brass band of the local Quebec Hussars played merrily as the grand procession snaked through the snowy streets toward the hall, and an honour guard of rowdy Laval University students, each carrying a lit torch, marched alongside Laurier's sleigh. It took a long time to get to the venue and get everyone settled after that, and it was not until a quarter to nine that the meeting finally came to order. Laurier, unlike Macdonald, liked to have his wife attend his rallies; Zoe was seated to the right of the platform, beaming at her husband. She was not, however, his most noteworthy supporter in attendance. Sitting beside the Liberal leader was the dapper Israël Tarte, the turncoat editor of *Le Canadien*, the man who knew all of the skeletons in the Tory closet. His presence among his newfound Liberal friends was an ominous development for the Conservatives.

Laurier rattled the Tories with more than the defection of Tarte. He delivered an unflinching attack on the Macdonald government, never vulgar, but certainly more hard-edged than his usually urbane and magnanimous oratory. Of the National Policy he had nothing good to say. Macdonald claimed he had brought prosperity to Canada, Laurier noted, but this was simply not true. "Where are the factories he was going to create?" he asked his audience. "They are yet to be erected." The exodus of Canadians to the United States in search of work, a painful fact of life in Quebec, was expounded upon.

Then, in the crux of his address, Laurier dealt directly with the charge of veiled treason that Sir John had made against Laurier and the Liberal Party. "In his manifesto Sir John, as usual, appeals to the loyalty of his British subjects against the prejudices of the Liberal Party. He says we are disloyal because we want reciprocity. Then he himself has been guilty of that crime, for formerly he advocated such a policy and recently, when he found out that the country was clamouring after free trade, he again committed the same crime by stealing from us that part of the program. No, gentlemen; as of yore we are still true and loyal to our Sovereign Lady the Queen."[33]

That received a hearty ovation from the crowd. So did the next line: "But if our interests were in opposition to those of England," Laurier insisted, refusing to back down on this oft-unspoken question, "we would stick to ours by all means. We are Canadians and we will watch Canada's welfare before all." Nor was that the end. The premature dissolution of Parliament was denounced as "a political crime" that the prime minister had knowingly committed. His charge that a direct tax would follow the adoption of unrestricted reciprocity was denied (though there was no explanation of where the lost tax revenue would come from). But the most striking words, the ones that stayed with his listeners, were those Laurier had uttered on the subject of loyalty and patriotism.

Laurier struck the same tone when he answered Macdonald in writing, with his own address to the electors, on February 13. This was a straight-to-the-point piece of work, shorter than that of Macdonald, and sharply focused on three topics: the premature dissolution, the failure of the National Policy, and the accusations of disloyalty made by the prime minister. The first was a reprehensible device used to disenfranchise thousands of honest Canadians and tilt the election to the Conservative Party. The second was "not only a failure but a fraud," and one that had instituted the very same tariff discrimination against Great Britain that was now being denounced by supposedly patriotic Tories. The third and most important issue, the loyalty cry, was "a totally uncalled for appeal, for in the present contest nothing is involved which in one way or another can affect the existing status of Canada."[34] Laurier's appeal to the voters lacked the ringing phrases of the Macdonald manifesto, to be sure. But the tone was defiant. The Liberal course—full speed ahead with U.R. nailed to the mast—was clear.

As the campaign moved into its third week, the debate was changing in important ways. First, it was becoming narrower. The Macdonald manifesto of February 9 and the Conservative offensive that followed it were designed to reduce the election to a flag-waving contest. If the loyalty cry were the only thing that mattered—if the Dominion was gravely endangered by the veiled treason of the Liberal party—then the Tories were in the driver's seat. And the Liberals seemed to agree that the election boiled down to a single issue. They were framing it differently, however, by arguing that the voters had a choice between the failed National Policy and their own unrestricted reciprocity. The shift of focus was in their interest, since the weakness of the economy and the years of mass emigration were strong evidence that the National Policy was failing Canadians. At the same time, the Liberals were holding their ground on the loyalty question, arguing that by putting the interests of Canada (not those of Great Britain) first, it was they, not the Tories, who were true patriots.

The concentration of both parties on this single issue was both good and bad. On the negative side, it was causing various issues that mattered to Canadians—temperance, poverty, women's suffrage, the right to strike, the state of public health, the quality of the civil service, and the McGreevy scandal, for example—to be neglected. On the positive side, it was pushing questions of race and religion onto the margins of campaign debates. Two years earlier, when the passage of Quebec's Jesuits' Estates Act had nearly incited a national crisis, it seemed inevitable that French and English Canadians would be pitted against each other in the next election. This much-dreaded racial conflict had failed to materialize, however, because the trade question and the loyalty cry were sucking up all the oxygen. Neither D'Alton McCarthy, running in Simcoe North, nor the Equal Rights Association had been able to attract more than passing attention in the early stages of the campaign. The E.R.A. released its own manifesto on February 11, urging Ontario voters to support candidates who took a hard line against the Catholic Church of Quebec, but outside of super-Protestant organs like the Toronto *Mail* and Montreal *Witness* it was largely ignored. At the same time, the hyper-Catholicism of the ultramontane clergy in Quebec was being similarly shunted aside, a welcome development for both political parties. Mercier himself was, for the most part, on his best behaviour. While he was hammering away on the theme of provincial rights, and thus embarrassing Laurier to some extent, he was not saying anything about race and religion that would aggravate English Canadians and injure Laurier and the federal Liberals.

The second major change in the campaign was in its tone. The language had become darker. There was little of the sportsmanship and humour that characterized healthy political debate in Canada. The charge of veiled treason was vicious and mean spirited, even if the Tories believed it to be true, and the Liberals responded with ratcheted-up rhetoric about their lying, despicable opponents. The Toronto *Mail*, which had done its share of poisoning the national debate in recent years, detected this shift before most other newspapers. Its editorial on February 12 struck a note of alarm and regret: "It is safe to say that a more violent campaign than that now pending has seldom been experienced in Canada. Though but a week old, it has called out all the accumulated bitterness of the past four years, and has created ill-feelings and animosities that it will take many months to allay."

The election was nearing its midway point, and the tone of the debate—already rancorous—was about to deteriorate even further. Sir John A. Macdonald, for so long cloistered at Earnscliffe by illness or the unrelenting crush of party business, was finally on the move. He was about to depart for Toronto, and there he would drop a bombshell on Laurier and the Liberals that would produce one of the most famous—or infamous—moments in the history of the Dominion.

EIGHT

The Academy of Music

The first indication that Tuesday, February 17, was to be an extraordinary day was a front-page announcement in the Saturday edition of the Toronto *Empire*:

THE PREMIER
Accompanied by Sir Charles Tupper
WILL SPEAK IN TORONTO

A monster Conservative rally was planned in the city on Tuesday evening, and that was not all. There was thrilling, mysterious news. Sir John would not just be giving his usual stump speech. Instead, the *Empire* hinted, he would reveal damning evidence of a treasonous Liberal conspiracy. But what evidence? What conspiracy? There were no further details other than the time of the rally (six o'clock) and the location (the Toronto Academy of Music, on King Street between

York and Simcoe). The exact nature of the Old Man's accusations was left to the fertile imaginations of the newspaper's readers.

There was an excited stir in the Queen City over the next three days. The *Empire*, plus the *World* and *News*, the lesser Tory-leaning papers, did their best to build suspense and tease their readers with hints of intrigue and scandal. On Monday, the day before the meeting, Macdonald and Tupper arrived together aboard a C.P.R. express and checked promptly into the Queen's Hotel. A vast red-brick building with a four-storey centre block and three-storey wings on either side, the Queen's Hotel on Front Street was *the* place to stay in Toronto. Its interior was elegant and extravagant, and the south-facing upper windows boasted a magnificent view beyond Union Station to the lapping waves of Lake Ontario. In its most infamous room, the Red Parlour, the prime minister had convened many secret meetings, brokered many deals, and collected vast campaign contributions over the years. On Tuesday morning, the day of the rally, he and Tupper held court for several hours, turning the hotel into what the Toronto *World* described as "the Mecca of scores of Conservative workers from all parts of the province."[1] In the afternoon, Sir John retired to his room to rest. He had a big night ahead.

As the working hours passed there was a great feeling of anticipation in the city. The sun was just going down on an unseasonably warm afternoon when, at five o'clock, people began to gather on the muddy brown thoroughfare of King Street. Within an hour thousands were milling about in front of the Academy of Music. Reporters from all the Toronto dailies weaved through the crowd, scribbling impressions that they knew would be splashed across the front pages in the morning. Young fellows in the crowd jostled for a good spot close to the front doors. There was considerable elbowing and shoving, and gentlemen and ladies frowned as their trousers and skirts were muddied to the knees in the mud, slush, and commotion. There was, of course, no shortage of gossip. According to one widely circulated rumour, Macdonald had documents proving that the *Globe* was linked to a conspiracy to sell out Canada to the

United States. If true, it was a delicious story indeed. But no one in the crowd knew for sure.

Only half a dozen men in Canada knew what document, and what incriminating evidence within its pages, was folded in the inside pocket of the prime minister's coat. It was, of course, the Farrer pamphlet, evidence of "veiled treason" that Macdonald had for two months kept hidden from the country. Tonight, at last, he would reveal its shocking contents in the most dramatic fashion possible. But for now he remained at the Queen's Hotel, patiently readying himself for the teeming humanity awaiting him at the Academy of Music.

Chaos on King Street

It was only six o'clock and already there was no hope of accommodating everyone who was waiting, with diminishing patience, amid the commotion outside the Academy of Music. A limited number of tickets had been made available to local Conservatives, and as the bells tolled six around the city, the stage door was opened early to admit them. The throng, sensing opportunity, made a sudden rush forward. The stage door was hurriedly closed, and those fortunate Tories with tickets were advised to go around the building to the side entrance off Dorset Street, which led to the basement. As they slipped into the theatre, largely unnoticed, the crowd out front strained against the front doors. A good-sized contingent of Toronto police was in attendance, but they were outnumbered so hopelessly that they had no chance of herding everyone into an orderly line to await the opening of the main doors. All the police could do was guard against trouble developing on the street, and so far, aside from the many sore ribs suffered among the thousands still outside, there had been no serious incidents. It was a rough-and-tumble crowd but the atmosphere was light. As the *Empire* cheerfully put it, those outside "surged and jostled in good nature."[2]

Seven o'clock arrived. There was a great shout, then an enormous surge to the front. The crowd charged through the front doors, much as a fast-flowing current might squeeze through narrow riverbanks, and within seconds the theatre was filled. Not for another twenty minutes did the organizers manage to push the front doors shut. About four thousand people were crammed inside, far beyond the hall's normal capacity, and still—by the excited estimate of the *Empire*, at least—fifteen or twenty thousand people hoped to get in, blocking carriage and streetcar traffic from York to Simcoe Street. There was a sign of frustration and impending trouble: a large gas lamp outside the hall was "carried away" by criminals, rupturing the gas main beneath it.[3] The lamps inside were rendered unusable, and the organizers were forced to throw the switch on the relatively untested electric lighting for the rest of the evening.

The atmosphere inside was exciting and expectant. The seats were filled, of course, and many people had been stuffed into the aisles, the limited standing room at the rear and sides, and even in the window embrasures. Some seats had been ripped from their moorings, and the blue plush railings at the back of the theatre had been badly muddied by dirty feet. Windowpanes had been smashed; door fastenings had been broken. Three hundred leading Conservatives were assembling on the stage and not everybody, it appeared, was friendly to their cause. The reporter from the *News* spotted one bald, grey-whiskered gentleman making himself particularly obnoxious, having "made it his special business to shout in drunken tones at the members of the committee who were arranging the people on the platform."[4] An unruly pack of young men, somewhat out of control, dominated the orchestra pit. A contingent of young Tories hustled about, frantically trying to maintain order.

All of the reporters observed that hundreds of ladies were in attendance. (Several who remained trapped in the throng outside had actually fainted, leading the *News* to state the next day, rather piggishly, that "many a woman learned what it is to take an active part in politics.")[5] The dresses of those seated inside lent welcome colour to an audience that was otherwise a sea of dark suits and hats. The decorating committee, always important at these events, had spared no expense. All pillars and boxes bore signs inscribed with patriotic mottoes such as "God Save the Queen" and "Disloyalty is at a Discount." Behind the stage hung huge banners reading "Hail to Our Chieftain" and, in a special dig at Erastus Wiman and Sir Richard Cartwright, "No United States Senators Need Apply." Each banner depicted three shields across its centre, one for each of "The Old Flag," "The Old Leader," and "The Old Policy." Along the balcony ran a sign that summed up the theme of the evening. "Ottawa, Not Washington, Our Capital," it defiantly read. "Canada for the Canadians."[6]

Outside, an anxious John Willison, being jostled like everyone else, worried that if the crowd became too restless there might be a riot. The *Globe* offices at Yonge and Melinda streets were only a short march to the east, and later in the evening Willison would arrange for fifty police officers to guard the building. For the time being, however, good humour prevailed. The people had come there to see Sir John, and they would stay until they saw him. They did not have much longer to wait. Just past seven-thirty, the prime minister's horse-drawn carriage finally came into view.

It was a remarkable achievement that the carriage even got as far as the Academy before it was completely hemmed in by the pressing crowd. Inside sat a calm Macdonald and four others: Harry Brock, a local party man who would introduce the prime minister; Col. Fred Denison, provincial M.P.P. and brother of George Denison, the police magistrate and president of the Imperial Federation League; and two very fortunate members of the Young Men's Liberal-Conservative Club of Toronto. None of them, for the moment at least, was going anywhere. Appeals were made to the crowd to make way for the prime minister. Instead, there were cries for him to make a speech. Ten long claustrophobic minutes passed during which Macdonald and his entourage were trapped in the carriage. Eventually Harry Brock, showing some dash, took matters into his own hands. He stepped out and, with the assistance of the police, formed a wedge that managed to shepherd the prime minister—not without some uncomfortable bumping and jostling—through the cheering crowd and into the theatre. Denison and the two young Conservatives were not quick enough, however, and had to remain sitting helplessly in their carriage as the crowd again closed ranks around it.

Inside the Academy

There was a thunderous ovation when Macdonald entered the theatre. It sustained itself for several minutes as he was slowly ushered to the stage, and as he moved forward he smiled and bowed several times to acknowledge the cheers. As the *Empire* fervently described the occasion, "Whirlwind after whirlwind of applause and cheers shook the building. Hats, handkerchiefs, flags were waved in indescribable enthusiasm."[7] When he stepped onto the platform the audience burst spontaneously into a rendition of "For He's a Jolly Good Fellow," accompanied by a booming drum that someone had come upon, and ten minutes passed before the serenade petered out. All along Macdonald smiled and remained quiet, seated prominently among the luminaries on the stage. The time was approaching eight o'clock. It was time for the great meeting to get under way.

Unfortunately, there was a small problem. Sir Charles Tupper was scheduled to speak before Sir John, but when Harry Brock called the meeting to order the War Horse of Cumberland was nowhere to be found. In fact he was, like so many others, stuck in the crowd outside. His carriage had arrived too late for him to get entry through the main doors, and without much ado Sir Charles began scouring the building for an alternative route inside. The same idea, of course, had occurred to others. One enterprising fellow had located an open cellar window and was letting people in for the exorbitant sum of twenty-five cents, leading them one at a time through the building, up a back stair, and into the rigging and rafters above the stage. Another young man (or three young men; there were conflicting reports) had come across a ladder that, for a relatively modest charge of ten cents, allowed people to scale a ten-foot wooden fence and try a back door. (Those without tickets were refused entry anyway and found, to their dismay, that it would cost them another ten cents to climb back out.)

Tupper was a broad and beefy customer, and he was not about to squeeze through any cellar windows. But going up the ladder, though not terribly dignified, was feasible. So it was that the former minister of finance, incumbent high commissioner to London, and future prime minister began climbing. When he reached the top Tupper was forced to balance uneasily on the fence as the ladder was hoisted over, then set up again on the other side. It was a perilous business—Sir Charles was wearing a cumbersome greatcoat and was, after all, just shy of his seventieth birthday—but he managed not to fall before the ladder was ready for him to descend. He almost crashed onto a pile of loose bricks on his way down, but was helped to a safe landing. Then, collecting his dignity, Sir Charles strode into the Academy of Music to deliver the opening address. The amused reporters who observed this spectacle did not find out, apparently, whether he had been forced to give over his ten cents for the use of the ladder.

Sir Charles entered the theatre just as Harry Brock, the chairman of the meeting, was making his introductory remarks. Brock was doing his best to whip the people up. He praised the "loyal citizens of Toronto," not surprisingly, and thanked the prime minister for coming to address them. Then he taunted their opponents: "Where are the leaders of the Opposition?" The audience liked that. "In the soup!" they cried. "In Washington!"[8] Brock continued speaking until Tupper finally pushed his way through the crowd and onto the stage. Seeing that Sir Charles was somewhat out of breath, one of the local members of Parliament, Emerson Coatsworth, thoughtfully rose and addressed the meeting for a few moments to allow him to recover.

When Tupper finally stepped to the front of the stage, there was practically pandemonium.

So much commotion was made, in fact, that Tupper could not begin his speech for several minutes. He attempted several times to get under way, but the clamour was too great. He urged the crowd to think of the reputation of Toronto for hearing a man out. He joked that they ought to adopt "a little unrestricted reciprocity in the way of order."[9] Finally, Tupper sat down in frustration. He stayed there for a few minutes until the police were able to physically eject some of the leading troublemakers. As the fracas went on Sir John remained seated, still smiling, but with a look of mild annoyance on his face. He never liked to see meetings get out of control like this.

When things at last settled down, Harry Brock reintroduced Tupper—"the most eloquent man on the continent of America"—and Sir Charles delivered one of his classic bludgeoning speeches. He touted the National Policy and the Canadian Pacific Railway, and bashed the Liberals, who had been too short-sighted to support them. He singled out Sir Richard Cartwright, sarcastically observing that he was a "man of marked ability" and "unquestionable courage" so that the audience could shout back, "But he is no good!" He asked them what unrestricted reciprocity, which was the same thing as commercial union, really meant. "Annexation!" And where had it come from? "The head, leader and front of commercial union is Mr. Erastus Wiman," Tupper intoned. The crowd hissed. "Mr. Erastus Wiman is a very clever man," he continued, "and he has laboured night and day for years for the purpose of undermining the loyalty and the integrity of Canada. It is not disguised." Sir Charles then claimed that in a recent speech Wiman had given in the United States, the "Dictator from New York" had declared, "I have got some young Canadian statesmen on the Liberal side that I can mould like putty"—the audience laughed—"and I can make them do just what I want."

Tupper kept hammering at Wiman for some time. Perhaps, he

admitted, Wiman had enslaved Sir Richard Cartwright and John Charlton. But Conservatives, even most sensible Liberals, would never fall for his attempts to "break down this glorious Canada of ours from its high, exalted and noble position to one of serfdom to the United States." Across the country the good citizens of Canada were rallying against those Liberals who had fallen for the evil deception of unrestricted reciprocity. A Conservative victory was assured. And on it went. Tupper was accustomed to being the final speaker of the night, and he found it hard to let go of his audience. At one point he stopped, remembering that the people were there to see the prime minister, and conceded, "I must not take up more of your time." The crowd dutifully cried, "Go on!" So he went on. He couldn't help it. He was, after all, Sir Charles Tupper.

At last the War Horse sat down, to a generous ovation mixed with a few errant catcalls, and the great moment arrived. Harry Brock made a brief introduction, and when Macdonald leaned forward in his chair the place went wild. Hats, handkerchiefs, walking sticks, umbrellas, and programs were waved in the air, and hoarse cheering throughout the hall blended into a deafening roar. Sir John stood silently, his eyes perhaps glistening a little, his mouth turned slightly upward in an appreciative smile. At one point the cheers faded somewhat, only to have someone shout, "For He's a Jolly Good Fellow!" The whole audience broke into the song, the ladies' voices soaring clearly above the din. When that died down Sir John seemed ready to speak, but a member of Parliament from Toronto, George Ferguson, leapt from his seat and pinned a buttonhole bouquet on the prime minister's lapel. Into his arms Ferguson placed a heap of lilies, orchids, and chrysanthemums, and there Sir John stood, laden with flowers, as he finally began to address the crowd.

Unveiling the Conspiracy

At first the people were somewhat startled. Sir John was dressed sharply, wearing a bold red tie and cameo pin, but he looked distressingly frail and he sounded even worse. He could not be heard beyond the first few rows. "Mr. Chairman, Ladies and Gentlemen," he started softly, "I need scarcely hope that my feeble and aged voice will reach to the extremities of this hall." As everyone strained to hear, he complimented Sir Charles on a fine speech. He then said, "It is always a great pleasure for me to come to Toronto," and the hometown crowd burst into proud and relieved applause.

He dwelled on Toronto for a while, musing that it was here that the effects of the National Policy had been most pronounced. "Every time I visit it," he said grandly, "I see palaces springing up; I see magnificent edifices devoted to Canadian industry." He was now speaking with more force. "I see evidences of wealth and prosperity ... Look at the villages and towns of Ontario; the hamlets have grown up to be villages and the villages to be towns, and the towns are now aspiring to be cities, all through the action of the National Policy." That drew fervent cheers. "I would want no greater praise than that there should be engraved on my tombstone," he continued, making a heartstring-tugging allusion to his fading strength, "that I introduced and carried into Parliament the National Policy, giving protection to native industries and making the country prosperous." It was not the whole truth, not to an impartial observer at least. The National Policy had not been such a resounding success. But this was no time for splitting hairs, and anyway, there were few impartial observers inside the theatre.

Macdonald praised the Canadian Pacific Railway, the greatest accomplishment of his party, for opening up the country. He now pledged to subsidize the construction of a line of fast steamships that could carry Canadian goods across the Pacific to the markets of China and Japan. (That was an eye-popper of a promise, sure to cost millions, but it was predictably well received by the crowd.) These new trade links would insulate Canada against any trade slowdown caused by the petulant behaviour of the Americans, should they choose to maintain their ludicrous McKinley Tariff. Then there was, most importantly, the

British connection. Canadians had always been able to rely on the British market, and they could do so still. Under his watch there would be no weakening of trade relations with the mother country, no tariff discrimination against Great Britain, as the Liberals were shamefully proposing.

Macdonald was edging toward the main thrust of his speech. Now the crowd was quiet as he spoke. Sir John explained the circumstances of the dissolution of Parliament, reminding his audience that it was James Blaine, not himself, who had been in the wrong. Then, addressing the thousands of supporters in the theatre and the hundreds of thousands who would read his words the next day in the newspapers, the prime minister launched his extraordinary accusation against the Liberal Party.

> Canadian traitors, as Sir Charles Tupper has truly called them, have gone to Washington, have told them, You should not concede to Canada anything; if you do not put the screws to Canada, if you do not put every possible obstruction upon her trade, if you do not coerce them, bulldoze them in every possible way, you will not get Canada; we will assist you, and with our assistance you will get Canada. That is a very strong statement for me to make, but I make it. I now take the opportunity of making the charge.
>
> I say that there is a deliberate conspiracy, in which some of the leaders of the Opposition are more or less compromised, I say that there is a deliberate conspiracy, by force, by fraud, or by both, to force Canada into the American union.[10]

There it was—the charge upon which Sir John had decided to stake the election. Now was the moment for elaboration. First, he wondered, had anyone ever heard of an Opposition agent meeting secretly with the leaders of a foreign power and advising them against the interests of Canada's elected government?

"Never!" cried the audience. "Name him!"

"Yes," Macdonald replied, "I will name him." The audience waited expectantly. "In the first place," he asked, "you know Mr. Farrer?"

"Hear, hear!"

"People know who Mr. Farrer is. He was once the editor of the *Mail*, when it was a Tory paper." Sir John was getting to the best part. "He is now the editor, philosopher, and friend of Sir Richard Cartwright, and the controlling influence over that great, that glorious and consistent newspaper—the *Globe*.

"Mr. Farrer," Macdonald continued, building the suspense, "has been down to Washington several times. Perhaps he is there tonight."

Someone called out from the crowd, "He is here tonight."

It was true. Farrer had strolled by the great throng on King Street earlier, seen by countless people, and stopped with John Willison to watch what was unfolding. The *Empire* reporter had since spotted them in the hall together. Farrer was sitting with Willison, nonplussed, watching calmly as the prime minister brought the crowd to a fever pitch by accusing him of committing treason.

"I am very glad that he is," Macdonald answered, not missing a beat, "because he will hear what I have to say."

The prime minister connected the dots between Farrer and Sir Richard Cartwright, portraying the latter, and not Wilfrid Laurier, as the driving force behind the madness that had overtaken the Liberal Party. Already he had drawn laughs for referring to Cartwright as "Mr. Richard" accidentally, then joking, "I do not think he can, in any decency, keep the title he got from the Queen when he becomes Senator for Ontario." His conduct, however, had been no laughing matter. Macdonald accused Cartwright of having "sneaked down to Washington, sneaked down, coaxed by Wiman," then skulking about, inquiring about "whether he could not sell Canada and sell me." The audience guffawed at that ridiculous thought.

What was the evidence of his sinister intent? Macdonald explained that Edward Farrer, "the conscience-keeper of Sir Richard Cartwright," had written a pamphlet for his anonymous American friends, explaining what measures the United States should take to force Canada into annexation. A loyal man with knowledge of the pamphlet had brought it to the attention of the government. He had obtained galley proofs of certain pages, and the police were now searching for the rest.

"Hear, hear!" shouted the crowd.

"I will read to you the last paragraph of that paper," Macdonald continued, building up to the critical moment, "and you will see the charge that I make that all this negotiation at Washington is merely leading up to a result which they consider inevitable—the annexation of Canada to the United States."

"Hear, hear!"

Sir John slid his hand into his breast pocket. It came out brandishing the proofs, the evidence itself, and from it he read aloud about the punitive measures that the United States could use to bring Canadian business to its knees and thus soften up the country for annexation. There were also disparaging remarks about the Canadian political system. Farrer described it—and by extension, the people and the country—as corrupt, pathetic, and held together only by the cleverness of the prime minister.

"The writer pays me a great compliment," Macdonald said. "He says annexation cannot make great progress as long as I am at the head of affairs."

That triggered more cheers.

"But then, he says," Sir John grinned, "I am 75 years old." He corrected Farrer: "I am 76 years old." There was more laughter. Joking aside, Sir John intoned, Farrer had written, "It is plain that Sir John's disappearance from the stage is to be the signal for a movement towards annexation ... a leader will be forthcoming when the hour arrives."

Shouts from the crowd: "That's Cartwright!"

Indeed it was, Sir John acknowledged. He was building toward his conclusion, carrying everyone in the room with him. "I believe that this election," he said earnestly, "which is a great crisis and upon which so much depends, will show the Americans that we prize our country as much as they do, that we would fight for our existence as much as they fought for the preservation of their independence."

"Hear, hear!"

There was one final, poignant line from the Old Man. It reflected his hope, his enduring belief, "that the spirit of our fathers, which fought and won battle after battle, still exists in their sons; and if I thought it was otherwise I would say the sooner the grass was growing over my grave the better, rather than that I should see the degradation of the country which I have loved so much and which I have served so long."

Macdonald sat down. He had given the last great speech of his life. The crowd exploded into raucous cheers, and from the platform, the Conservative leaders around him led the crowd in a chorus of an improvised song, "We Will Hang Ned Farrer on a Sour Apple Tree." A thunderous rendition of "God Save the Queen" followed, and the meeting was officially concluded. Sir John lingered on the platform for a while, shaking hands, receiving congratulations, and waiting for the crowd to thin out before riding back with Joseph Pope to the Queen's Hotel. Tomorrow there would be a speech to deliver, and another the day after that. There would be days of travel and constant demands from the party upon his precious time, away from Agnes and Mary and Earnscliffe, where he needed to rest. But tonight, for a moment, Macdonald could pause and savour what the *Empire* would correctly regard, in its morning edition, as "the greatest political meeting ever held in Canada."

The Aftermath

Not until after eleven o'clock did the assembly at the Academy of Music disperse. The great crowd left the theatre in a more peaceful manner than it had arrived, despite the inflammatory nature of the revelations made by the prime minister. The more headstrong characters might have been expected to charge out calling for blood, and to perhaps storm the *Globe* building, where fifty police officers summoned by Willison now stood guard. But all remained quiet at Yonge and Melinda streets, and the officers, seeing that they were not needed, soon went back to their regular duties. The euphoria that resulted from having witnessed a unique and remarkable moment in Canadian history, it appeared, had outweighed the indignation and hostility that swelled in many a breast when Macdonald revealed the Farrer pamphlet.

John Willison, the beleaguered *Globe* editor, could at least be thankful for that as he walked out of the Academy of Music. He was accompanied by Ned Farrer, for whom he must have been having mixed feelings at that moment. Farrer, however, was in his usual good humour. He seemed to be totally unaffected by the charges made against him, having sat calmly and quietly as thousands of people had been whipped into a frenzy and encouraged to sing about hanging him from a sour apple tree. Even now he did not seem at all worried about giving the appearance of disloyalty. An *Empire* reporter, tailing the two men as they left the theatre, overheard Farrer say, "I say, Willison, have you time to come around and see Ritchie with me?" He was referring to Sam Ritchie, the American businessman who was deeply involved in the alleged conspiracy that Macdonald had just exposed. This hardly seemed like the best moment for such a meeting. "Where is he?" Willison queried. "He is at the Rossin House," Farrer replied. Whether their meeting took place, however, the *Empire* reporter could not be sure. At that point he apparently lost them in the crowd.

A reporter from the *World*, however, caught up to Willison some time after the meeting had ended. "Have you any statement to make regarding Sir John's charge?" he asked. Willison, a bit wearily, answered, "We have no statement to make." That was not true, of course. He did have a statement to make, as did Farrer, but those were going to appear the next day in the columns of the *Globe*, and not those of their rival newspapers. The fallout from the exposure of the Farrer pamphlet could be disastrous for the Liberal Party, and as a loyal party man, Willison would do everything in his power to salvage the situation or, at least, limit the damage that had been done. He would have to get back to the *Globe* offices to draft an editorial response to the charges made against Farrer, and of course to oversee the paper as it went to press.

It was going to be a long night for John Willison. He knew there would be hell to pay in the morning.

NINE

The Turn of the Tide

February 18 was a banner day for Conservative journalists. Their patriotic fury was such that the largest available type had to be called into service, the better to work up monster headlines, and all their efforts were focused on inciting public outrage against Ned Farrer and the Liberal Party. The Toronto *Empire*, leading the charge, devoted prime space on its front page to the most delicious story of the campaign.

THE TREASON UNVEILED

Sir John Unmasks a Treasonous Conspiracy

IT WAS AN ATROCIOUS PLOT.

Canadians Can Form Their Own Estimate of the Participators.

Farrer intriguing with the Yankees—He writes a Pamphlet Supporting Their Views—A Great Meeting at the Academy of Music Last Evening—The Crowd Too Great for the Building—The Old War Horse of the Cumberland Makes a Brilliant and Effective Address—Sir John Received with Great Acclaim—It was a Grand Gathering.

Similar headlines screamed from the front pages of the leading Tory newspapers in every part of the country. "A VILE GRIT CONSPIRACY," cried the Halifax *Herald*. "FARRER—THE TRAITOR," thundered the Manitoba *Free Press*, adding, "SIR JOHN SAYS THE POLICE ARE AFTER HIM." Even the distant Victoria *Colonist*, drawing on reports sent to it by telegraph, greeted readers the next day with breathless headlines. "GREAT GUNS!" its lead story exclaimed, "Sir John and Sir Charles Fire Hot Shot Into the Ranks of the Opposition." In all of these organs there was not only excitement and satisfaction but also relief. Before Macdonald's speech, the Liberals had not seemed intimidated by the charge of "veiled treason," and it had been an uncomfortably close campaign. Now, surely, the Conservatives were headed for victory. Firm evidence of treason had been laid on the table. What could the Liberal newspapers possibly say to extricate the party from this valley of humiliation?

Explanations and Excuses

The Grit press was, not surprisingly, unenthusiastic about reporting Macdonald's speech. Some newspapers adopted what could only be called a head-in-the-sand approach, opting to ignore the story of the Farrer pamphlet altogether. The editorial staff of the Halifax *Chronicle* went this route, though the telegraph wires certainly reached their province and it was hard to believe that they were unaware of what had transpired. The *Chronicle* focused instead on a fiery speech delivered by J.W. Longley in Lunenburg County—a happy event for the Liberals, but insignificant compared to the aftershocks that were still rippling out from Toronto. Several Liberal newspapers in Quebec preferred to lavish attention on an address that Laurier had made in Montreal the same evening.

But not even the most determined neglect of the subject could make it go away. The response that mattered most was that of the Toronto *Globe*, whose man Edward Farrer was at the heart of the scandal. How would it answer the charges? And what would happen to Farrer? It seemed that the Liberals had been caught off guard by the exposure of the pamphlet, and there had not been time yet for Laurier or Cartwright to properly confer with Willison or Farrer. The *Globe* was acting on its own, and the suddenly precarious prospects of the Liberal Party hung on its reaction to the crisis.

The front page of the February 18 edition of the *Globe* conformed to the head-in-the-sand approach adopted by other Liberal papers. The lead article was devoted to the Laurier speech, which, in fairness, would have been a major story on any other morning. Rather incredibly, there was no mention at all of the Conservative rally in Toronto. Not until page 4, the editorial page, did the newspaper acknowledge the accusations made against its most eminent writer. This was done in a terse editorial, most likely written by Willison, which lamented that the prime minister had chosen to throw around charges of treason that no thoughtful person could take seriously. The editorial implied that this was just another desperate attempt to distract attention from the failure of the National Policy and the weakness of the Conservative position, and observed, "It is a sad sight to see the Premier of Canada driven on an occasion like this to make his battle on appeals to ignorance and prejudice."

The charge of treason was answered by Edward Farrer himself in a column that was matter-of-factly titled "What there is in the charges made by Sir John Macdonald." He did not shirk responsibility for the pamphlet. "The police need not trouble themselves about looking for evidence," he wrote. "I admit that I was the writer and sole author of the brochure." He had written it at the request of an American friend who was curious, if Farrer were to take the American point of view, about what position he might adopt regarding the fisheries dispute with Canada. It had been written from that vantage point for this person and for no one else. None of the twelve copies printed had been circulated to American politicians. Neither the *Globe* nor any Liberal leader had any knowledge of it, and there certainly was no grand conspiracy against Canada. Farrer's tone was defiant. He had no regrets and saw no reason to make an apology. "This is a free country," he insisted, "and I propose living up to the rights of the individual so far as I can." He called the bluff of the prime minister (who he correctly suspected did not believe that there was any real evidence of criminal wrongdoing) and urged the Old Man to put him on trial for treason. "My own view, but I am no judge," Farrer concluded, "is that intelligent men will feel sorry that Sir John should have been driven by the stress of the battle he has on his hands to resort to so poor a subterfuge."

This was a bold statement, and it was hard not to admire Farrer for having the courage of his convictions. But the attitude he had assumed was pointlessly obstinate, combative, and unapologetic, and it was not going to help the Liberals to fend off the charge that their man was an avowed annexationist. Where was the retraction of his statements in the pamphlet? Where was the remorse? Where, many Canadians surely wondered, was the punishment for his actions? Neither John Willison, the executive board of the *Globe*, nor the Liberal leaders seemed to believe that there was anything wrong with employing an editor who secretly advised Americans about the best way to force Canada into annexation. Leaving Farrer at his desk, unpunished, would not help the Liberal Party to reclaim the patriotic high ground, nor to limit the damage that his pamphlet was doing to their chances of winning the election.

In fact the most stirring reply to the prime minister did not come from Laurier, Cartwright, or anyone else in the federal party. It came from the premier of Ontario, Oliver Mowat, who had already been scheduled to deliver a speech at the Horticultural Pavilion in Toronto on February 18. It was the perfect opportunity for him to defend his Liberal allies. Mowat did not care for unrestricted reciprocity, but he had been a good party man about it. He had shelved his personal reservations, publicly supported Laurier, and put forth a respectable (if not very enthusiastic) effort to aid the federal party during the campaign. The best thing that he could do for Laurier now was to stand at his side and denounce the charge of veiled treason. Mowat had impeccable patriotic credentials—even the imperialist George Denison thought him a loyal man—and if he argued that Macdonald was talking rubbish it would, at least, have a morale-boosting effect on the Liberal Party.

The Horticultural Pavilion was packed to the rafters, with an unlucky overflow crowd of several thousand left roaming the grounds outside. The hall was decorated with the usual patriotic flags and banners, the largest of which, a weather-beaten Union Jack, floated high above the platform. The Liberals were obviously feeling tender about the charge laid by Macdonald, for an accompanying sign carried the cumbersome slogan "Loyalty will not allow the Old Flag to be used to make a wigwam for Old Tomorrow and his tribe of boodlers."[1] The audience was in a serious mood, the *Globe* reported, "marked by a steady, enlightened patriotism" and warmly receptive to the premier when he arrived at about half past seven.

In many ways Oliver Mowat, who had once clerked in Macdonald's law office, was cut from the same cloth as the prime minister. His greatest strengths were his natural moderation, tolerance, and patience, and like the Old Man, he was averse to sticking his neck out unnecessarily. Mowat had declined to endorse Laurier with much enthusiasm in 1889, when they had shared the platform at the Horticultural Pavilion. At the time he had wondered whether the new leader would help or hurt his own position in Ontario. Now, when it counted most, he rallied strongly behind Laurier. He lambasted the Conservative government on the battle-tested subjects of the premature dissolution, corruption, and the failure of the National Policy. He reserved his toughest language, however, for a rebuttal to Macdonald on the question of loyalty to Great Britain.

What annoyed Mowat most was the implication that Conservatives were a more loyal breed than Liberals. "There is but a fragment of our people," he declared, "either Conservatives or Reformers, who do not love British connection." That triggered warm applause. In fact there were, the premier continued, just as many loyal Liberals as there were Conservatives.

"More!" cried a voice in the crowd.

"My friend here says more," noted Mowat. "I dare say he is right in saying more." To renewed cheers the premier warmed to his theme, in language that deliberately echoed the words of the prime minister the night before.

> For myself I am a true Briton. [Hear, hear!] I love the old land very dearly. [Hear, hear!] I am glad I was born a British subject. A British subject I have lived for three-score years, and something more—[Hear, hear!]—I hope to live my life a British subject and as a British subject die. [Hear, hear and cheers!] I trust and I hope that my children and grandchildren, who have also been born British subjects, will live their lives as British subjects and as British subjects die.

Mowat wanted to make sure that his fellow Liberals were not discouraged by the charge of the prime minister. He repudiated the notion that unrestricted reciprocity with the United States would spark annexationist sentiment in Canada. That was nonsense. "We are not afraid of being Yankeefied by any such thing," he asserted. What faith did the Tories have in the Canadian people, implying that they would fail in open competition with the Americans and, even worse, that they would abandon their ties to Great Britain just because they were trading freely with their neighbours?

He did not shy away, either, from the subject of Edward Farrer. Mowat did not like Farrer's views and steadfastly denied that they were the views of the Liberal Party. But Farrer was a good writer, and it was better to have him working for the party than against it. Mowat treated the issue with a light touch, joking that Farrer had become an annexationist during his time at the *Mail* when it was a Conservative newspaper. His pamphlet was a trivial thing, the detached thoughts of a paid journalist, and it was sad that the Tories had stooped to trying to make it anything more than that.

It was a resounding performance and a welcome shot in the arm for the Liberal Party. The *Globe* needed twelve pages the next morning to accommodate its massive coverage of the event. None of the arguments were new, really. Mowat had hit on the same points that Laurier and Cartwright had been stressing in their campaign speeches. But it was important that he was willing to put his reputation on the line for Laurier, especially among those Ontario Liberal voters who might be undecided. He had not matched the sheer drama produced by the Old Man the night before. But for a shell-shocked Liberal Party it was a step in the right direction.

Pressing the Advantage

Macdonald and Tupper did not stay in Toronto to hear what Mowat had to say. The two old war horses were taking their show on the road—the "Veiled Treason Tour," one might call it—and just past noon on February 18 they were at Union Station to catch the westbound train to Hamilton. A sizeable crowd gathered to catch a glimpse of the Old Man, and he doffed his fur cap to them from the rear platform of their private car, the *Cumberland*. He had managed to get some sleep at the Queen's Hotel, and looked happy and refreshed as he shook hands with supporters before the train got under way. There was a stop along the route, at Oakville, where boisterous Conservatives assembled in the hope that Sir John might emerge briefly from his car. He obligingly stepped onto the rear platform, bareheaded and smiling, and addressed them for a few minutes about loyalty to Queen and country. A clamour ensued as children and adults pressed forward, reaching out to touch the Old Man before he departed.

Another eager crowd awaited Macdonald when his train pulled into Hamilton that afternoon. The city, with a population of fifty thousand, was one of the largest industrial centres in the Dominion. It had a proud working-class tradition, and to get elected here it was necessary to be seen as the "workingman's friend." Macdonald had never had much sympathy for organized labour—in his opinion, unions challenged the established order of things—but the National Policy had done the workers an important service by protecting their employers from foreign competition. Tariff protection had kept the factories running and helped new ones to spring up, providing steady jobs and wages for thousands of Hamilton workers and their families. The voters had narrowly elected two Tories in 1887, and it was for their benefit that Sir John and Sir Charles had travelled this evening.

Hamilton welcomed its honoured guests by dressing up not only the Palace Rink, where they were scheduled to speak, but also the entire city. British flags fluttered from buildings, and big banners ("Unrestricted Reciprocity is Death," "Good Old Tory, Grand Old Man—To The Devil with Wiman and Uncle Sam") enlivened the atmosphere. The triangular city park on King Street, "The Gore," was strung with lights and decorations. Brass bands were everywhere. The main event, a torchlight procession, followed a leisurely path from the train station through the main city streets. By early evening the Tory papers estimated that thirty thousand people had lined the sidewalks to see the prime minister. Fireworks burst overhead, assisting the gas street lamps in illuminating the proceedings, and a line of horse-drawn carts sponsored by Hamilton manufacturers made up the bulk of the procession. One hundred and fifty workers from the Gurney stove foundry marched together, as did two hundred from the Tuckett & Son tobacco factory and four hundred from the Ontario Rolling Mills. These men were a walking testament to the success of the National Policy, and it was fitting that they should escort the prime minister to the Palace Rink.

The speeches were basically the same ones that Macdonald and Tupper had made the night before. The most noteworthy aspect of the meeting lay not in what was said, but in the size of the crowd. The two thousand seats inside the Palace Rink were filled, and so many were stranded outside that a second venue, the nearby Arcade Hall, was opened to accommodate the overflow. Macdonald spoke at the rink—he finished early, so that he could get some sleep—while Tupper was dispatched to address the impromptu gathering at the Arcade Hall. Then the War Horse was shuttled back to the rink, where he delivered another fiery speech. Only then, after celebratory rounds of flag-waving and the traditional solemn swearing of loyalty to Queen and country, did the proceedings in Hamilton come to an end.

There was little time to rest. The next day Tupper and Macdonald headlined a rally in Strathroy, in the Tory-held bellwether constituency of Middlesex West, and Tupper was again called upon to address an overflow crowd in an adjoining building. From there the two knights travelled to London, where their old friend John Carling, the minister of agriculture, was in danger of losing the seat he had held since Confederation. If "Honest John" Carling was in trouble, then the Tories were in trouble throughout southwestern Ontario. It was essential that London be defended, and Macdonald and Tupper rose to the occasion. The rally held there on the evening of Friday, February 20, was a capital success, giving every impression that there were enough votes yet to return the minister of agriculture to Ottawa.

Because they were being deluged with requests to speak and sensed the need to cover as much territory as possible, Sir John and Sir Charles parted ways on Saturday, February 21. Tupper headed west to Windsor, where he would speak on Monday night. Macdonald travelled east, appearing twice in Stratford early in the day before moving on to speak in St. Mary's, Guelph, Acton, and Brampton, all key constituencies that were held by either a vulnerable Conservative or a beatable Liberal. It was an exhausting schedule—Macdonald didn't arrive in Toronto until 10 P.M.—and Joseph Pope thought he seemed more weary than usual at the end of the day.

On Sunday, Macdonald rested at the Queen's Hotel, though he was hardly resting at all, because it was necessary for him to deal with the continuous stream of letters and telegrams that followed him from one place to the next. Most constituencies had chosen their candidates by now, but too many still needed something from him. Some asked for a soothing telegram to be sent to a waffling supporter, or a letter of endorsement for their local candidate to read at a public meeting. Others were desperate for Sir John to make a speech, or to sort out some personal rivalry in the local party association. In Lincoln and Niagara, for example, there was "serious dissension" in the ranks that only a visit from Macdonald could resolve.[2] A typical example of the pettiness he was dealing with was the demand made in a telegram to Pope from W.F. Maclean, a Tory journalist who was running against Alexander Mackenzie in East York: "Get old man to write letter to EA Macdonald to the effect that he wishes him to accept decision of convention to turn in and help Maclean—and by this action qualify himself for the first vacancy that may occur that he recognizes his ability and influence and that he wants him to stand by the party in this struggle. This will straighten him out. Do it to-day and wire me."[3]

A problem in many Ontario constituencies was the wobbling Catholic vote. Catholic clergymen had not forgotten the strident rhetoric of D'Alton McCarthy, and the fact that many Conservative candidates were Orangemen was not helping the cause. Sam Hughes, a bilious super-Protestant from Victoria North, feared that the "vindictive" Catholics would defeat him even though his opponent, Liberal M.P. John Barron, had voted to disallow the Jesuits' Estates Act.[4] In Bruce East, near Georgian Bay, some local priests seemed to favour annexation. Could Macdonald persuade the local bishop to straighten them out? The prime minister had cultivated a good relationship with most of the Catholic clergy in Ontario, and he did not mind prevailing upon them to assist him politically. Bishop Dowling of Hamilton, for example, promised to rein in the priests in a half-dozen neighbouring constituencies. Some supported the Liberal Party, he confided; "however a word from me will keep them quiet."[5]

If securing the Catholic vote was a problem in Ontario, it was a matter of political life and death in Quebec. Macdonald knew that Laurier was infinitely better established in Quebec than any previous Liberal leader. The Liberals, moreover, had the full might of the Mercier government on their side. Sir John was getting slightly more encouraging reports from his lieutenants in Quebec than he had earlier in the campaign, but there was still bickering and confusion. A letter forwarded to him, written by a frustrated organizer to Chapleau, highlighted the continuing damage caused by party disunity in the province: "We are having a hard enough time in the county of Megantic trying to run an election without a candidate but Sir Hector or somebody interfering with the appointment of the returning officer has disgruntled the whole English section of the county & made it utterly impossible to succeed ... I see no use now in attempting a fight there. This last move has settled the case against us."[6]

With the Conservative party machine in such a troubled state, it was essential that the Catholic Church exert its vast influence in the province on behalf of the government. In the past this support had been automatic, but since the hanging of Riel and the rise of Honoré Mercier, the relationship between the Church and the Tories had been strained. Macdonald could not hope for a ringing endorsement from Édouard-Charles Fabre, the archbishop of Montreal, but perhaps the Liberal policy of unrestricted reciprocity—with its worrisome overtones of annexation to the United States—would persuade him to give at least tacit support to the government.

Fabre was a deeply moral and conscientious man, as one might expect of a bishop, and generally believed that religious leaders should keep out of politics. Still, the spectre of annexation alarmed him. On Sunday, February 22, he issued a pastoral letter that was read from the pulpit to parishioners through the vast Archdiocese of Montreal. He took care not to specifically endorse either of the political parties, but his theme was clear. Fabre reviewed the history of Quebec and, while lamenting the Conquest, depicted life under the British flag as a blessing for French Canadians: "When, after a series of grievous disasters, it pleased God to make us pass under the aegis of the British Empire, affairs were providentially arranged so as to assure us a national and a religious life as complete as we had then any grounds to hope for. In the shadow of the flag which shelters us—protecting rather than dominating—we enjoy a precious liberty, sanctioned by solemn treaties, which enables us to preserve intact our laws, our institutions, our nationality, our language, and above all, our holy religion."[7] In the midst of a campaign that revolved around loyalty, the words of the archbishop were greeted in Conservative circles with the greatest relief and gratitude.

Laurier was chagrined by the message, which appeared in the press throughout the province the next morning, but he knew better than to pick a fight with the archbishop of Montreal. At least the letter had not explicitly instructed parishioners to vote for the Conservatives. The Liberals would simply have to redouble their efforts to present unrestricted reciprocity as a safe, patriotic policy. Downplaying the pastoral letter was the sensible course and, frankly, the only one available to mitigate the harm done to the Liberal cause.

Circling the Wagons

Worse news was in store for Laurier and the Liberals. Two other traditional allies of the Conservative Party, the manufacturing interests and the Canadian Pacific Railway, were stepping up their efforts as the campaign passed its midway point.

The manufacturers, the premier beneficiaries of the National Policy, had been out in force from the beginning. They had assembled in Toronto and Montreal and deposited substantial sums—just how large was kept secret—into Conservative party coffers. They had collectively and individually denounced unrestricted reciprocity as the absolute ruin of Canada. Plus, perhaps most visibly, they had helped to get out the propaganda. The Tories were doing plenty of this themselves, having assigned to a government statistician, George Johnson, the responsibility of distributing hundreds of thousands of manifestos, stump speeches, almanacs, and other materials that would promote the party. The great contribution of the Industrial League, a group of manufacturers in close contact with Macdonald, was to sponsor a series of colour cartoons lampooning the Liberal leaders and their continentalist allies. For these cartoons alone, Macdonald owed his friends in the manufacturing sector a debt of gratitude.

The Industrial League cartoons were blunt and mean. They depicted Laurier and Cartwright, especially Cartwright, as sinister traitors. One, "Laying Out the Grit Campaign," had the two men hunched over a "Map of the Canadian States" around a table with President Harrison, Secretary of State Blaine, Laurier, Farrer, and Wiman. Another, mocking the "dignified attitude of the Liberals," showed Laurier and Cartwright kneeling and begging at the feet of Blaine and Uncle Sam, who was crowing, "Blaine, if these fellers git into office, Canady is ours!" Numerous others forecast economic and political disaster for Canada under a regime of unrestricted reciprocity. "The Grit Toboggan Slide" depicted Laurier, Cartwright, and "Lady Canada" hurtling off a cliff toward an American flag, while Macdonald pulled on the rear of the sled to rescue her. The depiction of the country as a damsel in distress was a common theme in the cartoons and featured in the crudest of them all. In "Canada for Sale" Cartwright was garbed as a slave trader, selling a bound and helpless Miss Canada to a rapacious-looking Uncle Sam.[8]

Some of the cartoons were a little more positive, and these featured the Old Man defending the country from Liberal annexationists. In one of the better ones Macdonald was a night patrolman guarding the "N.P. Lock" out front of a Canadian bank and factory complex, while Wiman and Cartwright heaved moneybags over the brick tariff wall that was protecting it. Most famous, however, was the depiction of the prime minister hoisted on the shoulders of two supporters—symbolically, a farmer and a factory worker—and wrapped in the folds of a British flag. The caption read, "THE OLD FLAG, THE OLD POLICY, THE OLD LEADER." The poster was a heavy-handed, desperate, heart-tugging appeal to the electorate, and it worked. It was the greatest piece of election propaganda in Canadian political history.

The cartoons reminded everyone that the manufacturers were solidly in the corner of the Conservative Party. Meanwhile, the greatest company of all, the Canadian Pacific Railway—known to Liberals as the "Tory party on wheels"—had been less forthcoming. The relationship between the railway and the government had been strained of late, and some Liberals were optimistic that the company would withhold its assistance from the Conservative cause. They were wrong. On February 23 the Montreal *Gazette* and other Tory organs published a letter from William Van Horne, addressed to Montreal financier George Drummond, that clarified the position of the C.P.R. in the present campaign.

> I am not in favor of unrestricted reciprocity or anything of the kind. I am well enough acquainted with the trade and industries of Canada to know that unrestricted reciprocity would bring prostration or ruin. I realize that for saying this I may be accused of meddling in politics; but with me this is a business question and not a political one, and it so vitally affects the interests that have been entrusted to me that I feel justified in expressing my opinion plainly ...
>
> [Unrestricted reciprocity] would ruin three-fourths of our manufactories; would fill our streets with the unemployed; would make Eastern Canada the dumping ground for the grain and flour of the Western states to the injury of our own Northwest, and would make Canada generally the slaughter market for the manufactures of the United States. All of which would be bad for the Canadian Pacific Railway company, as well as for the country at large; and this is my excuse for saying so much.

Van Horne, a businessman and not a politician, was reluctant to make his support of the Conservatives so obvious. Later in the campaign he would confess to Macdonald that he regretted doing it. It was, however, necessary. The interests of the railway had to be protected, and for that matter, so did the interests of the Dominion. For his decisive action Van Horne, an American who had made Canada his homeland, was called a traitor in certain U.S. newspapers. That did not seem to bother him. Nor did it deter him from applying exactly the same label to the Canadian opponents of the National Policy. His decision to intervene in the campaign was, the Conservatives hoped, a further nail in the coffin of the Liberal Party.

Two Bites on the Cherry

If the publication of the letters written by Archbishop Fabre and William Van Horne was bad news for the Liberals, there was still worse to come. That night Sir Charles Tupper addressed a meeting at the Windsor Opera House that drew an estimated five thousand people, a huge crowd considering that Windsor had a population of only ten thousand. The city sat at the southwest tip of the Ontario peninsula, and nowhere was unrestricted reciprocity more popular. (George Denison, for example, regarded Essex as Canada's most disloyal county.) J.C. Patterson, the Conservative M.P. for Essex North, was in grave peril of losing re-election despite having easily held the constituency for the last thirteen years.

The meeting was kicked off by Patterson, who bragged to the cheering crowd that he had never lost in Essex North and was not going to start now. He then gave the floor to Tupper, who delivered the same thundering speech that he had given in Toronto and London, with one important addition. Savouring the moment, and milking it for all it was worth, Sir Charles revealed two private letters from the alleged annexationist conspirators in the Liberal camp. The first was from Edward Farrer to Erastus Wiman, dated April 22, 1889, and its contents were even more incriminating than the Farrer pamphlet had been. The commercial union movement had stalled in 1889, Farrer wrote in this letter, because of the Jesuits' Estates distraction and the fact that Canadians were not convinced that the Republicans believed in it. Instead of pushing the lame-duck policy of commercial union any further, Farrer had a startling alternative plan.

> A very large number of people are inclined to think that we had better make for annexation at once, instead of making two bites on the cherry ...
>
> ... The old parties here are rapidly breaking up, and when Sir John goes we shall be adrift without a port in sight, save annexation ...
>
> ... The littleness and half-heartedness of the Liberals is also very disheartening. Then again, the truth is that every man who preaches C.U. would prefer annexation, so that the party is virtually wearing a mask. Can't you come around this way and have a talk?

The two most memorable phrases in the letter—"two bites on the cherry" and "the party is virtually wearing a mask" were disasters for the Liberal Party. Farrer was now unquestionably in favour of annexation, and other passages suggested that he was actually working with American politicians to promote that unworthy cause. He also seemed to confirm—with that "wearing a mask" line—the suspicion that the Liberals were only championing unrestricted reciprocity as the first step toward political union with the United States.

The second letter Tupper read aloud at the Opera House had been written by Congressman Robert Hitt of Illinois, also in April 1889, and addressed to Erastus Wiman. Hitt confirmed that Farrer wanted to campaign for annexation, but disagreed with his tactics. Better, Hitt thought, to hammer at commercial union until it took hold with the "slow-moving popular mind," thus softening the ground for annexation. It was clear from this letter that Hitt assumed Wiman was also an annexationist. It did not prove that he was, but in the hands of Sir Charles Tupper in front of a raucous Conservative crowd, such distinctions hardly mattered.

The two letters appeared in the Toronto *Empire* the next morning, in large type, accompanied by larger headlines that read, "PEOPLE OF CANADA READ THIS!" and more thoroughly:

> TREASON!
>
> Of the Rankest Kind. Proofs Unearthed that Put the Matter Beyond All Doubt. The Traitor Farrer Is Fairly Caught and Thoroughly Exposed By Sir Charles Tupper

The rest of the Conservative press followed the *Empire*'s lead, and suddenly the Liberals were dealing with the Farrer pamphlet scandal all over again. In a way it was even worse this time, because the letters revealed not just a hypothetical discussion of annexation but that Farrer had conspired with—indeed, pressured—American politicians to bring it about. There was nothing the Liberals could do but denounce the words and deeds of their wayward editor while—somewhat straining credibility—maintaining that their party, oblivious to his actions, had done nothing wrong. The *Globe* put some distance between itself and Farrer, condemning him in its editorials but still, amazingly, keeping him on staff. It also raised questions about the letters and how the Conservatives had obtained them. It pointed out that it was shabby of the government to be stealing and revealing private correspondence—particularly that of a U.S. congressman—in a tacky attempt to avoid defeat.

In fact, though this was not public knowledge, the letters had been in the possession of Erastus Wiman, who was horrified by their publication and suspected that someone had stolen them from his gripsack. The truth was even worse. His cousin William McDougall had taken the letters and handed them to Sir Charles Tupper in exchange for the promise of a Senate seat. McDougall could justify his own actions, perhaps, on the grounds that the future of Canada was at stake and the scheming of Ned Farrer had to be exposed. But it was a stark betrayal of his cousin Erastus, who had been supporting McDougall financially and who trusted him implicitly.

Whatever the story behind its exposure, the "two bites on the cherry" correspondence put the Liberals back on the defensive. Then yet another letter, this one a private missive by John Charlton of North Norfolk, appeared in the Conservative press. The "member from Michigan," a self-righteous Presbyterian and supporter of the Equal Rights Association, had never fully accepted Laurier's leadership, and in the letter's most important passage, wrote bitterly that "a French Catholic leader" could never win the election. Gleeful Tory journalists seized upon that disloyal nugget as fresh evidence that Liberals such as Charlton were intolerant of French Catholics or, in other words, of Quebec itself. It was another embarrassment for the party.

The Toronto *Mail*, scrutinizing the campaign from its independent vantage point, sensed that the Farrer pamphlet was having an undeniable effect and the momentum was with the Conservatives. On February 25, it published a front-page report from its Montreal correspondent on the state of affairs in Quebec. His assessment might well have applied to the Dominion as a whole: "There is no question that the action of the church will prove a very serious matter for the Liberals, and many of the most enthusiastic Liberals now admit that their chances are not nearly as good as they were a week ago ... The Liberals are now on the defensive all along the line, and will have to fight not only the Government, with the Old Flag raised aloft and the cry of treason, but the much more powerful influence of the Church and the great railway trust of the country."

The *Mail* then put down in black and white what many Canadians were thinking. "Will the Liberals be able to win against such odds as these?" it asked. The paper did not dare to answer its own question, but added, "Even their most devoted friends say that the struggle will be a terrible one."

The Last Stand

The same morning, Macdonald left Kingston for a hastily arranged meeting in Napanee, a small town thirty miles away in the constituency of Lennox. Sir John was already worn out, having braved stormy weather the night before to address another meeting. He probably should have stayed in the city, but the party organizers in Lennox needed him. The constituency was in Conservative hands, but its member of Parliament, a merchant named Uriah Wilson, had won in 1887 by just twenty-three votes. Wilson's supporters had called on the prime minister as he rested at his brother-in-law's home in Kingston, and he had eventually bowed to their entreaties and agreed to go. Macdonald had once lived in Napanee, and Lennox was the sort of iffy constituency that had to be held if the Conservatives were to win the election. Joseph Pope, at his side as always, would have preferred to see the Old Man rest in Kingston. Now there would be no rest. It was to be a grave mistake.

Macdonald and Pope travelled by train to Napanee and then were driven through the main street of the town slowly, in an open carriage, to let the cheering crowds catch a glimpse of the prime minister. Pope was disgusted that the party organizers had not made better preparations. Everything seemed to have been thrown together in haste, and it was inexcusable that Macdonald was riding in an open carriage in freezing weather. The meeting itself was even more poorly planned. Too many people were crammed into the building, and boisterous youngsters had been allowed to encroach onto the platform. Sir John sat uneasily in the stale, nauseatingly warm air, flushed and sweating, as local ladies sang the national anthem, Uriah Wilson made the opening remarks, and a letter of thanks from the Lennox Liberal-Conservative association was read to the crowd.

When Macdonald finally rose to speak, it was clear that he was in some distress. He gave the same speech that he had been making since the Toronto meeting, but his delivery lacked the deftness and light touch that he usually employed on the platform. "I fear that I will greatly disappoint you today," he began weakly, "because I will not be able to address you at any length or with a clear voice." He was seventy-six years old, he reminded them, in feeble health, suffering from a hoarse voice. He denounced the Liberals, in an uncharacteristically crude attack. Then, in the middle of a recitation of figures about the economy under the National Policy, Sir John abruptly stopped, said, "I thank you for your kind and courteous hearing," and sat down, exhausted.[9] The oblivious crowd responded with thunderous applause.

Joseph Pope was alarmed. He urged the event organizers to allow him to escort the prime minister back to his private railcar, so that he could rest and recover before going back to Kingston. The local Tories insisted, instead, on taking Macdonald across town to another meeting. He was put in the open carriage again, where his sweat-soaked skin was chilled by the wind, and driven out to the second event. Sir John dutifully went through the motions, giving the same speech again, to the same oblivious cheers. There was another drive through the town, yet again in the open carriage, and finally Pope was able to shepherd the weary, seemingly disoriented prime minister into the private car that had been waiting for him at the station.

Leaving Sir John for a few moments, Pope checked to see whether any telegrams had arrived in the short time they had been away from the wire service. Some had, of course, and several required the urgent attention of the prime minister. Pope opened the door to his room and saw that Sir John was stretched on the bed, hardly moving. His face was ashen grey. "I am exhausted," Macdonald said simply, and nothing more.[10] Pope feared that this was something more than mere exhaustion—he had seen that ashen look before—and he was right. Sir John A. Macdonald had made his last stand. He had given his final speech in the campaign, and there was nothing that Pope could do but get him back to Kingston and into bed. The Conservatives, who had depended on the Old Man so heavily in every campaign over the past four decades, would have to fight on without his active leadership. There was a week left until election day.

The Final Sprint

On the morning of February 26, Macdonald was resting in the spare bedroom at his brother-in-law's home in Kingston. It was a lonely scene, with just his brother-in-law, his secretary, and a physician, Dr. Sullivan, at his side. The bare, cheerless decor, which Pope thought was badly in need of a woman's touch, seemed to contribute to a general sense of foreboding. Here in this bed, in these sad and spartan surroundings, Macdonald would be confined until election day. His indisposition was not advertised in the newspapers, of course. The Conservative press did its best to quell fast-spreading rumours and play down his sudden absence. The Liberal organs were less discreet, but even they seemed unsure of what to say. The loss of Macdonald from active duty was a blow to the Conservatives, but the apparent seriousness of his condition made it unseemly for his opponents to celebrate.

After a thorough examination, the doctor determined that the prime minister was suffering from a weak heart and, most likely, congested lungs. There was no prescription but rest, and that placed his loyal secretary in an impossible position. Urgent reports and requests were still streaming in from party members across the country. How much of it could be shown to Sir John without putting his health in further jeopardy? How much of it actually needed to be handled by him anyway? In the days to come Pope was forced to play it by ear. He took care of the routine business himself, while more important material was shown to Macdonald only in those moments when he seemed strong enough to bear it. Though he tried to remain upbeat, the strain was telling on the Old Man. At one point he complained to Pope, "If you would know the depth of meanness of human nature, you have got to be a prime minister during a general election."[11] That self-pitying remark, out of character for Sir John, spoke volumes about his weary condition.

Meanwhile the campaign was fought without him. February 26 was nomination day, when the candidates were formally presented to their discerning constituents. It was the one day on which there were big rallies in every constituency in the Dominion, and it was a fabulously hectic occasion. In some places the two parties held joint meetings, giving the opposing candidates the opportunity to debate each other directly, and that made for considerable excitement even in constituencies where the race was not close. At the nomination meeting in North Norfolk, for example, John Charlton and his Conservative opponent, Lachlin Sinclair, agreed to meet in the upstairs room of a local hall. The crowd was boisterous, and Charlton noticed with alarm that the floor had sagged six inches under its weight. "I warned the audience to refrain from stamping," he later recalled, "and was gratified when the meeting closed without a catastrophe and loss of life."[12]

The sagging floor and the risk it posed was, happily, a far cry from the bad old days of Canadian politics, when public meetings were often marred by violence. There were still, however, occasional incidents. One involved the most prominent Conservative who was still stumping on the campaign trail. Sir Charles Tupper was in Quebec City on nomination day, making a brief stop on his way to the Maritime provinces. He took the opportunity to confer privately with Adolphe Caron about party organization, and then gave a speech to an overwhelmingly friendly crowd at the local Tara Hall. Trouble began when a young man (identified by the Montreal *Gazette* as an employee of the Mercier government) disrupted the meeting by waving his arms and hollering in support of Laurier whenever Tupper began to speak. The War Horse first ignored him, then tried to talk over him, but without success. Eventually he sat down in frustration.

Something had to be done. A dozen police officers stood near the platform, and the chairman urged them to remove the heckler. They remained silent and motionless. The chairman, flustered, asked the officers if they were there only to serve as ornaments. Still there was silence. "Then we must take the law into our own hands," declared the chairman, and within moments a "Physical Force Committee" had been assembled. The rowdy man was grabbed, hollering all the while, and forcibly ejected from the building. There was a scuffle at the exit as some supporters of the heckler fought back against the "committee," but eventually they too were pushed out into the street. There, according to the *Gazette*, these disturbers cheered so vociferously for Laurier that they could still be heard inside.

None of this was terribly out of the ordinary. Public meetings were, as the name made clear, open to the public. Hecklers were common, though this one in Quebec City was particularly determined. Things began to get out of hand, however, once Tupper had finished his speech. The audience let out into the streets, and a torchlight parade saw his carriage to a ferry down at the wharf. Someone on the street heaved a large chunk of ice at the procession, and a young Tory was struck on the back of the head. "When the procession reached the market wharf," the Montreal *Gazette* reported, "it was met by a crowd of bullies who meant business. One of them ran up to the carriage and commenced striking out left and right among the young men who surrounded it. In a moment there was a free fight, sticks and lighted torches being brought into requisition. The crowds were mixed up in a dense, struggling mass, and everyone seemed to be striking at random."[13]

Tupper himself was not involved in this frightening melee, having boarded his ferry just before it broke out. No one was killed, but several were injured, including a young boy who had been struck in the face. The Conservatives were infuriated that the police, who they had to assume were sympathetic to the Liberals, had done nothing to stop the fight. The incident was prominently covered in the Tory press, but the Liberal organs were sceptical of the *Gazette*'s version and reported merely that the meeting had been interrupted. In fact it was impossible for the voters to know what had really happened, because the heightened partisanship on both sides meant that newspaper reports could not be taken at face value. Something had happened in Quebec City, however, and it was hard to believe that the Liberals had not been at the root of the disturbance in Tara Hall, if not the violence in the streets afterward.

There were no entirely innocent parties, certainly, in the final week of this hard-fought campaign.

The pace picked up in the final days. February 28 was the last day of the short month, and March 1, a Sunday, was a customary day of rest. Suddenly there were only three days left before the vote. Both parties were hunkering down, with less time now for the monster meetings that had characterized the early part of the campaign. The prominent figures in both parties were concentrating their efforts on winning their own constituencies, with two great exceptions. Sir Charles Tupper, who was not running anywhere, would spend the final days in his native Nova Scotia, firming up party support from Amherst to Halifax. And Wilfrid Laurier was a free agent, having been acclaimed on nomination day in Quebec East. The failure of the Conservatives to run someone against him, an oversight that Chapleau angrily blamed on Langevin and Caron, was a considerable relief to the Liberal leader. It allowed him to continue to rally the party in close constituencies right up to election day.

Laurier had spent virtually the entire campaign in his native province, but now, at the last minute, he decided to make a couple of stops in eastern Ontario. On the evening of March 2 he headlined an overcrowded rally in Cobourg, halfway between Toronto and Kingston. The following night he was a bit farther east, in Cornwall, and spoke in both English and French in front of a friendly audience that the Toronto *Globe* estimated at five or six thousand people. On both occasions the Grits arranged the requisite torchlight procession and a phalanx of supporters to cheer every word. The meetings were deemed a great success in the Liberal newspapers, of course, and as he headed back to Montreal, Laurier could feel heartened by the warmth of his reception in both towns.

Laurier had not actually been at his best in Cobourg or Cornwall. He had looked tired, his voice was husky from overuse, and his speeches contained nothing new. Still, the Toronto *Globe* mused, it was striking to see this French Canadian politician treated with such unrestrained affection and respect in Ontario, and by predominantly English Canadian audiences. Laurier was fading somewhat physically, but he had stood up well—better than expected—to the stresses of his first campaign as a national leader. Even the rival *Mail*, not known for its sympathy toward French Canadian Catholics, admitted that there was something elegant about the man: "Not since the opening of the campaign has he uttered a harsh word against his opponents. He has dealt with the issue on its merits, and to all the cries that have been raised he has made a dignified reply. Even his bitterest opponents admit he is fighting the campaign like a man, and that his conduct is in remarkable contrast to some of the leading public men who are now parading the country."[14]

The Conservatives were hardly falling over themselves to praise Laurier, but their campaign suggested that they also harboured a grudging respect for him. From the outset they had concentrated their attacks not on Laurier, the actual Liberal leader, but on Sir Richard Cartwright, Edward Farrer, Goldwin Smith, and Erastus Wiman. Those names provoked a much more intense emotional reaction from voters in the English Canadian provinces. Men such as George Denison truly believed that the Dominion was in grave danger from these annexationists and that they ought to be executed for treason. William Kirby, a fellow loyalist, was not kidding when he wrote Denison that annexation would be achieved only "over the dead bodies of thousands of loyal Canadians."[15]

That view was extreme, but the Conservatives knew the majority of Canadians shared at least some of Denison and Kirby's animosity toward annexationists. They had spent the whole campaign insinuating that the Liberals were willing accomplices of traitors, and in the final week they ramped up their attacks. Just after nomination day, Denison gave a speech in Toronto on the subject of loyalty, condemning the Liberals generally and especially his one-time friend Goldwin Smith. The point was to rally loyalists behind the Conservatives, and it appeared to work. Kirby, for one, loved the speech. "I am glad you give Goldwin

Smith his own," he wrote his friend, adding, "That man ought to be sat upon until he is as flat as a dead cat in a public highway."[16]

Erastus Wiman was also the target of Conservative attacks as election day neared. In the Maritime provinces the Tory press referred to all Liberals as "Wimanites," and his every attempt to persuade Congress to pass a resolution favouring unrestricted reciprocity was brought to the immediate attention of their readers. Circulars that he had sent out to American politicians and businesses, asking for their support, were quoted time and again to demonstrate Wiman's craven attachment to powerful interests in the United States. Outlandish estimates were published of the amount of Yankee money that he was supposedly funnelling into Liberal coffers. And the morning before the election, March 4, various Tory newspapers featured a story about a passing acquaintance of Wiman who swore that he had once privately confessed to being an annexationist. That was dubious journalism, but it stoked loyalist sentiment and aided the Conservative cause.

Notwithstanding these attacks, the tempo of the campaign changed as it entered its final hours. Wednesday evening, March 4, was curiously quiet. Rallies were held in certain constituencies, but the focus was now shifting to the actual business of getting out the vote, and extensive preparations were being made behind the scenes by multitudes of party workers who were responsible for coordinating this "ground game." The horses were treated to additional oats, girding them for the strenuous task of shuttling voters to the polls the next day. Voters lists were checked and rechecked. Speeches were made, but they were made mostly in committee rooms, behind closed doors, exhorting fellow Liberals or Conservatives to fan out the next morning and do everything that could be done to ensure victory.

Election day had arrived.

TEN

The Fifth of March

The morning of the election "broke bright and clear," noted the Toronto *Mail*, adding with its typical sarcasm that "on such occasions it always either 'breaks' or 'dawns.' On ordinary days it simply gets light."[1] The independent newspaper, contemplating the struggle with more detachment than the party organs, also offered this cheerful account of the private scenes that it suggested were already playing out across the country: "Young men got up and put on red and blue neckties with considerable hauteur, and old men got up and [said] their prayers. For the Day had come at last, a day that was to be remembered for years, a day when the good old flag was to have one more wave and the 'traitor' one more execration; when voters were to hurry to the polling places on the wings of steam, or in the vibrating buggy, or merely on a pair of nervously hastening legs."

The two party leaders, of course, deserved special mention. "Sir John Macdonald, paraphrasing Hamlet in a merry way, as he left his bed in a springy manner, said—'The air bites shrewdly! I have got a cold.' Mr Laurier somersaulted from between the blankets with the good old remark about who would fire the last rifle in defence of Canadian loyalty, and the day was begun."

Such humorous stuff was, most definitely, the exception to the rule in the Canadian press. For the bulk of journalists whose newspapers supported one party or the other, election day was a deadly serious affair. The morning editions featured dramatic headlines and screaming editorials, all designed not to win support—very few voters were undecided at this late stage—but rather to inspire the party faithful to do everything possible to ensure victory.

The Conservative press adopted a tone that was, somehow, both optimistic and apocalyptic. "Ready!" the Toronto *Empire* exhorted its readers, "After a Quiet Day of Hard Work, For the Polls and the Victory That Will This Day Be Won." That was pretty cheerful for an *Empire* headline. The page 4 editorial, reiterating the central theme of the Conservative campaign, reverted to the familiar dark observations: "It is not a case of Grit versus Tory, of one party against another, a battle of the ins and outs. It is whether Canada shall be preserved for Canadians, whether this Dominion shall remain an integral part of the British Empire, or whether the government of its affairs shall pass into the hands of a clique leagued with foreigners, associated with a treasonable conspiracy, and pledged to a policy that presages the commercial and political extinction of the country." Vote early, urged the *Empire*, "so as to make the overthrow of the party of treason and annexation as complete as possible."

Its Tory brethren agreed that the survival of the Dominion was at stake. "Shall We Be An American State?" wondered the Saskatchewan *Herald*. In case readers somehow missed the point, it added helpfully, "Unrestricted Reciprocity Means Annexation." The little Charlottetown *Examiner* was of the same mind, urging all Islanders to be "Anti-Annexationists" (and "Tunnel Men," of course, in keeping with local priorities). The Halifax *Herald*, which always strove to outdo the competition in the area of editorial hysterics, took the talk of treason most seriously. "The traitors are at our gates," it warned, "and every true citizen is expected to do his duty." The Montreal *Gazette* warned constituency workers that the greatest enemy now was overconfidence. That advice might well have been addressed to the editors of the Victoria *Colonist*, which treated readers to a front-page reprint of the "Old Flag, the Old Policy, the Old Leader" cartoon. "VICTORY IS ASSURED," it happily proclaimed. "The Opposition Practically Give Up The Ghost." The only question left unanswered was the size of the Tory majority; the *Colonist* predicted that every single farmer in the country would vote for the Old Man. The Manitoba *Free Press* anticipated a majority of at least fifteen for the government, but admitted with surprising candour that in the West, "the restless feeling which was cultivated among the farmers by the opposition ... has not been altogether overcome by the Conservatives."

The Liberal press was hopeful, but not quite certain, that unrestricted reciprocity was popular enough to offset the energetic flag-waving of the Tories. The Toronto *Globe* tried to exude quiet confidence, opting to forgo dramatic headlines in favour of positive stories about the preparations being made by Liberal armies for the great struggle ahead. All omens were good for the party, the newspaper claimed, particularly the outcome of a provincial by-election held the previous day in North Bruce in which the Liberal member had been re-elected with an increased majority. There was some withering criticism of Sir John A. Macdonald, of course, but it seemed that the editors were consciously trying to suppress the typically negative tone of an opposition newspaper. "The Liberals have fought this campaign not only with courage and enthusiasm," the *Globe* declared, "but with a dignity which has commended their cause to intelligent men ... we say that victory is to all appearance assured."

Few other Liberal newspapers had such reservations about going negative. The Halifax *Chronicle*, which led the way in this regard, offered a mocking summary of the Conservative program:

THE TORY PLATFORM:
THE OLD MAN
THE OLD POLICY
THE OLD BOODLERS
THE OLD VOTERS' LISTS
THE OLD BUSINESS STAGNATION
THE OLD HUMBUG
THE OLD HARD TIMES

Though they tried hard to conceal it, there was an undercurrent of anxiety in Grit editorials that reflected the bitter disappointments of the past. Alarms were raised against Tory dirty tricks. The influence of the Canadian Pacific Railway and the pervasive use of boodle to bribe the electorate were denounced, as were the premature dissolution and the outdated state of the voters lists. It almost seemed that the Liberals, consciously or not, were already justifying their own expected defeat. In Manitoba, the weekly Brandon *Sun* was so resigned to another loss that it published the results before even an evening paper could have possibly obtained them, under the depressing headline, "Manitobans Willing To Remain Serfs." For some gloomy Liberals, it seemed, the institutional advantages of the Macdonald government made the outcome inevitable.

If the press of both parties agreed on one thing, it was the need to ensure that their supporters knew when, where, and how to cast their ballots. Basic information about the hours in which votes could be cast, the location of polling stations, and even the look of the ballot were common newspaper features. There were also warnings to look out for opposition tricks. The Quebec *Chronicle* urged Tory readers not to fall for the scam of "pairing," in which two voters of opposing parties agreed not to vote to save themselves the time and trouble of going to the polling station. "Poll your own vote and let him look out for his," it suggested. Voters were also advised that bribery was a criminal offence, and that ballots could be nullified if their owners had been given inducements to vote, including travel expenses.

That much was obvious. There were, however, many more rules and regulations. Some were intended to ensure fairness, some were there to restrict the franchise to those Canadians deemed properly qualified, and some were just bewildering.

The Rules of the Game

The circumstances under which Canadians were to cast their ballots were fairly consistent throughout the Dominion.[2] Each constituency had one returning officer, a public official appointed by the Macdonald government to ensure a fair election—the Liberals were naturally sceptical about that—and dozens of deputy returning officers, one for each of the polling stations located at strategic points around that constituency. The secret ballot was standard in all but four constituencies; only in the North-West Territories would the open ballot still be used. Every ballot would be deposited by its elector into a ballot box and stored in that box, unseen, until the polls closed. Local candidates were permitted to appoint scrutineers to observe the votes being cast at each polling station, the point being to satisfy both sides that the ballot box had not been tampered with and that only properly qualified electors had been allowed to cast ballots.

It was the latter task, determining who was entitled to vote, that would lead to confusion and conflict at the polling stations. The Franchise Act of 1885, under which this election was being held, specified that three basic criteria had to be satisfied in order for a person to vote. The first and most important qualification, in terms of the number of Canadians that it excluded from participating, was that voters must be male British subjects. The massive disenfranchisement of women and some ethnic minorities that resulted from this had been totally ignored as an issue during the campaign, as had been the case since the pre-Confederation days when it had first been enforced. Macdonald had floated the idea of extending the franchise to women in recent years, but his musings had remained only musings. "Chinese and Mongolian" individuals were not permitted to vote, and native people were largely disenfranchised by a complicated set of rules that related to whether they were naturalized citizens, lived on or off a reserve, or received any assistance from the government. Despite its far-reaching impact, however, it was unlikely that this qualification for voting would cause trouble at the polling stations. Past instances of members of these unfortunate categories trying to pass themselves off as "legitimate" voters, with the exception of some natives, had been rare in Canadian elections.

The second qualification was that electors must be at least twenty-one years of age on election day. This was going to be far more controversial, because the voters lists had not been updated since 1889, and those who had turned twenty-one since were, therefore, missing from the lists. The Conservatives, masters of the lists, had said little about this, but the Liberals estimated that at least fifty thousand men had been disenfranchised in this way. Even if a young man was willing to swear an oath at the polling station to prove that he was twenty-one, he would still have no hope of being enfranchised. The voters list was, by law, the final determinant of who could vote. The deputy returning officer had no discretion in the matter. He could accept a sworn oath only if another person on the list swore to the fact that the prospective voter actually was who he said he was. Impersonation was a big problem in Canadian elections, and it was primarily on those grounds that scrutineers would be demanding that voters make sworn statements before depositing their ballots.

The last criterion, the property qualification, was easily the most complicated. Macdonald did not believe in the universal franchise, and neither did most Tories. It was their view that the property holders of society, those who had the greatest stake in its development, were the only ones informed and responsible enough to vote for the character of their government. When the voters lists had last been compiled, it had been necessary for would-be electors to demonstrate that they owned a specific amount of property. (It was too late to try to do so at the polling station on election day; once again, the voters lists were final.) The trouble with this qualification, not even taking into account its restrictive effect on the right to vote, was that there was no one constant amount. In cities it was three hundred dollars' worth of property, but in towns it was two hundred, and in rural areas it was one hundred and fifty. Tenants qualified if the property they were renting was worth the proper amount in the proper location, or if their rent was at least two dollars per month or twenty dollars per year. Alternatively, one could satisfy the property qualification by earning annual income of three hundred dollars. Also, if an elector met any of these criteria in two or more constituencies, he could cast two or more votes on election day, one in every one of those constituencies!

It only got more complex from there. Men who more than met the property qualification, or widows who had inherited property, could convey the right to vote to their sons. The number of sons who qualified depended on the amount of property, which theoretically would be divided equally among them, with only the number of sons who consequently had enough to meet the minimum qualification in their area being awarded the franchise. For example, if the parent had nine hundred dollars of property to spread among five sons, and if the family lived in an urban area in which the minimum was three hundred dollars, only three of the sons would be permitted to vote—if, that is, those sons could each prove residency in the house of the parent for at least twelve months, with no break in that residency for longer than four months during that period.

Then there were exceptions for British Columbia and Prince Edward Island, the only two provinces that had not required any sort of property qualification before the Franchise Act took effect. People who had voted in those provinces in previous elections, but who did not have enough property under the newer laws, were grandfathered in and would still have the right to vote in future elections. The property qualification would apply, however, to those who were voting for the first time in these provinces and every time thereafter. And, of course, if these unlucky young men had turned twenty-one later than the 1889 revision of the voters lists, they—like young men everywhere else in the Dominion—would be disenfranchised in the election of 1891.

One other problem loomed, one that was destined to lead to many challenges of impersonation at the polling stations. According to Liberal estimates, at least, thirty to forty thousand Canadians whose names appeared on the 1889 lists were, unfortunately, dead. This was what the press called the "cemetery vote." The *Mail*, with its usual cheek, reported that this election was so exciting that it "even roused dead men and took them to the polling places, where they recorded their votes with their old-time alacrity."[3] Which party would benefit most from the cemetery vote was anyone's guess.

Aside from the Franchise Act's bewildering complexity, there would be other significant influences on the election results. The exact timing of the election was slightly different in some parts of the country, but generally the polls opened at nine o'clock in the morning and closed at five or six o'clock in the evening. Bars and saloons were closed in many constituencies, the reason being to keep people from voting while drunk, but it was difficult to enforce the no-drinking rule, and many municipalities could not be bothered to try. Some businesses would shut themselves down for a few hours during the day to allow their workers to vote—a considerate gesture, but one practised unevenly from one constituency to the next.

Sometimes there would be a police presence at the polls. That would ostensibly be to keep order, but possibly—if the provincial or municipal government was interfering in the election—the police might be used to intimidate voters, influence the decisions of deputy returning officers, or otherwise create an advantage for one party.

Finally, there was the weather. There had been a major snowstorm in Quebec on the fourth of March, and in the newspapers of Montreal and

Quebec City this was being much talked about as a worrisome factor. Party supporters who could not get out the vote themselves were being urged to donate their sleighs to the cause, and voters who might think better of voting were being strenuously encouraged to do their duty to the country and make the chilly trek to the polls. In the early morning a snowstorm had battered New Brunswick, too, and the same pleas were being made in that province.

The Polls Open

After four years of speculation and thirty-one days of intense campaigning, the polls opened at nine o'clock sharp in the three easternmost provinces: Nova Scotia, New Brunswick, and Prince Edward Island. Because of the use of standard time—this was just the second election to be conducted under its auspices—the Maritime provinces would begin voting exactly one hour before the polls opened in Ontario and Quebec. Manitoba would follow an hour later, the North-West Territories an hour after that, and British Columbia an hour after that, four hours from the moment the first votes had been cast.

In the three Maritime provinces the polls opened without fanfare. There was little point in blowing the trumpets now, for the overriding concern of party workers was to get out the vote, and that was not a raucous business. Organizing committees on both sides had spent many laborious hours in the previous weeks identifying their supporters, and now horse-drawn sleighs and carriages clogged city streets and rural roads, hustling them to the polls. A storm was rumbling through Nova Scotia, making travel precarious, but in New Brunswick and Prince Edward Island the weather was fine. Things were particularly quiet on the Island, where civic pride ran high and most people chose to vote early. The Charlottetown *Guardian*, trying hard to gather newsworthy stories, reported the arrest of three drunks later in the day. That was three drunks too many for the pious *Guardian*, but it was a rare tale of disorder on an otherwise orderly day.

The streets of Nova Scotia were peaceful, but partisan journalists, both Grit and Tory, were sure that shameless shenanigans were being employed to prejudice the vote right under the noses of the returning officers. Physical intimidation, the crudest form of electoral persuasion, was thankfully at a minimum. Vote-buying was completely out of control, however, if the newspapers were to be believed. The fact that the secret ballot prevented parties from checking on whether bribed voters were in fact supporting them was apparently no deterrent to the practice. The Halifax *Chronicle* was certain that the Tories were spending an average of two to ten dollars per vote bought, and in Antigonish, where the party was straining to save Sir John Thompson, individual votes were said to be going for a hundred dollars apiece. The Halifax *Herald* countered that the Grits were doing some vote-buying of their own, drawing on a million-dollar slush fund that Erastus Wiman had collected from American friends in Boston and New York. Neither paper, unsurprisingly, produced hard evidence of its claims.

There was tremendous anticipation when the polls opened in Quebec, where the outcome was the source of hope and anxiety in both camps. No one could tell which way the votes would go in the rural reaches of the province, where the French language and Catholic faith were most deeply entrenched. It was in those teetering constituencies that the election in the province would likely be decided. It was easier to predict the results in the two great cities, Montreal (Conservative) and Quebec City (Liberal). In both there was clamour and commotion in the streets, but a happy absence of real trouble. In Montreal the police were called to investigate an empty house on St. André Lane that was allegedly being used as a staging point to dress up loafers and use them as impersonators, but it turned out to be deserted. The Conservatives claimed that the Grand Trunk Railway was aiding the Liberals by giving free transport to their voters, but the company had declared neutrality in the campaign, and it was employees of the Canadian Pacific Railway who were most conspicuously rushing about the city.

The most striking developments in the streets of Quebec City were the three feet of snow that had fallen the night before, and the colossal police presence. Every man on the city force was on duty, reinforced by volunteer reserves and jail guards, and several officers stood guard at each polling station. The official explanation was that they were there in response to rumours that Tory roughnecks were planning to cause chaos at the polls. Conservatives charged, however, that the police had been dispatched to intimidate their voters. That was possible. The premier had very actively supported the Liberals throughout the campaign and was playing host at his own residence to Wilfrid Laurier later in the evening. Laurier, already acclaimed in Quebec East, was spending the day touring constituencies in the city along with his friend Ernest Pacaud, editor of the Liberal organ *L'Electeur*. He was dressed as elegantly as always, and bowed whenever supporters cheered him as they passed in the streets. Though he was not speaking to the press, on the previous day he had bantered briefly with a reporter from the Montreal *Gazette*. Asked to make a prediction, Laurier was coy. "As Sir John says," he said wryly, "there is nothing so uncertain as a general election or a horse race."[4]

The "horse race" was nowhere being more closely fought than in Ontario. The Conservatives had won a comfortable majority of seats here in 1887, but every pundit outside of the most slavish Tory organs was anticipating a closer contest this time. The province was several elections removed now from the bad old days of open voting, and there was far less likelihood of disturbances arising between the parties while they were shepherding their supporters to the polls. As in Quebec, accusations were soon flying about the Canadian Pacific Railway aiding the Conservatives, and the Grand Trunk (and American conspirators) giving assistance to the Liberals. But the most interesting story of the day was a heartening one for the Conservatives. Sir John A. Macdonald was on the move again, having departed Kingston by train for Ottawa early in the morning. He would rest at Earnscliffe for the remainder of the day, back in the relieved company of Lady Macdonald. A telegraph wire had been run to the house to keep him constantly updated as events unfolded.

Only in western Canada were there a considerable number of reports of trouble at polling stations. In the constituency of Selkirk, Manitoba, the C.P.R. was rumoured to be blatantly intimidating its employees. William Van Horne had recently wired the prime minister, promising that "the CPR vote will be practically unanimous—not one in one hundred even doubtful."[5] The tactics used to achieve this improbable result were clear to the Brandon *Sun*, which was amassing witness statements from C.P.R. employees who claimed that their managers were taking them to the polls to observe how they voted, under threat of termination if they did not support the Conservative candidate. The *Sun* also reported that hundreds of voters were being brought in by rail to cast votes in the North-West Territories. Many of these men, it was implied, were not legitimate voters, and some were not Canadians at all.

The Polls Close

The voting was still under way in the rest of the country when the ballots began to be counted in the Maritimes. The newspapers waited breathlessly as the first ballot boxes were opened, the votes counted, and the results passed along by the returning officer of each constituency. This was an exciting day to be a journalist, for the importance of the press was never more clear and immediate than on election night. It was an age long before radio or television brought the news into people's homes, and newspaper buildings, with their access to the telegraph and their custom of posting up-to-the-minute results outside, were the ideal place to congregate. The results started to come in from the cities at first, and more slowly from rural constituencies.

The early returns were a shock. The Conservatives, who had appeared to be on the ropes during the campaign, were routing the Liberals. In Prince County, Prince Edward Island, their star candidate, George Howlan, was defeated. But they had made inroads on the Island, taking both seats in King's County in the eastern section of the province. In New Brunswick, where the Liberals had expected to make big gains, the Tories had held their ground everywhere but Carleton and possibly King's, where Minister of Finance George Foster had expected trouble and seemed to be going down to defeat. In the riding of the City of Saint John, the most hated Liberal politician in the Maritimes, the reputed annexationist John V. Ellis, was soundly defeated by almost six hundred votes. The Tories had also picked up one of the seats in the double constituency of the City and County of Saint John. That was also a satisfying victory for the Conservatives because the ousted member of Parliament was Charles W. Weldon, who had directed the campaign for the Liberals in the province. Overall, the Conservative Party claimed twelve of sixteen seats in New Brunswick. The last one to move firmly into the Tory column was King's, which George Foster would eventually hold by seventy-three votes. At the office of the Saint John *Sun*, a leading party organ in the province, relieved and exhilarated Conservatives were still whooping it up at two o'clock the next morning.

Nova Scotia also responded to the loyalty cry. Instead of losing seats, the Tories managed a net gain of two, winning sixteen of twenty-one. They lost Digby and Queen's but shocked the Liberals by redeeming Lunenburg, Richmond, Shelburne, and one of the two seats in the double constituency of Halifax. Again, as in Saint John, the defeated Liberal, A.G. Jones, was a party leader and director of the campaign in the province. None of the leading Conservatives had been beaten in Nova Scotia. Charles Hibbert Tupper had cruised to victory in Pictou, and Sir John Thompson, who had half expected to be defeated in Antigonish, had triumphed by a comfortable 237 votes.

In Halifax the Conservatives—buoyed by the arrival of Sir Charles Tupper—had assembled at the Lyceum while the Liberals gathered at the provincial government building. The *Herald* described the scene at the Lyceum with the unrestrained joy of a loyal party newspaper: "A dense mass of humanity packed the building. It was a scene of wild enthusiasm ... Yes, it was indeed a happy multitude that filled the Lyceum. They were joyful, they were exultant, they had triumphed in a righteous cause and they could not be otherwise than happy." The *Herald* could not resist adding, "What a contrast to the crowd that assembled at the province building. It was too dismal to endure."[6]

This was a sweet moment for the Conservatives in the Maritimes, who knew early on that they were heading for a good smashing of the "Annexationist Party." In all, the Conservatives had won thirty of forty-three seats in the region. That gave the Macdonald government an edge of seventeen, a substantial lead as the focus of election night shifted to Quebec and Ontario.

In neither of those provinces, in which 157 seats were in play, did a clear winner emerge for some time after the polls closed. In Quebec the only obvious development was that traditional voting patterns were holding up in the cities. Montreal was as Tory as ever. Chapleau was in the city, weary and sick but still on duty, and so was the eminent businessman Donald Smith, who had won his race in Montreal West by more than thirty-seven hundred votes, the largest margin in any constituency in the country. As the *Gazette* proudly explained the outcome, "The millionaire, the merchant, the clerk and the workman all vied with each other in working to ensure the success of the National Policy candidates."[7] On St. James Street there was a splendid rally and procession for Smith, who obliged jubilant supporters with a victory speech, and throughout the city, government candidates and their constituents enjoyed good-natured celebrations.

The Conservatives could also be proud that none of the leading Quebec ministers had been defeated. Chapleau had easily won Terrebonne, and though Adolphe Caron had lost Chicoutimi, he had redeemed Rimouski, which was good enough to send him back to Ottawa. Sir Hector Langevin, despite the McGreevy scandal, had won both seats he had contested, Three Rivers and Richelieu. Thomas McGreevy, the man at the centre of the scandal, had somehow won Quebec West (a massive disappointment to the Liberal press, which could only guess that "the most frightful boodle" had been spread around to defy the will of the people[8]). As a bonus, in the toss-up Eastern Townships constituency of Richmond and Wolfe, Wilfrid Laurier himself had gone down to defeat.

Laurier, who was camped out with Mercier in the premier's residence in Quebec City, received the results immediately through a telegraph wire that had been connected there for the evening. He could shrug off his personal defeat in Richmond and Wolfe, embarrassing though it was, because of his earlier acclamation in Quebec East. He was also hearing good news for the Liberal Party from almost everywhere but the Montreal region. Quebec City remained a Liberal stronghold: only McGreevy had resisted a rising red tide in the capital, and Israël Tarte, elected in Montmorency, could now hurl charges at him from a seat in the House of Commons. Charles Colby, a second-tier Conservative cabinet minister, had been ousted in Stanstead. Six Liberal seats had been lost across the province, but thirteen had been gained from the Conservatives, giving the Liberal Party a sizeable majority in Quebec for the first time since Confederation. On election night the results were uncertain enough to allow both *bleus* and *rouges* to celebrate into the wee hours. But the final tally—thirty-seven seats won out of sixty-five in the province—was a groundbreaking triumph for Laurier and the Liberals.

In Ontario, where the day was cold and clear in most constituencies, people began gathering in the streets outside the newspaper buildings even before the polls had closed. The largest crowds were in Toronto, where, according to the *Globe*, a surprisingly genial atmosphere prevailed among the thousands of onlookers who were waiting patiently for the telegraphs to start clicking. There was a good deal of wandering to and from the various newspaper offices, and Tories and Grits could be found together in each of these spontaneous crowds, bantering nervously and hoping for a good outcome for their respective parties.

At about five-thirty the first results began to stream in, and—in part because the cities tended to report first—the news was encouraging for the government. Ottawa and Hamilton were still solidly Tory. In Toronto the party had retained all its present seats and even seemed to be on the verge of defeating Alexander Mackenzie in York East, one of the grittiest Grit constituencies. Four seats east of Toronto had been regained from the Liberals, plus Halton, a surprise pick-up in the west. Most heartening for the Tories was the result in Kingston City, where Sir John A. Macdonald had cruised to re-election, 483 votes ahead of the overmatched Alex Gunn. Cheers went up in the Tory ranks across the province when the outcome was announced. Even the party workers in Kingston were surprised by the margin of victory, and set off on a triumphant parade even before most of the Ontario results had come in. John McIntyre, who had kept Macdonald posted on the situation, telegraphed soon after seven o'clock with a jubilant message. "The city is in a tremendous excitement," he reported, "our overwhelming victory has set the people frantic. I hope you are much better."[9]

It was welcome news, but Macdonald was not much better. He was lying in his upstairs bedroom at Earnscliffe, following the results alertly, but with a curious absence of excitement or emotion. There was still a long way to go in Ontario, and as the rural constituencies began to report more fully, the momentum began to swing back to the Liberals. John Carling was badly defeated in London, an ominous sign. In Windsor, J.C. Patterson had been crushed by the huge margin of eight hundred votes.

Now the appeal of unrestricted reciprocity to the farmers of Ontario began to weigh in fully, and many seats, in the western marches especially, began to change hands. The southwestern end of the peninsula was going solidly red, and a few eastern constituencies had similarly turned away from the National Policy. Northumberland West, where Laurier had spoken three days before, had flipped by hundreds of votes from the result in 1887 to elect the Liberal candidate. Lennox, which Macdonald had compromised his frail health trying to defend, was lost anyway by fifty-seven votes. By the time the polls closed in Manitoba, it was evident that Ontario had been split down the middle, neither party having scored a clear victory.

Manitoba had only five constituencies, but given the tiny lead of the Conservative Party through the Maritimes and Quebec—fewer than ten seats—and the creeping gains made by the Liberals in Ontario, the importance of every contest was magnified. Two were easy Conservative wins, but three had been considered too close to call before the polls closed. Marquette, the only seat held by the Liberals, was retained by the popular incumbent, Robert Watson. Selkirk went the other way, with the Conservative member Thomas Daly defeating Joseph Martin, the high-profile provincial attorney general and author of the Manitoba Schools Act.

The third intriguing contest was in Winnipeg, where Sir John's son, Hugh John Macdonald, had agreed to run as a Conservative candidate with just two weeks left in the campaign. The betting the night before had offered a two-to-one payout for a Macdonald victory, and Conservatives had been taking those odds, confident that he would squeak out the win. The result was known soon after the polls closed, and it was a surprise to everyone in the city. Hugh John had been elected by more than five hundred votes, a colossal and entirely unexpected margin of victory. The Winnipeg Tories paraded to city hall, which had plenty of room for big crowds, and Hugh John was there to thank his exhilarated supporters. They carried him on their shoulders to the *Free Press* office, where another speech and hearty cheering for the prime minister and the Queen followed. Onto their shoulders he went again, then into a sleigh pulled not by horses, but by party workers. Boys set fire to brooms to make torches, more singing and marching ensued on the way to the Opera House, and eventually a bonfire was lit on Main Street. Hugh John retired to his home in the wee hours, happy and tired, only to be serenaded from the street by an overenthusiastic brass band.

The news from Winnipeg was the source of raucous celebration for Conservatives across the Dominion. The election of Hugh John was a victory not just for the party, but for the prime minister, whose health still concerned them so gravely. Perhaps he would be reinvigorated by the knowledge that his son had triumphed so magnificently. Sir John was, in fact, lying in bed when Pope brought him, just after eight o'clock, the telegraphed results from Winnipeg. He seemed to be cheered by it, as he had been by the news of his own election in Kingston. But there was little energy or enthusiasm in the Old Man. For two more hours he lay quietly in bed, receiving frequent updates from his secretary. The Conservatives were ahead when the clock tolled ten, but the results in constituencies across the Dominion were still coming in, and many were still too close to call. Pope estimated that only half the seats in the new House of Commons had been definitely settled when Macdonald said, simply, "I think that will do for tonight."[10] He then turned on his side and went to sleep.

As the night progressed, and the results from the North-West Territories and British Columbia began to be tallied, the Liberals saw their hopes of forming the government begin to slip away. They were doing quite well in Quebec and Ontario, but probably not well enough to make up for the beating they had taken in the Maritime provinces. Unless the Liberals were at least ten or fifteen seats ahead by the time western Canada began to weigh in, the Macdonald government would certainly be re-elected. Manitoba had elected four Tories, and as the results from the more distant west streamed in over the wires, there was more excellent news for the Conservatives. In the North-West it had almost literally been no contest. Two of the four races had featured Tories against Tories, without even token opposition from the Liberals. In the two that had genuine competition, the Liberal candidates were losing by hundreds of votes.

It was a similar story in British Columbia. Two of six Conservative candidates had been acclaimed, and it shortly became obvious that the other four were on their way to re-election. This overall domination of the Western constituencies was going to boost the Conservative total by fourteen or fifteen seats. Across Canada, there was a growing realization in both camps of what had happened—what was still happening as the hours passed—in the election of 1891. There would be no days of confusion after the polling, no conflicting claims of who had won and who had lost. Liberal journalists resigned themselves to the task of preparing the morning editions, with nothing to cheer about but moral victories and a reduced Conservative majority. Conservative journalists, of course, revelled in their victory as they fired up the presses.

The counting continued long into the night in many constituencies, but the result was in. Sir John A. Macdonald and the Conservative Party had won the election. The "loyalty cry" had saved the day.

ELEVEN

The Empty Saddle

When the sun rose over Earnscliffe on the morning of March 6, Sir John A. Macdonald was still prime minister of Canada. It was a momentous accomplishment. But there was little celebration in the quiet upstairs bedroom where the Old Man still lay. Agnes was there by his bedside, keeping an anxious vigil, watching her husband struggle to recover from the exhaustion—or perhaps something worse—that had caused his collapse the week before. He could hardly move, as if he were pinned by some invisible weight. There was pain in the left side of his chest. His pulse was erratic, and he had developed a hard, recurring cough. As the days passed, Macdonald was very slow to improve. It was not until March 9 that he felt well enough to brave the stairs and start into the mountain of correspondence that had been accumulating in his study. There he finally could sit down and reflect upon the landscape, now that the dust had settled.

The overall result was a Conservative majority of about thirty seats, pending the outcome of a handful of court challenges in the closest ridings. Congratulations had poured in from Conservative members of

Parliament, of course, and from the big manufacturers who had supported the campaign. The most heart-warming letters had come from the rank and file, the ordinary party workers who had put up posters and organized meetings and worked long, unpaid hours to elect Tory candidates. To them the reason for the party's success was clear: Sir John A. himself had rescued the Dominion. "Accept our heartiest congratulations on your personal triumph ... our people are jubilant," wired D.R. Hannington from Dorchester, New Brunswick, "for your courage wisdom and judgment have saved Canada." "From the bottom of my heart you have saved the Dominion and the old flag," Thomas Howard applauded from Montreal; "CANADA FOR EVER" was scrawled across the top of his letter. From the prime minister's own constituency of Kingston, J.M. Fenwick wrote, "I hope the victory will act on you as an 'Elixir of Life' so that the country will not lose your services for many years to come. Canada can't spare you."[1] There was a touch of anxiety, even sadness, to that one.

The Conservative Party's fortunes had varied considerably across the country. In the West it had been a total rout. "British Columbia is solid," cabled Gordon Corbould, re-elected by more than a thousand votes in New Westminster. That was an understatement. Only Cariboo riding, sprawling in size but tiny in population, had been even close. One triumphant candidate, D.W. Gordon, wired Sir John, "Accept my congratulations ... felt sure Canada would speak with emphasis today from ocean to ocean in vindication of your policy." It was the same in the North-West. From Red Deer, Alberta, Macdonald learned from party worker Leo Gaetz that "your grand record, and most patriotic policy, have touched and influenced the remotest constituency in the entire Dominion." There the winning candidate took 80 percent of the votes; his opponent, James Reilly, was a fellow (but apparently less popular) Conservative. "We did our work in this district," reported a North-West Mounted Police officer in Calgary, "and think Reilly will lose his deposit." The officer wondered if his detachment might be sent a portrait of the prime minister as its reward.[2]

In Manitoba, the only Liberal victory, in Marquette, was won by just thirty-six votes, and the defeated Conservative candidate assured Macdonald that a recount was coming. At any rate, he observed, "the West has done its duty nobly." The Canadian Pacific Railway Company had evidently exerted its mighty influence on behalf of the Conservatives; William Van Horne reported to Macdonald that Marquette had been lost "purely by oversight."

At the other end of the country the results had been almost as one-sided, and even more pleasantly surprising. The Conservatives had triumphed in thirty-one of forty-three Maritime constituencies. Sir Charles Tupper received much of the credit for the rout, but more than any individual, it was the "loyalty cry" that had determined the outcome. The people of the Maritimes were the closest to Great Britain geographically, of course, and more than that, in their outlook on the world and habitual patterns of thinking. The Old Policy and the Old Leader had never been loved in the Maritimes as they may have been in central Canada, but the Old Flag was sacred. The Conservative appeal to patriotism had been extremely effective there.

The news had not been as good for the Conservatives in the heart of the country. In Ontario they had actually lost the popular vote and retained only a slight edge in seats of forty-eight to forty-four. In the western part of the province the Liberals had swept the rural constituencies and made a casualty of John Carling. A stove manufacturer, one of thousands of party volunteers who had canvassed for the Tories across Ontario, reported unhappily to Macdonald, "I do not regard the result in this province with much comfort. We are weak where we ought to be strong and have lost some of your ablest supporters. It ought not to have been so."[3]

That letter was representative of an uneasy post-election mood within the party as the results sunk in. Their calamitous showing west of Toronto was attributed by some to the evildoing of the Liberals, variously described as "a most unscrupulous opposition" and, more colourfully, "the traitorous band who have fought like demons."[4] These were not terribly enlightening explanations, though there was a touch of truth to hypocritical Tory complaints that the Liberals had "boodled heavily" and imported Canadians from the United States to vote in the border constituencies.[5] There was also, in a grudging way, some acknowledgment of the obvious. Unrestricted reciprocity had won over the majority of the province's farmers. As a loyal Conservative wrote from Amherstburg, just across the river from Detroit, "There is no doubt that the farming community has been greatly disturbed and coaxed to try the Grits again by U.R. with the States. It came very near being a great wave which would have swept our party if it had not been for your great popularity and the idea most people had that after all you were the safest bet."[6]

The news from Quebec was even worse. The province had been the Conservative Party's fortress since Confederation, but this time the Liberals had won the majority of the constituencies, thirty-seven seats to twenty-eight. From the Tory point of view the result was a complete disaster. Though all the important Quebec ministers had survived, Charles Colby, a junior minister, had been beaten in the Eastern Townships, and the party had done poorly in the predominantly French-speaking constituencies. The still-lurking ghost of Louis Riel, the odious McGreevy scandal, and the popularity of Honoré Mercier and Wilfrid Laurier had clearly assisted the Liberal cause. Conservatives could not help but feel the ground shifting beneath their feet in the province. George Drummond, the rich Tory from Montreal, best expressed the feelings of shock and disappointment of the party's old guard. "Quebec," he sniffed in a letter to Macdonald, "has disgraced itself."[7]

As he scrutinized the results, Sir John A. found too few reasons to celebrate. His majority of thirty seats was uncomfortably slim, and the court challenges to come might give more seats to the Liberals. The mandate from the people was not a resounding one, and he was not sure what legislation to introduce in the next session of Parliament.

Most distressingly, if the results in Quebec and Ontario were combined, the government had lost in central Canada—by far the most populous region—by the narrow margin of eighty-one seats to seventy-six. To his old friend George Stephen, a former C.P.R. president, the prime minister revealed his apprehension about the political situation. "If our election had been postponed until another harvest, we should have been swept out of existence," he confessed. "I was surprised and grieved to find the hold unrestricted reciprocity had got of our farmers." The Tories had benefited from the foolishness of the Liberals and their allies, which had allowed Sir John to "raise the loyalty cry, which had considerable effect. Still," he concluded grimly, "the farmers' defection, and the large sums sent, *beyond a doubt*, from the United States, have left us with a diminished majority and an uncertain future."[8]

The Liberal Reaction

Their future might be uncertain, but the Tories had won the election. The Liberals had no such consolation and, besides, they had Edward Blake. Laurier had prevented him from publishing his West Durham letter in the midst of the campaign, but there was no stopping him now. Laurier tried. Two days before the vote, he had written to Blake again, urging him to wait longer before revealing his inflammatory views. "Do you not believe," he pleaded, "that ... it would be preferable to be heard by a less prejudiced public in a less excitable moment?" The answer was a cold refusal. "My feeling is that the sooner the last painful stage is over the better for all concerned," Blake replied flatly. He added, with unbecoming self-pity, "God only knows what I have suffered in these last days."[9]

So it was that the day after the election, the Toronto *Globe* dutifully carried the West Durham letter that Blake had signed his name to the month before. It was buried on page 4 but it consumed most of the page—thirty-five paragraphs, all told—and there was no hiding its extraordinary contents. Blake's argument started off on familiar ground with a denunciation of the Conservatives and the National Policy. There was no surprise there, but then he went off the Liberal script completely. He dismissed unrestricted reciprocity as an unrealistic proposal that the United States would never accept. Commercial union, far reaching and entangling though it might be, was in Blake's mind the only kind of free trade that might realistically be agreed upon by both countries. And if commercial union was achieved, he prophesied, "the tendency, in Canada ... would be towards political union, and the more successful the plan the stronger the tendency ... our hopes and fears alike would draw one way. We would then indeed be 'looking to Washington.'"[10] Most scandalously, Blake seemed to imply that if political annexation was Canada's future, then Canadians ought to accept that fact and seek the best terms possible with the United States. That, to most Canadians, was sacrilege.

Blake probably felt better, at least at first, to finally get his long-suppressed feelings off his chest. Still, he must have known that this was an absolute betrayal of the party that had followed him faithfully for many years. Blake was implying that their trade policy would lead to annexation, and though he vouched for their loyalty—suggesting that his colleagues did not appreciate the consequences of their policy—that defence rang hollow in the ears of his old supporters. They were outraged. They had endured long years of putting up with his neurasthenia and indecisiveness and, most of all, his habit of leaving when they needed him most. How could he have done this to them?

The Liberal reaction to the West Durham letter was swift. The same issue of the *Globe* ran an editorial that called Blake's opinions "wholly distasteful." Going further, it asserted that the *Globe* would prefer to hope for the future of Canada, "rather than to share with Mr. Blake the responsibility of advocating political union." That was a low blow, insinuating that he had been *promoting*, instead of warning against, annexation. Blake was furious. The *Globe*, apparently with the consent of the party leadership, had purposely twisted his words to turn him into a traitor. He was permitted to publish a one-sentence denial in the paper five days later, itself a marvel of cryptic ambiguity, but the damage had been done and the Liberal Party was washing its hands of him. Sir Richard Cartwright was so angry that he never spoke to Blake again. Other prominent Liberals avoided contact with their former leader for several months.

Wilfrid Laurier was personally hurt by Blake's action. Many years later he would still recall vividly the feeling of having been stabbed in the back. What upset him most, however, was not the personal slight but the fact that Blake had discredited unrestricted reciprocity without suggesting a constructive alternative. Laurier was no doubt relieved to discover, in the days that followed, that many Liberals shared his view. A Manitoba party worker observed that "Mr. Blake suggests nothing & throws up his hands."[11] George Casey, an Ontarian, was an especially disgruntled former Blake man. On March 12 he reported defiantly that "it makes no difference whatever to my voters in this region what E Blake thinks about the situation."[12] Two weeks later, he was more reflective. "Blake's letter has not caused the commotion I expected," Casey informed Laurier. "People are tired of criticism. They want something done and someone to do it." Summing up the tortured reasoning that had led Blake to publish the letter, he said simply, "It is sad to see such a gigantic mind made impotent for patriotic use, by fighting its own microscopic scruples."[13]

That comment about the "microscopic scruples," from the pen of a disillusioned former supporter, was a telling insight into Edward Blake's maddening, disappointing, and now utterly finished career in Canadian politics. That he was astonished by the response of the Liberals to his letter—to Laurier he later complained that the party had treated him as if he were dead—spoke volumes about his capacity for self-absorption and his inability to connect emotionally with the party's rank and file. Even so, it was a sad departure from the national stage. For all his faults he had always tried to put the best interest of the country first, and that awful self-pitying line, "God only knows what I have suffered," might well have applied to his whole political career.

In the summer of 1891 there was nothing for Blake to do but focus on his legal practice and lament the loss of friendships. There would eventually be reconciliation with Laurier, who magnanimously revived their personal correspondence that August, but not with the Liberal Party. A year later Blake was offered a safe seat in the British Parliament, representing the Irish Nationalist cause, and gladly took it. He would spend fifteen years there, mellowing with age and finding steadily more time for friends and family. Some of the old political wounds probably never healed. But Blake could be proud that he had left the Liberal Party a more tolerant, genuinely national party than he had found it in the early 1880s. And, he liked to boast, he had been a great success in his choice of a successor.

On that vital point, the quality of leadership offered by Wilfrid Laurier, Blake and the Liberals were in agreement. It would have been easy for them to declare it a mistake—"a fearful blunder," as J.D. Edgar had once put it—to have been led into the election by a French Canadian Roman Catholic. They might well have concluded that the prejudices of English Canadians would henceforth have to be pandered to. After the election there were, indeed, some grumbles about how hard it was for the Laurier-led Liberals to woo hidebound Ontario Protestants. But the grumblers were in the minority. After the election of 1891, most Liberals expressed unreserved confidence in Wilfrid Laurier. They had lost, but not because of his leadership, his race, or his religion. They applauded his performance on the campaign trail and his calm defence against the charges hurled at him by the Tories. Some of the sentiments that emerged from Ontario, where there had been the most initial opposition to his leadership, were remarkable. A Liberal from Hamilton who described himself as a "humble foot soldier" reported proudly that he had made speeches at eighteen meetings in thirteen days, for at least two hours each time. The name that he had heard most often, even more than those of local candidates, was Laurier. What he wrote next was inspired, and inspiring.

> Fifteen months ago it was said in Ontario that no "Frenchman" could lead the liberals of Ontario. Today such a remark is impossible in our Province. I regard your capture of Ontario, and heart and respect of Ontario, as marvellous. For the first time in many years the reform party of Ontario speak *lovingly* of their Chief. I have seen it with my eyes, from the Georgian Bay to Prescott. Mark you I was a prejudiced onlooker believing that a leader from Ontario must come from thence. Not so! Your hold upon the affections of Ontario is marvellous ... I write to cheer you on. Victory is within sight.[14]

With this kind of support, it was clear that Laurier was going to remain the leader.

The fate of unrestricted reciprocity was less clear. Again, it would have been easy to appreciate the reasoning of the Liberals if they had decided that the policy was just too inflammatory. Many of them had been stung by those charges of treason, and in the campaign post-mortems that Laurier received in March 1891 this was a complaint, particularly in the Maritimes. Louis Davies reported from P.E.I. that the sentimental appeals of the Tories had been effective, and John Ellis, who had lost his seat in a mean-spirited contest in Saint John, ruefully remarked that "the main thing was the loyalty cry. The charges were rung upon it in every way ... it really surprised me in the end that we had any votes left."[15]

Still, there was broader support among the Liberals for sticking with unrestricted reciprocity. The policy itself was not flawed, its proponents argued; in fact it was more popular than the National Policy. They would just have to take greater care next time to prevent the Conservatives from twisting the question into a false choice between loyalty and disloyalty. They must also do a better job of countering the effects of Conservative boodle. The Halifax *Morning Chronicle* reported under a decidedly sore-loser headline, "THE TORIES DID THEIR DIRTY WORK IN NOVA

SCOTIA AND NEW BRUNSWICK," that in Sir John Thompson's constituency of Antigonish votes had been purchased for the staggering sum of one hundred dollars apiece.[16] George Mitchell of Nova Scotia informed Laurier that "Sir Charles Tupper is the most accomplished villain in Canadian politics today," adding that while Nova Scotia's Liberals had presented the more popular policy to the voters, at Tupper's instigation "the Tories ... having no policy to present, presented cash instead." These and other Conservative dirty tricks, rather than unrestricted reciprocity, were held by Liberals across Canada to be the reason for their narrow defeat.[17]

But the Boodle Brigade could not march forever. Macdonald was an old man leading an old party that was utterly spent of energy and ideas. The Liberals might yet defeat the Tories if they could trigger another election soon. Sir Richard Cartwright, after consulting with Laurier, began preparing dozens of court challenges in the constituencies where fraud and corruption had allegedly prevailed. This strategy might put additional seats in the Liberal column, and perhaps even overturn the Tory majority in the House. The party also determined to attack the National Policy more aggressively. The tide of public opinion had turned against it—David Mills cheerfully told Laurier that "the NP is as dead as Louis XIV"[18]—and the Liberals were sure that time was on their side. "The trade question is *the* question," Laurier wrote to J.D. Edgar, "and upon it we must hammer, hammer, hammer."[19] His supporters agreed, and they marched confidently forward—still united under Laurier, still champions of unrestricted reciprocity—into the spring session of Parliament.

The Last Days

By the beginning of April 1891, Sir John A. Macdonald was feeling well enough to make little ventures into town and attend more regularly to his prime ministerial duties. Agnes, however, was still fearful. She knew that her husband was not the same as he had been before his collapse in Kingston, and she did her best to limit his exertions as he readied for the next session of Parliament. The two of them spent quiet hours in the sunshine on the terrace overlooking the Ottawa River at Earnscliffe, and he devoted precious time to Mary, who always delighted in his company. But there was, as there had always been, the call of politics. Sir John A. had known it long before he had known Earnscliffe, or Agnes, or even Ottawa. He had always responded, and there was never any real doubt that he would do so now.

Perhaps it would be all right. Joseph Pope would be there to lighten the burden of his correspondence, and his parliamentary colleagues could surely do most of the heavy lifting in the upcoming House debates. Sir Charles Tupper was gone, however. Before leaving for London he had stopped in at Earnscliffe and found the prime minister at his desk, looking haggard and dispirited, buried as always in paperwork. "I wish to God you were in my place," Sir John A. had said. That was an impossibility, of course. He could not have meant it seriously. But these two old Tories—one so slim and slight, the other burly and bombastic—had weathered countless political storms over their long careers. They were practically the last of their generation, and of all the Conservatives, Tupper knew best how wearying it was to be in Sir John A.'s place. "Thank God I am not," he had replied.[20] Tupper then sailed for England.

Macdonald stayed, and the seventh Parliament of Canada met on April 29. The day had special significance for him, and not merely for the obvious reason that he was being reconfirmed as prime minister. For the first time Macdonald would sit together in the House of Commons with Hugh John, the newly elected member for Winnipeg. The father and son had never been close—even in their private letters, there was always a kind of sad formality between them—but it was one of the more memorable moments in the history of the House when they took their oaths and signed the register together, then walked arm in arm to a rousing ovation.

Then there was the usual partisan jousting. During the debate on the speech from the throne, for example, Laurier drew attention to the reduced government majority, only to be reminded by the grinning prime minister that he had a majority still. But the good humour did not last. The Opposition was confident and aggressive, and began probing eagerly for weaknesses in the Tories' armour. Sir Richard Cartwright orchestrated the Liberal attack with enthusiasm, and they were set to humiliate the government with the McGreevy scandal. On May 11 Israël Tarte, the new member from Montmorency, took his seat in the House holding a little black bag, the contents of which he claimed he had been offered over a hundred thousand dollars for. Inside were what he called his "little papers": long-accumulated evidence of corruption in the Department of Public Works involving the McGreevy brothers and Hector Langevin, the responsible minister. Tarte rose and levelled sixty-three charges against these three distinguished Conservatives. The charges were promptly referred to the Select Standing Committee on Privileges and Elections, and that was where the real action would take place throughout the session. In two weeks the committee would begin a circus-like investigation that would embarrass the government, cause Thomas McGreevy to be expelled from the House, and destroy the political career of Hector Langevin.

Meanwhile, however, it was evident that something was not right with Sir John A. Macdonald. He was trying hard to appear his old self, but the act was not convincing. He had been sitting listlessly in the House, rarely contributing to debates, and a dismal speech delivered on May 1 had left even members of the Opposition concerned. Over the years the Liberals, to a greater extent than the Tories or the general public, had witnessed all that was good and bad in the Old Man. They had admired his intelligence and ability, but loathed his dismissive sarcasm, aggressive partisanship, and ruthless management of patronage and power. As they saw it the prime minister had used every dirty trick in the book to keep himself in office, and the best interests of the country had often suffered in consequence. Some Liberals, like Sir Richard Cartwright, genuinely hated him. They all had good reason to resent the charges of treason that Macdonald had flung at them in the recent campaign.

Even so, they could not help but be distressed to see him fading before their eyes. Sir John A. Macdonald was not just the prime minister. In a country that was desperately short of unifying symbols, he had been one of the few constants, someone whom Canadians felt they had always known and relied on and, at critical moments, rallied around. He had become a national institution, and there was not a Liberal who would fail to acknowledge that. Typical was the attitude of John Charlton, whom Macdonald had long mocked as the "member from Michigan." During the session, Charlton bitterly scolded the prime minister for his "most discreditable and dishonest" tactics on the campaign trail. But he was deeply affected by the feebleness of Sir John A.'s speech on May 1, and soon afterward crossed the floor to shake his hand and inquire about his health. Sir John looked up at Charlton and managed a weak smile. "My dear fellow," he said sadly, "I feel that I shall not trouble you long."[21]

That was prophetic. On the afternoon of May 12, just before a scheduled meeting between Macdonald, Sir John Thompson, and the Governor General, Joseph Pope noticed that Macdonald was suddenly having difficulty speaking. When Pope informed him that Thompson was on his way, the prime minister replied that he must come immediately and speak for him to the Governor General. "I cannot talk," he struggled to explain, "there is something the matter with my speech." Lord Stanley was distressed to see Macdonald like this, and worried that he was showing signs of paralysis. After their meeting Sir John admitted to Pope, "I am afraid of paralysis; both my parents died from it, and I seem to feel it creeping over me." It was the only time that Pope ever saw him look frightened. But by the time they reached the cab that had been summoned outside, the Old Man seemed to have improved. He declined Pope's help getting into the carriage and assured his anxious secretary that he was feeling fine. He then instructed Pope soberly, "You must be careful not to mention this to Lady Macdonald."[22]

For a little while it seemed that the attack he had suffered was a false alarm, an isolated and unexplained medical anomaly. His powers of speech soon recovered, and on Saturday, May 16, he hosted his usual weekend dinner party at Earnscliffe. He was in his seat in the House of Commons through the next week, and appeared to have regained some of his old jauntiness. On Friday, May 22, in what would turn out to be his final appearance in the House of Commons, he spent little time listening to the debate. Instead he moved among the government benches, stopping to talk to the backbench members, spinning old stories and insisting that he was feeling better. The next evening, against his wife's wishes—Agnes feared that he was pushing himself too hard—Macdonald hosted another elaborate dinner party. It was too much, and for several days afterward Sir John was confined to Earnscliffe, feeling miserable and ill.

At half past two in the morning on May 28, Agnes was awoken by her husband's alarmed calls for help. His condition was serious; his left arm appeared to be partly paralyzed. By morning things had improved, but this time Sir John A. seemed to sense that his time was running out. He began to put his personal affairs in order—"now, while there is time," he matter-of-factly informed Pope[23]—affixing his signature to documents requiring prompt attention. He saw Sir John Thompson, and they spent an hour discussing matters of state. At that meeting, Thompson later observed, the prime minister was mentally just as sharp as he had ever been. The next morning, Wednesday, May 29, although Macdonald was still feeling weak, he busied himself by answering correspondence brought by Pope, and relaxed with some quiet reading in his bedroom.

At four o'clock that afternoon, Macdonald was engaged in pleasant conversation with his doctor, Robert Powell. As they chatted, Sir John rather abruptly lay back on his pillow, yawned once or twice, and then lost consciousness. The action seemed harmless enough, and a moment passed before Dr. Powell sprang forward, realizing what had just happened. Macdonald had suffered a second stroke, far more devastating than the first. Agnes and Hugh John were immediately summoned, as were two additional doctors of distinguished reputation whose expertise might somehow remedy his desperate condition. Examining the patient, Dr. Powell surmised that he had suffered a hemorrhage into the brain, causing paralysis on his right side. When Macdonald regained consciousness, it became clear that his vocal chords had seized up. His eyes were alert, however, and terrible hours passed as he struggled to speak to Agnes and Hugh John.

The doctors could do nothing. They had seen strokes of this severity before, and they judged that the prime minister was beyond their care. Their grim prognosis was that he had hours to live. At eight o'clock they issued a bulletin informing the public of the relapse and stating that the situation was "most critical." A reporter from the Toronto *Empire* was sent with a note to the House of Commons, which was debating a Liberal motion condemning Sir Charles Tupper's participation in the recent campaign. As Sir Richard Cartwright made a spirited attack on Macdonald's conduct in recalling Tupper, the reporter passed the note to Hector Langevin, the prime minister's deskmate. Silently he absorbed the crushing news—"entire loss of speech, haemorrhage into the brain, condition quite hopeless"—and the expression on his face stirred anxious whispers on the government side of the House. The *Empire* reporter observed that "it was pathetic to observe the pain which came over the faces of the Conservative members." As the debate continued, members on both sides withdrew to the lobby in search of information. A Liberal member soon brought the news to his colleagues in the chamber, and similarly anxious conversations spread quickly through the Opposition benches.[24]

It fell to Langevin to officially deliver the news to the House. After conferring briefly with the other Conservative ministers, he crossed the floor and spoke to Laurier. The two agreed to adjourn for the evening. Langevin then quietly addressed the House, which listened in silence as he informed them that the prime minister's condition was grave and that he was expected by his doctors to live only hours longer. Laurier seconded his motion, and the House adjourned. Members from both sides met on the floor to talk in small groups, shaking their heads in seeming disbelief, all of them having essentially the same conversation. The minister of customs, Mackenzie Bowell, was seen dabbing his eyes with a handkerchief. Langevin sat alone, distracted, beside the prime minister's empty chair. Tears streamed down the old man's face. To no one in particular he murmured softly, "For thirty-three years I have been his follower." He repeated this sentence again and again, as if he could not bring himself to believe the news that he had just delivered.[25]

Those who knew Macdonald well hurried over to Earnscliffe, but Dr. Powell kept his bedroom door closed to all but an intimate circle that included Agnes, Hugh John, and the faithful Joseph Pope. A broad-shouldered Dominion policeman was on hand to guard the door and, when needed, turn the patient in his bed. There was little change in Sir John's condition as night passed into morning. He was in and out of consciousness, but when he was definitely awake, his mind functioned well enough. Through his eyes, and by faintly pressing on the hands of those by his bedside, he managed to convey simple messages. But there was no reason to hope that his condition was going to improve. There at Earnscliffe, and throughout the stunned Dominion, there was nothing to do but wait for the end.

A day passed, then another, and another after that. Regular bulletins were posted on the front gates at Earnscliffe, where a hushed crowd awaited them, and every possible detail about the situation was rushed by telegraph—a special tent was set up by the gates with the required equipment—to the newspapers. Telegrams of concern flooded the wires. Family and friends started immediately for Ottawa, hoping to arrive in time for a final goodbye. Churches that held evening services provided parishioners with reports on Macdonald's condition, and countless prayers—fittingly, from Protestants and Catholics alike—were whispered on his behalf in all parts of the Dominion.

On June 6, the doctors at Earnscliffe noticed a decline in Macdonald's vital signs. He was conscious less and less often, and then finally, in the afternoon, not at all. His breath was coming in short gasps. At seven o'clock that evening, a bulletin posted on the front gate of Earnscliffe said simply, "Sir John's end is fast approaching, has been unconscious since 4pm." The family gathered in the bedroom at nine o'clock, when the doctors saw that he was breathing more slowly. An indescribably long hour followed, during which Agnes and the others watched him peacefully slip away, never regaining consciousness. At twenty-five minutes past ten, reporters lingering outside Earnscliffe saw Joseph Pope walking up the path from the house. "Gentlemen," he announced quietly, "Sir John Macdonald is dead. He died at a quarter past ten, without pain and in peace."[26]

The Empty Saddle

The bell in Ottawa's city tower tolled into the night, seventy-six times in all, wordlessly informing residents of Sir John's passing. Inside Earnscliffe the atmosphere was solemn, and preparations for the funeral began almost immediately. Agnes, who had kept her vigil to the end, was finally persuaded to seek some rest. An undertaker was summoned within the hour; the June weather was warm, and there was no time to be lost embalming the body. It would then be brought down to the spacious dining room, where private visitors would pay their last respects over the next three days. A messenger was sent to Rideau Hall to inform Lord Stanley, who dutifully cabled the news to Queen Victoria and Lord Salisbury, the prime minister of Great Britain. Edgar Dewdney, Macdonald's trusted North-West lieutenant, was dispatched to inform the cabinet. To the rest of the country, which had kept its own distant vigil during the prime minister's final days, the news travelled quickly along the telegraph wires. The next day was a Sunday, however, so there were no newspapers to read. Not until Monday, June 8, did many Canadians learn in their morning dailies of the death of Sir John A. Macdonald.

The tone of the newspapers, Liberal and Conservative, was remarkably alike. The sense of emotional loss, of the terrible finality of the moment, was reflected in the front pages. The last moments of the prime minister were reported in extraordinary depth, as if paying special attention to even the slightest and most inconsequential details might in some way assist the grieving process of the readers. They could, from these pages, learn the precise timeline of events on June 6, and what the weather had been like in Ottawa, and how Sir John's breathing had altered over the course of the day, and who had been with him when he died, and what the scene had been like outside Earnscliffe immediately afterward. Even the sound of the bell in the city tower and how many times it had tolled—once for each year of his life—were reported in emotional language that might normally have caused responsible journalists to blush.

Most newspapers included thorough biographical information as well, reviewing Macdonald's greatest achievements and tactfully dodging, even to a respectful extent in the Liberal press, the subject of his less glorious political methods. There were scores of anecdotes. The old stories that Canadians already knew well were told one last time, as were lesser-known observations that journalists had collected over decades of covering the Old Man. The Toronto *Globe*, the newspaper that had probably tormented him most during his lifetime, recalled his talent for parliamentary debate with grudging admiration. It talked of his habit of turning his back on the Opposition and speaking chummily to his own followers, for example, and of the pleasant personal relations that Macdonald had so often maintained with his greatest opponents in the House of Commons.

It was also on Monday that Macdonald's passing was acknowledged in the House itself. All the members were aware of it, of course.

They were meeting only to authorize a state funeral and to formally adjourn for eight days to give the country, and themselves, a respectful time for mourning. It was the duty of Hector Langevin to deliver the formal announcement, and a difficult duty it was. He planned to read from a prepared text, he informed the Speaker, because he did not trust his memory to get things right. That was a breach of parliamentary etiquette, but forgivable under the circumstances. He began by remembering his old friend's great political longevity, and his central place in the history of the young country. Of future historians who would assess his impact Langevin said, in a measured way, "They may not agree with all of his public acts, but they cannot fail to say that he was a great man, a most distinguished statesman, and that his whole life was spent in the service of his country," until death had claimed him before he could rest even briefly from the burden of leadership.

Langevin then tried to express his personal feelings, but his emotions swelled and it was becoming harder to keep speaking. "Having spent half of my life with him as his follower and as his friend," he informed the House, "his departure is the same as if I had lost half of my existence." He tried to go on, to explain the nature of the special bond between Macdonald and French Canadians such as himself, a bond that had allowed for Confederation to take place and then kept the nation together as nothing else could have done. But it was too much. "Mr Speaker," Langevin suddenly said, in a choked voice, "I should have wished to continue to speak of our dear departed friend, and spoken to you about his goodness of heart, the witness of which I have been so often, but I feel that I must stop; my heart is full of tears. I cannot proceed further."[27]

Langevin sat down with tears in his eyes, and there was a long moment before another member rose to speak. It was Wilfrid Laurier, tall and elegant as always, now facing the delicate task of eulogizing a man he had not known well personally, who had been his political enemy, and who had only three months ago called him a traitor. The

House hung on every word, and he did not disappoint. The Liberals "did not believe in his policy, nor his methods of government," he admitted candidly, yet they shared the sense of loss that the Conservatives were feeling. "It is in every respect a great national loss," he observed solemnly, "for he is no more who was, in many respects, Canada's most illustrious son, and in every sense Canada's foremost citizen and statesman." It was impossible to believe that his chair would remain empty, that his voice would not be heard in the House ever again, whether in the midst of a serious address or a humorous interjection. "In fact," Laurier continued, "the place of Sir John Macdonald in this country was so large and so absorbing that it is almost impossible to conceive that the political life of this country, the fate of this country, can continue without him. His loss overwhelms us."[28]

Laurier spoke for a few more minutes, but those words best captured the acute sense of loss that had overtaken the House. Across the country the feeling was much the same. There was intense interest in the particulars of Sir John's funeral, which was easily the most elaborate that had ever been planned for a Canadian statesman. The route to be taken, the order of precedence for the funeral procession, and even a meticulous description of the coffin could be gleaned from the newspapers. On June 9 the body was taken from Earnscliffe, where Agnes said her final farewell, to the Senate Chamber of Parliament. There Sir John lay in state, and thousands lined up patiently, long into the night, to shuffle solemnly past his open coffin. The next morning, June 10, the funeral began. A lengthy procession of police and militia officers, friends and family, political colleagues, and other dignitaries was set in motion at about half past one by the tolling of city and church bells. These continued for the full length of the journey from Parliament to St. Alban's Church on King Edward Street, about a mile away. The heat was oppressive and a thunderstorm threatened, but sixty thousand people lined the route—some atop temporary platforms specially built to give mourners a better look—and bared their heads as Macdonald's hearse, pulled by four plumed horses, slowly made its way forward. It was a unique and extraordinary spectacle.

After the funeral ceremony at St. Alban's the procession headed to the train station, where the coffin was to be placed aboard a special car and taken to Kingston for the burial. Along the way the skies darkened, and as the long line of mourners passed the Parliament Buildings, the clouds rumbled and finally opened up. A drenching rain scattered some pedestrians, but the procession continued without interruption until it reached the station. It was not until after ten in the evening that the train, which had been stopped several times to accommodate crowds of mourners along the route, arrived at the Kingston city hall. The body again lay in state, and again the people waited patiently to pay their final respects. The next day, June 11, the actual interment took place after a procession of about three miles to Cataraqui Cemetery. Though somewhat smaller than that at Ottawa, the crowd of mourners that lined Princess Street was more densely packed and no less orderly and respectful. Many made the long walk beyond the city limits to the cemetery. There, beneath its gently undulating green grounds, the body of Sir John A. Macdonald was laid to rest.

The Old Man was now a memory. Canadians mourned their loss with a kind of intensity, even urgency, that surprised even the most cynical journalists. The drawn-out funeral had been moving not just for its grandeur and solemnity but also for the respects paid by so many thousands of ordinary folks along the routes through Ottawa and Kingston. At train stations between the two cities people gathered as well, and as the train carrying the body travelled through the countryside, many solitary figures could be seen standing in the fields at the side of the tracks. These Canadians, their heads bowed as Sir John passed their farms, gave his death as much dignity and gravity as all the assembled dignitaries had managed to do. They had shared in a moment of collective national grief. On those two days in June 1891, all across the Dominion businesses and public schools had been closed, memorial services had been held, and the church bells had tolled at the same time that they had in Ottawa and Kingston.

This remarkable outpouring was the product of deep affection for Macdonald and an appreciation of his contribution to the history of Canada. But the people had not been overcome by grief alone. In the newspapers of the day, and the correspondence of those who left private papers behind, there was a real sense of anxiety as well. Macdonald had occupied an incomparable place in Canadian politics, and therein lay the problem. He had been a master of men and he had used all of his ability, all these years, to keep this divided country together. Could it be kept together without him? This sense of unease and uncertainty was best captured by J.W. Bengough, the *Grip* cartoonist who had made a career of caricaturing the prime minister. He had often reserved his harshest criticism for the Old Man, but the first Bengough cartoon that appeared after his death took a very different, simple, and moving approach. The June 10 edition of *Grip* featured a cartoon that was striking for its emptiness but for a mournful, riderless old horse set against a slowly rising sun. The caption read simply, "The Empty Saddle."

It was the most fitting tribute of all.

EPILOGUE

The Destiny of Canada

The nation mourned. Grief hung in the air like a fog as Canadians resumed the rhythms of everyday life. The loss of Sir John A. Macdonald would be felt for a long time, and nowhere more painfully than among the leading Conservatives, who were not prepared to face the "uncertain future" that his passing had made even less certain. Macdonald had often talked of retirement, and his health had been failing before the election. Always, however, he had balked at the question of who else could lead the warring factions of the party and the country. Always it had seemed, to himself and his party, that he was the only man for the job. So Macdonald had stayed on—for just a little longer, he would say—but the successor who should have been ready to take over had never emerged.

Now the question had been thrust upon them. Who could fill the "empty saddle"? Technically there had been no government since June 6 because Lord Stanley considered it improper to set up a new one before

Macdonald had been buried. The delay only made the situation more tense, but even if Stanley had been inclined to do so, there was no one for him to call upon. Only on June 12, the day after the funeral, did party elders assemble in Ottawa to select a new leader. John Thompson summed up their challenge to a friend. "Few even in Ottawa realize the difficulty of the situation that now presents itself," he judged. "It will be a very difficult task to reorganize the Government as we have a great number of conflicting interests and ambitions."[1]

Sometimes Macdonald had seemed to favour Hector Langevin, whose claim to the leadership was premised upon unswerving loyalty to the Old Man and long years of service to the party. Once, in 1888, Joseph Pope had asked the prime minister about his successor. "Oh, Langevin, there is no one else," he had replied. Pope, who thought him a decent minister but not leadership material, had pressed for an explanation. Macdonald had said simply, "He has always been true to me."[2] But the McGreevy scandal had made Langevin a liability to the party. On June 12 he waited impatiently for someone to ask him to form the new government. No one did. Pope later recalled that "the moment Sir John Macdonald's support was taken away, he fell."[3]

A more impressive candidate was Sir Charles Tupper, the fearsome, indestructible "War Horse of Cumberland." He had given four decades of service to the Tory cause, and possessed the energy and bombast of a man half his seventy years of age. Some Tories loved him, but others found his self-promotion—the pursuit of the "glory of Tupperdom," one historian would later call it[4]—unbecoming of a future prime minister. Tupper also liked being Canadian high commissioner in London, and as he saw it the party would have to show that it wanted him badly before he would resign that plum post. What transpired behind closed doors was not made clear to the public, but Sir Charles did not become prime minister—not now, at least. He sailed for England a few days after the funeral.

Another heir apparent was Sir John Thompson, the most indispensable minister in the government. Thompson was easy to like and greatly respected for his intelligence and legal expertise. He was a bit of an odd fit within the Conservative Party in that he disliked politics, especially the thuggish partisan combat that his colleagues relished. He was lonely in Ottawa and preferred life back in Halifax, where he could be with his wife, Annie. Still, Thompson had always answered the call when Macdonald had asked him to remain, and there was little doubt that he would say yes if the party enlisted him to become prime minister.

The trouble with Thompson was that he was unacceptable to the ultra-Protestant Orangemen of English Canada. They still sniggered about his conversion to Catholicism and referred to him as a "pervert" because of it. That kind of bigotry was depressing, but it was a legitimate concern for the Conservative Party. Like it or not, they needed Orange votes to maintain their position in English Canada. When the name of Thompson was floated as successor, D'Alton McCarthy—he of the one-nation, one-language, one-religion vision of Canada—stated flatly that he would never serve under him. That was enough to convince Thompson that there was no sense in the party's choosing him as prime minister. He did not want the burden anyway. He would get his wish, for now.

Who else was there? McCarthy, once such a bright light, had burned his bridges with French Canada and could never unify the party. Joseph-Adolphe Chapleau should have been considered, not just because of his charisma and oratorical talent but because of his hard slogging to keep the Conservatives relevant in Quebec even as they had lost ground to the Liberals. Yet Macdonald had never quite trusted him, and now there was no real consideration of him for the leadership. Within a year Chapleau, his ambitions frustrated and foreseeing dark times ahead for the Conservatives, would leave politics to become the lieutenant-governor of Quebec.

The job of prime minister was finally entrusted as a caretaker position to Sir John Abbott, a grumbling cabinet minister from Montreal. He was hardly the party's leading light. Abbott was a very successful lawyer and businessman and a capable minister, but he was seventy years old and sat in the arthritic, appointed Senate rather than the elected House of Commons. He lacked Macdonald's charm and he certainly did not possess his enthusiasm for public life. (His only famous saying about politics was "I hate politics.")[5] Personally he would have rather seen John Thompson form the government. Still, Macdonald had noted that Abbott was "distinguished for his lack of animosity and personal bitterness," and before his death Sir John had confided to Thompson, "When I am gone, you will have to rally around Abbott; he is your only man."[6] It fell to Thompson to persuade Abbott to become prime minister, and Abbott finally agreed, on the condition that he would lead the government in the Senate while Thompson would lead it in the House. On June 15, 1891, the Abbott-Thompson Conservative government was formed.

The Interregnum

No man could replace Macdonald, but perhaps these two men could. Abbott and Thompson worked well together, shepherding the government through heavy weather in Parliament in the summer and fall of 1891. The Liberals, sensing opportunity, threw everything they had at them. They concentrated on the McGreevy scandal, and the vast corruption in the Department of Public Works was exposed in all its putridity. The parliamentary committee that investigated the charges produced fifteen hundred pages of evidence, much of it damning. There were stories of contracts awarded to firms that did not exist, of trap doors to secret offices, of confidential documents shown to favoured contractors, and of kickbacks paid to the Conservative Party. Langevin denied it all, but on August 11, even before the committee had reported, he bowed to the inevitable and resigned from the cabinet.

The humiliation of the McGreevy scandal was a low moment in the history of the Conservative Party. It should have been in real political trouble, and not just because of the scandal: the economy remained depressed, and in February 1892 an attempt to restart trade talks with the United States ended in deadlock. It seemed like the perfect time for the Liberals to strike, and they got their chance. An extraordinary *sixty-one* by-elections, most triggered by cases of voter fraud, were held across Canada between January 1892 and January 1893. The Liberals had expected to benefit from the results, but instead the Conservatives crushed them, winning forty-nine contests including sixteen Liberal constituencies, increasing their majority in the House to sixty seats.[7] It was a shockingly one-sided outcome, especially given the gloomy political outlook over the course of the year.

The main problem for the Liberals had been the waning popularity of unrestricted reciprocity, which had been affected by a modest annexationist movement—championed by Goldwin Smith and Edward Farrer—that was active in Ontario in the summer and fall of 1891. Eventually that situation had been dealt with by Oliver Mowat, who anxiously advised Laurier that "Farrer seems to have made lively annexationists of the whole Globe staff and directorate."[8] Mowat declared that annexationists had no place in the Liberal Party, made life miserable for Smith whenever he tried to hold meetings, and likely had something to do with Farrer abruptly leaving his position at the *Globe* in the summer of 1892. But Canadians had not forgotten that Smith and Farrer had once been prominent supporters of unrestricted reciprocity, under obviously false pretenses, and U.R. was a badly tarnished commodity as a result.

The Conservatives had gotten a lucky break, but their fortunes began to decline in July 1892 because of the re-emergence of the poisonous Manitoba Schools Question. The Judicial Committee of the Privy Council (the British supreme court that had the final say over Canadian laws) ruled that month that the Manitoba government did have the right to abolish public funding for Catholic schools. That put the federal Conservatives in an awkward position, because they would have to decide whether or not to save the schools by imposing remedial legislation upon the province. Saving them would infuriate many English Protestants across the country, but allowing them to be abolished would outrage French Catholics in Quebec. What were the Tories to do? Thompson, who took over as prime minister when Abbott retired in November 1892, stalled for time. He referred the question of whether the federal government *could* legally intervene to the Judicial Committee, and hoped some sensible solution might be found in the meantime.

It was a terrible mistake. The Manitoba Schools Question festered for two years while the Judicial Committee made up its mind, and when it did, in January 1895, the court confirmed that the federal government could use its constitutional powers to restore public funding to the Catholic schools. By then, though, the Conservatives had suffered an irreplaceable loss. In October 1894 Thompson, stressed and overweight, had gone to England to visit doctors and enjoy a rare holiday. On December 12, while lunching with the Queen at Windsor Castle, he died suddenly of a heart attack. Canadians mourned the loss deeply, and the Conservatives most of all. From the shallow pool of possible successors they selected Mackenzie Bowell, their mediocre seventy-year-old minister of trade and commerce. "Grandpa Bowell," as he was called, got the job based on seniority.

Bowell proved to be an incompetent leader who, as a former Grand Master of the Orange Order, hardly possessed the background to tactfully handle the Manitoba Schools Question. To his great credit he eventually decided—after a year of endless dithering—to use remedial legislation to restore publicly funded Catholic schools in Manitoba. But by then it was too late. In January 1896, after Bowell brought the legislation forward and then withdrew it, half of his ministers resigned in protest of his waffling leadership. He bitterly called them a "nest of traitors," but bowed to the inevitable.[9] Bowell stayed on as a nominal prime minister for the rest of the session, but the real leader of the party after January 1896 was Sir Charles Tupper, who returned from London to take charge of the government and shepherd the remedial legislation through the House of Commons.

The Changing of the Guard

Tupper found, to his dismay, that he was facing a Liberal Party that had put its house in order while the Conservatives had slowly disintegrated. The turning point for the Liberals was a grand party convention in Ottawa in June 1893, ostensibly to craft a new party platform. More than twenty-five hundred delegates from across the country poured into the Rideau Rink and found themselves building a sense of camaraderie that would help the Liberal Party to become, for the first time, a truly national organization. Laurier, who carefully stage-managed the proceedings, quietly abandoned unrestricted reciprocity by arranging a unanimous resolution in favour of "liberal trade intercourse" with the United States. This bland policy made the Liberals safe on the trade question again, and the party emerged from the convention confident and united.

His experience with unrestricted reciprocity had also taught Laurier, perhaps, that adopting bold policies was not always the best course in Canadian politics. On Manitoba Schools, to the immense frustration of the Conservatives, he refused to be pinned down to a specific position. With the advice and support of Israël Tarte, who formally joined the Liberals in 1893, Laurier devised the strategy of *opposing* remedial legislation because it was intruding in the affairs of the province. Forcing Manitobans to reverse their policy, he argued, would only stoke tensions in the province and create a harmful backlash. But what, then, was his solution? Negotiations that would satisfy everyone, Laurier replied. When pressed, he recounted a fable about the best way to separate a traveller from his coat. A chill wind would only cause him to clutch his coat closer, but warm sunshine would persuade him to take it off. As prime minister, Laurier promised, he would find a "sunny way" to resolve the crisis.

The parliamentary session of January to April 1896 was one of the most bizarre in Canadian history. The Conservative government led by Tupper, an English Protestant, tried to pass remedial legislation that would restore public funding to French Catholic schools in Manitoba. And incredibly, the Liberal opposition led by Wilfrid Laurier, a French Catholic, fought to *prevent* the legislation from passing. Tupper did not give up without a fight. He resolved to wear down the opposition through a battle of willpower and physical stamina, trying to keep the House of Commons in session constantly until the remedial bill passed. This put a horrendous strain on the Tories, who were already exhausted from the stress induced by the crisis (one Quebec Conservative, Guillaume Amyot, died of a stroke during the debate). The Liberals were assisted by D'Alton McCarthy and his band of ultra-Protestant supporters, who opposed the bill because it undermined their plans for an English-only Canada. This unholy alliance of Liberals and McCarthyites rotated through eight-hour shifts in the House of Commons, obstructing the vote at every turn. Tupper kept the session going continuously, except for dinner breaks and one Sunday of rest, for ten days and nights. Members slept at their desks, got drunk, listened to excruciating speeches—one was about the adventures of Tom Sawyer—and had passed just 12 of the 115 sections of the remedial bill when the clock ran out on the session. The Liberal filibuster had stymied the Conservatives.

Tupper conceded defeat, formally replaced Bowell as prime minister, dissolved Parliament, and called a general election for June 23, 1896. The campaign that followed was fought along the same lines as the parliamentary debate over the Manitoba Schools Question. The Conservatives ran on their support for remedial legislation, even while many in the ranks opposed it, and everywhere he went, Tupper faced hecklers from within his own party.

Laurier and the Liberals ran on "sunny ways," one of the least heroic platforms in the history of Canadian elections. Because they opposed remedial legislation, however, they won the support of many English Protestants. And because they also proposed to protect the schools through negotiation, they also won the support of many French Catholics. On election day the Conservatives narrowly won the popular vote, and in English Canada the outcome was evenly divided between the two parties. In Quebec, however, the Liberals won forty-nine of sixty-five seats, giving them a majority of over twenty in the House of Commons. What Laurier himself had not believed possible had come to pass. For the first time in their history, Canadians had elected a French Catholic as their prime minister.

In fact Laurier, for all his superficial differences from Sir John A. Macdonald, proved to be a very similar prime minister. His economic policy was a continuation of the National Policy, tweaked to offer a preference to British imports. His immigration policy pursued the same goal of filling up western Canada with hard-working peasant farmers, with far greater success. Toward Great Britain he was always deferential—he accepted a knighthood in 1897—but like Macdonald, Laurier looked after Canadian interests first. His handling of delicate questions of language and religion was also reminiscent of Sir John. Both recognized the need for cooler heads and compromise when passions were inflamed, and both tacitly conceded that sometimes there was little sense in pressing the rights of the minority to the point of enraging the majority.

Laurier had learned other things from Macdonald. He was cautious when making his cabinet, giving plum posts to Oliver Mowat and other British loyalist types, and for a politician who was once considered lazy by his colleagues, he took a remarkable interest in exerting personal control over patronage appointments. The Canadian political system functioned under Laurier just as it had under Macdonald, with all its inglorious emphasis on the scratching of backs and rewarding of friends. The difference was that the Liberals were now the ones getting the government jobs. There was corruption under Laurier as well, and though he was not personally tainted by it, he showed no inclination to improve a flawed political system that was working for him.

Laurier would serve as prime minister for fifteen years, winning four consecutive elections and presiding over a period of unprecedented growth and prosperity in Canada. He was eventually defeated—ironically, after he had decided to resurrect the policy of free trade with the United States—in the election of 1911. Like Macdonald, however, Laurier never left Parliament. His last years as Liberal leader were tumultuous and sad; he could only watch helplessly as Canadians were traumatized by the horrors of the First World War overseas, then brutally divided between French and English by a crisis over mandatory conscription for military service. When he died in 1919 the country mourned Laurier as deeply as it had Macdonald. And it was a testament to his political talents, and those of Macdonald before him, that Canada—in spite of the pain and tension caused by the war—held together, and healed, and prospered again. The country, and its people, had come a long way since the despairing years of the late nineteenth century.

The Lost Legacy of 1891

By the early twentieth century the election of 1891 was already receding from popular memory in Canada. There were several good reasons for that. The election of 1911 superseded it as the cautionary tale of what happened to Canadian parties that pursued free trade with the Yankees. Laurier served so long as prime minister that he became an icon of national unity and prosperity, and few people remembered the self-doubting young leader he had once been. And none of the notorious continentalists of the late nineteenth century remained prominent long after the election of 1891. Edward Farrer, ironically, developed a friendly association with the Laurier government. The prime minister liked Farrer, forgave him his past indiscretions, and entrusted him with various secret missions as a reporter and political troubleshooter for the Liberal Party. Farrer prospered and lived comfortably in Ottawa with his wife, Annie, until his death in 1916.

Goldwin Smith met a more bitter end. Behind the walls of the Grange he railed against society in general and the failure of annexation in particular, never accepting that Canadians did not want to be

Americans. As time passed he became isolated from old friends. W.T.R. Preston wrote in his memoirs that Smith was "almost pathetic," trying in vain to convert his dwindling houseguests into annexationists. "The last time I was there he offered me $60,000 to organize a campaign in favour of annexation," Preston claimed. "I never went again."[10] When Goldwin Smith died in 1910, the obituaries heralded his literary talents, but few Canadians were moved by his passing.

Much sadder was the plight of Erastus Wiman, who suffered defeats and tragedies throughout the later years of his life. His finances evaporated when economic depression struck the United States in the early months of 1893. A year later he was arrested on two charges of forgery, and the trial that ensued resulted in his conviction and imprisonment. He was exonerated two years later, but his career and reputation had been destroyed. Wiman then pleaded with Laurier for a job as an advocate for reciprocity, confessing, "I am not a beggar, but I cannot now work for nothing."[11] His plea fell on deaf ears. He ran for New York city council, hoping to jump from there into Congress, but the voters of Staten Island rejected him. The death of his son Frank in 1896 left him devastated. He suffered a crippling stroke in 1901, and after he died in 1904 Wiman faded quietly into historical obscurity.

The election of 1891, the great moment of truth for each of these continentalists, has never been forgotten by the Canadian people quite so utterly as they have forgotten Wiman. But what traces of the contest linger in our histories are sadly one-dimensional. Even the most fair-minded historians have tended to portray the campaign along the same lines that Macdonald shrewdly drew in the heat of battle. The election of 1891, the story goes, was the great "loyalty election," a climactic battle between the heroic nationalism of the Conservatives and the "veiled treason" of the Liberals. The poster of Macdonald hoisted on the shoulders of supporters, wrapped in the British flag—"The Old Flag, the Old Policy, the Old Leader"—has been the most enduring image of the campaign. And the collapse of the Old Man on the campaign trail, followed by his death only months afterward, has fostered the legend that he literally died saving Canada from being sold out to the United States.

The election of 1891 was a turning point in Canadian history, but *not* because Sir John A. Macdonald saved the Dominion from the veiled treason of Wilfrid Laurier and the Liberal Party. The truth is that the campaign was a struggle between two competing yet equally patriotic visions of the destiny of Canada. Macdonald and the Conservatives sincerely believed that the only way to build a great country was to nurture the British connection, develop a prosperous industrial economy with the help of the National Policy and Canadian Pacific Railway, and resist the assimilating pressure of the United States. There was room in this vision for both English and French Canadians, though the former were naturally more responsive to appeals to the Union Jack. This vision triumphed in 1891, and in consequence the pro-British, anti-American nationalism of the Old Man has been accepted as the definitive expression of Canadian patriotism in the late nineteenth century.

This was not, however, the only brand of nationalism that inspired Canadians in 1891. Wilfrid Laurier and the Liberal Party did not run on a platform of veiled treason. They simply did not accept the national vision of the prime minister, which in their eyes called for dependence on Great Britain, a tariff policy that unfairly favoured an elite class of manufacturers rather than ordinary Canadians, and an irrational fear of the United States. The latter point was the most important. Many Liberals—many Canadians—in the late nineteenth century adopted a continentalist view of the future. They believed that free trade with the United States offered the best chance to achieve the prosperity that had eluded them since Confederation. They still retained an emotional attachment to Great Britain, but they were not swayed by sentiment when they considered what was best for Canada.

These continentalists also saw no reason to fear more intimate relations with the United States. The Conservatives worried constantly that moving Canada closer to the American colossus would ruin the dream of developing not only an independent national economy but also a distinctive national culture and identity. Continentalists such as Erastus Wiman and Sir Richard Cartwright believed that was nonsense. They saw no threat either to Canada's political sovereignty or its national identity in simply trading freely with the United States. Why would Canadians suffer on a level playing field, if they were the equals of the Americans in industry and intelligence? And why would Canadian culture be diminished under free trade, so long as those who valued it were determined to protect and nurture it? The irony of this striking brand of nationalism—this "confident continentalism"—was that it actually made Macdonald out to be the pessimist, the man who seemed to believe that loyalty was, as Erastus Wiman once complained, "an article so precious that it should be put in a glass case to be gazed at, rather than to be in every-day use."[12]

This is what the election of 1891 was really about. It was a struggle between two nationalisms, two visions of the destiny of Canada, and each was patriotic and sincere in its own way. Some schemers really did hope for annexation, and these individuals—Farrer, Smith, and U.S. politicians such as Ben Butterworth—did an untold amount of damage to the continentalist movement in Canada. That does not change the fact that men like Wiman and Cartwright championed free trade, and free trade only. It was not a platform that repelled all Canadians. On the contrary, it is worth remembering that the election of 1891 was a very close contest. Nearly half of the Canadian electorate voted for continentalism, and they did not do so because they were traitors.

There had never been such an intense debate about the destiny of Canada in the course of a federal election, and that alone made the election of 1891 memorable and important. No less important, however, was what the election was *not* about. It was the first time that either a French Canadian or a Roman Catholic had led a federal party into a national campaign, and that historic development came to pass at a time when the race-and-religion question was so toxic that Laurier himself believed his party was doomed under his leadership. He was convinced that no English Canadian Protestant, or too few of them anyway, would support him, simply because that was the way that things were in nineteenth-century Canada. If he had been proved right—if the Liberal Party had been crushed in a campaign that revolved around the ethnicity of its leader—then both parties might well have deduced that in the future only an English Canadian, and preferably one from Ontario where the most voters resided, could lead a national party. The damage to national unity that would have been wrought by such a cynical assumption is all too easy to imagine.

The election of 1891 proved Laurier wrong. It demonstrated beyond a doubt that it was possible for a French Canadian and a Roman Catholic to lead a federal party into a national campaign. The Liberals did not win, but they did not lose because of Laurier. They were defeated on the trade question and by the institutional advantages enjoyed by the Conservatives—their access to patronage, superior campaign funds, an advantage in the party press, and control of the voters lists. English Canadian Liberals did not desert the party because of Laurier. On the contrary, the predominant feeling in the ranks was that he had performed admirably. John Willison, watching Laurier confront the Jesuits' Estates Act controversy directly in 1889, had written, "This man would be a giant in some national crisis."[13] In a letter to Laurier three weeks after the election, Willison expressed his conviction that the Ontario Liberals now shared his views: "But be sure of this, you have now a wonderfully enthusiastic following in Ontario and it is of first-rate importance that you should be in this province as often as possible. You are now in a pre-eminent sense the leader of the party, our people, and I know what I am talking about, are more than proud of the way you managed the campaign, and they want to meet you, cheer you, and encourage you."[14]

The Liberals deserved credit for having the courage to accept Laurier as their leader, but no less important was the fact that the Conservatives resisted the temptation to make him the issue in the election of 1891. In many English Canadian constituencies, it must be remembered, an appeal to prejudice would have played well with the electorate, and the Conservatives felt constant pressure to pander to D'Alton McCarthy, the Orange Order, and the Equal Rights Association.

Sir John A. Macdonald refused to entertain that notion even for a moment. He had spent his life holding the young country together, and it was a measure of his success as a nation-builder—perhaps one of the greatest achievements of his career—that he had lived long enough to see a French Canadian battle him for the office of prime minister. On the trade question, Macdonald fought dirty and made scandalous accusations. Every Canadian knows that he was no paragon of virtue. But he confined the debate to the trade question, and by doing so he prevented race and religion from becoming the main issue during the election of 1891. There was, beneath all the knavery and opportunism, some genuine nobility in Sir John A. Macdonald.

It is important to remember that this nobility, this determination to fight the forces of intolerance that would have happily broken the country, was not confined to Laurier or Macdonald. Canadian politicians had a pretty low reputation among their constituents in the late nineteenth century. The boodling of the era has been well documented, and the sleaziness of certain public figures—McGreevy comes to mind—was certainly nothing to celebrate. Nevertheless, there was a consensus among most federal politicians that preserving the fragile unity of a nation composed of English and French, Protestant and Catholics, was worth risking their political futures. That was a crucial phenomenon, and it transcended party lines even in the heat of the campaign.

No example was more inspiring than that of George Dickinson, the rookie M.P. who voted with Macdonald against disallowance of the Jesuits' Estates Act in the pivotal parliamentary debate of March 1889. Dickinson was aware that he was, as Macdonald lamented, "committing political suicide." He voted with the prime minister anyway, and he did lose his seat in the election of 1891. Dickinson never made it back into the House of Commons. But he was a brave politician, and there were countless brave Canadians who refused to give in to the easy temptation of sticking to their own race or religion in a country that could not survive if they did. That story, no less important than the struggle over the trade question that has always defined the election of 1891, is one that can only be read between the lines.

One more aspect of the campaign seems extraordinary from the jaded perspective of the twenty-first century. Canadians cared about politics then. They lived and breathed it, many of them, from the moment they picked up the morning edition of their preferred party's newspaper to their happy participation in the torchlight processions and massive rallies that marked the evenings of the campaign. There were good reasons to be repelled by politics: the system was saturated with partisanship, down to the least consequential post office job, and it must have been difficult for Canadians to keep faith in the fairness of the process. Corruption was endemic, and the exclusion of so many of the people from voting based on their race, sex, or class was grossly unfair.

Still, Canadians went out and voted. They took trains, hitched up teams of horses, or walked for miles, whatever they had to do, to cast ballots that had only recently been made secret. A greater proportion of them voted in the election of 1891, notwithstanding the difficulties of getting to the polls, than would exercise their democratic right a century later. Thousands packed the raucous, unpredictable campaign events, becoming a part of scenes that can hardly be imagined today by Canadians whose politicians struggle to put a hundred bored supporters into their spontaneity-free, made-for-television, no-questions-from-the-audience "rallies." Perhaps Canadians in 1891 were so engaged because there was not much other entertainment available to them. But that was certainly not the entire explanation. There was a closer connection between the politicians and the people in those days. Constituencies had smaller populations, and candidates knew many of their constituents personally. It was possible to write the prime minister directly and get a response. It was an imperfect political system, but the people believed in it, participated in it, and never took their democratic rights for granted. Not all Canadians since have been able to say the same.

The election of 1891 can be remembered for much that should never have been forgotten. It was a genuinely exciting event, generously endowed as it was with suspense and intrigue and colourful characters. It featured a clash of the titans, for it was the only occasion in which Sir John A. Macdonald and Wilfrid Laurier, two legendary Canadian statesmen, contested a federal election as opposing party leaders. It was the setting for a wrenching, emotional debate about the destiny of the country. And it gave us proof that most Canadian political leaders, and the ordinary Canadians who supported them, were determined to set aside racial and religious differences and fight for an inclusive national idea. That idea anticipated the values of tolerance and multiculturalism that have come to define the country in the twenty-first century. This all happened a long time ago. But it is hard not to be inspired by the election of 1891.

NOTES

PREFACE

1. K.A. MacKirdy, "The Loyalty Issue in the 1891 Federal Election Campaign, and an Ironic Footnote," *Ontario History*, vol. 15 (1963): 143–54; J.R. Miller, "'This saving remnant': Macdonald and the Catholic Vote in the 1891 Election," CCHA *Study Sessions*, 1974, vol. 41: 33–52; Miller, "The election in Western Canada," *Prairie Forum*, vol. 10, no. 1 (1985); Ben Forster, Malcolm Davidson, and Robert Craig Brown, "The Franchise, Personators, and Dead Men: An Inquiry into the Voters' Lists and the Election of 1891," *Canadian Historical Review*, vol. 68, no 1 (March 1986): 17–41; Patricia K. Wood, "Defining 'Canadian': Anti-Americanism and Identity in Sir John A. Macdonald's Nationalism," *Journal of Canadian Studies*, vol. 36, no. 2 (2001): 49–69. The election of 1891 is also covered in P.B. Waite's survey of the period, *Canada 1874–1896: Arduous Destiny* (Toronto: McClelland and Stewart, 1971); a chapter is devoted to it in J.M. Beck's *Pendulum of Power: Canada's Federal Elections* (Scarborough: Prentice Hall, 1968); and the most exciting account of the campaign is found in Carman Cumming's *Secret Craft: The Journalism of Edward Farrer* (Toronto: University of Toronto Press, 1992). At least a page or two on the election can be found in biographies of the leading politicians of the day, as well as in the memoirs of some politicians, notably Sir John A. Macdonald (whose memoirs were assembled posthumously by his secretary, Joseph Pope), Sir Charles Tupper, and Sir Richard Cartwright, as well as a few other participants in the election such as the police magistrate George Denison and journalist John Willison.
2. John Duffy, *Fights of Our Lives: Elections, Leadership, and the Making of Canada* (Toronto: HarperCollins, 2002), 26. Though this introduction is hard on Duffy on this particular point, *Fights of Our Lives* is in general a worthy and interesting book, and a very welcome addition to the thin shelf of material, scholarly, journalistic, or otherwise, on the history of Canadian election campaigns.

3. Though Macdonald and Laurier are always credited for attempting to preserve harmony along racial and religious lines throughout their careers, and rightly so, their specific efforts to do so before and during the election of 1891—not to mention those of their rank-and-file supporters, some of whom sacrificed their political careers by following their leaders—tend to be obscured by the standard characterization that this was the "Loyalty Election."
4. Stephen Leacock, from a 1907 article, but summarizing just as well the previous generation of Canadian politicians, quoted in Gerald Lynch, *Stephen Leacock: Humour and Humanity* (Montreal and Kingston: McGill-Queen's University Press, 1988), 10.

ONE: THE MARCH OF THE BOODLE BRIGADE

1. Sir Joseph Pope, ed., *Memoirs of the Right Honourable Sir John Alexander Macdonald* (Toronto: Oxford University Press, 1894, revised 1930), 628.
2. Canadians today know him universally as "Sir John A.," but in the 1880s most Canadians referred to the prime minister simply as "Sir John." The "A." had originally come into usage to help distinguish Sir John A. from Sir John Sandfield Macdonald, a Liberal politician who served as the first premier of Ontario. Sir John S. had retired from public life in the 1870s.
3. Though the general practice in this book is to limit endnote clutter by citing only direct quotations, this is a proper moment to acknowledge that the most thorough and accurate history of Macdonald's movements throughout his lengthy career remains the magisterial two-volume biography written by Donald Creighton, one of the best-known books in all of Canadian historiography. Creighton, *John A. Macdonald: The Young Politician, The Old Chieftain* (Toronto: Macmillan, 1952 and 1955, reprinted with an introduction by P.B. Waite, University of Toronto Press, 1998).
4. A word is needed here about party terminology. Officially, Sir John A. Macdonald's party was named the Liberal-Conservative Party, but in the late nineteenth century most party members referred to themselves as Conservatives. They were also nicknamed the "Tories," a label borrowed from the British political system that was used in Canada, depending on the political leanings of the speaker, as either a term of endearment or a disparaging insult. In this book "Tory" is used as a neutral term, simply because people used it often and because it is much less tiresome to repeat than "Liberal-Conservative." The Liberals were sometimes called Reformers, their original moniker, or Grits, a reference to a one-time faction of the party called the Clear Grits. This was a reference to the ideal material used in masonry work, "all sand and no dirt: clear all the way through," and it was meant to symbolize purity and incorruptibility. Instead of using the term Grit to disparage their opponents, the Conservatives usually preferred harsher stuff like "traitor."
5. One might wonder why Macdonald was not accused of being anti-British as well, since the tariffs applied equally to British goods coming into the country. The Liberals tirelessly and correctly pointed out that Sir John, a man who loved to wrap himself in the Union Jack, was pursuing a trade policy that was injurious to

the economic interests of Great Britain. Macdonald just shrugged off their criticisms. He judged that most Canadians would care more deeply about their own economic interests, as he did himself, and he was right.

6. Thomas Shaw, "A Farmer's View of Commercial Union," in Commercial Union Club of Toronto, *Handbook of Commercial Union: a collection of papers read before the Commercial Union Club of Toronto* (Toronto: Hunter, Rose & Co., 1888), 59.
7. Toronto Board of Trade, 1886 Annual Report, Toronto Board of Trade fonds, vol. 9, MF C-9850, Library and Archives Canada (hereafter LAC).
8. The Métis were the product of relationships between French fur traders and aboriginal "country wives"; similar relationships between English fur traders and aboriginal women produced offspring referred to matter-of-factly as "half-breeds." By the time of Confederation there were several thousand Métis and half-breeds in western Canada, living a semi-nomadic life pursuing the immense buffalo herds across the prairies or putting down roots in the Red River Settlement.
9. Quoted in George F.G. Stanley, *Louis Riel* (Toronto: Ryerson Press, 1963), 114.
10. One of Macdonald's most infamous quotations. An early citation is found in George Parkin, *Sir John A. Macdonald* (London and Toronto, 1908), 244.
11. There are many slightly different versions of this story, which was being told even in Macdonald's day, but there is no definitive record of where and when this happened or, for that matter, if it happened at all. The British historian Ged Martin, a Macdonald expert, suspects that it might have occurred while he was campaigning in an 1864 by-election in Ontario. That would have been fitting because Macdonald was on the stump with D'Arcy McGee, one of the most famous drinkers of the period. See Ged Martin, "John A. Macdonald and the Bottle," *Journal of Canadian Studies*, vol. 40, no. 3 (Fall 2006): 162–85.
12. These two famous drinking-related quotations, paraphrased here, are investigated in Martin's "John A. Macdonald and the Bottle," 162–85.
13. Earnscliffe, a mid-nineteenth century greystone Victorian house not quite large enough to call a mansion, was purchased by the Macdonalds in the early 1880s. It still occupies its magnificent perch atop the bluffs overlooking the Ottawa River, and since 1930 it has served as official residence of the High Commissioner of the United Kingdom in Canada.
14. Peter B. Waite, "The Political Ideas of John A. Macdonald," in Marcel Hamelin, ed., *The Political Ideas of the Prime Ministers of Canada*, The Vanier Lectures, 1968 (Ottawa: University of Ottawa, 1969), 66. Though Macdonald cheerfully sloughed off most of the slings and arrows of political debate, he could not stand to be called a liar. That always enraged him, and his response could be primal and violent. He once challenged an opponent to a duel—yes, a gunfight—over something he had said. He also raced across the floor of the Legislature in the old Province of Canada after being chastised by Oliver Mowat. "You damned pup," Macdonald exclaimed angrily, "I'll slap your chops!" Before the promised slapping of chops could occur, however, another member stepped between the two men and an unbecoming fistfight on the Legislature floor was avoided. Waite, *Macdonald: His Life and World* (Toronto: McGraw-Hill Ryerson, 1975), 13.

15. Michael Bliss, *Right Honourable Men: The Descent of Canadian Politics from Macdonald to Chrétien*, rev. ed. (Toronto: HarperCollins, 2004), 25.
16. Much of our knowledge of Macdonald's private thoughts and habits in his later years comes from Pope, who wrote two invaluable biographies of the Old Man and further discussed their working relationship in his own memoirs. Pope's love and admiration for his mentor shines through in these works, which are in some places very touching, and though they can hardly be called impartial, his remembrances of the prime minister make for fascinating reading.
17. John Charlton, draft autobiography, John Charlton papers, MSS100, vol. 17, 638–41, Fisher Rare Books Library, University of Toronto Libraries. Charlton, a fierce critic of Macdonald, reflected the bitter feelings of many Liberals toward the prime minister when he judged, "His mistakes were many and grievous. Many of the most reprehensible of his acts were not mistakes, but were deliberate measures adopted for the purpose of securing political advantages ... I give Sir John credit for having a desire to do right, but I fear that I shall be compelled to acknowledge that when he found he could not do right and retain office, he did as near right as he thought was advantageous to his political interests." Even so, he could appreciate Macdonald's unique talents. "I recognized him as a great leader," Charlton admitted. "I have felt the charm of his magnetic personality, and I realize ... the nature of that subtle influence which attached his followers to him with bands of steel."
18. Macdonald famously dubbed himself a "cabinet-maker" when signing the guest book at the first of the three political meetings that led to Confederation, the Charlottetown Conference of September 1864.
19. Peter B. Waite, "The Political Ideas of John A. Macdonald," 54.
20. Sir John A. Macdonald to Sir Charles Tupper, Private, 15 October 1886, Sir Charles Tupper fonds, Political Correspondence, 3393–94, MG26F, LAC.
21. Pope, *Memoirs of the Right Honourable Sir John Alexander Macdonald*, 639, 791.
22. "Men versus women" is conspicuously absent from this list, and an explanation is necessary. Canada was a man's world in the late nineteenth century. Women were not permitted to vote, nor were they expected to contribute in any way to public life other than to appear as decorative ornaments at political meetings (or as faithful and supportive political spouses). There was a consensus among Canadian politicians that this was the proper state of affairs. So it was that despite gender-specific problems being prevalent in the Dominion, such as domestic abuse, the political voice of women was muted in the late nineteenth century.
23. Waite, *Macdonald*, 81.
24. J.K. Johnson and Peter B. Waite, "Sir John Alexander Macdonald," in *Dictionary of Canadian Biography*, vol. 12, eds. Francess G. Halpenny and Marcel Hamelin (Toronto: University of Toronto Press, 1990), 591–612.
25. An excellent analysis of how the patronage-dispensing machine operated in the Macdonald era is Gordon T. Stewart, "Political Patronage under Macdonald and Laurier, 1878–1911," *American Review of Canadian Studies*, vol. 10 (1980): 3–26.
26. Bliss, *Right Honourable Men*, 5.
27. Gordon T. Stewart, "Sir John A. Macdonald's Greatest Triumph," *Canadian Historical Review*, vol. 63, no. 1 (1982): 3–33.

28. Halifax *Morning Chronicle*, 12 February 1887.
29. Printed repeatedly in various Liberal newspapers during the election of 1887; one of its first appearances was in the Halifax *Morning Chronicle*, 9 February 1887.
30. The electoral results from 1887 and all other Canadian general elections are available online, through the Parliament of Canada website, at http://www2.parl.gc.ca/Sites/LOP/HFER/HFER.asp.
31. The saga of Haldimand riding offers a classic example of the electoral misconduct and bitter party warfare that were depressingly common features of nineteenth-century Canadian political life. Coulter petitioned to have his victorious Conservative opponent, Walter Montague, unseated for committing electoral fraud. (In a contest this close, petitions were almost always filed against the winner.) The courts agreed with Coulter, and a by-election was held in November 1887. Montague won this time by seventeen votes. Coulter again successfully petitioned the courts, another by-election was held in January 1889, and this time Coulter won by forty-three votes. Montague then petitioned the courts, Coulter was unseated, and a *third* by-election on the grounds of electoral fraud was held in February 1890. Montague was returned to office, with the votes strangely being left unrecorded in the official register. There things rested in Haldimand, but only until the election of 1891, a year later, when the two candidates did battle again. It is not hard to imagine, given this sordid record of five elections in a five-year period in a single riding, why many nineteenth-century Canadians viewed politics as a crooked business.

TWO: THE FEARFUL BLUNDER

1. Edward Blake to Wilfrid Laurier, Confidential, 28 February 1887, Sir Wilfrid Laurier fonds, MG26G, 2, 403–4, LAC.
2. Louis Davies to Blake, 15 March 1887; C.W. Weldon to Blake, 19 March 1887; James Fisher to Blake, 8 April 1887; Laurier to Blake, 16 March 1887; and J.D. Edgar to Blake, 9 March 1887, all in Edward Blake fonds, F2, Series B, Archives of Ontario (hereafter AO). A copy of the Edgar letter is found in Laurier fonds, 2, 420–21, LAC, and the Laurier letter of 16 March is reproduced in F.H. Underhill, "Laurier and Blake, 1882–1891," *Canadian Historical Review*, vol. 20, no. 4 (December 1939): 399–400.
3. This firm, Blake & Blake, was in the 1880s a partnership between Edward and his brother Samuel. Today it is one of the largest firms in Canada, has offices around the world, and is still colloquially dubbed "Blakes."
4. W.T.R. Preston, *My Generation of Politics and Politicians* (Toronto: D.A. Rose Publishing Company, 1927), 173–74.
5. Classical liberalism in nineteenth-century Canada preached a focus on preserving and expanding personal freedom, limited government, and global free trade. It was a far cry from the ambitious and interventionist welfare-state liberalism that eventually came to define the Liberal Party of Canada in the second half of the twentieth century.

6. These personal demons are investigated in a fine article by J.D. Livermore, "The Personal Agonies of Edward Blake," *Canadian Historical Review*, vol. 56, no. 1 (1975): 45–58.
7. John Crerar to Laurier, 14 November 1892, Sir Wilfrid Laurier fonds, vol. 6, 2291–94, LAC.
8. Edgar to Blake, 9 March 1887, Blake fonds, AO; a copy is found in a letter from Edgar to Laurier, 9 March 1887, Laurier fonds, 2, 421–22, LAC.
9. Draft letter of Edward Blake, 28 March 1887, Blake fonds, AO, reprinted in Margaret A. Banks, "The Change in Liberal Leadership, 1887," *Canadian Historical Review*, vol. 38, no. 2 (1957): 114.
10. Blake circular, 28 March 1887, Laurier fonds, 2, 433, LAC.
11. Sir Richard Cartwright to Laurier, 29 October 1887, Laurier fonds, 2, 579–83, LAC.
12. Montreal *Gazette*, 24 June 1887, quoted in Banks, "The Change in Liberal Leadership," 118.
13. *Grip*, 30 May 1891 and 28 January 1893. The former is reproduced in Carman Cumming, *Sketches of a Young Country: The Images of* Grip *Magazine* (Toronto: University of Toronto Press, 1988), 112. The latter is mentioned in Waite, *Canada 1874–1896*, 18.
14. Joseph Schull, *Edward Blake: Leader and Exile, 1881–1912* (Toronto: Macmillan, 1976), 90.
15. Schull, *Laurier: The First Canadian* (Toronto: Macmillan, 1965), 57.
16. Schull, *Laurier*, 178. The famous "shouldered a musket" quote is sometimes translated from the original French to mean "taken up arms" instead. See for example Réal Bélanger, "Wilfrid Laurier," in *Dictionary of Canadian Biography*, vol. 14, ed. Ramsay Cook (Toronto: University of Toronto Press, 1998), 616.
17. Though the existing evidence suggests that Wilfrid and Zoe were a reasonably happy couple, he did have a close relationship with another woman, Emilie Lavergne, the wife of his legal partner Joseph Lavergne. Wilfrid and Emilie insisted that this was a platonic friendship, but it was suspected—though never proven—to have become a romantic one at some point. Evidence of this alleged affair is highly circumstantial, with the most frequently cited "proof" being the fact that Emilie and Joseph's son, Armand, bore quite a striking resemblance to Laurier. Wilfrid and Zoe, for the record, had no children.
18. Laurier to Ernest Pacaud, 11 June 1887, quoted in Bélanger, "Wilfrid Laurier," 617.
19. François Langelier to Blake, 7 March 1887, quoted in Banks, "The Change in Liberal Leadership," 118–19.
20. J.W. Dafoe, *Laurier: A Study in Canadian Politics* (Toronto: Thomas Allen, 1922), 31.
21. Bélanger, "Wilfrid Laurier," 617.
22. Bliss, *Right Honourable Men*, 37.
23. Laurier L. Lapierre, *Sir Wilfrid Laurier and the Romance of Canada* (Toronto: Stoddart, 1996), 57.

24. Laurier to Blake, 18 June 1887, Edward Blake fonds, Series B, AO, reproduced in Banks, "The Change in Liberal Leadership," 122.
25. Wm. M. Gray to Sir Richard Cartwright, 25 June 1887, Sir Richard Cartwright fonds, F24, Series F24-1, AO.
26. Edgar to Matilda Edgar, 6 June 1887, Sir James David Edgar family fonds, F65, Correspondence, Series A-1-3, AO.

THREE: THE BUSINESS PROPOSITION

1. Sir Richard Cartwright to Wilfrid Laurier, Confidential, 8 July 1887, Laurier fonds, 2, 459–61, LAC.
2. Sir John A. Macdonald to Sir Charles Tupper, 28 June 1884, Tupper fonds, MG26F, 2672–75, LAC.
3. Though it is difficult to believe in the early twenty-first century, for the balance of its existence the United States has been reluctant to wade too deeply into the murky seas of international relations. Most famously, President George Washington warned his successors of the danger of "foreign entanglements" (though he did not in fact use that precise phrase) in his Farewell Address of 1796.
4. New York *Times*, 28 May 1887.
5. Congressional Record, 50th Congress, 1st Session, H.R. 6668, introduced by Benjamin Butterworth, 14 February 1887, "Bill to extend the trade and commerce of the United States and to provide for full reciprocity between the United States and the Dominion of Canada," 984.
6. Clipping, Chicago *Tribune*, 23 February 1888, Benjamin Butterworth papers, Manuscript Group 120, Box 2, Folder 8, Sterling Memorial Library, Yale University.
7. The remarkable career and character of Farrer are delightfully brought to life in Carman Cumming's *Secret Craft*.
8. The *Globe* had never been the same since 1880, when its founding publisher, George Brown, was shot in his office by a drunken, recently discharged employee. He survived the initial attack but succumbed to the gunshot wound in his leg six weeks later, leaving the *Globe* without the powerful and bombastic editor who had guided the newspaper since its founding in 1844. Though his death is rarely considered to have been an assassination, given that he was long out of politics and his assailant had no political motive, the murder of George Brown should be rightly regarded as one of the great tragedies of nineteenth-century Canadian political history.
9. Smith used this phrase frequently in his writings and public speeches; his argument on behalf of this North American "re-union" is most thoroughly expounded in the polemical *Canada and the Canadian Question* (London and New York: Macmillan, 1891).
10. Walter Dymond Gregory, draft autobiography, Walter Dymond Gregory fonds, Box 9, B-1, 126–27, Queen's University Archives.

11. A useful outline of Wiman's career is Robert Craig Brown, "Erastus Wiman," in *Dictionary of Canadian Biography*, vol. 13, ed. Ramsay Cook (Toronto: University of Toronto Press, 1994), 1101–2.
12. Washington *Post*, 17 July 1886.
13. Belleville *Intelligencer*, 27 June 1887.
14. David Macpherson to Macdonald, 19 and 20 May 1887; Samuel Leonard Tilley to Macdonald, 22 June 1887, Confidential; and George Johnson, Memorandum on Erastus Wiman, 1891, Macdonald fonds, 250, 113155–60; 277p1, 127307–14; and 68, 27460, LAC.
15. Henry Norman, *Commercial Union as photographed by an intelligent English visitor to Canada* (New York: Erastus Wiman, undated), 7.
16. Washington *Post*, 17 July 1886.
17. Halifax *Chronicle*, 16 July 1887.
18. Ian Hodson, "Commercial Union, Unrestricted Reciprocity, and the Background to the Election of 1891" (master's thesis, University of Western Ontario, 1952), 25.
19. Clipping, Ottawa *Journal*, 4 July 1890, Macdonald fonds, 68, 27405, LAC.
20. Norman, *Commercial Union*, 7.
21. J.H. Beaty to Macdonald, 22 May 1887, Macdonald fonds, 444, 219745–47, LAC.
22. Wiman and Macdonald had been acquainted for years, and some pleasant correspondence is found in the Macdonald fonds from the spring of 1887 in which the prime minister gently resists Wiman's attempts to sell him on commercial union. See for example Wiman to Macdonald, 23 and 25 July 1887, Macdonald fonds, 325, 147248, and 44, 17215, LAC.
23. Toronto *Globe*, 5 May 1887.
24. Erastus Wiman, "The Advantages of Commercial Union to Canada and the United States," in G.M. Fairchild, *Canadian Leaves: History, Art, Science, Literature, Commerce: A Series of New Papers Read Before the Canadian Club of New York* (New York: Thompson & Co. Publishers, 1887), 279.
25. Ibid., 276.
26. Ingersoll *Chronicle*, 7 July 1887.
27. Toronto *Globe*, 2 July 1887.
28. The speech was widely quoted in Canadian newspapers, and its full text, from which this quotation is drawn, was quickly reprinted by Wiman himself in a pamphlet, *Commercial Union between the United States and Canada: Speech of Erastus Wiman at Lake Dufferin, Ontario, July 1 1887* (Toronto: Toronto News Company, 1887).
29. Toronto *Globe*, 30 June 1887.
30. Ibid., 2 July 1887.
31. Ibid., 4 July 1887.
32. Ibid., 5 July 1887.
33. James Young to Laurier, 19 November 1887, Laurier fonds, 737, 208153, LAC; Young, *Our National Future: being five letters by James Young in opposition to*

commercial union (as proposed) and imperial federation, and pointing out what the writer believes to be the true future of Canada as part of North America (R.G. McLean, 1888).

34. Alexander Mackenzie to Cartwright, 27 September 1887, Private, Sir Richard Cartwright fonds, Correspondence 1884–1899, F24-1, AO.
35. Thomas R. McInnes to Laurier, 16 July 1887, Laurier fonds, 737, 208105, LAC.
36. The English translation of the speech varied significantly in the papers of the day; this particular wording is taken from Joseph Schull, *Laurier*, 205–8.
37. *Proceedings of the Inter-provincial Conference held at the City of Quebec, from the 20th to the 28th October inclusively*, 38; clipping, Halifax *Herald*, 27 October 1887, George Foster fonds, 82, Scrapbook: Unrestricted Reciprocity 1887–89, MG27-IID7, LAC; Toronto *Globe*, 24, 28 October 1887; Halifax *Morning Chronicle*, 25 October 1887.
38. Toronto *Globe*, 14 October 1887.
39. Edgar to Laurier, 14 October 1887, Private, Laurier fonds, 2, 571–72, LAC.
40. Sir James David Edgar, *The Wiman-Edgar Letters: a series of open letters between Mr. J.D. Edgar, M.P., Toronto, and Mr. Erastus Wiman, New York: Unrestricted Reciprocity as Distinguished from Commercial Union*, 1887.
41. Cartwright to Laurier, 29 October 1887, Confidential, Laurier fonds, 2, 579–83, LAC.
42. Laurier to Edgar, 9 December 1887, Private, Edgar fonds, Correspondence, Series A-1-1, AO.
43. Cartwright to Laurier, 2 January 1888, Private, Laurier fonds, 737, 208190, LAC.
44. Cartwright to Laurier, 23 January 1888, Private, Laurier fonds, 737, 208203, LAC.
45. Joseph Pope, *The Day of Sir John Macdonald: A Chronicle of the First Prime Minister of the Dominion* (Toronto: University of Toronto Press, 1914, reprinted 1964), 165.
46. Hansard, 14 March 1888, 144–61.
47. Saint John *Globe* and Ottawa *Citizen*, quoted in Washington *Post*, 30 March 1888.
48. Wiman to Laurier, 13 April 1888, Laurier fonds, 3, 718, LAC.

FOUR: THE BASTARD NATIONALITY

1. Sir Richard Cartwright to Wilfrid Laurier, 29 October 1887, Laurier fonds, 2, 579, LAC.
2. Laurier to Blake, 29 March 1888, Blake fonds, AO, reprinted in Underhill, "Laurier and Blake, 1882–1891," 402–3.
3. Laurier to Edgar, 27 March 1888, Edgar fonds, Correspondence, Series A-1-1, AO.
4. Laurier to Blake, 29 March 1888.

5. Laurier to Blake, 31 May 1890, Blake fonds, Series B, AO; reprinted in Underhill, "Laurier and Blake, 1882–1891," 404–5.
6. Laurier to Edgar, Private, 27 June 1888, Edgar fonds, Correspondence, Series A-1-1, AO.
7. Edgar to Laurier, 18 July 1888, Laurier fonds, 2, 742–44, LAC.
8. J.S. Willison, *Reminiscences: political and personal* (Toronto: McClelland and Stewart, 1919), 164.
9. Sir John A. Macdonald to Sir Charles Tupper, 15 October 1885, Private, reprinted in Pope, *Correspondence of Sir John Macdonald* (New York and Toronto: Doubleday, Page and Company, 1921), 386.
10. J.R. Miller, *Equal Rights: The Jesuits' Estates Act Controversy* (Montreal and Kingston: McGill-Queen's University Press, 1979), 42.
11. Pope, *The Day of Sir John Macdonald*, 164.
12. Miller, *Equal Rights*, 55.
13. J.S. Willison, *Sir Wilfrid Laurier and the Liberal Party: A Political History*, vol. 2 (Toronto: Morang, 1903), 56.
14. G.P. Browne, "Guy Carleton, 1st Baron Dorchester," in *Dictionary of Canadian Biography*, vol. 5, ed. Francess G. Halpenny (Toronto: University of Toronto Press, 1983), 143.
15. D'Alton McCarthy to Macdonald, 17 April 1889, reprinted in Pope, *Correspondence of Sir John Macdonald*, 443.
16. Pope, *Memoirs of the Right Honourable Sir John A. Macdonald*, 665.
17. All quotations from this speech and the ensuing House of Commons debate are drawn from the original parliamentary record, Hansard, which—in an indication of the particular significance of this debate—was soon published in pamphlet form, *A Complete and Revised Edition of the Debate on the Jesuits' Estates Act in the House of Commons, Ottawa, March, 1889* (Montreal: Senecal & Fils, 1889).
18. Miller, *Equal Rights*, 76.
19. David Creighton to Macdonald, 1 April 1889, Macdonald fonds, 208, 88444, LAC, also quoted in Miller, *Equal Rights*, 81.
20. Pierre Dufour and Jean Hamelin, "Honoré Mercier," in *Dictionary of Canadian Biography*, vol. 12, 726.
21. The Glorious Twelfth commemorated the victory of King William of Orange, the Protestant claimant to the thrones of England, Scotland, and Ireland, over the Roman Catholic King James, thereby ensuring that Ireland would remain under Protestant control. That this battle took place in July 1690 is an indication of the long memories and historical grudges that were a defining feature of the Protestant-Catholic divide in Canada in the late nineteenth century.
22. Miller, *Equal Rights*, 108; Larry L. Kulisek, "D'Alton McCarthy and the True Nationalization of Canada" (Ph.D. diss., Wayne State University, 1973), 238–39.
23. Kulisek, "D'Alton McCarthy," 240.
24. E.W. Thomson to Laurier, 30 June 1889, Laurier fonds, 3, 950–57, LAC.
25. David Mills to Laurier, 3 July 1889, Laurier fonds, 3, 962–64, LAC.

26. Edgar to Laurier, 30 July 1889, Laurier fonds, 3, 992–94, LAC.
27. Thomson to Laurier, 25 July 1889, Laurier fonds, 3, 980–84, LAC.
28. Toronto *Globe*, 1 October 1889; the full text of the Toronto speech is also found in Ulric Barthe, *Wilfrid Laurier on the Platform* (Quebec: Turcotte & Menard's, 1890), 534–69.
29. Barthe, *Wilfrid Laurier on the Platform*, 554.
30. Schull, *Laurier*, 234.
31. J.S. Willison, introduction to *Wilfrid Laurier on the Platform* by Barthe, xix.

FIVE: THE GATHERING STORM

1. Kulisek, "D'Alton McCarthy," 245.
2. Lapierre, *Sir Wilfrid Laurier and the Romance of Canada*, 163.
3. P.B. Waite, *The Man from Halifax: Sir John Thompson, Prime Minister* (Toronto: University of Toronto Press, 1985), 254–55.
4. Speech of John Sherman, Congressional Record, 50th Congress, 1st Session, 7 August 1888, 7286.
5. Clipping, New York *World*, vol. 29, no. 9965, Denison fonds, Scrapbook, Container 33, LAC.
6. Clipping, New York *World*, 3 December 1888, Robert R. Hitt papers, MSS26104, Container 10, Library of Congress.
7. Benjamin Butterworth, House Resolution 240, 13 December 1888, Congressional Record, 50th Congress, 2nd Session, 234; New York *Times*, 14 and 15 December 1888.
8. Clipping, Toronto *Empire*, 17 May 1888, George Foster fonds, MG27-IID7, vol. 82, Scrapbook: Unrestricted Reciprocity, 1887–1889, LAC.
9. J. Armstrong to Wilfrid Laurier, 18 January 1889, Laurier fonds, 3, 846, LAC.
10. Erastus Wiman to Laurier, 29 December 1889, Laurier fonds, 3, 1161–63, LAC; Congressional Record, 51st Congress, 1st Session, 18 December 1889, Benjamin Butterworth, HR 678, 249.
11. John Willison to Laurier, 5 January 1890, Laurier fonds, 4, 1197–204, LAC.
12. Wiman, "concluding portion of letter to E.W. Thomson, apparently about 5 January 1890," Denison fonds, Container 4, 1773, LAC.
13. Sir Richard Cartwright, *So Near, and Yet So Far: the United States and Canada; speech to the Board of Trade and Transportation of New York, 21 February 1890* (New York: Wiman, 1890); New York *Times*, 22 February 1890.
14. David Creighton to Sir John A. Macdonald, 29 March 1890, Macdonald fonds, 208, 88542–44, LAC.
15. Cartwright to Edgar, 9 August 1886, Edgar fonds, Correspondence, Series A-1-1, AO.
16. Laurier to Willison, 26 June 1890, Confidential, Sir John Willison fonds, MG30-D29, vol. 24, folder 179a, 17687–92, LAC.

17. For a concise explanation of the background to the scandal and the role of *Le Canadien*'s editor in exposing it, see Laurier L. Lapierre, "Joseph Israel Tarte and the McGreevy-Langevin Scandal," *Report of the Annual Meeting of the Canadian Historical Association*, vol. 40, no. 1 (1961): 47–57.
18. *Grip*, 29 November 1890, quoted in Waite, *Macdonald*, 206.
19. Pope, *Memoirs of the Right Honourable Sir John A. Macdonald*, 665.
20. Ibid., 626.
21. Christopher St. George Clark to Goldwin Smith, 21 and 23 August 1895, Goldwin Smith Papers, 14/17/134, Correspondence, Canadian-American relations, Collection of Regional History and University Archives, Albert R. Mann Library, Cornell University.
22. George Taylor Denison, *The Struggle for Imperial Unity* (Toronto: Macmillan, 1909), 165–66.

SIX: THE CALL TO ARMS

1. James G. Blaine to Benjamin Harrison, 23 September 1891, in Albert T. Volwiler, *The Correspondence between Benjamin Harrison and James G. Blaine* (Philadelphia: American Philosophical Society, 1940), 193–94.
2. Toronto *Empire*, 30 January 1891.
3. Telegram, Sir John A. Macdonald to Sir Charles Tupper, 21 January 1891, Tupper fonds, 4306 and 4308, LAC (the original encrypted telegram accompanies the decoded version).
4. Clipping, Toronto *Globe*, 16 December 1890, Macdonald fonds, 288, 132220, LAC.
5. Joseph-Adolphe Chapleau to Macdonald, 11 August 1890, Macdonald fonds, 205, 87256–73, LAC.
6. Pope, *Memoirs of the Right Honourable John Alexander Macdonald*, 627.
7. J.D. Cameron to Edward Blake, 4 February 1891, Laurier fonds, 5, 1595–97, LAC.
8. J.W. Longley to Laurier, 10 February 1891, Laurier fonds, 5, 1601–3, LAC.
9. Laurier to Blake, 31 May 1890, Blake fonds, Series B, AO; Underhill, "Laurier and Blake, 1882–1891," 404–5.
10. W.H. Montague to Macdonald, 16 October 1890, Private, Macdonald fonds, 68, 27411, LAC.
11. George Johnson, Memorandum on Erastus Wiman, 1891, Macdonald fonds, 68, 27457–58 and 27460, LAC.
12. Erastus Wiman, "The Capture of Canada," *North American Review*, vol. 151, no. 405 (August 1890): 212.
13. Toronto *Empire*, 16 January 1891.
14. Boston *Globe*, 31 January 1891.

15. Cartwright to Laurier, 13 December 1890, Confidential, Laurier fonds, 737, 208419–20, LAC.
16. The fullest story is told in Willison's *Reminiscences*, but some aspects of this frantic effort to prevent Blake from publishing his letter can be gleaned from other memoirs of that era, though not from Laurier or Blake themselves.
17. Laurier to Blake, 2 February 1891, reprinted in Underhill, "Laurier and Blake, 1882–1891," 405–6.
18. Blake to Laurier, 7 February 1891, Confidential, Laurier fonds, 5, 1598–600, LAC.

SEVEN: THE APPEAL TO THE PEOPLE

1. Chapleau to Macdonald, 22 December 1890, Private, Macdonald fonds, 205, 87432–35, LAC.
2. Telegram, John McIntyre to Macdonald, 6 February 1891, Macdonald fonds, 494, 247715, LAC.
3. Toronto *Empire*, 5 February 1891.
4. Toronto *Mail*, 10 February 1891.
5. A. McNeill to Macdonald, 7 February 1891, Private and Confidential, Macdonald fonds, 495, 247857–58, LAC.
6. G.E. Sanford to Macdonald, 7 February 1891, Private, Macdonald fonds, 495, 247870–72, LAC.
7. C.R. Smith to Macdonald, 7 February 1891, Private, Macdonald fonds, 495, 247876–78, LAC.
8. W.P. Purver to Macdonald, 6 February 1891, Macdonald fonds, 494, 247772–73, LAC.
9. Telegram, John Boyd to Macdonald, 9 February 1891, Macdonald fonds, 495, 247933, LAC. The time of this particular telegram, 10:58 P.M., implies the urgency with which these messages were flowing toward the prime minister's study at Earnscliffe.
10. A.W. Ross to Macdonald, 9 February 1891, Macdonald fonds, 495, 248047–50, LAC.
11. Van Horne to Macdonald, 11 February 1891, Confidential, Macdonald fonds, 288, 132240, LAC.
12. Chapleau to Macdonald, 22 December 1890, Private.
13. In the nineteenth century it was permissible for an individual to contest more than one constituency, and party leaders often did so to better ensure their re-election to the House (though they could take only one seat). In 1878, for example, Macdonald ran in no fewer than three constituencies—Victoria, Marquette, and Kingston. This was a prescient strategy, for Sir John unexpectedly lost his seat in Kingston but won the other two races, and thus had his choice of representing either Victoria or Marquette. He chose Victoria and thus became the first prime minister to hold a British Columbia seat, though he did not actually visit the constituency during his four years as its M.P.

14. McIntyre to Macdonald, 7 February 1891, Macdonald fonds, 495, 247855, LAC.

15. James Shannon to Macdonald, 9 February 1891, Macdonald fonds, 495, 248056–57, LAC.

16. Toronto *Mail*, 7 February 1891. The Conservative press covered the rally too, of course, but the *Mail*'s account is useful because of its relatively impartial tone, and the quotations used here are from that paper.

17. Whether there was any credibility to this charge is unknown; the story simply disappeared from the news, and Tupper, who was very careful about protecting his legacy and reputation, certainly would not have left any incriminating documents in his personal papers that might have implicated him in such a scandal. The evidence is just not there one way or the other, and whether one believes that Tupper impregnated and then abandoned this woman really depends, frankly, on what one thinks of Tupper as a human being.

18. Macdonald to Tupper, 6 February 1891, reprinted in Tupper, *Recollections of Sixty Years in Canada* (London, New York, Toronto, Melbourne: Cassell and Company, 1914), 212–13.

19. The full text of Macdonald's address appears as an appendix in Pope, *Memoirs of the Right Honourable Sir John A. Macdonald*, 772–77.

20. Toronto *Mail*, 10 February 1891.

21. Lord Stanley to Macdonald, 3 January 1891, Macdonald fonds, 90, 35276–77, LAC.

22. Clipping, Peterborough *Daily Review*, 10 February 1891, Macdonald fonds, 495, 248213, LAC.

23. Telegram, Foster to Macdonald, 9 February 1891, Macdonald fonds, 215, 92036, LAC.

24. George A. Drummond to Macdonald, 9 February 1891, Macdonald fonds, 495, 247952–55, LAC.

25. Montreal *Gazette*, 13 February 1891 (the last quotation comes from this issue); Toronto *Mail*, 9 and 11 February 1891.

26. Chapleau to Macdonald, 13 February 1891, Private, Macdonald fonds, 205, 87466–68, LAC. This report was seconded by Joseph Tasse, a former M.P. who hurriedly wired Macdonald that the Montreal rally had been a success and that "everywhere are good friends enthusiastic fully satisfied with your address" (Telegram, Joseph Tasse to Macdonald, 11 February 1891, Macdonald fonds, 495, 24899, LAC). Tasse had good reason to work hard for the Conservative cause. On the ninth, the same day that the manifesto had come out, Macdonald had appointed him to the Senate.

27. Halifax *Herald*, 16 February 1891.

28. Ibid., 11 February 1891.

29. Ibid., 16 February 1891.

30. Toronto *Globe*, 10 February 1891.

31. Montreal *Witness*, 10 February 1891.

32. Toronto *Mail*, 10 February 1891. This quote from the *Mail*, a paper that was usually impartial or slightly leaning toward the Liberals, reflects its preoccupation with the Jesuits' Estates Act controversy and general antagonism toward Mercier and his alleged schemes of "French domination."
33. Montreal *Gazette*, 12 February 1891.
34. Toronto *Globe*, 13 February 1891.

EIGHT: THE ACADEMY OF MUSIC

1. Toronto *World*, 18 February 1891. All of the Toronto newspapers provided copious and quite similar coverage of the Academy of Music rally in their issues of 18 February, and the endnotes in this chapter generally cite tidbits of information or editorial opinions in a specific newspaper that did not appear in the others. The Macdonald speech itself is quoted from the Toronto *Empire*, 18 February 1891. It should be pointed out that Carman Cumming has drawn on mainly the same sources to recreate this grand rally, in slightly less detail but in highly entertaining fashion, in *Secret Craft*, 1–11. This narrative along with a personal conversation with the gracious Mr. Cumming in Ottawa in the fall of 2004 was very helpful in the early development of this chapter.
2. Toronto *Empire*, 18 February 1891.
3. Ibid.
4. Toronto *News*, 18 February 1891.
5. Ibid.
6. Toronto *Empire*, 18 February 1891.
7. Ibid.
8. Toronto *Mail*, 18 February 1891.
9. Toronto *Empire*, 18 February 1891.
10. Ibid.

NINE: THE TURN OF THE TIDE

1. Toronto *Globe*, 19 February 1891. The following speech by Mowat is drawn from the same edition; not surprisingly, similar accounts appeared in other Liberal organs across Ontario on 19 and 20 February.
2. Telegram, S. Neelon to Macdonald, 14 February 1891, Macdonald fonds, 496, 248570, LAC.
3. Telegram, W.F. Maclean to Pope, 18 February 1891, Macdonald fonds, 496, 248851, LAC.
4. Sam Hughes to Macdonald, 15 February 1891, Private and Confidential, Macdonald fonds, 496, 248605–9, LAC.

5. Bishop Dowling to Macdonald, 13 February 1891, Macdonald fonds, 496, 248426–29, LAC; Miller, "'This saving remnant,'" 33–52.
6. W.B. Ives to Chapleau, 14 February 1891, Macdonald fonds, 496, 248562–63, LAC.
7. Montreal *Gazette*, 23 February 1891.
8. The original cartoons are preserved in volumes 68 to 70 of the Macdonald fonds; some are reprinted in MacKirdy, "The Loyalty Issue," and in Cumming, *Secret Craft*.
9. Toronto *Empire*, 26 February 1891.
10. Pope, *Memoirs of the Right Honourable Sir John Alexander Macdonald*, 628.
11. Pope, *Public Servant: The Memoirs of Sir Joseph Pope*, edited and completed by Maurice Pope (Toronto: Oxford, 1960), 77–78.
12. Charlton, draft autobiography, 633.
13. Montreal *Gazette*, 27 February 1891.
14. Toronto *Mail*, 25 February 1891.
15. William Kirby to Denison, 21 February 1891, Denison fonds, Container 5, 1936–39, LAC.
16. Kirby to Denison, 1 March 1891, Denison fonds, Container 5, 1947–56, LAC.

TEN: THE FIFTH OF MARCH

1. Toronto *Mail*, 6 March 1891.
2. The electoral rules outlined in this section are drawn principally from Elections Canada, *A History of the Vote in Canada*, 2nd ed. (Ottawa: Office of the Chief Electoral Officer of Canada, 2007); Stewart, "Sir John A. Macdonald's Greatest Triumph," 3–33; and Forster, Davidson, and Brown, "The Franchise, Personators, and Dead Men," 17–41. Generally, it should be noted, the newspapers of the day did a better job of protesting against alleged misconduct at the polls—an invaluable role, to be sure—than explaining the complexities of the Franchise Act that was governing the polling itself.
3. Toronto *Mail*, 6 March 1891.
4. Montreal *Gazette*, 6 March 1891.
5. Van Horne to Macdonald, 28 February 1891, Macdonald fonds, 288, 132278, LAC.
6. Halifax *Herald*, 6 March 1891.
7. Montreal *Gazette*, 6 March 1891.
8. Montreal *Daily Witness*, 6 March 1891.
9. Telegram, McIntyre to Macdonald, Kingston, 5 March 1891.
10. Pope, *Memoirs of the Right Honourable Sir John Alexander Macdonald*, 628.

ELEVEN: THE EMPTY SADDLE

1. Telegram, D.R. Hannington to Macdonald, 5 March 1891; Telegram, Thomas Howard to Macdonald, 6 March 1891; and J.M. Fenwick to Macdonald, 6 March 1891, all Macdonald fonds, 71, 27619, 27864, and 27827, LAC.
2. Telegram, G.E. Corbould to Macdonald, 5 March 1891; Telegram, D.W. Gordon to Macdonald, 5 March 1891; Leo Gaetz to Macdonald, 6 March 1891; and W.S. Hercheuer to Macdonald, 6 March 1891, all Macdonald fonds, 71, 27609, 27617, 27836, and 27859, LAC.
3. J.L. Larke to Macdonald, 6 March 1891, Macdonald fonds, 71, 27879., LAC.
4. William Anderson to Macdonald, 6 March 1891, and Telegram, Robert Birmingham to Macdonald, 6 March 1891, Macdonald fonds, 71, 27747 and 27765, LAC.
5. N.A. Coste to Macdonald, 6 March 1891, Macdonald fonds, 71, 27796-97, LAC.
6. Ibid.
7. Drummond to Macdonald, 7 March 1891, Macdonald fonds, 72, 28044, LAC.
8. Macdonald to George Stephen, 31 March 1891, in Sir Joseph Pope, ed., *Correspondence of Sir John Macdonald*, 485–87.
9. These and other relevant letters between Blake and Laurier are conveniently reprinted in F.H. Underhill, "Laurier and Blake, 1882–1891," 392–408.
10. Toronto *Globe*, 6 March 1891.
11. William Rhind to Wilfrid Laurier, 19 March 1891, Laurier fonds, 5, 1711–20, LAC.
12. George Casey to Laurier, 12 March 1891, Laurier fonds, 5, 1675–79, LAC.
13. Casey to Laurier, 26 March 1891, Laurier fonds, 5, 1747–59, LAC.
14. John Crerar to Laurier, 9 March 1891, Laurier fonds, 5, 1659, LAC.
15. Louis Davies to Laurier, John V. Ellis to Laurier, 7 March 1891, Laurier fonds, 5, 1651–54, LAC.
16. Halifax *Morning Chronicle*, 6 March 1891.
17. George Mitchell to Laurier, 23 March 1891, Laurier fonds, 5, 1729–43, LAC.
18. David Mills to Laurier, 18 March 1891, Laurier fonds, 5, 1702–5, LAC.
19. Laurier to Edgar, 27 March 1891, Edgar fonds, Correspondence, A-1-1, AO, also quoted in Stevens, "Laurier and the Liberal Party in Ontario, 1887–1911" (Ph.D. diss., University of Toronto, 1966), 67–68.
20. Waite, *Macdonald*, 211.
21. Charlton, draft autobiography, 635–36.
22. Pope, *Memoirs of the Right Honourable Sir John A. Macdonald*, 628–29.
23. Ibid., 630.
24. G. Mercer Adam, *Canada's Patriot Statesman: The Life and Career of the Right Honourable Sir John A. Macdonald* (Toronto: C.R. Parish and Company, 1891), 487–88; Waite, *Macdonald*, 213.

25. This dramatic moment is quite poignantly captured in Creighton, *John A. Macdonald*, 571.
26. Toronto *Globe*, 7 June 1891.
27. Pope, *Memoirs of the Right Honourable Sir John A. Macdonald*, 634, 778–79.
28. Ibid., 780–83.

EPILOGUE: THE DESTINY OF CANADA

1. Waite, *The Man from Halifax*, 296.
2. Pope, *The Day of Sir John Macdonald*, 142.
3. Ibid., 141.
4. P.B. Waite, "Sir Charles Hibbert Tupper," *Dictionary of Canadian Biography*, vol. 15, ed. Ramsay Cook (Toronto: University of Toronto, 2005), 1016–18.
5. Carman Miller, "Sir John Joseph Caldwell Abbott," *Dictionary of Canadian Biography*, vol. 12, 7.
6. Ibid., 8; Waite, *The Man from Halifax*, 290. It is worth observing that Macdonald changed his mind in his final conversation with Thompson, advising him just hours before his final incapacitating stroke that Abbott was "too damned selfish."
7. The story of the 1891–93 by-elections is carefully told in Lovell C. Clark, "A History of the Conservative Administrations, 1891 to 1896" (Ph.D. diss., University of Toronto, 1968), 71–75. Each result can be accessed online at the Parliament of Canada website "History of Federal Ridings Since 1867," http://www2.parl.gc.ca/Sites/LOP/HFER/HFER.asp.
8. Mowat to Laurier, 31 December 1891, Laurier fonds, 5, 2042–43, LAC.
9. The fall of Bowell, who has the hard lot of being consistently ranked as one of the worst prime ministers in Canadian history, is amusingly told in Waite, *Canada 1874–1896*, 252–71.
10. Preston, *My Generation of Politics and Politicians*, 185.
11. Wiman to Laurier, 23 March 1896, Laurier fonds, 70, 21945–46, LAC.
12. Wiman, "The Struggle in Canada," *North American Review*, vol. 152, no. 412 (March 1891): 343.
13. Willison, introduction to *Wilfrid Laurier on the Platform* by Barthe, xix.
14. Willison to Laurier, 26 March 1891, Laurier fonds, 5, 1764–68, LAC.

BIBLIOGRAPHY

When I set out to research this book, I had the great advantage of having explored this era of Canadian politics in my doctoral dissertation, "The Politics of the Continentalist Movement in Canada and the United States, 1887–1894." Much of the secondary reading conducted for this book thus overlapped with that of the dissertation, and so did some of the primary research, though not nearly as much as I expected. It turned out that the best information on the election of 1891 came from two sources: the personal papers of many of the politicians involved—especially Macdonald and Laurier—often in correspondence that I had not consulted previously, and the newspapers of the day, which were the only source of the marvellous blow-by-blow accounts of the campaign that were indispensable to the second half of this book. So essential to the narrative were these newspapers that I have listed the most important of them here first, roughly in order of importance, rather than observing the usual custom of starting with archival materials.

NEWSPAPERS

Toronto *Globe*
Toronto *Empire*
Toronto *Mail*
Montreal *Gazette*
La Minerve (Montreal)

Montreal *Witness*
La Patrie (Montreal)
New York *Times*
New York *Sun*
New York *Herald*
Halifax *Chronicle*
Halifax *Herald*
Hamilton *Spectator*
Ottawa *Free Press*
Ottawa *Citizen*
London *Free Press*
Toronto *World*
Toronto *News*
Grip (Toronto)
London *Advertiser*
Manitoba *Free Press*
Quebec *Chronicle*
Quebec *Mercury*
Charlottetown *Guardian*
Charlottetown *Examiner*
Saint John *Globe*
Saint John *Sun*
Saskatchewan *Herald*
Calgary *Herald*
Brandon *Sun*
Victoria *Daily Colonist*
London *Times* (England)
Washington *Post*
Chicago *Tribune*
Boston *Globe*
New York *World*
The Bystander (Toronto)
Le Monde (Quebec)

ARCHIVAL SOURCES, CANADA

LIBRARY AND ARCHIVES CANADA (OTTAWA, ONTARIO)

Sir John J.C. Abbott fonds
Sir Mackenzie Bowell fonds

Christopher St. George Clark fonds
Colonial Office fonds
Consular Records, U.S. Department of State
George Taylor Denison fonds
Edward Farrer fonds
George E. Foster fonds
Sir Sam Hughes fonds
Justice File, Records Relating to American Annexationists, 1893–94
Lord Lansdowne fonds
Sir Wilfrid Laurier fonds
Sir John A. Macdonald fonds
D'Alton McCarthy fonds
William McDougall fonds
Montreal Board of Trade fonds
Sir John S.D. Thompson fonds
Toronto Board of Trade fonds
Sir Charles Tupper fonds
Sir Charles Hibbert Tupper fonds
John S. Willison fonds

ARCHIVES OF ONTARIO (TORONTO, ONTARIO)

Edward Blake fonds
Alexander Campbell fonds
Sir Richard Cartwright fonds
Sir James David Edgar fonds
J. Castell Hopkins fonds
William Kirby fonds
Goldwin Smith fonds
John Willison fonds

QUEEN'S UNIVERSITY ARCHIVES (KINGSTON, ONTARIO)

Walter Dymond Gregory fonds

THOMAS FISHER LIBRARY, UNIVERSITY OF TORONTO (TORONTO, ONTARIO)

John Charlton papers

UNIVERSITY OF WESTERN ONTARIO (LONDON, ONTARIO)

David Mills papers

ARCHIVAL SOURCES, UNITED STATES

LIBRARY OF CONGRESS (WASHINGTON, D.C.)

Wharton Barker papers
Thomas F. Bayard papers
James G. Blaine papers
Andrew Carnegie papers
Grover Cleveland papers
Benjamin Harrison papers
Robert R. Hitt papers
John Sherman papers

GEORGE WASHINGTON UNIVERSITY (WASHINGTON, D.C.)

Chauncey M. Depew papers

WESTERN RESERVE HISTORICAL SOCIETY (CLEVELAND, OHIO)

Samuel J. Ritchie papers

NEW YORK PUBLIC LIBRARY (NEW YORK CITY)

William Bourke Cockran papers
Chauncey M. Depew papers
Miscellaneous file (Erastus Wiman)

STATEN ISLAND HISTORICAL SOCIETY (NEW YORK CITY)

Erastus Wiman papers

STATEN ISLAND INSTITUTE OF ARTS AND SCIENCES (NEW YORK CITY)

Erastus Wiman collection

CORNELL UNIVERSITY (ITHACA, NEW YORK)

Goldwin Smith papers (accessed by diffusion microfilm at the Archives of Ontario)

YALE UNIVERSITY LIBRARY (NEW HAVEN, CONNECTICUT)

Benjamin Butterworth papers

PUBLISHED GOVERNMENT SOURCES

Canada. Elections Canada. *A History of the Vote in Canada*, 2nd ed. Ottawa: Office of the Chief Electoral Officer of Canada, 2007.

Canada. Government of Canada. Electoral Atlas of the Dominion of Canada, as divided for the revision of the voters' lists made in the year 1894. Ottawa: Government Printing Bureau, 1895.

Canada. Parliament. "History of Federal Ridings Since 1867," http://www2.parl.gc.ca/Sites/LOP/HFER/HFER.asp.

Canada. Parliament. House of Commons. Debates (Hansard).

United States. Congress. Congressional Record.

United States. Government. Papers Relating to the Foreign Relations of the United States. Washington: Government Printing Office, 1887–1891.

United States. Senate. Select Committee on Relations with Canada. Testimony taken by the Select Committee on Relations with Canada, submitted by Mr. Hoar, 21 July 1890. Washington: Government Printing Office, 1890.

United States. Senate Committee on Interstate Commerce. Transportation interests of the United States and Canada: Report, submitted by Mr. Cullom, and statements taken before the Committee. Washington: Government Printing Office, 1890.

CONTEMPORARY PUBLICATIONS

Adam, G. Mercer. *Canada's Patriot Statesman: The Life and Career of the Right Honourable Sir John A. Macdonald*. Toronto: C.R. Parish & Company, 1891.

Aitken, William Benford. *The Dominion of Canada: a study of annexation*. New York: Van Siclen, c. 1890.

Barker, Wharton. *Letter to Henry A. DuPont*. Philadelphia, 1891.

———. *Memorandum on the commercial relations of the Dominion of Canada to the United States of America*. Philadelphia, 1880.

———. *Our Canadian Relations: A Letter to Hon. James A. Garfield by Wharton Barker*, 27 April 1880. Philadelphia, 1880.

———. *Surplus Revenue and Canadian relations*. Philadelphia, 1887.

Barthe, Ulric. *Wilfrid Laurier on the Platform*. Quebec: Turcotte & Menard's, 1890.

"Bastion Old." *An open letter on the question, Do you want annexation to the United States?: written to an American friend*, by "Bastion Old." Toronto: J. Ferguson, 1890.

Beers, George. *Young Canada's reply to "Annexation."* Montreal: Blaiklock, 1888.

Blake, Edward. *Letter of the Hon. Edward Blake to the West Durham Reform Convention*. Toronto: Budget, 1891.

Butterworth, Benjamin. *Commercial Union between Canada and the United States: an address delivered before the Canadian Club of New York*. New York: Erastus Wiman, 1887.

Canadian Manufacturer's Association. *The Canadian Manufacturer's Association*. Toronto: 1890?

Carnegie, Andrew. "A Look Ahead." *North American Review*, June 1893, vol. 156, no. 439, 685–711.

Cartwright, Sir Richard. *So Near, and Yet So Far: the United States and Canada; speech to the Board of Trade and Transportation of New York*, 21 February 1890. New York: Wiman, 1890.

Charlton, John. *Speeches and Addresses: Political, Literary and Religious*. Toronto: Morang & Co, 1905.

Clarke, S.R. *A New Light on Annexation: A Political Brochure*. Toronto: James Murray & Co, 1891.

Commercial Union Club of Toronto. *Handbook of Commercial Union: a collection of papers read before the Commercial Union Club of Toronto*. Toronto: Hunter, Rose & Co., 1888.

Commercial Union between the United States and Canada: some letters, papers, and speeches. New York: Erastus Wiman, 1888.

A Complete and Revised Edition of the Debate on the Jesuits' Estates Act in the House of Commons, Ottawa, March, 1889. Montreal: Senecal & Fils, 1889.

Continental Union Association of Ontario. *Continental Union: A Short Study of its Economic Side*. Toronto: Continental Union, 1893.

———. *Our Best Policy*. Toronto: Hunter, Rose & Co., 1895.

Edgar, Sir James David. *The Canadian Trade Question, an open letter to the constituents of West Ontario*, 23 January 1893. Toronto, 1893.

———. *The Wiman-Edgar Letters: a series of open letters between Mr. J.D. Edgar, M.P., Toronto, and Mr. Erastus Wiman*, New York: Unrestricted Reciprocity as Distinguished from Commercial Union, 1887.

Equal Rights Association of Ontario. *D'Alton McCarthy's Great Speech, Delivered in Ottawa, December 12, 1889*. Toronto: Equal Rights Association of Ontario, undated (likely 1890).

Fairchild, G.M. *Canadian Leaves: History, Art, Science, Literature, Commerce: A Series of New Papers Read Before the Canadian Club of New York*. New York: Thompson & Co. Publishers, 1887.

Glen, Francis Wayland. *Continental Union versus Reciprocity: Erastus Wiman answered by an Ex-Member of the Canadian Parliament*. New York: 1893.

———. *The Political Reunion of the United States and Canada*. New York: 1893. Reprinted from the *American Journal of Politics*, December 1893.

Hoar, George. *The fisheries treaty: speech in the Senate of the United States, Tuesday, July 10, 1888*. Washington: 1888.

Hopkins, J. Castell. *Continental influences in Canadian development*. Toronto: W. Briggs, 1908.

Inter-provincial Conference. *Proceedings of the Inter-provincial Conference held at the City of Quebec, from the 20th to the 28th October inclusively*. Quebec: 1887.

Johnson, George. *Information given regarding annexation and other matters*. 1889.

Longley, J.W. *Commercial union between the United States and Canada: speech by J.W. Longley, delivered in the House of Assembly of Nova Scotia, May 2, 1887*. 1887.

———. *The Future of Canada*. Toronto: Lake Magazine, 1891.

Macdonald, *Sir John A. Address to the people of Canada*. 7 February 1891.

Mowat, Oliver. *The Reform Party and Canada's Future: an open letter from the Hon. Oliver Mowat, Premier of Ontario, to the Hon. Alexander Mackenzie, M.P. for East York, and formerly Premier of Canada*. Toronto: Hunter, Rose & Co., 1891.

Nimmo, Joseph. *Canadian protection compared with the provisions of the McKinley Tariff Act: a reply to Sir John Macdonald's speech at Halifax*. Washington: 1890.

———. *A Canadian scheme of aggression upon American commerce, and how it should be treated*. Washington: Gibson, 1889.

———. *The chimera of commercial union with the Dominion of Canada*. Washington: 1890.

———. *Our relations with Canada: statement by Joseph Nimmo Jr. before the Select Committee of the Senate on relations with Canada, April 28, 1890*. Washington: Government Printing Office, 1890.

———. *What is the Dominion of Canada, and what are its relations to Great Britain and to the United States?* Washington: Gibson, 1888.

National Liberal Federation of Canada. *Reciprocity: a retrospect*. Central Information Office, 1915.

Norman, Henry. *Commercial Union as photographed by an intelligent English visitor to Canada*. New York: Erastus Wiman, undated (likely 1889).

Patrons of Industry. *Hand-book introducing facts and figures in support of the Patron platform and principles*. Toronto: 1895.

Shaw, Thomas. *Plain talks on commercial union between Canada and the United States*. Hamilton: Griffin & Kidner, 1887.

Smith, Goldwin. "Anglo-Saxon Union: A Response to Mr. Carnegie." *North American Review*, August 1893, vol. 157, no. 44, 170–88.

———. *Canada and the Canadian Question*. Toronto: University of Toronto Press, 1971. Reprinted from the 1891 edition, with an introduction by Carl Berger.

———. "Canada and the United States." *North American Review*, July 1880, vol. 131, no. 284, 14–26.

———. *Loyalty, aristocracy, and jingoism: three lectures, delivered before the Young Men's Liberal Club*, new ed. Toronto: Hunter, Rose & Co., 1896.

———. *A Political Destiny of Canada*, with a reply by Sir Francis Hincks. Toronto: Belford, 1877.

Tupper, Sir Charles. "The Wiman Conspiracy Unmasked." *North American Review*, May 1891, vol. 152, no. 414, 549–57.

Willison, Sir John. *Sir Wilfrid Laurier and the Liberal Party: A Political History*. Toronto: G.N. Morang, 1903.

Wilson, James H. *Remarks of Gen. James H. Wilson in Joint Debate with Erastus Wiman, before the Board of Trade and the Citizens of Wilmington, Delaware, on Our Relations with the Dominion of Canada*. Wilmington: Delaware Printing Company, 1890.

Wiman, Erastus. "Can we Coerce Canada?" *North American Review*, January 1891, vol. 152, no. 410, 91–102.

———. *The Canadian Club, Its Purpose and Policy*. New York: 1885.

———. "The Capture of Canada." *North American Review*, August 1890, vol. 151, no. 405, 212–223.

———. *Chances of Success: Observations in the Life of a Busy Man*. New York and Toronto: 1893.

———. *Commercial Union between the United States and Canada: Speech of Erastus Wiman at Lake Dufferin, Ontario, July 1 1887*. Toronto: Toronto News Company, 1887.

———. "Impossibility of Canadian Annexation." From the *Brooklyn Eagle*, 26 September 1891. New York: Erastus Wiman, 1891.

———. "The Feasibility of a Commercial Union between the United States and Canada: interview with Erastus Wiman" in the *Chicago Tribune*, 5 October 1889. New York: Erastus Wiman, 1889.

———. "The Greater Half of the Continent." *North American Review*, January 1889, vol. 148, no. 386, 54–73.

———. *The perfect development of Canada: is it consistent with British welfare?* New York: Erastus Wiman, 1887.

———. *Points Made in a Maritime Province Tour: Closest Trade Relations between the United States and Canada*. Toronto: National Publishing Company, 1892.

———. "The Struggle in Canada," *North American Review*, March 1891, vol. 152, no. 412, 342–43.

———. "Union between the United States and Canada: Political or Commercial; which is desirable and which is presently possible?" Speech of 9 December 1891, reprinted from the *Brooklyn Standard-Union*, 10 December 1891. New York: Wiman, 1891.

———. "What is the Destiny of Canada?" *North American Review*, June 1889, vol. 148, no. 391, 665–676.

Young, James. *Our National Future: being five letters by James Young in opposition to commercial union (as proposed) and imperial federation, and pointing out what the writer believes to be the true future of Canada as part of North America*. R.G. McLean, 1888.

PUBLISHED CORRESPONDENCE AND MEMOIRS

Cartwright, Sir Richard J. *Reminiscences*. Toronto: William Briggs, 1912.

Colquhoun, A.H.U., ed. *Press, Politics and People: The Life and Letters of Sir John Willison*. Toronto: Macmillan, 1935.

Denison, George Taylor. *Recollections of a Police Magistrate*. Toronto: Musson, 1920.

———. *The Struggle for Imperial Unity*. Toronto: Macmillan, 1909.

Haultain, Arnold. *Goldwin Smith: his life and opinions*. Toronto: McClelland, c. 1910.

———, ed. *A Selection from Goldwin Smith's Correspondence*. Toronto: McClelland and Goodchild, c. 1910.

Hincks, Sir Francis. *Reminiscences of his public life*. Montreal: Drysdale, 1884.

Pope, Sir Joseph, ed. *Correspondence of Sir John Macdonald.* New York, Toronto: Doubleday, Page, & Company, 1921.

———. *The Day of Sir John Macdonald: A Chronicle of the First Prime Minister of the Dominion.* Toronto: University of Toronto Press, 1914, reprinted 1964.

———. *Memoirs of the Right Honourable Sir John Alexander Macdonald.* Toronto: Oxford University Press, 1894, revised 1930.

———. *Public Servant: The Memoirs of Sir Joseph Pope.* Edited and completed by Maurice Pope. Toronto: Oxford University Press, 1960.

Preston, W.T.R. *My Generation of Politics and Politicians.* Toronto: D.A. Rose, 1927.

Sherman, John. *Recollections of Forty Years in the House, Senate, and Cabinet.* Columbus: Estill, 1900.

Smith, Goldwin. *Reminiscences.* New York: Macmillan, 1910.

Tupper, Sir Charles. *The life and letters of the Rt. Hon. Sir Charles Tupper.* Edited by E.M. Saunders, with an introduction by the Rt. Hon. Sir R.L. Borden. London, Toronto: Cassell and Company, 1916.

———. *Recollections of Sixty Years in Canada.* London, New York, Toronto, and Melbourne: Cassell and Company, 1914.

Volwiler, Albert T. *The Correspondence between Benjamin Harrison and James G. Blaine.* Philadelphia: American Philosophical Society, 1940.

Willison, Sir John. *Reminiscences: political and personal.* Toronto: McClelland and Stewart, 1919.

Young, James. *Public Men and Public Life in Canada.* Toronto: William Briggs, 1912.

BOOKS AND THESES

Allin, Cephas D., and George M. Jones. *Annexation, Preferential Trade, and Reciprocity.* London: Hazell, Watson and Viney, 1912.

Beaven, Brian. "A Last Hurrah: Studies in Liberal Party Development and Ideology in Ontario, 1878–1893." Ph.D. diss., University of Toronto, 1982.

Beck, J.M. *Pendulum of Power: Canada's Federal Elections.* Scarborough: Prentice-Hall, 1968.

Berger, Carl, ed. *Imperialism and Nationalism, 1884–1914: A Conflict in Canadian Thought.* Toronto: Copp Clark, 1969.

———. *The Sense of Power: Studies in the Ideas of Canadian Imperialism, 1867–1914.* Toronto: University of Toronto Press, 1970.

Bliss, Michael. *A Living Profit: Studies in the Social History of Canadian Business, 1883–1911.* Toronto: McClelland and Stewart, 1974.

———. *Northern Enterprise: Five Centuries of Canadian Business.* Toronto: McClelland and Stewart, 1990.

———. *Right Honourable Men: The Descent of Canadian Politics from Macdonald to Chrétien*, rev. ed. Toronto: HarperCollins, 2004.

Bothwell, Robert. *Canada and the United States: The Politics of Partnership*. New York: Maxwell Macmillan, 1992.

Brown, Robert Craig. *Canada's National Policy, 1883–1900: A Study in Canadian-American Relations*. Princeton: Princeton University Press, 1964.

———. "Canadian-American Relations in the Latter Part of the Nineteenth Century." Ph.D. diss., University of Toronto, 1962.

Bumsted, J.M. *The Red River Rebellion*. Manitoba: Watson & Dyer, 1996.

Carrigan, D. Owen. *Canadian Party Platforms, 1867–1968*. Toronto: Copp Clark, 1968.

Clark, Lovell Crosby. "A History of the Conservative Administrations, 1891 to 1896." Ph.D. diss., University of Toronto, 1968.

Clark, Robert J. "The Making of the Laurier Ministry, 1896–1911." M.A. thesis, University of Western Ontario, 1969.

Clippingdale, Richard. "J.S. Willison, Political Journalist: From Liberalism to Independence, 1881–1905." Ph.D. diss., University of Toronto, 1970.

———. *Laurier, His Life and World*. Toronto: McGraw-Hill Ryerson, 1979.

Creighton, Donald. *John A. Macdonald: The Young Politician* and *The Old Chieftain* Toronto: Macmillan, 1952 and 1955, reprinted with an introduction by P.B. Waite, University of Toronto Press, 1998.

Cumming, Carman. *Secret Craft: The Journalism of Edward Farrer*. Toronto: University of Toronto Press, 1992.

———. *Sketches of a Young Country: The Images of* Grip *Magazine*. Toronto: University of Toronto Press, 1988.

Curnoe, Lorne J. "John Charlton and Canadian-American Relations." M.A. thesis, University of Toronto, 1938.

Dafoe, John W. *Laurier: A Study in Politics*. Toronto: Thomas Allen, 1922.

Duffy, John. *Fights of Our Lives: Elections, Leadership, and the Making of Canada*. Toronto: HarperCollins, 2002.

Easterbrook, W.T., and Hugh G.J. Aitken. *Canadian Economic History*. Toronto: University of Toronto Press, 1988.

Evans, Margaret. *Sir Oliver Mowat*. Toronto: University of Toronto Press, 1992.

Fergusson, Charles Bruce. *Hon. W.S. Fielding*. Windsor, NS: Lancelot Press, 1970.

Forster, Ben. *A Conjunction of Interests: Business, Politics, and Tariffs 1825–1879*. Toronto: University of Toronto Press, 1986.

Graham, W.R. "Sir Richard Cartwright and the Liberal Party." Ph.D. diss., University of Toronto, 1950.

Greening, William Edward. "The *Globe* and Canadian Politics, 1890–1902." M.A. thesis, University of Toronto, 1939.

Halpenny, Francess P. (vols. 3–12) and Ramsay Cook (vols. 13–15), general eds. *Dictionary of Canadian Biography*. Toronto: University of Toronto Press, 1974–2005.

Heisler, J.P. "Sir John Thompson, 1844–1894." Ph.D. diss., University of Toronto, 1955.

Hillmer, Norman, and J.L. Granatstein. *For Better or for Worse: Canada and the United States into the Twenty-First Century.* Toronto: Thomson Nelson, 2007.

Hodson, Ian Albert. "Commercial Union, Unrestricted Reciprocity and the Background to the Election of 1891." M.A. thesis, University of Western Ontario, 1952.

Hunt, Michael H. *Ideology and U.S. Foreign Policy.* New Haven: Yale University Press, 1987.

Jeffers, H. Paul. *An Honest President: The Life and Presidencies of Grover Cleveland.* New York: Morrow, 2000.

Kulisek, Larry. "D'Alton McCarthy and the True Nationalization of Canada." Ph.D. diss., Wayne State University, 1973.

Lapierre, Laurier L. Sir *Wilfrid Laurier and the Romance of Canada.* Toronto: Stoddart, 1996.

Lynch, Gerald. *Stephen Leacock: Humour and Humanity.* Montreal and Kingston: McGill-Queen's University Press, 1988.

Macleod, John T. "The Political Thought of Sir Wilfrid Laurier." Ph.D. diss., University of Toronto, 1965.

Masters, Donald C. *Reciprocity 1846–1911.* Ottawa: Canadian Historical Association Booklet No. 12, 1961.

———. *The Reciprocity Treaty of 1854.* Toronto: McClelland and Stewart, 1963.

Matthews, John Herbert. "John Sherman and American Foreign Relations, 1883–1898." Ph.D. diss., Emory University, 1976.

Miller, J.R. *Equal Rights: The Jesuits' Estates Act Controversy.* Montreal and Kingston: McGill-Queen's University Press, 1979.

Morton, W.B. *The Critical Years: The Union of British North America, 1857–1873.* Toronto: McClelland and Stewart, 1968.

Neatby, H. Blair. *Laurier and a Liberal Quebec: A Study in Political Management.* Edited and with an introduction by Richard T. Clippingdale. Toronto: McClelland and Stewart, 1973.

Noel, S.J.R. *Patrons, Clients, Brokers: Ontario Society and Politics, 1791–1896.* Toronto: University of Toronto Press, 1990.

Norrie, Kenneth, Douglas Owram, and J.C. Herbert Emery. *History of the Canadian Economy*, 4th ed. Toronto: Nelson, 2007.

Norris, James D. *R.G. Dun and Co., 1841–1900: The Development of Credit-reporting in the Nineteenth Century.* Westport: Greenwood Press, 1978.

Parkin, George. *Sir John A. Macdonald.* Toronto: Morang & Co., 1908.

Pennington, Christopher John. "The Politics of the Continentalist Movement in Canada and the United States, 1887–1894." Ph.D. diss., University of Toronto, 2007.

Pierce, Lorne. *William Kirby: The Portrait of a Tory Loyalist.* Toronto: Macmillan, 1929.

Phillips, Paul T. *The Controversialist: An Intellectual Life of Goldwin Smith.* Westport: Praeger, 2002.

Rumilly, Robert. *Honoré Mercier et son temps.* Montreal: Fides, 1975.

Rutherford, Paul. "The New Nationality, 1864–97: A Study of the National Aims and Ideas of English Canada in the Late Nineteenth Century." Ph.D. diss., University of Toronto, 1973.

Schull, Joseph. *Edward Blake: Leader and Exile, 1881–1912.* Toronto: Macmillan, 1976.

———. *Laurier: The First Canadian.* Toronto: Macmillan, 1965.

Skelton, O.D. *Life and Letters of Sir Wilfrid Laurier.* New York: Century Co., 1922.

Socolofsky, Homer Edward. *The Presidency of Benjamin Harrison.* Lawrence: University Press of Kansas, 1987.

Stacey, C.P. *Canada and the Age of Conflict.* Vol. 1, *1867–1921.* Toronto: University of Toronto Press, 1984.

———. *The Undefended Border: The Myth and the Reality.* Ottawa: Canadian Historical Association, Historical Booklet No. 1, 1960.

Stamp, Robert. "The Public Career of Sir James David Edgar." M.A. thesis, University of Toronto, 1962.

Stanley, George F.G. *Louis Riel.* Toronto: Ryerson Press, 1963.

Stephanson, Anders. *Manifest Destiny: American Expansionism and the Empire of Right.* New York: Hill and Wang, 1996.

Stevens, Paul. "Laurier and the Liberal Party in Ontario, 1887–1911." Ph.D. diss., University of Toronto, 1966.

———, ed. *The 1911 General Election: A Study in Canadian Politics.* Toronto: Copp Clark, 1970.

Stuart, Reginald C. *United States Expansionism and British North America, 1775–1871.* Chapel Hill and London: University of North Carolina Press, 1991.

Swainson, Donald. *John A. Macdonald: The Man and the Politician.* Toronto: Oxford University Press, 1971.

Tansill, Charles Callan. *Canadian-American Relations, 1875–1911.* New Haven: Yale University Press, 1943.

———. *The Foreign Policy of Thomas F. Bayard, 1885–1897.* New York: Fordham University Press, 1940.

Tennant, Glen. "The Policy of the *Mail*, 1882–1892." M.A. thesis, University of Toronto, 1946.

Thompson, John, and Stephen Randall. *Canada and the United States: Ambivalent Allies.* Athens: University of Georgia Press, 2002.

Waite, Peter B. *Canada 1874–1896: Arduous Destiny.* Toronto: McClelland and Stewart, 1971.

———. *Macdonald: His Life and World.* Toronto: McGraw-Hill Ryerson, 1975.

———. *The Man from Halifax: Sir John Thompson, Prime Minister.* Toronto: University of Toronto Press, 1985.

Wallace, Elizabeth. *Goldwin Smith: Victorian Liberal.* Toronto: University of Toronto Press, 1957.

Warner, Donald. *The Idea of Continental Union.* Lexington: University Press of Kentucky, 1960.

Welch, Richard E. *The Presidencies of Grover Cleveland.* Lawrence: University Press of Kansas, 1988.

Willison, J.S. *Sir Wilfrid Laurier and the Liberal Party.* Vol. 2, *A Political History.* Toronto: Morang, 1903.

SCHOLARLY ARTICLES

Banks, Margaret. "The Change in Liberal Party Leadership, 1887." *Canadian Historical Review*, June 1957, vol. 38, no. 2, 109–28.

Beaven, Brian P.N. "Partisanship, Patronage, and the Press in Ontario, 1880–1914: Myths and Realities." *Canadian Historical Review*, September 1983, vol. 64, no. 3, 317–51.

Bélanger, Réal. "Sir Wilfrid Laurier." In *Dictionary of Canadian Biography*, vol. 14, general editor Ramsay Cook, 610–28. Toronto: University of Toronto Press, 1998.

Bliss, Michael. "Canadianizing American Business: The Roots of the Branch Plant." In *Closing the 49th Parallel: The Americanization of Canada*, edited by Ian Lumsden. Toronto: University of Toronto Press, 1970: 26–42.

Bray, Matt. "Samuel J. Ritchie." In *Dictionary of Canadian Biography*, vol. 13, general editor Ramsay Cook, 873–76. Toronto: University of Toronto Press, 1994.

Brown, Robert Craig. "The Commercial Unionists in Canada and the United States." *Canadian Historical Association Report*, 1963, 116–24.

———. "Erastus Wiman." In *Dictionary of Canadian Biography*, vol. 13, general editor Ramsay Cook, 1101–2. Toronto: University of Toronto Press, 1994.

———. "The Nationalism of the National Policy." In *Readings in Canadian History: Post-Confederation*, 2nd ed., edited by R. Douglas Francis and Donald B. Smith, 44–51. Toronto: Holt, Rinehart and Winston, 1986.

Browne, G.P. "Guy Carleton, 1st Baron Dorchester." In *Dictionary of Canadian Biography*, vol. 5, general editor Francess G. Halpenny, 146–47. Toronto: University of Toronto Press, 1983.

Campbell, Charles S. "American Tariff Interests and the Northeastern Fisheries, 1883–1888." *Canadian Historical Review*, September 1964, vol. 45, no. 3, 212–28.

———. "The Anglo-American Crisis in the Bering Sea, 1890–1891." *Mississippi Valley Historical Review*, 1961, vol. 48, no. 3, 393–414.

Carr, Graham. "Imperialism and Nationalism in Revisionalist Historiography: A Critique of Some Recent Trends." *Journal of Canadian Studies*, 1982, vol. 17, no. 2, 91–99.

Carroll, Francis M. "The Passionate Canadians: The Historical Debate about the Eastern Canadian-American Boundary." *New England Quarterly*, 1997, vol. 70, no. 1, 83–101.

Clark, Lovell C. "The Conservative Party in the 1890s." *Canadian Historical Association Report*, 1961, 58–74.

Cole, Douglas. "Canada's 'Nationalistic' Imperialists." *Journal of Canadian Studies*, 1970, vol. 5, no. 3, 44–49.

Cook, Ramsay. "Goldwin Smith." In *Dictionary of Canadian Biography*, vol. 13, general editor Ramsay Cook, 968–74. Toronto: University of Toronto Press, 1994.

Cumming, Carman. "The Plot to Buy the Canadian Northwest." *Beaver*, Autumn 1984, 4–9.

———. "The Toronto *Daily Mail*, Edward Farrer, and the Question of Canadian-American Union." *Journal of Canadian Studies*, 1989, vol. 24, no. 1, 121–39.

Dales, John. "Canada's National Policies." In *Readings in Canadian History: Post-Confederation*, 2nd ed., edited by R. Douglas Francis and Donald B. Smith, 52–62. Toronto: Holt, Rinehart and Winston, 1986.

Dufour, Pierre, and Jean Hamelin. "Honoré Mercier." In *Dictionary of Canadian Biography*, vol. 12, general editor Francess G. Halpenny, 726–27. Toronto: University of Toronto Press, 1990.

Ferns, Thomas H., and Robert Craig Brown. "John Charlton." In *Dictionary of Canadian Biography*, vol. 13, general editors Ramsay Cook and Jean Hamelin, 187–90. Toronto: University of Toronto Press, 1994.

Forster, Ben, and Jonathan Swainger. "Edward Blake." In *Dictionary of Canadian Biography*, vol. 14, general editor Ramsay Cook, 81. Toronto: University of Toronto Press, 1998.

Forster, Ben, Malcolm Davidson, and R. Craig Brown. "The Franchise, Personators, and Dead Men: An Inquiry into the Voters' Lists and the Election of 1891." *Canadian Historical Review*, March 1986, vol. 67, no. 1, 17–41.

Fridley, Russell W. "When Minnesota Coveted Canada." *Minnesota History*, 1968, vol. 41, no. 2, 76–79.

Gagan, David P. "A Prophet without Honour: George Taylor Denison III, Cavalry Historian." *Military Affairs*, 1970, vol. 34, no. 2, 56–59.

Gluek, Alvin. "The Riel Rebellion and Canadian-American Relations." *Canadian Historical Review*, September 1955, vol. 36, no. 3, 199–221.

Graham, W.R. "Liberal Nationalism in the Eighteen-Seventies." *Canadian Historical Association Report*, 1946, 101–19.

———. "Sir Richard Cartwright, Wilfrid Laurier, and Liberal Party Trade Policy, 1887." *Canadian Historical Review*, March 1952, vol. 33, no. 1, 1–18.

Grant, Ian. "Erastus Wiman: A Continentalist Replies to Canadian Imperialism." *Canadian Historical Review*, March 1972, vol. 53, no. 1, 1–20.

Hafter, Ruth. "The Riel Rebellion and Manifest Destiny." *Dalhousie Review*, 1965, vol. 45, no. 4, 447–56.

Howell, Colin D. "W.S. Fielding and the Repeal Elections of 1886 and 1887 in Nova Scotia." *Acadiensis*, Spring 1979, vol. 8, no. 2, 28–46.

Johnson, J.K., and Peter B. Waite. "Sir John Alexander Macdonald." In *Dictionary of Canadian Biography*, vol. 12, general editors Francess G. Halpenny and Marcel Hamelin, 591–613. Toronto: University of Toronto Press, 1990.

Kohn, Edward. "The Member from Michigan: The Unofficial Diplomacy and Political Isolation of John Charlton, 1892–1908." *Canadian Historical Review*, June 2001, vol. 82, no. 2, 283–306.

Lapierre, Laurier L. "Joseph Israel Tarte and the McGreevy-Langevin Scandal." *Report of the Annual Meeting of the Canadian Historical Association*, 1961, vol. 40, no. 1, 47–57.

Lederle, John. "The Liberal Convention of 1893." *Canadian Journal of Economic and Political Science*, 1950, vol. 16, 42–52.

Livermore, J.D. "The Personal Agonies of Edward Blake." *Canadian Historical Review*, March 1975, vol. 56, no. 1, 45–58.

MacKirdy, K.A. "The Loyalty Issue in the 1891 Federal Election Campaign, and an Ironic Footnote." *Ontario History*, 1963, vol. 15, 143–54.

McLaughlin, K.M. "W.S. Fielding and the Liberal Party in Nova Scotia, 1891–1896." *Acadiensis*, 1974, vol. 3, no. 2, 65–79.

Martin, Ged. "John A. Macdonald and the Bottle." *Journal of Canadian Studies*, Fall 2006, vol. 40, no. 3, 162–85.

Martin, Lawrence. "Continental Union." *Annals of the American Academy of Political and Social Science*, 1995, vol. 538, 143–50.

Miller, Carman. "Sir John Joseph Caldwell Abbott." In *Dictionary of Canadian Biography*, vol. 12, general editor Francess G. Halpenny, 7. Toronto: University of Toronto Press, 1990.

Miller, J.R. "As a Politician He Is a Great Enigma: The Social and Political Ideas of D'Alton McCarthy." *Canadian Historical Review*, December 1977, vol. 58, no. 4, 399–422.

———. "The 1891 Election in Western Canada." *Prairie Forum*, 1985, vol. 10, no. 6, 147–67.

———. "'This Saving Remnant': Macdonald and the Catholic Vote in the 1891 Election." CCHA *Study Sessions,* 1974, vol. 41, 33–52.

Morgan, Cecilia, and Robert Craig Brown. "Sir Richard Cartwright." In *Dictionary of Canadian Biography*, vol. 14, general editor Ramsay Cook, 200–205. Toronto: University of Toronto Press, 1998.

Morton, Desmond. "The Divisive Dream: Reciprocity in 1854." *Beaver,* December 2002–January 2003, vol. 82, no. 6, 16–21.

Neatby, H. Blair, and John T. Saywell. "Chapleau and the Conservative Party in Quebec." *Canadian Historical Review*, March 1956, vol. 37, no. 1, 1–22.

Pannekoek, Frits. "The Flock Divided: Factions and Feuds at Red River." *Beaver*, December 1990–January 1991, vol. 70, no. 6, 29–37.

Pennanen, Gary. "American Interest in Commercial Union with Canada, 1854–1898." *Mid-America*, 1965, vol. 47, no. 1, 24–39.

———. "Goldwin Smith, Wharton Barker, and Erastus Wiman: Architects of Commercial Union." *Journal of Canadian Studies*, 1979, vol. 14, no. 3, 50–62.

Richardson, Lynn E. "James Young." In *Dictionary of Canadian Biography*, vol. 14, general editor Ramsay Cook, 1087–89. Toronto: University of Toronto Press, 1998.

Schlup, Leonard. "Benjamin Butterworth." *American National Biography Online*, February 2000. http://www.anb.org/articles/05/05–00112.html. Accessed 30 May 2006.

Shortt, S.E.D. "Social Change and Political Crisis in Rural Ontario: The Patrons of Industry, 1889–1896." In *Oliver Mowat's Ontario*, edited by D. Swainson, 211–35. Toronto: Macmillan, 1972.

Spetter, Allan. "Harrison and Blaine: No Reciprocity for Canada." *Canadian Review of American Studies*, 1985, vol. 12, no. 2, 143–56.

Stamp, Robert M. "J.D. Edgar and the Liberal Party: 1867–1896." *Canadian Historical Review*, June 1964, vol. 45, no. 2, 93–115.

Stewart, Gordon. "Political Patronage under Macdonald and Laurier, 1878–1911." *American Review of Canadian Studies*, 1980, vol. 10, 3–26.

———. "Sir John A. Macdonald's Greatest Triumph." *Canadian Historical Review*, January 1982, vol. 63, no. 1, 3–33.

Terrill, David A. "David A. Wells, the Democracy, and Tariff Reduction, 1877–1894." *Journal of American History*, 1969, vol. 56, no. 3, 540–55.

Tulchinsky, Gerald, and Brian J. Young. "John Young." In *Dictionary of Canadian Biography*, vol. 10, general editor Francess G. Halpenny, 722–28. Toronto: University of Toronto Press, 1972.

Underhill, F.H. *Canadian Political Parties*. Ottawa: Canadian Historical Association Booklet No. 8, 1957.

———. "Edward Blake, the Liberal Party, and Unrestricted Reciprocity." *Canadian Historical Association Report*, 1939, 133–41.

———. "Laurier and Blake, 1882–1891." *Canadian Historical Review*, December 1939, vol. 20, no. 4, 392–408.

———. "Laurier and Blake, 1891–1892." *Canadian Historical Review*, June 1943, vol. 24, no. 2, 135–55.

Waite, Peter B. "The Political Ideas of John A. Macdonald." In *The Political Ideas of the Prime Ministers of Canada*, The Vanier Lectures, 1968, edited by Marcel Hamelin. Ottawa: University of Ottawa, 1969.

———. "Sir Charles Hibbert Tupper." In *Dictionary of Canadian Biography*, vol. 15, general editor Ramsay Cook, 1016–18. Toronto: University of Toronto Press, 2005.

Wood, Patricia K. "Defining 'Canadian': Anti-Americanism and Identity in Sir John A. Macdonald's Nationalism." *Journal of Canadian Studies*, 2001, vol. 36, no. 2, 49–69.

Young, D. Murray. "Alexander Gibson." In *Dictionary of Canadian Biography*, vol. 14, general editor Ramsay Cook, 400–404. Toronto: University of Toronto Press, 1998.

ACKNOWLEDGMENTS

First, I wish to express my heartfelt appreciation to the marvellous and inimitable Robert Bothwell, without whom this book would never have been written. Bob has been a tremendous mentor and supporter over the years, and it was he who first proposed, as I was finishing my dissertation in 2006, that I write one of the books in a Canadian History series published by Penguin Canada. This was a fantastical leap of faith on his part—it truly was, believe me—and for his tireless, unfailing support as this book inched toward completion, I will always be in his debt.

Margaret Macmillan, who along with Bob edits this series, was obliged to make the same leap of faith, and in the past four years I have been a constant, extremely grateful recipient of her wise guidance and rock-solid support. Margaret is not only a brilliant historian but also a remarkably gracious and generous person, as I learned many times over in the course of writing this book. For her editorial talents, and even more so for her warm and unflinching moral support, I wish to express my sincere appreciation.

Without Penguin Canada, of course, there would have been no series to write for. Of the many good people with whom I have been in contact, Diane Turbide, the principal editor, must be singled out for special recognition. I really had no idea what to expect in my first encounter with an editor at a major publishing company, and was thrilled to find that Diane was as pleasant, accessible—and above all, patient, when the birth of our twins threatened to delay the entire series—as I could have possibly hoped for. Also at Penguin Canada, I wish to thank Jonathan Webb and Sandra Tooze, as well as freelance editor Shaun Oakey, for their assistance and expertise at the successive stages of the publishing process.

Among scholars who have influenced my views about late nineteenth-century Canadian politics in general, most important has always been Michael Bliss, my doctoral supervisor from 2001 to 2006. He remains a fine mentor and friend, and I never cease to admire his many contributions to Canadian political history. Robert Craig Brown and Ian Robertson each deserve special mention for being generous with their time and expertise when this book was in its early stages. For their personal insights, scholarly advice, or special assistance and support over the course of this project, I would also like to express my appreciation to Carman Cumming, John English, Arne Kislenko, Marcel Martel, Philip Papas, Ian Radforth, and Paul Stevens.

Those who know me at the University of Toronto, my academic home since 2001, know that I frequently need help with things. For their tireless and cheerful assistance over the years, and especially more recently while I juggled the book and my professorial duties, I am indebted to the excellent staff at the St. George and Scarborough campuses. There isn't room here to mention everyone, but I would particularly like to thank Arthus Bihis, Marilyn Laville, Milene Neves, Sean Ramrattan, and Laurel Wheeler. At every one of the archives visited for my research, as well, the staff was similarly courteous and professional. To all those who assisted me, too many to list here, unfortunately, I am much indebted.

Those who had to put up with me the most while I was writing the book were, of course, my friends and family. Once again the list is too long to mention everyone, but I first want to single out those who took a special interest in this project in one way or another. For their assistance with my research, or for putting me up during research trips, I extend my thanks to Veronica Abbass, Kyra Abbott, Wendy McCaul, Bob McCron, and Maxie, Monique, and Surantha Rodrigo. For their advice about the manuscript, or for especially supportive friendship as I was in the rather stressful final stages of writing the book, I wish to thank Lana Armstrong, Yayoi and Bobby-Joe Breitkreutz, Ryan Edwards, Alec Steinwall, and Andrew Steinwall.

I always say that I have terrific in-laws, and I am extremely grateful to Stan and Dee Steinwall, my wife's parents, for their extraordinary support not only while I wrote the book but also during the epic length of my doctoral studies. In particular I thank them for all their help with the kids on those days when it was necessary for me to burrow myself away and keep working on the manuscript. To my sister-in-law Vanessa Steinwall and her partner, Kevin Corbin, I express thanks for their long-time friendship, as well as the sympathetic ears that they often lent me when all I wanted to talk about was my book.

Without my parents, Jack and Linda Pennington, I obviously would not be writing these acknowledgments. They have always been wonderful parents in every way, full of love and wisdom and support, and in particular, they have been encouraging me to write since I could hardly hold a pencil. They are the first to read every manuscript I produce, and this one was no exception (though, curiously, they seemed to like everything about it, and had no serious criticisms!). The first copy of this book that comes into my hands is going straight to them, and I am immensely looking forward to the moment when they proudly put it on their bookshelf. My brothers, Mike and Paul Pennington, also deserve a special mention here for all the long years of friendship and support that they have given to their little brother.

Finally, and most important, I am glad for the opportunity to put in writing my deep love and admiration for my wife, Christine Steinwall. She bore the greatest burden as I worked at the Scarborough Campus by day, then on the manuscript at night, for long weeks and months at a time. She also had two children along the way, after a harrowing pregnancy in early 2008 that demonstrated what incredible resources of strength and will she possesses. Her unfailing love and support, and her extraordinary devotion to our sons Ian, Emmett, and Winston, were without any doubt the most important components in the completion of this book. This book is dedicated to her and to them.

INDEX